WELCOME TO AMERICASTAN

WELCOME TO AMERICASTAN

Jabeen Akhtar

PENGUIN
VIKING

VIKING
Published by the Penguin Group
Penguin Books India Pvt. Ltd, 11 Community Centre, Panchsheel Park,
New Delhi 110 017, India
Penguin Group (USA) Inc., 375 Hudson Street, New York, New York 10014, USA
Penguin Group (Canada), 90 Eglinton Avenue East, Suite 700, Toronto,
Ontario, M4P 2Y3, Canada (a division of Pearson Penguin Canada Inc.)
Penguin Books Ltd, 80 Strand, London WC2R 0RL, England
Penguin Ireland, 25 St Stephen's Green, Dublin 2, Ireland
(a division of Penguin Books Ltd)
Penguin Group (Australia), 250 Camberwell Road, Camberwell,
Victoria 3124, Australia (a division of Pearson Australia Group Pty Ltd)
Penguin Group (NZ), 67 Apollo Drive, Rosedale, Auckland 0632,
New Zealand (a division of Pearson New Zealand Ltd)
Penguin Group (South Africa) (Pty) Ltd, 24 Sturdee Avenue, Rosebank,
Johannesburg 2196, South Africa

Penguin Books Ltd, Registered Offices: 80 Strand, London WC2R 0RL, England

First published in Viking by Penguin Books India 2011

10 9 8 7 6 5 4 3 2 1

This is a work of fiction. Names, characters, places and incidents are either the product of the author's imagination or are used fictitiously and any resemblance to any actual person, living or dead, events or locales is entirely coincidental.

ISBN 9780670085316

For sale in India and Pakistan only

Typeset in Scala by SÜRYA, New Delhi
Printed at Thomson Press India Ltd, New Delhi

For my parents, Hanif and Zahida

Part 1

I

I had only been home eighteen minutes when the cursing started.

You churail! Haram zadi! Awarra! Bey waqoof!

She was cursing at me in Urdu, the national language of Pakistan. Urdu was not to be confused with Punjabi, my parents explained, that other language of Pakistan, the language of grungy and unfiltered-cigarette-smoking rickshaw drivers. Urdu was spoken by the elite and the educated—the people who lived in the pink barricaded palaces on Mall Road in Lahore. The ones with cooks and drivers and invitations to have afternoon chai near the crystal staircase of the downtown Avari Hotel. Urdu had history. Urdu was an epic classical language of the Persian and Mughal dynasties in which the most eloquent philosophical principles were inspired and the most stirring poetry was scribed.

Urdu was also a language my parents never bothered teaching me, so I had no idea what profanities my mother was hurling my way. But I could guess—you devil child, you vagabond, you spoiled, ugly-looking witch.

I glanced over at the living room windows.

'I'm talking to you!' she said, this time in English.

I couldn't figure out where she was. Maybe outside by the water fountain with the green fibreglass cherubs? The fountain was on and the sound of splashing, gurgling water was nice. Like there was a creek nearby. I looked at the wrought-iron bench behind the fountain but she wasn't there either.

'Samira! Do you hear me?'

A bead of sweat rolled down the back of my neck. I was roasting in the little oven that was my Honda Civic. All the windows were open but there was no cross-breeze. Two wasps flew in and out of my car, in and out, in and out, whirling around my head several times before settling on the windshield for a hump session. I watched the mounting, the penetration at lightning speed—allowing myself some of this interspecies voyeurism—and then not a few seconds later the lovers up and flew onto my older brother's car to hump on his roof. Khalid still hadn't fixed that boulder-sized dent on the passenger-side door. I wondered why. My father could get it fixed for free. But I guess it didn't matter now that Khalid was leaving the country. Khalid wouldn't need a car where he was going.

I rested my elbows on the steering wheel and put my fingers to my head, massaging the temples.

'Samira!' she screamed. 'Do you hear me? I need your damn help!'

My mother didn't seem to care that I had just driven five long hours from Washington, D.C. to our house in Cary, North Carolina, with my car stuffed with eleven trash bags of clothes, three suitcases and three boxes. Of course, she didn't know my car was stuffed with boxes and suitcases and bags and that the rest of my apartment, my entire life, actually, had been hastily thrown into a D.C. storage unit two days ago.

'Looks like you're gettin' the hell out of dodge,' the manager at Founding Father Storage up on 16th Street, S.E. told me, inspecting the jumble of furniture and household goods that piled to the ceiling of my 5' x 15' unit. 'Cops bust you for drugs or somethin'?'

Not exactly.

I looked up from my seat, still wearing my seat belt, and saw my younger sister's heavily lined cat eyes peering down at me from an upstairs window. She was chatting on her cell phone, the little diamond in her nose twinkling. Meena was twenty-five and home from grad school for the weekend and everything about her was twinkly, even the cell phone she was talking into. Twinkly, sparkly pink. Her advancing age be damned. She waved to me and I waved back.

'For the last time, Samira. Are you going to help me or not?'

I curled my fingers around the back of my neck and squeezed to relieve the tension. This was the first time I was back home since spring when we celebrated my twenty-seventh birthday. Ethan, my parent's favourite green-eyed Appalachian with size twelve feet and, until recently, my boyfriend, had scooted a tiny velvet box across the dinner table. Everyone held their breath as I opened it, but inside was a tiny emerald, my birthstone, pressed in the middle of a heart on a platinum chain. Ethan and I had already discussed marriage and when it would happen for us—the following spring we would get engaged, after work cooled down for me and he paid off some of his law school debt and we would have time and a little more money to plan the wedding. Having an engagement ring? A technicality. A minor detail for two people who had spent eight years together and knew marriage was certain. My parents didn't say anything, but they were visibly disappointed when I opened the box. I wasn't. I thought the necklace was beautiful.

I lifted the chain from my neck now, letting the thin metal slip between my fingers. If history was any indication, my mother would not stop yelling and cursing until she had me in her grip. I didn't know what she needed help with or why there was any urgency to it, but whatever it was, I dreaded it. Whatever those five feet of anger had in store made me want to slink under the mat and pretend I wasn't really there, sitting in my parents' driveway.

A few days back, I had told my parents that things were slow at work and I had more vacation days than expected so I was using it to come home for a week.

'Such a good girl,' my father had said, pleased his busy daughter could have travelled anywhere with her time but used all of it to come home.

I was going to have to coast on this goodwill until I figured out how and in what order to tell him and my mother the following: I moved out of D.C.; I tried to kill Ethan; the US government thinks I'm a terrorist; and I need my old room back.

'Fine. Stay there,' my mother cried out. 'Don't help me then. Just stay there and keeping sitting in that driveway like a bump!'

The belt swooshed past my chest. I pressed the unlock button. Taking one gulp of moist air for fortitude, I finally stepped out.

'You mean bump-on-a-log,' I said to no one in particular as I followed the flagstones to the front door. 'It's bump-on-a-log.'

2

Merlin was at my feet the minute I was in the foyer, meowing and curling his black satin body around my ankles. I picked him up and nuzzled my face in his neck and kissed it, and carried him through the house with me. In the kitchen, multiple pots gurgled on the stove. Rice boiled in one and coriander-scented steam threatened to pop open the lid of another. Our nicer dinnerware had been stacked on the counter by the sink and some pink roses from the garden were thrown together in a clear vase. All of this meant one thing.

'Oh, no.' I put Merlin on a bar stool and approached the stove. My mother was hunched over the counter, grating cucumbers. 'Who's coming?' I asked.

My mother's eyes stayed on the cucumbers. 'Who's coming? I haven't seen my daughter in months and all she has for me is "Who's coming." How about a hug, a hello. Honestly, do you even miss me when you are over there in that Washington?'

I walked over to her. I was a good five inches taller than my mother and had to be careful not to constrain her arms as they were busy with the cucumbers, so I bent down and hugged her hips. 'Of course I miss you, Mom.'

She turned around, slipping past me. 'Well, I'm glad you're home. I invited your Aunty Fozia and Uncle Akbar for dinner. Fozia's brother is visiting so the whole family is coming over.'

'The whole family?' I asked, anxiously. 'How many?'

'Samira, I don't know how many people are coming. I just need your help. And if you don't want to help me then leave and stop being in my way,' she said as she picked up the pot of boiling rice and drained it in the sink.

My lower lip shot forth at the prospect of having to talk to these people who were not my real aunts and uncles but were, nevertheless, as culture dictates, endearingly labelled family. 'What do you want me to do?' I asked.

'You can stop asking a million questions and put the dishes away.'

I did as my mother asked and unloaded the dishwasher and not a thing more. This dinner party couldn't have happened on a worse night. The whole drive to Cary was made possible by the idea that as soon as I arrived home I could lie on my bed, read any old pile of crap I could find and shut the door to the rest of the world for the rest of the evening. I didn't feel like socializing with my own family, let alone a bunch of desis I didn't know who would sit in the living room and stare at me all night out of mild curiosity but mostly boredom.

I perched on a bar stool and watched my mother work her away around the kitchen. She reached for the pot with the anxious lid and lifted it open, then poured in a bowl of red lentils. Two stirs. Then, over a deep frying pan full of chopped onions, she tipped a bulk-size bottle of olive oil and let it fall in three large blobs. While the onions sizzled, she tossed in spoonfuls of turmeric, coriander and red chilli powder.

It always took me a few days to get used to the smell of Pakistani cooking at home. The smell pervades everything—the curtains, your clothes, your hair. I had no idea how to cook, so I especially had no idea how to cook anything as complicated as Pakistani food. For me it was microwavable frozen pot pies and take-out, or when I did cook—spaghetti. Nothing ever made the air in my kitchen smell different.

My mother took a handful of green beans and dropped them in the frying pan. Through the steam of the cookers, she looked at me for the first time, eyeing the khaki shorts and damp T-shirt I had on. 'Why don't you change your clothes and put some make-up on? You're looking haggard. So pale and gangly,' she said, crinkling her eyebrows and getting back to her pots. Then she looked at me again and put her spatula down.

'Wait. Come here,' she said.

'Why?'

'Just come here.'

I walked over. She held my face with her hands, the onions caramellizing below us. Strands of frizzy hair poked out of her bun and her black kohl was smeared. Even in the midst of all her cooking and stress, my mother was still such a pretty little thing. Dark eyes. Delicate hands. Skin the colour of tea with cream and sugar. She studied me now, looking at my face, over twenty years younger than hers, but dry, bony and lifeless.

'You don't look well. Is everything all right?'

I turned my face away. 'Everything's fine.'

'You look like you've lost weight.'

'Just some stress from work,' I said. 'But it's over now.'

'Well, I've never seen you this skinny. You don't look good at all. If you knew how to cook, you could take better care of yourself. You'll keep wasting away like this if you don't learn how to cook. While you're here this week, you should learn how to make shorba. Come here. I'll show you right now.'

'Not now,' I said.

'If not now, then when?'

'I'm too tired.'

'You're always too tired.'

'No, Mom. I really am tired.'

'I know. And like I said, you're always too tired.'

The phone rang, interrupting this typical mother-daughter bottomless pit of a conversation. When I reached behind me and answered, I could barely make out my father's voice amongst people talking and engines being started. He was saying something about a folder of paperwork he needed.

'I'll bring it, Dad,' I said, grateful for a chance to get out of the house and escape my mother again.

Joe Tanweer Honda was located in what was considered 'Auto Alley'—a ten-mile stretch of auto-dealers like Chrysler, Hummer, Toyota, Volkswagen and Rolls Royce in the middle of an otherwise heavily forested area. The Honda dealership was one of the largest and most successful in North Carolina, certainly the most successful in the Triangle. An average of 150 units was sold there each month. The 'Joe' was my father's idea, thinking 'Tariq Mohammed Tanweer Honda' might scare potential customers away.

It looked like business was slow as I pulled up to the dealership. Abdul and Bilal, both of whom who had been working there since I was a kid, stood together by the entrance. They were joined by a young, lanky blonde who looked unsure of himself in his collared shirt and tie. He must have been a new hire, someone from one of the universities who would stay for a few weeks and leave, unlike the rest of the salesmen who knew they had a good thing working for my father and would probably stay there for the rest of their lives.

'Hi guys!' I said, trying to hurry past them.

'Wait, wait,' Abdul said, quickly exhaling his cigarette and flicking it twice. 'Not so fast. How are you doing? How's the white boy?'

'Ethan? He's fine.'

'What are you doing here?' Bilal asked. 'Home for a vacation?'

'Yeah,' I said. 'For a vacation. But, um, I may be here a little longer this time around.'

'Got fired, did you?'

My whole body tightened, and it took me a second to realize Bilal was making a joke. They both laughed, the new guy awkwardly laughing with them, and I tried laughing along too.

'Got something for your father?' Bilal asked, pointing to the folder.

'Yes. Have you seen him?'

'He's upstairs,' Abdul said. 'But stop by on the way out. Talk to us a little more.'

I told them I would, having no intention of actually doing so, and went inside. There was some initial shock as I looked around in there—apparently my father had made some changes since the last time I came out to the dealership. He had added a flat screen television in the reception area and upgraded the desks, chairs and carpeting on the display floor. The whole place looked cleaner, more upscale—a sure sign of my father's continual success. I passed the showroom and walked upstairs to the offices, where, to my disappointment, I noticed the upgrades were limited to the first floor. The white hallways had pen marks and dirty hand smudges and the offices remained sparse and windowless. I found my father behind his faux pine desk, his gold-rimmed glasses halfway down his nose, a bottle of Tums by the telephone, stacked papers and folders all around him.

'Mera laal. My baby's home!' he shouted. He took the folder from me and extended his cheek over the desk. 'You're late on your taxes.'

I leaned in and gave him a kiss.

'Much better,' he said. 'Paid in full. How was your drive home?'

'It was fine, Dad,' I said, lowering myself on to a metal stack chair.

'Did you take your car for the 60,000-mile service like I told you to?'

'Uh . . . no. But I'll do that later.'

My father picked up the bottle of Tums and shook it. 'You need to do it now. You can't let these things go. Especially with these long drives. You need to make sure your car is in good condition. I worry about you making those long drives alone, with all those killers and murderers on the highway. They sit and wait for girls like you, you know. I read these things in the papers. They'll pull over and pretend they need help. Then these girls stop and you know what they do? They rape and kill them. Then they throw their bodies in rivers and trash cans.' He flipped the cap off the bottle and tossed two pale blue tablets into his mouth.

'I know, Dad,' I assured him. 'I won't stop for anyone.'

'I would feel better if Ethan had driven with you.'

I tapped my fingers on the faux pine.

'So how's your job going?'

'Well . . . um . . . you see . . .' My mouth went dry and my throat tightened. I released a wan little cough, looked up at my father and wondered if I should just come clean right then and there. Just lay it all out and get it over with. But I was exhausted. Unable to think clearly. It would be better to come clean after a meal and a good night's sleep, I reasoned. Nourishment and rest. And perhaps a shower. Yes, definitely a shower. Cleanliness was key. 'Job's going fine, Dad.'

My father shook his head and grabbed a napkin. 'Blah,' he said, spitting out the remnants of the tablet into the napkin. He stuffed the moistened napkin into the bottle and with a loud thud and perfect aim, threw the bottle into a trash can across the room. 'Most disgusting thing in the world,' he said, grabbing another napkin to spit into—'this Tums. Don't know why your mother gave me such an awful remedy for my stomach. This is your Aunty Rajni's fault, you know. Your mother and I ate at their house two days ago and such a filthy kitchen they had! Shoo! Smelled like rotting turnips! I kept telling your mother that woman was trying to poison us. But your mother didn't believe me. I don't know why she insists on going to Rajni and Fundi's house. Rajni and Fundi sit alone in their home and take no part in the desi community, attend no functions and contribute nothing to society, so why should I have to sit in a filthy kitchen and eat with these nobody people?' My father wiped his mouth once more and nodded. 'Yes, Congressman Bailey. A powerful man. You should be thankful to have such a prestigious job and work with such important people. When I was a young student in Pakistan, I dreamed of having such an opportunity. To walk beside the leaders of America. To be among those steering the course of the entire world . . .'

He suddenly paused, taking a moment to eye me up and down. 'You're not decently dressed. You need to change before your Aunty Fozia comes over. You shouldn't wear shorts around these people. I don't like it when you and your sister wear shorts, but what can I do? You girls were raised here. If you were raised in Pakistan,' he said, pointing directly to my T-shirt, 'you wouldn't even wear shirts like that.'

I looked down at my shirt. A burqa with an eye grill would get me more wolf whistles on a Kabul street corner than my oversized T-shirt with fluorescent green aliens that said 'Our Planet!' But my sleeves were rolled up, scandalously exposing my naked arms. 'Yes, Dad,' I obeyed. 'I'll go change my clothes so I can look like a decent person.' 'Good girl,' he said, not having detected the sarcasm in my voice. He told me to tell my mother he'd be home in an hour and to have some green tea ready to calm his stomach before the guests arrived. I gave him another kiss on the cheek, and when I walked back into the hallway, I rounded the corner and almost slammed right into Cody, Khalid's best friend since second grade.

'Little Sammer's back!' he bellowed, wrapping his bear arms around me, lifting me off the ground. 'What's going on, girl? How ya been?'

My back was still a little damp when he hugged me, but I didn't think it was enough for him to notice. I breathed in his cologne—orangey-citrus with a hint of bergamot. I was careful not to crush the Ray-Bans that hung from his neck.

Meena and I both had crushes on Cody when we were growing up. We loved his all-American presence whenever he came to our house—his spiked dirty blonde hair and jeans with holes in both knees. He had a troubled past with drugs and petty theft that gave me the most illicit fantasies of us running away together, living a life of sex and crime. My father was credited with stepping in and saving Cody after his last attempted robbery—that time he pulled a knife on a PetSmart employee who was in the middle of shaving a Scottish collie. Dad bailed him out of jail and immediately took Cody under his wing, paying for his accounting degree at the local community college and eventually giving him the lead finance position at the dealership. My crush died a slow, agonizing death.

'Haven't seen you forever, Sammer,' Cody said, putting me back on the ground. 'Khal told me you were coming home. Hey, he said you got arrested?'

My hands flew up and landed on his stomach. Cody was double the length, width and height of me but somehow I was able to push him three steps back until he was flat against the smudged wall.

'No one knows about it. It was just an accident. A traffic accident. It wasn't a big deal. They let me go. And my parents don't know about me and Ethan so don't say anything about that either . . .'

'Slow down there, missy,' Cody said, appearing somewhat startled by my reaction. He made a zipper motion at his mouth. 'Lips are sealed. I won't say a thing.'

I looked over at my father's office to ensure we were out of earshot. 'Let's not talk about it here. We'll catch up later. I'll give you all the juicy details.' I poked him in the stomach and noticed how soft it had gotten. 'What's new with you?'

Cody threw his head back. 'Can't complain. Just put money on a house off Lawyer's Road. I'm part of the man now.'

'That's crazy,' I said. 'Whatever happened to reckless Cody?'

'He grew up, gained weight, got himself a woman.'

'A woman? Who is she?'

'Agh, no one special,' he said with a dismissive wave of his hand. 'She's uh . . . she's okay. Mug's a little rough, but she's got a kick-ass bod, you know? So did you hear what your Dad said to us the other day?' Cody asked, shifting on his feet, growing increasingly animated. 'We were all hanging out at the office, getting to know the new manager your Dad hired for the Greensboro lot, and he's like, to everybody, "This is Carl Scavo. He's the new head of the development project in Greensboro. Like the head of my dick",' Cody said, laughing heartily. 'I mean, your Dad . . . he really yelled that out.' Cody cupped his hands in front of his mouth and parted his lips wide. 'LIKE THE HEAD OF MY DICK!'

I cringed, not enjoying the story one bit. Cody was bent over, laughing even harder than before. 'Your Dad was just trying to be one of us, you know, one of the guys,' he said. 'But, oh man, we were dying!' Cody's perpetually sunburned face was even brighter red from his laughter. I also noticed he had developed a double chin.

'Sorry to cut this short,' I told him, catching another whiff of his cologne. 'But I have to get going. We're having guests tonight and I need to get home and help my mother.'

'Why don't you come out with me and Khal tonight,' he said. 'We're meeting at the Town Centre around eight. Three-dollar drafts on Thursdays!'

Cody didn't know it, but he had just outed my brother.

'That's not fair,' I told Khalid when I got back to the house. Meena was in the basement with us, giving herself a pedicure. 'I don't want to be here tonight anymore than you do. Why don't you stay and serve guests tea while I go out drinking?'

Khalid shook his head. 'No way, rat. I'm outta here. What—you think you can keep me from going out? And what's the point of not telling Mom and Dad what happened to you in D.C.? Just tell them. Don't you think they'll know something's up when a year passes and you're still in your room?' Khalid cracked up, lifting a hand for Meena to high-five, but she was too busy scraping back the cuticle of her big toe to notice.

'When *are* you going to tell Mom and Dad about everything?' Meena said, now scraping her other big toe. 'Don't you think they deserve to know?'

'Of course they do,' I replied. 'But you know how they are. They'll both have heart attacks before I even get past the part about me and Ethan. And that's not even the worst of it. Best to tell them in increments.'

My cell phone started ringing in my pocket. It was my father.

'Hi, baby. I'm on my way home,' he said. 'Please tell your mother to serve dinner late. I have to bring your car back to the dealership.'

'My car? Why?'

'The service guys said they would do your 60,000-mile service today before they close.'

A mild panic set in. I still had all those suitcases and trash bags in my car, and it would take some time to get them out. And I certainly couldn't start now. Not with guests coming over any minute and before I had a chance to even explain why I had so many personal belongings when I was supposedly staying only a week.

'I appreciate that, Dad,' I said. 'But there's no need for you to come home and then drive my car back. I'll take it there myself.'

'No. I want to test-drive it.'

'But, Dad, can't it wait until later? We're having guests tonight, remember?'

'The service department is booked solid for the next week. You're only staying the week, right?'

I gulped hard, and told him I was.

'Well then, this is the only time they can do it.'

I was about to say something back, offer an alternative plan for getting my car serviced at another time, but my father was a busy man and his mind was made up, so he had already hung up on me. I threw my phone onto the couch and looked back at Meena and Khalid. 'Dad's said he's coming over to take my car for inspection and I have all those suitcases and trash bags in there. I gotta get that shit out now before he sees it!'

Khalid was grinning. 'Aww. Sure sounds like you could use my help.'

'Listen, Khalid. If you help me I won't tell Mom you're going out tonight.'

'Nope.'

'Okay, fine. I'll forget about the seventy dollars you owe me.'

Khalid scratched his short, rough black hair, and I watched as the thought of helping me for seventy dollars flickered briefly across his face before melting away. He stood in the middle of a rancid mess of dirty clothes and junk food wrappers and I wondered how my mother had been tolerating him for the last two months. Khalid was back in my parents' basement while the house he shared with Ashley, his fiancée, was up for sale. Ashley was in Vødesværk, Denmark, having recently transferred there with the satellite company she worked for. The plan was for Khalid to join her there after their wedding in early spring. In the meantime, Khalid worked busily at home creating a Vødesværk office for the software company he worked for, and, because Ashley was so far away, being in charge of the wedding planning here. At least that's the impression he gave Ashley.

Khalid, thirty-years old going on twelve, plopped onto what looked like a giant black worm with a '$195' price tag dangling from the side. 'Check it out,' he said. 'I got my cup holder here, my controls right here, X-box over there. And look.' He tried to build suspense as he slowly pulled a plastic-wrapped box from the floor. 'The next generation of Halo. Got it early 'cause I got connections. Do you know how many people have this version? Six. That's it. My friend Martin Anders knew a software developer over at Bungie and he hooked me up. This is some special shit, man. I've been waiting sixteen months to get my hands on this. And what does the love of my life have to say about it? 'Why don't you do something more productive with your time?' Khalid squeaked in high-pitched mockery of Ashley's voice. 'Why don't you spend the money on things we really need? Like ramekins? We need ramekins. We can't live without ramekins!'

I was getting nervous. I could hear my mother spraying cleaner on the kitchen counters upstairs. She had entered the final stages of preparing for company, indicating their arrival was imminent.

'Do you even know what ramekins are?' Khalid asked. 'They're these little white cups for cooking pudding. Last night I was on the phone with her and I was like, "Ash, Danish people don't eat pudding. They eat danishes. We'll use these things once when we're married, if that. Compared to Halo, which supplies hours upon hours of entertainment and pure joy." I was being so reasonable about it and all she had to say to me was, "It's crème brulee" and then we got disconnected.'

Meena rubbed lotion on her heels and ankles. 'Right. I'm sure you were *disconnected.*'

'Khalid,' I said to him. 'If you help me I will pay *you* seventy dollars.'

'I'll tell you this,' Khalid continued. 'I'm not spending my last few days as a free man worrying about it. If Ash tries one more time to rain on my Halo parade and tell me how to spend my hard-earned money, I'm going to tell her she can take her cups of pudding and go suck it. You just wait. Next time she calls that's what I'm going to tell her.'

Khalid settled into his game chair and placed an empty 7-Eleven cup in his cup holder. He practised picking it up and putting it back while he punched buttons on the control with his other hand. Meena was concentrating on her toes as she brushed her toenails with pink polish. She paused briefly to twist her heavy waist-length hair into a bun, then resumed her painting.

'Can one of you please get up and help me?' I said, a hint of hysteria developing in my voice.

Khalid studied the text on the back of the Halo game and tore the plastic off. 'Let's make sure this baby works,' he said, sliding the disc into the X-box. Meena removed the foam between her toes and blew on the polish.

'This is awful,' I said. 'I'm just asking for one little favour. How often do I ask you guys for favours? How often?' I felt it coming on, that stiffening in the back of the throat, the tingling in my nostrils. Standing right there in front of them, I thought I was going to cry. I knew it would have been overreacting to the situation and make me vulnerable to Khalid's teasing and Meena's eye rolling, but I hadn't exactly been in control of my emotions lately. I fought the tears back as hard as I could, and resorted to the last tactic I had in my arsenal. 'Forget it,' I said. 'Just forget it. But don't expect me to cover for you two anymore. Next time Mom and Dad ask where you are or who you're with . . .'

Meena's head snapped up after the 'who you're with' part, an unusually strong reaction to a threat I had been employing for years. She unravelled her bun and hastily brushed through her hair with her fingers, tearing through a tangle. 'Why would you go off telling Mom and Dad about something like that?' she piped in abruptly. 'It's none of their business who I'm with now. Like those two FOB's would even understand.' Meena began to tie her hair back up, and it seemed to slowly dawn on her that she had started to reveal something she didn't want revealed, because she fixed her feline gaze upon me and cracked a smile that only a sister would know was completely fake. 'Oh, whatever,' she said, with sudden composure. 'If you need help, I'll help you.'

'Thanks,' I replied, all too willing to leave the interpersonal drama brewing in her life unaddressed for now—drama that I was sure I would hear about in way too much detail at a later point anyway. 'Khalid, what about you?'

Khalid was turning over the disc in his hands. He looked up at me. 'Huh?'

'Can you help me unload my car? How many times do I have to ask you?'

He grunted a response, which I took as a yes, and I snatched the disc out of his hands. There was no time to waste. I concocted a shoddy little plan on the spot and gave them a quick run-down. Meanwhile, upstairs, salaam alaykums were being exchanged. The guests had arrived. Meena and I took a few minutes to help my mother serve tea while everyone gathered around the spread on the table—curried chickpea salad, fried onion pakoras, butter cookies, a pitcher of sweet tea pierced with a twig of lemon verbena from the garden—all just a quick snack before dinner.

Then, I snuck out.

The plan was that while my mother was occupied with the guests, Meena and I would grab everything from my car (we estimated this would take three trips), go around the left side of the house, away from the kitchen and living room windows, and sneak everything through a basement window. It was too risky to take my things upstairs, so we would hide everything in Khalid's room. When my parents were asleep, I would carry my things to my room little by little. We would have to work quickly because with guests here my mother would notice the absence of all three of us. Meena would make a quick stop inside after the first trip so as not to arouse suspicion.

As soon as I opened the trunk of my car, a blast of dense, hot air escaped. I picked up the first bag and saw Meena running towards me.

'Get all the bags first,' she ordered.

We grabbed as many trash bags as we could, pulling the yellow drawstrings over our arms like bracelets. They were heavy and the drawstrings dug into my skin. Khalid should have been the one doing this but he insisted he would be more helpful from the basement, taking the bags from us and hiding them immediately. Meena and I huffed as we crossed the front lawn. I could hear the muffled sounds of Urdu mixed with English mixed with clanking forks from the kitchen. Even from outside, it was easy to hear all the noises echoing on the main floor since my mother had pretty much torn down all the walls inside. My father had complied with this major renovation at the time. He really had no choice. When the family moved from New Jersey to North Carolina to live the quiet suburban life and for the growing South Asian population here, my mother saw an opportunity to buy an old, charming, southern fixer-upper with turrets and a wide wrap-around porch. That didn't sit well with my father. Old houses, no matter how charming, don't impress Pakistanis. Nothing old does. Old things aren't status symbols. But slick, modern houses are. This newly built house was a status symbol back in the day, with its yellow aluminum exterior and rust-coloured carpet in the basement, so we bought this instead of an old charmer. But for the rest of his life, my father was indebted to make whatever changes to the house my mother wanted.

Like the sunroom she added off the kitchen. She decorated it with a huge brown canvas couch and an earthy-toned marble table. My father, of course, hated all of it, so he struck a deal to get the formal living room designed more to his taste—maroon silk curtains, a sectional peacock couch under a crystal chandelier and some velvet Islamic art.

Then my mother built a second kitchen, complete with its own refrigerator, stove, sink and dishwasher. Why they needed this second kitchen will go down as one of the great mysteries of our family history. No one used it except Merlin and Ignatius Reilly, our two cats, who had their food and water bowls placed there.

Somewhere along the way, there was a turning point and my father jumped on the addition bandwagon. Because if there is anything that impresses Pakistanis more than a slick modern house, he came to realize, it's a slick modern house that's bigger. Upstairs, along with two small bedrooms for me and Meena was the master bedroom, which my parents decided needed an addition. After construction was over and they realized their room had practically doubled in size, they had to build a larger master bathroom to accommodate it. For some reason, my parents wouldn't just buy a larger house to suit their tastes and my father's growing income. They just kept building and building atop the modest one we had. From the front, the house looked just as it did when my parents first bought it—when the lawn was just a patchwork of freshly laid squares of turf. But as Meena and I rounded the side to the back, all the additions seemed to pop out of the walls like cancerous growths.

Finally, Meena and I reached the basement window. I caught my breath, looked down, and saw a major problem.

'Khalid,' I said through clenched teeth. 'You were supposed to remove the screen.'

Khalid was on his game chair wearing a wireless, space-age headset. On the television screen, animated soldiers were battling in what looked like an abandoned warehouse. 'Dude, take out their artillery first,' he said into his headset. 'What? What are you saying?' He jutted his head forward. 'Eragon, I can't understand . . . Butt-Chin needs to what? Kid, take the cock out of your mouth so I can understand you.'

'Khalid!' I full-out yelled as I crouched by the window. 'You stupid mother fucker. Khalid!' I was banging on the windows but, as I quickly realized, he couldn't hear me.

'What is all this?'

Meena and I looked up. Overstuffed trash bags dangling from our arms, we looked back at my mother clutching a pair of scissors and some pink roses, Uncle Akbar, Aunty Fozia, and two other adults and two children whose names I had learned a few minutes ago but had already forgotten. I saw my father coming down the hill on the other side of the house. Oblivious to the drama unfolding before the crowd by the basement windows, he waved enthusiastically to show he had my car keys.

'Well,' my mother repeated. 'What is this?'

I dropped the bags. I could taste salt dripping from my upper lip, and I wiped my face with my already sweaty alien T-shirt. It was time to admit defeat.

'Mom, Ethan and I broke up. I'm moving back home.'

I stayed in my room the rest of the night. After the guests left and the kitchen was cleaned and the living room was vacuumed, I quietly approached my parents' bedroom. Their television flickered pale white flashes into the hallway, and once inside their room, I could see their dark silhouettes on the bed. A movie was playing where some actress was on her hands and knees, holding the hand of what looked to be her mother, begging her about something while her mother screamed back, both women clearly distressed about whatever events had transpired. In the meantime, sitar music stretched mournfully in the background. If you walk into an Indian movie, chances are, you're going to walk into a scene just like this, and it was definitely not helping me. I thought about waiting another ten minutes or so for the movie to suddenly and inexplicably switch to a happy, crowd-filled dance number with women spinning in colourful saris and men jumping on car rooftops, but there was no point delaying it now. The truth was out and I had a lot of explaining to do.

But so much had happened, where to begin?

Ethan. The logical starting point. I would have to craft the story about him very carefully, convey everything that happened without getting too specific. Like the betrayal part. I myself couldn't believe I was somehow involved with betrayal—this concept that had always seemed so lofty before, so glamorous in a *Dynasty*-esque way. Yet there I was—betraying someone and being betrayed in return. There was sex and backstabbing and broken promises, but it was dirty and pathetic. A knock-off version of *Dynasty* played by a couple of twenty-somethings who bought household cleaners at dollar stores.

I crept over to my parents' bedside, wondering if they were still awake. My father was on his back—eyes closed and gently snoring—

his body stiff as he was obviously trapped between Ignatius' and Merlin's outstretched furry bodies on either side of him. The scene reminded me of a story my father once told me about the Prophet Muhammad—how Muhammad had nearly missed his call to prayer because his black cat, Muezza, had fallen asleep on the sleeve of his prayer robe. Muhammad loved this cat. It was said he delivered sermons with Muezza curled on his lap and that once Muezza saved an oversleeping Muhammad by awakening him just in time for the morning call to prayer. Though the rest of my family, especially my mother, didn't need a justification for keeping cats in our household, Islam's relationship with cats was often cited by my father as to why it was permissible, even honourable, to have them. There was even an Abu Hurayrah, my father explained—a 'Father of the Kittens' in Islam, and he was a very close friend of Muhammad's. Cats and Islam were like aloo and mutter. Potatoes and peas. Always together. A good pairing. But the bottom line, becoming more obvious as the years passed with pricey trips to holistic vets and a special order for catnip television, was that my father was just as cat co-dependent as anyone else. Even Muhammad, when faced with the prospect of disturbing his beloved Muezza that day, took a pair of shears and cut off the sleeve of his robe so his fuzzy companion could keep sleeping.

I sat on my parents' bed, carefully at the edge. My mother turned around when she heard me, then turned back towards the movie.

'Mom,' I said, 'do you want to talk about what happened?' For the longest time, she said nothing and didn't look at me. I watched the television for a little with her and it was still on that mother–daughter tragedy scene.

I took a deep breath. 'Mom . . .?'

She picked up the remote and turned off the television, leaving us in darkness but for the soft moonlight filtering through the sheer curtains. 'Okay, let's talk.'

I took another deep breath. 'Ethan and I have been having problems. For a while now. We both did some terrible things. It all started when I . . . um . . .'

'Samira, you and Ethan have been together for years,' my mother interjected. 'You two always have fights. Whatever happened, whosever fault it was, these things work out over time. You know what I'm saying? People forget things, they move on. So don't worry. Ethan is a good boy. I'm sure you two will work things out like you always do.'

I lowered my eyes. 'Not this time, Mom.'

'What about your job?' my father interjected. I didn't realize he had been awake, listening. 'Congressman Bailey. Did you leave your job?'

I slid further into the middle of the bed. I reached over and patted down Ignatius' abundant orange fur, tucking the fluff under his collar. Then I moved back to the edge and straightened my legs over the side. I was buying time. I knew my father would ask this question—that the focus of his inquiries would rest on my job, not my relationship. Boys may come and go, after all, but my father held reputation and career in the highest esteem, more sacred than his daughters' virginity. He didn't sacrifice everything to come to America so Meena and I could find husbands, he always said. There were plenty of husbands in Pakistan. We were lucky. We were privileged to be here. We had better not squander the opportunities most girls in Pakistan will never, ever have.

It could wait. My job with Congressman Bailey. And the truth about how I squandered it. I had just told my parents about Ethan and they had that to digest and that was enough for now. It wouldn't be fair to dump all of my failures onto their laps at one time—not when they were trying to go to bed.

'My job is fine, Dad,' I replied, avoiding eye contact with him as I said it. 'I just . . . need some time off. Be away from D.C. for a while. I wouldn't do this if I didn't really need to, Dad. Can't I just stay here?'

He paused to study my face. 'You know this is your home. Stay as long as you need. But if you're going to be here, use this time to figure things out. Be productive. That way when you go back, you can go stronger.'

My mother turned the television back on. 'Okay, now? You have nothing to worry about. Your father and I are fine with you being here.' She puckered her lips and kissed the air. 'Go on now. Go to sleep.'

I leaned over and kissed them both before getting up from their bed. I felt relief. Relief that they reacted more calmly than I had expected. At least about me moving back home. There was still so much they didn't know. But the rest of the story, I figured, like the fact that I was never going back to D.C, could come later.

3

I awoke in a panic, staring straight at the giant dead eyes of a giant teddy bear, shocked and momentarily confused as to why I was in a pink flowery bedroom and not in my apartment in D.C. Then the memories started to trickle back, as slowly as the sweat accumulated and beaded down my armpits and shoulders, pasting my cotton nightie to my skin.

Two months before I was arrested, Ethan called me one afternoon and said he had some good news to share. He sounded happy, peppy almost. We agreed to meet at my apartment in half an hour. I had just come from a used bookstore and was awkwardly holding six books I had just bought when I met him at my door. Once we were both inside, I put the books on the side table next to my couch and watched as Ethan's eyes watered over.

'I'm going to ask you this one last time,' he said, as I quickly realized the true purpose of this meeting. 'Did you cheat on me two years ago?' My heart started pounding. 'Why are you asking me this?' 'Answer the question!' he yelled, so loudly I knew my neighbours must have heard. 'Answer my question,' he repeated, more softly this time, in a forced calm.

I just stood there looking back at him, wondering what caused this door to open again.

'Answer me, Sam,' he said. 'Did you sleep with someone at that conference?'

I kept looking at him, and felt fear and panic and curiosity as to why this had come up again after all these years. We had had fights about this before. Ethan always suspected I had done something when I attended that conference in Atlanta. I told him nothing happened there—that we had been fighting before I left and my room was in a noisy, smoky hallway and I was dead tired and that was why I was acting strange when I returned. Ethan eventually stopped talking about it and I thought the issue had died.

But something had changed. Ethan must have learned the truth, to be confronting me like this. Learned it from someone. But she was to be dealt with later.

Ethan was standing in front of me now, waiting for an answer that he already had, so I turned my face towards him, looked in his eyes, and said yes.

'You lied to me!' he screamed, even louder than before. I was probably the only person who could ever make him scream that loud. 'You've lied to me all these years!'

He pressed his lips together and brusquely walked past me. He started hunting around my living room, picking up the pillows from my couch and throwing them off. The intricate beadwork on my favourite green pillow splintered against the hardwood floor, scattering into silver and copper bits.

'Where's the Emperor?' he yelled.

He knocked over a framed photo of the two of us and the glass shattered against the table.

'I want him back,' he said. 'Where is he?'

'I don't know.'

'Yes, you do!'

'I don't know.'

I stood paralysed with my back against my bookcase, hearing things crash in my bedroom. Ethan walked back out and tore everything from the shelf in my hallway closet. He threw a sheet set, still unopened in its clear plastic wrapping, right above my head, knocking over the books on the top shelf. He looked under my futon, found a CD cover and flung it across the room. Finally, he stopped. Only half his face was illuminated from the light in the living room, but somehow the whites of both his eyes glowed.

'You destroyed us,' he panted. 'Things will never be the same. Why did you do this to us?'

I slid my body to the right of the bed. The mattress was cooler there, cleaner. My pillow was wet, downright soaked from the night's tears. For the past three weeks, every night since I had moved back home, I lay awake and cried, on and off, usually between 1:30 a.m. and 4:00 a.m. One night I actually got out of bed and wandered through the house. I thought I'd watch television. I turned it on, then, my eyes stinging from the sudden brightness, turned it off. I went to all the bathrooms and quietly searched through the cabinets. Maybe there was something that could help me get back to sleep. I didn't find anything, other than some expired cold medicine, so I spent the rest of the night at my bedroom window, looking out at the dark shadows of the trees, waiting to see if something would appear from them—a deer, a fox, anything—before going back to bed.

I could hear the vacuum cleaner on downstairs, the clanking of dishes, my family awake. I checked my watch. It was almost eleven. I lay my head to the side, and the tears saturating the skin around my eyes easily rolled out. I had to breathe through my mouth because my nose was clogged. I needed a tissue bad. There were none around, and I couldn't bear the idea of getting out of bed, so whatever dripped out of my nose I wiped with my nightie or the pillow case.

I finally understood what self-mutilation was all about—why people sometimes slice their arms with razors or take sandpaper to their faces. They do it because they need outward manifestations of the pain they're feeling on the inside—physical proof to the world that they really are suffering. That's how I felt. I hadn't showered in four days. My hair was greasy with pieces of lint in it. My eyebrows were grown in. I wanted to look as disgusting as I felt on the inside.

'Hey, sleeping beauty!' my mother yelled as she pounded on my bedroom door. 'Were you the one who removed the plastic covers from the couch downstairs?'

I stayed quiet. I had no idea what she was talking about.

'I keep those covers on because Ignatius has been peeing on the couch. And do you know what happened last night? Ignatius peed on the couch! That's why I keep those covers there! You know, you kids move into this house and you think you're so smart. You think you can rearrange everything with no regard to how I run things.'

I could visualize my mother behind the door, wearing yellow rubber gloves and holding a small bucket of brown soapy water with a stained rag floating on top. I looked at the ceiling and willed her to go away.

'Were you the one who removed the covers?'

'No,' I said, my nose so clogged it sounded like 'dough'.

'What? I didn't hear you.'

'Dough!'

'Ni uth ja,' she said, with one last pound on the door. 'Get up. How long can one person sleep? Must be nice, being able to sleep all day like this.'

She cursed in Urdu as she thumped down the stairs. I felt a wave of relief that she was gone. With every ounce of energy I had, I leaned over the side of the bed and picked up a sock. My heart pounded from the stress of moving my body when it didn't want to move, and when I lay back down I thought I was going to pass out. I blew my nose into the sock and tossed it back on the floor.

I continued to lay there exhausted but at least now I could breathe. Cool air passed through my body and I felt relaxed again. I started to drift back to sleep, happy to have several more hours away from the world outside my bedroom door, when my cell phone rang.

'Meena,' I answered, trying to make my voice sound crisp as if I'd been awake all morning. 'What's up?'

'Hey, guess what?' she said, sounding chipper than the last time I saw her. 'I'm coming home again this weekend. But I won't stay at the house, so don't tell Mom and Dad. I'll be crashing at this friend's house in Raleigh. Freedom! Anyway, I'm on my way and I'll be in town in a few hours. My friend's at work until five so I thought we should grab lunch. Are you eating? I know you're not eating.'

'I eat plenty,' I replied, somewhat defensively. 'Three square meals a day.'

'Cereal's not a square meal,' she said.

I hated how well Meena knew about my over-reliance on cereal—my quick-fix answer to any question over what to eat. But I didn't want to talk about my diet. My weight and bad eating habits were reminders of how incapable I was of handling even the most basic requirements of life, something everyone else around me seemed to have mastered with ease. 'Who's this friend of yours?' I asked, trying to change the subject. 'Is this a guy?'

'Just a girlfriend,' she said. 'I met her a couple months ago at Jazzfest. Really cool chick. Anyway, where do you want to meet? There's this new Thai place that opened up in Raleigh. I heard it's good in spite of its name—Dungrats.'

I agreed to meet her at the restaurant in two hours. But right after I hung up, even before the phone was back on the nightstand, I questioned why I had agreed so easily. I felt bloated and full, in spite of not having eaten anything yet, and too tired to leave the house or drive anywhere. I felt so weak that when I finally turned the knobs in the shower, the force of the water hurt, like a thousand hot needles pricking my skin.

Meena sat at a table near a giant copper Buddha in the back of the room. She was halfway through a glass of red wine and was anxiously twirling her hair around her finger. Upon my arrival at the table, she put her finger down and examined me from top to bottom. 'Oh my god, you've lost so much weight,' she said. 'Wow. Skinny winny.'

I sat across from her and put my napkin on my lap. 'I was this same weight the last time you saw me,' I told her. 'Didn't notice before?'

'I was preoccupied last time I was home.'

'With what?' I asked.

She looked down at her menu. 'Oh, with nothing,' she said whimsically, scanning the lunch specials. 'Just . . . nothing. So how are you holding up?'

Meena glanced back up at me—with those big puffy eyes and eyelashes so thick and expansive they almost reached her eyebrows. My father always remarked about Meena's beauty, calling her his little Rajput princess—an image that brought to mind the women depicted in Mughal paintings and the rugs my parents had in the living room, with the lithe bodies in candy-coloured gowns twisting over balconies, their thick sheets of raven hair tumbling to the ground. When it was my turn to receive fatherly praise, it was usually in the vein of 'the most responsible daughter in the world' or 'the world's most intelligent daughter' or 'no one in the world has seen such a responsible and intelligent daughter.' The comments never bothered me. Meena really did look like a little princess, and I—I was a reasonably intelligent and responsible individual. At least I had played that role with perfection for years—the competent and wise big sister. And that was the reason Meena was looking up at me. She wanted me to probe, to ask her what was going on the last time she was home and insist she tell me in spite of her staged shrugging and nonchalant attitude. And then she would want me to analyse the situation for her and generate a solution.

And I would ask her what was going on. I would. But I still wasn't ready. Whatever she had in mind seemed deep and complicated and big sister needed a little break.

'I'm okay,' I answered. 'I'm still kind of in shock over everything. By the way, thanks for helping me get all my stuff upstairs that day. My head was so far up my ass, I don't think I ever thanked you.'

Meena laughed, indicating to my relief, that she was willing to drop whatever was on her mind. 'Don't worry about it. I'm sure you'd do the same for me if I get arrested for terrorism.'

She laughed again, and kept laughing, and I just sat there frozen. As soon as she had uttered those words, I realized a line had been crossed. Maybe it was the source. Meena was my sister, after all, and had it come from someone else I might have felt differently. But for the first time since the arrest, instead of cringing with embarrassment and guilt and wanting to escape to some mountain cabin to live out a Thoreau-inspired existence of isolation and agrarian dieting and naked bathing in nearby rivers, I wanted to join her in laughter. 'It's *expensive* being a terrorist,' I said, daring to have a little more fun with the incident. 'You know when they towed my car? On top of the $200 traffic fine, I had to pay a hundred twenty bucks to get my car back.' I took a few sips of water. 'And there was this weird powdery shit all over the inside. God knows what the cops did in there. It took hours to vacuum it out.'

'Are you ready to order?'

Our waitress was standing above our table. I wondered how much she had overheard. Meena gave her order first—she wanted the papaya salad, no peanuts, no lime dressing and no papaya. I ordered the red coconut curry, and when the dish arrived, I almost had to spit it out. I had become accustomed to eating bland, easily digestible foods. The curry was so spicy I had to take a big forkful of rice to help it go down.

'You're so skinny,' Meena said. 'Mom's surely not happy with that.'

'Let's not talk about my weight.'

'Okay. Have you talked to Natasha?'

'Jesus.'

I squirmed in my chair. Meena could certainly be blunt, seeing no need to pad a nasty topic of conversation with transitional words or circuitous phrasing. I hadn't heard the name 'Natasha' in weeks and would have been happy to have never heard it again, but deep down, I was wondering when it was going to finally come up. After all, no conversation about Ethan could be complete anymore without also mentioning Natasha. I suddenly felt a burning in my chest, unsure if it was from the mention of Natasha's name or acid reflux from the curry.

'I haven't heard from Natasha,' I replied. 'Of course not. Why would I?'

'Maybe to apologize for stealing your boyfriend?'

I poked at the mound of rice with my chopsticks. Natasha stealing my boyfriend? Ethan was no diamond necklace. The boy had a brain, a conscience. Nobody could steal him away if he didn't already want to leave. And he wanted to leave. I gave him a reason. I just never imagined he would walk straight into the waxed arms of a girl who wasn't just a friend to me—but another sister, another Meena.

I first met Natasha at a party and noticed everyone gathering to admire the mehndi patterns on her hands. I introduced myself. Natasha was extremely animated as she spoke back to me, the small purple birthmark near her right temple glistening under a thin layer of concealer. Her colourful hands flitted about as she delighted that we were both Pakistani. 'You must become doctor,' she said with a thick, rounded accent, mocking the stereotypical Pakistani parent. 'Or you are vurthless child!' She wore a 70's-style romper with an armful of black plastic bangles that managed to look both skanky mall tween and couture, and I knew I was going to unsuccessfully try to copy her style for as long as I knew her. We took to each other immediately, huddling on the couch, tuning out the party, bonding over our flawed lives as girls often do. Natasha told me about her family—about how she was shunned by her two sisters for marrying her white high school boyfriend at eighteen and divorcing him a year later. Her marriage to a gora and the subsequent divorce were blights on her family's reputation, obstacles to her sister's chances of finding suitors, so rather than being ignored in her own home or hearing the occasional 'slut' when passing one of them in the kitchen, Natasha did something inconceiveable in the Pakistani community—she left her family. If they were going to reject her, she was going to reject them first, so she dropped out of school and moved in with roommates in the city and never spoke to them again. She worked at bars and smoked and she didn't read Roll Call. She was different from my other friends. She didn't seem to play it safe, didn't care about reputation. She was a proud outcast, and I wanted to be like her. Even if I would never have the gumption to defy parental expectation or even just skip a day of work to nurse a hangover, hanging out with her for the next six years made me bold by association. In return, I gave Natasha family again.

Natasha was my only South Asian friend—evidence to my parents that there wasn't something wrong with me. That I did like my own people after all, could bond with them, socialize with them, and not just the goras I usually hung out with—and they were thrilled. Natasha spent every holiday with us. She would sleep in my bed, thread my eyebrows and reorganize my closets. My mother never spoke of her divorce and treated her like a third daughter, going to great lengths to prepare separate pots of curries with less spice because Natasha had a sensitive palate.

Then one night, Ethan came over for dinner. 'It really annoys me how she makes your mom go through so much trouble,' he whispered to me at the table. 'Why can't she find another family to cling to?'

Harsh words. Why was he being such a jerk, I wondered? Especially since my parents had taken him in like another child as well? The more time we all spent together, the more comments he made. Ethan thought Natasha was shallow, ignorant. She knew nothing about the world and couldn't engage in an intelligent conversation with him. What did I even have in common with her? Surely there were better friends out there for me, if I would spend a little less time with Natasha and give someone else a chance.

At the time, I questioned Ethan's antagonistic feelings toward her. What was the real reason he was so negative? Was it because, according to some twisted logic, he had feelings for her? I kept an eye on him. Sometimes when we all went out to dinner or to the beach on weekends, I watched for funny looks, lingering stares, anything that would indicate he wanted her.

'I don't want her,' Ethan would try to assure me when my paranoia kicked in.

'Then what's the problem,' I asked. 'Why are you so against Natasha?'

'It's just a feeling I get.'

'What feeling?'

'I don't trust her,' he said.

Meena put down her fork and picked up her drink. 'Maybe Natasha was a friend to you in the beginning, but once she realized you were another desi about to have the life she tried but failed to get—marriage to a gora that everyone approved of, a job that impressed the community, a family that loved you, she turned on you. She couldn't have your job, couldn't have your family. All you had that she could take from you was Ethan. And Atlanta gave her the perfect tool.'

I nibbled my rice. I appreciated Meena's attempt at rationalizing the behaviour of a girl who I spent almost every day with and unwisely trusted with my secrets. Meena was raising some good points, and perhaps it would comfort her if we could pinpoint a reason together, find an explanation for Natasha's behaviour. But there was nothing to be made out of the fact that a Pakistani commonality played a role in Natasha's backstabbing. No. I didn't believe it. Or maybe I didn't want to believe it. I didn't want to ascribe a motive to Natasha's actions. After everything she did, why should I be so charitable? There was another explanation I preferred, a simpler one—a universal label I could use to reduce Natasha to being nothing more than a tired old cliché unworthy of anyone's time and analysis.

'She's just a bitch,' I told Meena. 'A plain old bitch. You can't explain them, you can't understand them. That's why they're bitches. Let it go.'

Meena sighed and leaned back in her chair. I leaned back in mine. We sat that way for a second, thinking our own thoughts. An image popped into my head of what Ethan and Natasha's life looked like now. I could picture the two of them in bed—Natasha, tall and thickly built, probably having to lay next to Ethan instead of on top of him, and Ethan caressing her hair—frizzy and caramel-coloured from too many flat-iron attempts, feeling gratitude that she came forth and told him the truth about me, still astounded that I was the one he couldn't trust all along. I tried to block the thought. I couldn't tell if it was making me feel sad or enraged.

Meena scraped the last piece of carrot off her plate. 'Why don't you get a drink?' she said. 'Just one to take the edge off. It would be good for you.'

'No,' I emphatically replied. 'I'm in a state of mental distress. "Have *one* drink." That's like telling an obese kid who just got beat up at school to eat *one* chip.'

Meena sighed. She picked up her glass of wine and took a delicate little sip. 'You don't have to binge, you know. You can try to develop adult drinking habits.'

'That's not a priority at the moment,' I said. 'And I don't want to talk about Ethan or Natasha or the whole city of D.C., so tell me—what else is happening? What's going on with you?'

'Well . . .' Meena began, then looked at me seriously. 'I actually have something to ask you. Remember Chris Bennigan? You may not because he was in my class, and well . . . you didn't exactly swing with the popular crowd . . . but anyway, he was the quarterback who dated Patty Ronson. You're not going to believe this, but he came out of the closet last year. He's now living in Cary with his boyfriend. His boyfriend! Apparently living with him for three years. And he's white. So Chris is in a gay *and* interracial relationship. Can you believe that?'

The entire time Meena was relating this story, my mind was back on Natasha's frizzy hair. Natasha had always flat-ironed it in my bathroom before we went out. I didn't know why she flat-ironed so much. Her natural, silky curls would do just fine. But she would spend hours in front of the mirror, cooking every inch of her hair to within an inch of its life. I would always have to sweep the broken, crispy pieces off my linoleum floor the next morning.

God, how I hate her.

'Sam?'

'Sorry, I'm listening. Gays. Blacks. Whites. Go on.'

'So they're having a Halloween party at their house this weekend,' Meena continued. 'We should go. It has a theme—Halloween, 1986.' I furrowed my eyebrows. 'It's September. And why 1986?'

'It's Chris' partner's birthyear. They're moving in a week and they wanted a combined going-away-birthday bash,' she said. 'So the idea is this—it's a costume party, but it's supposed to be a costume party that takes place in 1986. So it's like . . . you're going to a Halloween party, but it's 1986, how would you dress? What kind of costume sensibilities would you have?'

I shook my head. 'This is all way too complicated.'

Meena looked at me sourly. 'Come on. We can leave whenever you want. It'll be good for you to get out of the house. Be around people having fun.'

More importantly than that, I thought, be around people who were not my parents. I was gradually warming to the idea and before I knew it, I shrugged my shoulders and smiled. 'All right,' I said. 'I have no idea what I'll wear, but whatever. Let's go.'

Around five o'clock on the Saturday of the party, Meena called me. 'I'll pick you up around eight. I'll drive up the street so Mom and Dad can't see my car, but I'll call when I'm in the neighbourhood. I'm gonna grab a case of beer on the way over too. Natty Light okay?'

Like a coward, I had waited passively all day for Meena to call me instead of picking up the phone and calling her to deliver the bad news.

'Hey, Meena?' I began. 'Um . . . I'm sorry to tell you this, and I probably should have called and told you earlier, but . . . it turns out I can't go to the party.'

'Oh, really?' she said, audibly disappointed. 'Why not?'

'I know this sounds awful,' I said, 'but I just don't feel like it anymore.'

'But didn't you go out and buy all that make-up and stuff for tonight?'

'Yes, but . . .'

'No buts, Sam,' she sternly replied, not accepting my excuse and making me regret that I didn't lie to her with a better excuse. 'You are *not* bagging on me tonight. Besides, it'll be good for you to be out again.'

I explained to Meena that my hair was greasy and my legs were hairy and I was wearing a stained T-shirt with the Soviet flag on it, pausing briefly to wonder where on earth I got it from, and all this meant I wasn't going anywhere.

'Sam. Eight o'clock. Be outside,' she said before hanging up.

Laid out before me on the bed were all the items I had purchased for my costume—tomato-red pants, a purple puffed-sleeved sweater, a pair of yellow hoop earrings from the thrift store and some dollar make-up.

First, I put my sweater on. The wool had a musty odour and scratched at my arms, and the pants weren't much better. For some reason, they seemed to come up higher on my ankles than they did at the thrift store, but for six dollars for the entire outfit, I couldn't complain. For my make-up, I had printed out a photo of an oiled and skinny Ban de Soleil model from the eighties and used it as a guide—half an eyelid with frosty pink shadow, the other half with frosty blue shadow, blue pencil all around and a swipe of pink lipstick. Then I unravelled my four braids and brushed through them vigorously to make my hair frizz out, and clipped one side up with a barrette. A pair of clear Jelly shoes made me a finished product. I hopped on my bed to get a full-length view of myself in my dressing table mirror. I looked ridiculous, but the overall effect was, if I may say so, startlingly realistic.

Meena had just sent me a text that said, 'in o'donnell's driveway'. I passed my mother as I walked by the kitchen to get to the front door.

'Where are *you* going?' my mother yelled over her bowl of atta.

I walked back to the kitchen and she eyed me up and down, a look of utter disappointment crossing her face. 'I don't like what you're wearing,' she said. 'Change into something else. We're having guests over.'

'Mom, this is a *costume*,' I said. 'And Jesus, don't you and Dad ever go to other people's homes?'

'It's different this time,' she said. 'These desis are important members of the community. If your father gets in good with them it'll be good for his business.'

'How many is it?'

'I don't know. Twenty or thirty.'

'Twenty or thirty? Christ Almighty!'

My mother kept pounding the atta, and I briefly wondered if she was a cruel enough woman to be picturing my face in the dough. 'Why are you being so dramatic, Samira?' she said, crossly. 'What's the matter with you? You know what I think? You really want to know what I think?'

I clasped my eyes shut to physically block her oncoming lecture. It was an unconscious response. I think it began as a child, when I would hold tea parties on the top of my father's car. Every time, without fail, a doll or stuffed monkey would inevitably slide off the blanket and I would go tumbling to the ground after it. The only way to endure my mother's red-hot castigation while she tended to my bloody knees afterwards was to pretend she wasn't there, that I couldn't really hear what she was saying.

'I think you don't like people anymore,' my mother began. 'You used to be such a sweet little girl, but now you're turning into a bitter, miserable woman. At such a young age too. Your father and I have been through so much, worse than you could ever imagine, and we never turned out this way. Look at your father. Hindus raided his village during the India–Pakistan partition. Lost both his parents. Had to hide under their bleeding, sliced bodies so the Hindus wouldn't find him. And they did.' She made a sweeping, then chopping motion with her arm. 'They found him. They moved his parents' bodies aside and wielded their swords and cut your poor father in the back. Left him there to die with everyone else. It's a miracle your father made it out alive. A miracle! You keep these things in mind as you live your life. Learn from us. Learn from our experiences. Gain perspective. If you don't change your attitude, you will become a miserable shrew just like your Aunty Sonia in Islamabad. She fought with everybody. She was always right. Everyone was always wrong. What kind of man would want to live with that? Nobody could stand her. She died alone three years ago. No husband. No children. I don't want that to happen to you. Listen to me, I'm your mother. You need to change your behaviour. Stop being so cynical. Socialize with people again. Get out of your bones.'

'You mean your shell.'

My mother didn't like that, being corrected. 'Don't try to be smart with me, Samira. You're in no position. I see what is happening with you. You sit up in your room all day, sulking around, crying. You and Ethan may not be together right now but you can't hide from people forever. These guests are bringing their kids so you'll have people to talk to.'

'Twelve-year-old kids don't have anything to talk to me about.'

For Pakistanis, everyone in the population falls into two categories—kids and parents. There are no 'young singles' or 'twenty-somethings' or 'thirty-somethings'. If you're nineteen years old and have a husband and a kid, you belong with the grown-ups. If you're twenty-seven like me and not married-with-children, you're in the 'kids' category, and belong in the same room with the screaming eight-year-olds and brooding fifteen-year-olds.

'I can't be here tonight,' I explained to her. 'I got invited to a party. Some old high school friends. It sounds like fun. It's a 1980s-style party.'

'So you won't be here to help me?'

'You just said you wanted me to socialize again. This party is going to be huge.'

I thought my mother was ignoring me. She sprinkled some dry wheat flour on a cutting board and began rolling out a handful of dough. 'Okay, go,' she said. 'Maybe it'll be good for you. Get you out of this depression. Just promise you'll help when you get back.'

My cell phone vibrated in my pocket. Meena had just sent me another text.

'Promise, Mom. But gotta go. My ride's here.' I gave my mother a quick peck on the cheek and headed for the door.

'Who's your ride?' I heard her say as I shut the door behind me.

When I got to the end of the driveway, I turned around to make sure my mother's face wasn't pressed against a window looking out, saw that it wasn't, turned left and jogged down the neighbourhood.

I was out of breath by the time I reached Meena's car. 'Jesus, why did you drive all the way to the O'Donnell's?' I said, letting myself in. 'I can barely catch my breath.'

'What took you so long to get here?' she said.

'Sorry. Mom trapped me with a lecture. She pulled the scar speech.'

Meena shook her head. 'I am so tired of them telling us that story. They do it just to lay guilt trips on us. I mean, what's the point in telling us other than to make us feel shitty? Is it our fault we didn't grow up in those conditions? And the story isn't even true! Remember last year they slipped up and told us he got the scar from a moped accident in Lahore and Mom was the nursing student who stitched him up? Remember? They were like, "and that's how we met".'

As Meena spoke, I looked over her costume. She had on black flip-flops, jeans and a black tank top.

'Why aren't you in a costume?' I barked.

Meena bit her lower lip, then widened her eyes. 'Yeah, about that. Well, look, I meant to get one but I had to finish this paper and I wasn't able to get to the mall like I planned . . .'

We were at a stop sign, so I reached for the door and stepped out. 'That's it,' I said, slamming the door behind me. 'I'm out.'

'What? Where are you going?' Meena put the car in reverse and slowly followed my path back to the house.

'I'm not going to this party looking like some fool,' I said. 'If you want to go to this party so bad you can go alone.'

'But you look so cute,' she pleaded out the window. 'I meant to tell you I wasn't in a costume earlier. But I got so busy. Come on. I'm sorry. I'll make it up to you. Please? I *really* want us to go to this party.'

I stopped walking, hesitated for a second, then got back in. 'You better make this up to me,' I warned her.

When we arrived at the party twenty minutes later, a whopping six people were there. They all sat together in the living room, tamely drinking beer from red plastic cups. A large orange and black banner swung across the ceiling that said, 'All Hallows Eve, 1986'.

'Hi everyone. I'm Meena,' Meena said, smiling generously. She seemed unfazed by the lack of people around us. She nudged me with her elbow.

'I'm Samira.'

'Hello,' the crowd said in unison, some throwing in an additional hand wave.

'Samira! Hey, Samira!'

At the top of the stairs, someone dressed as Elvira was calling out my name. I was pretty sure that underneath the wall of black hair and plastic cleavage was Peggy-Rae Cooper, one of my very few friends from high school. 'You came!' she yelled. 'Oh my god, look at you! You look great!'

'You look great too,' I replied. 'Nice boobs.'

'And Meena!' she shrieked, lifting her dress to scurry down the stairs. 'Oh my god! The Tanweer sisters! I haven't seen you guys in years. I totally can't believe it!'

Peggy-Rae needed to calm down. I remembered why she was one of the only girls who ever talked to me in high school. She was a little too desperate for friends, tried a little too hard. She grabbed my hand and led the three of us to a couch, where we spent the next twenty minutes catching up on our lives. It was mostly Meena and Peggy-Rae catching up on their lives while I listened in, and I was grateful to have Meena serve as a buffer between me and any other chatty former high school mates we might encounter. Meena was the popular one, after all. She knew, and did, everybody.

'Have you guys seen Chris?' Peggy-Rae asked.

'Not yet,' Meena replied. 'He's the host of this thing, right?'

'Yeah, I'll go get him.' Peggy-Rae got up from the couch, then lowered her head, her bubbly enthusiasm abating a little. 'You guys know about him right?'

'We heard,' I said. 'But it's no big deal.'

'Well, some of the people invited left rude messages on his Evite. Some of Chris's old friends said shit like, "I can only come fag, I mean stag." Mike Dern posted that one.'

'That's awful. Mike was one of his best friends,' Meena replied.

'And remember Joe Bennett?' Peggy-Rae asked. 'He said, "Hey Chris, going to dress like a man this Halloween?"'

'Stupid jocks,' I said, hoping Peggy-Rae wouldn't remember how much I pined over jocks in high school.

'Well, enough people responded who supported Chris and got back at those other guys. It was kind of like a war-of-the-words on Evite.' Peggy-Rae looked up the stairs. 'Let me get them. I think Dan's stressing over his costume. They're being very rude to their guests.'

I already wanted to leave. I was craving the comfort and solitude of my bed. The soft pink quilt, the stack of magazines by my freshly washed laundry-sheet-scented pillow. I was about to inform Meena—she did say we could leave whenever I wanted—but before I had the chance a short vampire waddled down the stairs, with Chris not far behind. Chris was wearing an oversized white T-shirt with red, shiny parachute pants, his hair shaved closely on the sides with a rectangular clump running down the middle of his scalp. Their outfits confirmed what I had suspected all along about this party—that people were either going to dress in the eighties' style or wear a Halloween costume. Not some combination of the two, whatever that would be.

'Oh my god,' Peggy-Rae yelled to Chris. 'What did you do to your hair?'

'It was my idea,' the vampire proudly stated. 'It's more Fresh Prince of Bell Air, which I'm afraid teeters dangerously on the 90s. But doesn't it look great? Oh hello, I'm Dan,' said Dan as he presented his hand to me. Meena and I introduced ourselves and Chris told us he was glad we could make it.

'I think it looks great. Incredibly authentic,' Dan continued about Chris's hair as he grazed his hand over the top of it.

'It looks okay. No need to get too excited now. I'm shaving it all off tomorrow so this is just for the party.' Chris smiled softly. 'Oh, you girls need drinks. Tell me what you want.'

'A Corona would be good,' said Meena.

'None for me,' I replied.

'Well, just make yourselves at home and let me know if you need anything,' Chris said. 'More people are expected so don't worry, this party will pick up. Meena, let me get your Corona.'

We both watched as Chris, heading for the kitchen, became entangled in a group of partiers. When it became clear he wasn't getting away from them anytime soon, Meena grabbed my hand. 'Let's get the drinks ourselves,' she said.

I reluctantly let her lead me to the kitchen. 'I don't know if I want a drink,' I said. 'Maybe after I get into this place a little. I don't want to risk it.'

Meena poured some rum and coke into a plastic cup. 'You sound like a virgin at a frat party.' She dipped a finger into her cup to stir, added a few ice cubes, and took a sip. 'Come on. Let's mingle.' About an hour later, Meena and I were separated. She went off, busily chatting with other guests and at one point, searching all the rooms, while I was content to stay in a corner of the living room and people-watch. Not many people from high school showed up, and the ones that came seemed to be from Meena's class. I felt partly relieved because it meant I wouldn't have to engage in any more conversations about what I had been up to all these years, which possibly included being a threat to national security. But still, I was kind of hoping *some* of the high school people I knew would show up, especially the popular kids, so I could decide they'd aged poorly and use that to feel better about myself.

Around midnight, I heard Meena calling out to me. Groups of people were streaming into the house. The crowd was getting so dense so quickly it was hard to even see her from where I was sitting.

'Come here. Come here,' she beckoned. She edged herself between a Mr T and a gorilla, and reached over to grab my arm. 'That bitch isn't here,' she hollered to me over her shoulder. 'I knew she wouldn't show up.'

'Who's not here?' I asked. 'Meena, what's going on?'

'Forget it,' she snapped. 'I'm already *so* over it and this stupid party. But there's someone else I want you to meet.'

With great difficulty, she tugged me through the crowd, both of us dodging devil forks and fairy wings and abandoned cups of beer on the ground until we were face to face with a guy wearing jeans, a Jackson Hole, Wyoming T-shirt and a rubber mask with an ax protruding from his cut open and oozing brain.

'Samira,' Meena said. 'This is Steve. Steve, Samira.'

'Nice to meet you,' Steve said through his rubber mask. 'Meena says you want some smoke?'

My eyes lit up. Alcohol was one thing. The liquid was some sort of portal that led me directly to a secluded area of deep thought and introspection, and no good ever came of thinking about my life that hard. Weed? It calmed me, erased my thoughts, made me pleasant, put the world in perspective. I hadn't told Meena I wanted any or asked her to find some for me, but I was glad she did and the party, the night, my entire life, just got better. 'I would love some,' I told him. 'Come with me, ladies.' Meena and I followed Steve onto the wooden deck outside, descending the stairs and discreetly looping around the side of the house. An icy dew on the grass seeped into my Jelly shoes and a cold breeze blew through the wool of my sweater. I crossed my arms tightly to keep the chill out as I watched Steve reach behind the air condenser and pull out the largest bong I had ever seen in my life. He dug in his pocket and retrieved a plastic ziplock bag that was half-full of the green stuff. I could see it well in the moonlight—dense, clumpy, studded with little crystals—good-quality pot. After crumbling some of it into the stem of the bong and patting it down, he offered it to me.

It took me a second—the bong was awkward and heavy and I wondered what possessed him to bring such a conspicuous and unnecessarily huge device out to a party—but I eventually steadied it and prepared myself. 'Thanks for sharing, Steve,' I said. 'I really appreciate it.'

'No problem. My pleasure, ladies,' he said, holding the flame of his cigarette lighter over the stem.

I stuck my lips inside the large glass tube and breathed in slowly and steadily, but noticed nothing came up. So I did it again, breathing deeper this time until I heard water bubbling and saw the white cloud of smoke approaching. I sucked in all the smoke and held it in, slowly breathing it back out. It burned as it came out and I started coughing uncontrollably, each cough making my throat burn more severely. I was coughing so hard I thought I was going to gag.

'That's good stuff,' I said, my voice sounding strained as I lurched over trying to get some oxygen.

'Have another one,' Steve generously offered. I took the bong in my hand and repeated the process, only this time, I seemed to be sucking in the white cloud forever. 'Whoa! You just took a huge hit, girl! You're gonna be so fuckin' stoned!' Steve said, seemingly very pleased. 'Have a little more.'

'No more,' I said, my voice barely audible. 'Been a while since I've done this much. But thanks.'

'Again, it was my pleasure. Meena, you gonna have some?' Meena turned to me. 'Samira, go on in. I'll catch up with you in a bit.' I looked at her puzzled. 'Why?'

'Go on,' she repeated, talking to me like I was her toddler. 'I'll be there in a minute.'

Whatever was going on with them, I didn't care. My throat was on fire and I was dying for some water. I went back into the house, which was now maximally occupied with the features of a good party evident—plastic cups scattered everywhere, people on every level of the house and out in the backyard, sticky hardwood floors, the musty odour of keg beer. I estimated eighty per cent of the people at the party wore some kind of costume.

Coming up with that rough statistic must have taken everything out of me, because rather suddenly, I could feel my eyelids slowly rolling down like projector screens. My feet felt heavy, leaden, and my toes tingled in a way that was ticklish and slightly painful. I felt like I might faint.

There were two stools over by the mini-bar—one with a pile of sweaters on top, the other unoccupied, which I sat down on. Not a bad spot. I could relax while enjoying good views of the kitchen, stairs and the impromptu dance floor in the middle of the living room. Monsters, ghosts and gay cops danced alongside Madonnas and Michael Jacksons to Rockewell's 'Somebody's Watching Me'. Someone came dressed as a scuba diver. Mesmerized, I watched the spectacle of him straining to dance about in his flippers.

A moustachioed Magnum P.I. put his unopened water bottle on the counter. The minute he turned away, I grabbed it, twisting off the cap. I cocked my head back and relished the cold sensation of liquid pouring down my burnt throat. As I leaned over to toss the empty bottle into the trash can, my hand brushed against the counter. It was the first time I noticed—the counter was made out of a strange material, not tile or wood or something like that, but a soft, shiny cloth. I scratched at it with my finger nail.

'Dude!' someone yelled from behind me. 'That's a person!'

A man dressed as a member of Kiss marched to the bar and started picking off the drinks. Then he picked up and took away the pile of sweaters and I realized it wasn't a pile of sweaters but a girl dressed as bumble bee. She had apparently passed out and people were setting their drinks on her wings.

'What's so funny?' Meena asked.

I didn't even realize I was laughing until Meena pointed it out to me. 'There was a bee,' I giggled, my cognitive abilities growing weaker by the second. 'A bee. Oh, fuck. Nevermind.'

Meena took her keys from her pocket. 'I'm tired. Ready to go?'

I was already heading for the door. We walked two blocks to Meena's car and I could still hear the noise and chatter coming from the house. A few minutes later, we were off down the highway.

'Well, Sam, did you have a good time?' Meena asked.

I was freezing. All the windows in the car were open. My frizzy hair tattered in bunches in the wind, but I didn't ask her to close the windows. The cold was sobering me up.

'I had a great time,' I replied. 'You were right. It was good for me to get out for the night. And the weed was perfect.'

Meena dug into her purse, then smiled as she held up a joint. 'Want some more? Parting gift from our little friend out back.'

I grabbed the joint from her. 'Thanks. I'll save some for you.'

'No need. I don't do pot.'

'You don't do pot?' I asked, slightly confused at her rejection of something she enabled me to get, and a little miffed with the undertone of superiority in Meena's voice as she said it. 'What's your problem with pot?'

'It's illegal,' she said, handing me a lighter. 'I don't want to do anything illegal.'

I quickly lit the joint and took a nice suck off it, the smoke disappearing quickly behind my head. 'That's good of you, Meena,' I replied. 'I'm not sure where your sudden love affair with the law came from, but I've already been arrested for much worse than pot possession. So . . .' I smiled excitedly. 'Guess who's smokin' up tonight?'

Meena chuckled and turned towards the window. She stuck her face out as far as she could and breathed in a big gulp of cold fog. Our car whizzed through a yellow light.

'Uh, hey, I know you're not stoned but are you drunk?' I asked her, feeling less worried about it than I should have been.

'I sobered up much earlier. Trust me. I wouldn't drive if I wasn't able to.'

I watched for signs from her driving that she really was sober—not too fast, not too slow, cautious when changing lanes. According to my little inebriated brain, everything was fine, so I sucked on my joint.

'Mmm,' I said, admiring the joint in my fingers. 'This is nice. I feel nice. Best I've felt in months. I need to thank that masked guy for his generosity. By the way, who was he? You still haven't said.'

'I have no idea who he was,' Meena replied. 'I never saw his face.'

'You never saw his face? You didn't know him? Why did he share his weed with us?'

Meena laughed. 'Like you said, he was just being generous.'

'I don't believe that for a second. Guys don't . . .' I paused mid-sentence as the new round of pot clouded over the connection between my brain and my tongue. All the lights we were driving by started to swirl together. Something seemed off. This didn't feel like normal pot. This didn't feel like pot at all. 'Guys don't . . .' I drifted off again.

'Yeah? Guys don't what? Having a little trouble there, Sam?'

'Shit,' was all I could muster in response to that.

When we pulled into my neighbourhood, Meena, without warning, declared, 'I gave him a blow-job.'

'What?' I stared back at her like she told me she missed her period. 'What did you just say?'

'BJ I gave him a BJ.'

Meena rolled up her window and turned the defogger on high. 'I told you I'd make it up to you for not wearing a costume,' she explained. 'Remember I promised? I'm good as my word.' She kept fiddling with the defogger, and muttered something about how it still wasn't working properly and she was going to defy my father and buy a Volkswagen. I wanted to slap her little brown hand away from the dashboard and make her look at me. She was acting so casual, so dismissive, I wasn't sure I was hearing properly.

'When I told you to make it up to me, I didn't mean give some random stranger a BJ,' I said, looking at her gravely. 'Do you realize the implications, Meena? That this, in fact, makes you a whore?'

'No, it doesn't,' she replied. 'I'm an engineering student.'

Meena giggled, a sparkly little laugh, and she told me to quit worrying. That I'm always worrying. And that we'd had a great time at the party and, 'Besides,' she said, 'aren't you enjoying your doobie?'

The doobie? Of course I was enjoying the doobie. I was enjoying it very much. I looked at it again, jostled between my fingers. Soft, white. Tube-like. I stuck it in my mouth and sucked one more time. One long, generous suck . . .

Wait a minute.

As I blew some white smoke out of the side of my mouth, I had a slight epiphany. I wasn't upset at Meena because she gave a blow-job to a guy whose face was obscured by a rubber mask. Meena was always a bit loose that way, lost her virginity back in junior high, always sneaking out of the house to make out with the gangly boys who worked the drive-through at the downtown Sunrise Biscuits. The reason I was upset was because this time, she acted this way for *me*. Out of compassion or generosity or some twisted sense of remuneration, she got on her knees for my happiness. I didn't appreciate having more guilt to pile on my already heavy conscience—now that I was a contributor to my kid sister's delinquency. If I didn't set her straight, Meena would pull something like this again. Something was obviously happening with her. A quarter-life crisis. Some kind of crisis. She seemed confused, lost in contradictions. Enabler and law-abiding citizen. Whore and designated driver. The girl needed help.

I searched for what to say as I looked over at Meena in the driver's seat—the centre of her billowy lips glowing pink and the gloss wiped off. I pictured a little Meena—a pair of long, black braids falling down her back, her feet swinging to and fro, two fat little lips wrapping themselves around a grape popsickle . . .

I shuddered at the thought. I knew that every suck off the joint from here on out was going to remind me of that image, make me feel like I was giving the masked pot-dealer a blow-job by association. I glanced at Meena disapprovingly before I took one last hit, put it out in the ashtray and then stuck it in my pocket for later use.

The weed may have been cursed but it was still good weed.

'Well, looks like its 'Party at Tanweer Central,' she said, excitedly.

As we pulled onto our street, I counted seven cars parked in front of our parents' house.

It took me a few seconds, but soon I realized those cars had brought people with them. And those people were in my house.

'Shit!' I yelled, panicking at this new problem before me. 'I can't go in there! Look at me!' I yanked down her passenger-side mirror. My normally straight and silky hair billowed out like Einstein. My pastel-coloured eye make-up had leaked into various crevices in my face, and my clothes looked ridiculous. Too much explaining would have to be done if I met any of the guests. The last thing I was capable of doing at that moment was explaining anything to anyone. 'They're all over the house!'

Meena spoke with an annoying sense of sobriety. 'Just sneak in through a basement window.'

'What time is it? Shouldn't they be gone by now?'

Meena checked her dashboard. 'It's 1:30.'

I was screwed. 1:30 a.m. white people time means 10:00 p.m. desi time. Too early for the guests to go home.

'Well,' Meena began. 'I gotta get out of here before anyone sees me. I was going to crash at my friend's house but turns out I'm not staying there after all, so I'm driving back to Wilmington.'

'No, you go,' I said. 'Just leave me here and I'll figure this all out.' I was being sarcastic but she took me seriously.

She stretched her arms out wide to give me a hug. 'Take care of yourself, sis. I'll be home again soon. Remember, though. Tonight, I was never here.'

I was half-heartedly hugging her back, too preoccupied with my next task. I got out of her car and crept to the basement windows, pulling the bushes out of the way. My father and all the male guests were sitting in the main room downstairs, chatting and inspecting Khalid's Halo equipment. None of the trees were tall enough for me to climb to an upstairs window. I walked back around. There was simply no escape. I had to go through the front door.

Someone's kid whizzed by as soon as I walked in, chasing another kid up the stairs. I heard the clanking of dishes in the kitchen and it reawakened a thought in me—I had promised my mother I would help clean up after the party. But the party was still going on. Surely she didn't expect me to help her clean this late?

'Oh, Samira!' my mother yelled. 'How was your party?'

I entered the kitchen, expecting to find my mother hovering over the sink surrounded by stacks of dirty dishes, but instead, the entire room was sparkling clean. A few Aunties were scurrying about, drying pots and teacups with towels.

'Here. I'm in the sunroom,' my mother hollered.

I found my mother lying on the carpet, sprawled over a giant silk pillow like a Roman empress. 'I want everyone to see your costume. Look everyone. She's supposed to be someone dressed from the 80s.'

Five women sat on the couch above my mother. Some of them stayed cold silent, either not getting the joke or not caring. But Aunty Ruby laughed. And that was the most important laugh to get. Aunty Ruby was the queen bee of the Aunties, married to one of the richest and most established men in the Pakistani community. No party, no decision, no gossip, was ever complete without her involvement. She sat in the centre of the couch, her hefty weight distributing itself around her, anchoring down the room.

'Come here, mera beta. Come, come. Oh, va va va!' She swung her head from side to side. 'Such interesting look. This was for party?'

'Yes, Aunty Ruby,' I said. 'I went to a party.'

'Sit down, mera laal,' she said, pushing me down next to her. 'We have missed you tonight. You mother made such delicious vegetable kofta balls. And daal, and chana and aloo. Your uncle would like this food. Always good food here . . . you know . . . your mother makes. I have just come back from Pakistan, where I stayed with my daughters Kahana and Salil. They have a servant who cooks baingan bharta, but it is not so good. Not as good as your mother makes. That is something I miss, having servants. We are getting maid but she is a very cold woman, not good in the house. I think I do not feel comfortable with this woman . . .'

As I listened to Aunty Ruby talk, I couldn't help but notice there was something terribly wrong with her face. I didn't know if she had always looked this way or if something had happened to her recently. A car accident? Did she get a facelift?

'But she, yes that one, she is very reliant servant,' Aunty Ruby continued. 'My daughters are okay. And if they are okay,' she smiled, 'you know, it makes me okay.' She pounded her chest. 'From the heart.'

It was Aunty Ruby's forehead. I had never seen one like hers before. It was all shiny and round. It was huge. And it seemed to be sloping towards me.

'There are too many people in the house at one time,' Aunty Ruby said. 'Too much noise, too much mess. In Pakistan they have separate quarters. It is good for them too, you know? To be away from the house . . .'

It was her whole head. Her cheeks, her eyes, her nose, her lips—everything was bulging out, inflating, stretching to the max, like someone had stuck an air hose in her neck and turned it on.

'. . . not very different, you know, from the others there . . .'

I felt my ears clog like someone stuffed cotton in them and I could barely hear anything but a faint whistle sound. I desperately tried to listen to what Aunty Ruby was saying, using every bit of will to concentrate, but all I could focus on was the flapping of her enormous fuschia lips, more pronounced as her speech slowed to a murmur.

'Need to say your thanksss . . . and . . . p . . . r . . . a . . . y . . . that . . . thossssse . . . you . . . knnoowwww . . .'

Her head was gently bobbing back and forth, tenuous, about to fly away . . . 'all . . . my . . . chil . . . drennnnnn . . . brrrrreak . . . fast . . . burrrr . . .'

I reached out and grabbed it.

A few years back, I had decided that before finishing grad school and joining the workforce where I could get randomly drug tested I was going to try every drug that existed. I didn't want to live out my life wondering so I did ecstasy at an outdoor War of 1812 overture concert. I spent the rest of the day rolling around on the ground behind some port-o-johns. Then one day I tried cocaine and it did the opposite. It kept me alert and chatty all night but that was it. Maybe it was bad coke and it was diluted or something but I didn't understand what all the hype was about. It wasn't much different from downing three espresso shots at one go. Then I tried mushrooms and the only thing I remember from that experience was that I could smell everything in the next room. That was actually pretty cool. Probably the coolest of all my experiences. The only other drug I was ever curious about was acid, but for some reason it was never available to me so I never tried it and I realized, now that my hands were clutching Aunty Ruby's head, I would never have to.

'Bissss . . . mill . . . aahhhh!' she yelled.

I lifted my hands off her, my movements feeling as thick and slow as molasses. I tried to speak, not sure at what speed it was coming out in reality, but I hoped it sounded like, 'I thought I saw a spider in your hair.'

She whacked at her head. 'Is it still there?'

I swallowed hard, relieved she accepted my explanation. 'No, Aunty. I think I got rid of it.' I looked up. The couch, the Persian rug, the marble coffee table—everything was spinning, and in the several twirls I saw three head-covered Aunties scornfully watching me but thankfully I didn't see my mother. My heart was racing. I felt nauseous and needed water bad. 'I'll be right back,' I said to all of them, using Aunty Ruby's chubby knee to balance myself as I got up and hobbled over to the kitchen. I practically threw myself over the sink, turning on the faucet. I waited for the water to turn cold, ice-cold, as cold as it could get. I cupped my hands under the stream and drank, then splashed some on my face. I rubbed my eyes until the rubber hole of the garbage disposal came into sharp focus. I took a deep breath and splashed myself once more. I was reaching for the hand towel hanging over the dish rack when a high-pitched yelp pierced the air, like a cat shrieking in heat. I dropped the towel and my knee lurched forward, striking the brass knob on the cabinet below the sink.

The pain spread like fire. I grabbed my knee, rubbing it furiously. Was it Merlin? Was it Ignatius? Is one of them hurt? I looked around. No, it was my mother. She was huddled in a dark corner, out of view of the other Aunties, singing to herself in Urdu.

'Jesus, Mom. I didn't see you standing there.'

On the counter in front of her was a big glass bowl with a curved spoon in the middle, floating atop a pink, foamy punch. She dipped the spoon in the bowl, past the foam and into the thin liquid underneath, and poured some in a glass. 'Samira, come here. I want you to try this.'

I stopped rubbing my knee and limped over to her. She handed me the glass and I took a quick sip. It was delicious, sugary and cold, like melted popsicles. 'Mom, this is yummy. What's in it?'

Whatever was in it, I felt my head clearing up immediately. I downed the whole glass and my mother poured me another. She casually stirred the punch, humming another Urdu tune.

'Mom,' I asked again, 'what's in it?'

She lowered her voice, almost to a whisper. 'Well,' she began, 'you see, it's my own special recipe. A little bit of Sprite, some fruit punch, some chunks of pineapple, a little food colouring to make it festive . . .' She stirred the bowl some more. '. . . and two cups of Captain Morgan rum.'

I peered down my empty glass. No wonder it was so good.

My mother leaned over and laid her hands on my chest, exploding into giggles. It was then I realized she had been enjoying the punch all night. 'How about that?' she said, barely able to contain herself. 'I've been serving it to these women all night, with their dupattas and their Islam. They've been drinking alcohol and they don't even know it.'

My eyes widened. I didn't know whether to laugh with her or freak out. My mother was serving these people alcohol? Was she crazy? I mean, it was kind of funny. Actually it was really funny and I was pretty impressed with her for pulling it off but what a stupid prank! What if someone found out? It would ruin my parents' reputation in the community, my father's business, everything. I sniffed my glass to see if I could smell the rum.

Then I realized . . . how would these women know what alcohol smelled like? Or tasted like? Or felt like if they never drank? George Bernard Shaw did say that thing about the Pope. About him giving advice on things like abortion and masturbation. If the Pope knew anything about sex, Shaw argued, he shouldn't.

'You know, Samira,' my mother said, 'back in the day, when your father and I were young college students in love, Lahore was such a romantic city. It was like Paris, with gardens everywhere and a river. Your father and I used to go canoeing on that river. Oh, we were so fashionable! The girls would wear the most beautiful saris from India. We would put flowers in our hair. Your father and I would picnic in the rose gardens with our friends. We would recite poetry. Oh, if you only knew Urdu! The most beautiful poetry in the world is in Urdu. Did you know we almost named you Shamah? It was too difficult for these Americans to say, so we chose Samira, a simpler name. But we wanted you to be Shamah. Hai hai! From the most beautiful poem in the world. Your father would hold my hand when he read it to me. 'Shamah herang main jalti hai sahar honetak.' The flame will burn no matter what until the dawn of light.'

'Mom,' I said, 'Maybe we should start cleaning up.'

'Hai hai hai,' she went on. 'Art and poetry and *romance*. This is how Pakistan used to be. We were cultured. My father—your Abbaji—he was a diplomat. He drank, he smoked. Before that terrible Zia took over and made everyone so religious. Just look at a picture of Zia if you don't believe me. Whereas Jinnah was an intellect, a peaceful man, a hero, Zia was a scoundrel. I'm telling you. Just look at pictures of him on that inter-*net*. With his evil eyes and that damn moustache. He *looks* like a crazy person. Oh, you were so young when he took over. You were living here, so far from where your father and I grew up. But I'm telling you, Samira, it used to be different. Look at these young women now—with their heads covered, barely saying a word to anyone. I won't accept this version of my Pakistan. I don't care what your father says or anyone in this community says. I won't accept it.'

There was a shudder of the basement door, and suddenly standing in the middle of the kitchen was Uncle Zafir. He had thin, side-swept hair and he rested his hands atop a boulder-sized stomach that balanced atop two pin legs. He smiled contentedly and spoke as if addressing an audience.

'I have come to say goodnight, as it is time for us to leave our gracious hosts. As usual, we have enjoyed an evening of great food, great conversation, and of course, exceptional hospitality . . .'

I looked around to see who he was talking to. My mother was stirring the punch, humming to herself again. The Aunties were all standing up in a circle, laughing together as one of them put her hand on another's shoulder, no doubt all of them feeling curiously good about the world.

I was glad the guests were leaving. I didn't like being stoned while all this was happening. I tried to keep my wits about me for the next ten minutes as my mother went upstairs and I took over for her, seeing people out. Luckily, no one seemed to notice anything amiss about the night or my mother's sudden headache.

'What's wrong with your mother?' my father asked, standing beside me in his striped pajamas and sleeping cap as I tucked my mother into bed.

'She's not feeling well, Dad,' I said. 'Tough day.'

'Poor woman. Yes, she works hard sometimes.'

I nodded. 'Yes, it is. I mean, she is. I mean, yes . . . she does.'

'Samira,' my mother wearily called out.

'Yes, Mom?'

She grabbed my purple puffed-sleeve and gently pulled me in towards her. 'Put the punch in a Tupperware.'

Part 2

4

For the next month, for the first time ever, my life came to a complete stop. There was no school, no work, no C-SPAN or BBC or CNN or any other print or electronic media that could tell me what was happening in the world because everything happening in the world reminded me of D.C. Even while reading a local alternative newspaper, I saw a blurb about my Congressman and boss, Jim Bailey from North Carolina, fourth district, member of the House Ways and Means Committee, whose tax reform policies were getting wide support from both parties and several favourable editorials from the *Washington Post* and the *New York Times.*

That was my work. Those reform policies. I was the legislative aide who spent a solid two years analysing existing policies, performing statistical analyses of proposed changes and crafting new policy language. Bailey acknowledged that and expressed his appreciation when he asked to see me in his office the day after I was arrested. I was grateful for his recognition of my work, and I was going to thank him—thank him profusely for coming to my aid the day before and getting me out of police custody. Two calls to the station had been made on my behalf—one of which was from Bailey. I had friends in high places, everyone said. And Bailey was a busy man. It was nice of him to make the call, vouching for my innocence. I was grateful, and I was going to tell him I was sorry for what I did and hoped it didn't inconvenience him or cause him any embarrassment, but I was eager to put the whole incident behind me and get right back to my analysis of the latest fiscal stimulus package.

'As you know, Samira,' he said as he sat atop his mahogany desk, swinging his stout legs in front of me, 'this next election is going to be tough. Real tough. I'll be up against the former governor, and we all know he plays dirty politics. I'll need as clean a slate as possible going into this race.'

He nodded for validation and I nodded back.

'We managed to keep this story out of the media, write it off as a traffic incident. But that doesn't mean it's gone forever. You know how gossipy Capitol Hill is,' he chuckled. 'People could hear about it and twist it around, in all sorts of ways. After all, your name still appears on that FBI list. People might say I have a security risk on my staff.' He grabbed his belly and full-out laughed. 'You and I . . . you and I know that's just not true about you. But you understand how these things go, right? It's the way of the world, I guess. Daggone it! It just ain't pretty.'

I nodded again in agreement.

'You've been a great asset to this office, Samira. A solid analyst. After the election, I'd love to have you back.'

He stuck his hand out and I politely shook it. Then I gave my office-issued laptop back to the secretary and cleared out my cubicle. Election was a year away.

I was unemployed. After what I had done, possibly unemployable. A statistic on a government chart, like The Police sang, and I don't ever want to play the part. But the problem I didn't want to admit to anyone, especially to myself, was that in this state of zero purpose and zero contribution to the economy, I was surprisingly quite content. I was happy to wake up at ten each day, eat breakfast at ten-thirty, wear the exact same clothes I had been wearing for the past three days and generally keep my world as small as possible. But I wasn't useless during this time either. I still did chores around the house and helped out my father at the dealership. He had tasked me with mundane administrative work—data entry, answering the phone on the main floor, fetching keys for the sales guys doing test drives. One day I overheard Abdul make a sales pitch for the newest Honda Pilot SUVs. Plush, velvety cloth interior, he said. Sound proofing. Quiet enough to not wake the baby, he said, nodding to the yuppie couple's bundle of DNA clumsily strapped and dangling from the husband's chest.

That did it for me. Later that afternoon when no one was looking, I took a pair of keys from the rack. It was a cool afternoon and I had finished most of my work anyway, so I discreetly walked to the farthest Pilot on the lot and let myself in. I readily inhaled the delicious vapours of polish, cleaners and other volatile organic compounds that comprise 'new car smell' and crawled into the back seat. I took off my grey cardigan and laid it behind my head. Oh, *hell yes*, I thought. I nudged off my shoes and stretched my legs all the way out. I lay my right arm over my head and took a few deep breaths. Abdul was right. Couldn't hear a peep from outside.

I wasn't sure how long I had fallen asleep for exactly, but by the time I woke up, it was dark. Not pitch black, but fall was descending upon us quickly and the days were getting shorter. It must have been five or six in the evening. There was a crisp chill as I grabbed my sweater and got out of the car, walking briskly across the parking lot towards the office and towards the flashing lights in front of the main entrance. Upon closer inspection, I realized the flashing lights were from a police car and that my father, Abdul, Bilal and a police officer holding a small pad and pen were standing in front of it. I walked up behind them and said to my father, 'Hey Dad,' and they all turned around.

'What's going on?' I asked.

My father's face crumpled. He gripped his whole head in his hands, the tip of his tie fluttering in the wind, and started rocking back and forth, saying, 'Oh, my god, oh my god' and the cop pointed to me and asked if 'that was her.'

Apparently when I left the building and left my wallet and cell phone behind and never came back, the sales guys started asking about my whereabouts and then someone told someone who told someone who told someone they saw me getting into an SUV four hours earlier. By the time this bit of information travelled back to my father, the story had morphed into someone pulling up to me in a black SUV and asking me to get in the car with him and me getting in and us driving away. The cops were called and everyone at Joe Tanweer Honda was deployed in my search. Cody was still out apparently—patrolling the streets for any sign of this mysterious SUV.

My father was furious on the way home, in spite of my apology for the afternoon nap and protestations that I was too old to still be lured into strangers' cars. But he was unassailable, refusing to even look at me. And although he didn't say it, he didn't actually come out and *disinvite* me from the dealership, I knew I wasn't exactly welcome back there again.

So I started going to the public library. There was a computer off in the corner there, far behind the circulation desk, obscured by some large scrolls of aquatic maps, where I looked up everything related to the FBI Terror Watch list. My name was on there, after all. Somehow, for some reason, it was on there, and since there was no time like the present and I found myself with nothing else to do, I could learn just how badly this was going to screw up my life.

My initial research produced some interesting results. Created in the aftermath of September 11, the watchlist had swelled to almost a million names of suspected terrorists—the number only an estimate and the list itself heavily classified. I found dozens of articles and blogs dedicated to it—people complaining about finding their names on the list and not knowing how they got on there. Names and names and names. Some foreign, some Muslim-sounding, and many as white as Wonder Bread. Adam McCauley. Jamie Hughes. Someone named Little Paige Wimble. Names of famous people. Nelson Mandela. Senator Ted Kennedy. Names of two-year-old kids. Names of dead people.

In other words, the list was generally regarded as useless—its sole purpose to provide headaches for the hundreds of thousands of upstanding citizens who up until the moment they discovered their names on the list had no beef with the United States government. While everyone scrambled for answers, for solutions to getting their names pulled from the list, I learned there were some universal, common-sense approaches everyone took to make their lives easier in the meantime. The first and foremost of which involved drawing zero attention to yourself—steps you could take to avoid getting into any more trouble. I thought of what, in practical terms, that would mean for me:

No more trying to kill significant others. Or anything else that would get the attention of the police, including shoplifting and urinating in public.

No more flying. I didn't imagine that would be a problem, since I had no money and no one to travel with. I hadn't flown since that trip to Atlanta, and no one searched my body cavities or looked at me suspiciously when I checked in, so maybe my name wasn't on the list at that point. But from here on out, travel was to be done by car, train, or air balloon only.

No protests. Just be a quiet, obedient individual and never question an authority figure or entity. No signing petitions either, or adding my name to activist mailing lists, just to be on the safe side.

Don't do anything that would require a background check. In other words, don't apply for a job, anywhere, ever again.

Swoosh!

Swoosh!

Swoosh!

I zipped my head around. One by one, the maps on the shelf next to me tumbled onto the floor. They fell all by themselves. No one was around, no one else could hear. Was this a message? From who or where I didn't know. But this seemed like a message. A warning. *We're watching you, young lady,* they were trying to tell me. *We're judging your every step.*

I picked up the maps off the floor, and a fury swept through me as I put them back on the shelf. I couldn't live out the rest of my life like this, in this oppressive state. Aside from one little indiscretion I had been a dutiful, tax-paying citizen my entire adult life. There must be some recourse, some due process for getting my name removed from the list.

This was America, after all. What in the hell was all that Revolutionary War fuss about in the first place? Declaration of this and Bill of that. What was the point of it all if an upstanding citizen like myself couldn't defend my good name in the eyes of the American government?

I turned back to the computer. On the FBI and Homeland Security websites, I learned I could fill out a form, put in a request to get my name removed. But investigators were inundated with such requests already. It could take years, they warned, to respond to your case. So after reading more articles and going to the ACLU website and the chorus of blogs written by individuals who were detained for hours while trying to catch their evening flights to Minneapolis or Philly, everyone seemed to be in agreement that the request form was bullshit and the only real path to getting your name removed from the list was this:

Write to your Congressman.

As my Congressman made clear he wanted no further association with me, I was, quite simply, fucked.

On top of that I had run out of things to research. My internet quest for everything 'fbi terror watch list' was exhausted by the middle of the first day at the library, so I got up from the computer and started wandering around. I discovered that the library had an extensive collection of brand-new, gold-bound encyclopedias and in the audio-visuals department I could watch movies on small, cold-war era television monitors. Here was my chance to watch all those foreign-language films I'd see on Oscar night—the ones I swore I would rent but would always forsake for the newest, violent blockbuster.

Mostly, though, instead of these noble pursuits, I spent the next month reading back issues of *Gourmet Magazine* on microfiche and taking naps in the children's reading room. Deep down, I knew if something didn't change for me soon, this would easily become my life forever.

'I need a job,' I told Khalid as I lay on the couch in the basement, watching him type on his computer. 'Something. Anything. But nothing that would require a background check.'

'What about working for Dad?' he said.

'You mean at the dealership? Already tried that.'

'No, something else,' Khalid said. 'I heard Mom and Dad talking about it the other day.'

I immediately sat up. 'Talking about what the other day?'

'Dad said he thinks you're wasting away.'

I scoffed at the suggestion. 'Says who? I'm doing peferctly fine. Don't you think I'm doing fine?'

Khalid sighed, not turning from his computer. 'This little issue of yours is already so beyond my realm of caring.'

'But what did they say?' I demanded.

'Huh? Oh, you're still talking to me?'

I searched the floor. I snatched up a piece of paper and was about to crumple it into a ball and throw it at Khalid when I looked down at what it was.

'When did you go to Victoria's Secret?' I asked him.

That made Khalid turn around. 'What? Mind your own business.'

I read the items on the receipt. 'Are you having an affair?'

'No, rat. I'm not having an affair. I bought some stuff for Ashley.' I continued to look at him suspiciously.

'All right,' he said, tossing me a black and pink striped box. 'Look at the box. The card inside has her name on it.'

I carefully opened the box and peeled back layers of pink tissue. I read the card inside. It said, 'For my love, can't wait for your return—he he' with a crude drawing of a devil's face with horns. Sprawled inside was a red lace teddy and matching red thong.

'Eww! I don't want to see this!' I dropped the box onto the floor.

'Watch it, rat.' Khalid carefully refolded the tissue and slid the box under the couch. 'Feel better now?'

'Will you just tell me what Mom and Dad said?'

Khalid sneered. 'You'll find out soon enough.'

Right at that moment, almost as if it had all been planned, my father called out to me from upstairs. 'Baby,' he said. 'Can you come upstairs please? I need to talk to you.'

I scrambled for the remote and turned on the television, upping the volume until I was sure his voice would be drowned out. Nervously, I pressed the up arrow on the remote in a repetitive fashion.

'Now!' he screamed.

I shot Khalid a look of contempt and tossed the remote on the couch. Once I appeared in the kitchen, to my surprise, but not to my relief, my father's face lit up.

'Samira, I have a new job for you,' he announced. 'Something I think would be a most wonderful opportunity. I want you to join me at PAC-PAC. You will learn how to run an organization like I do and learn the issues that affect the Pakistani community. Fahim Kureshi is letting us use his office while he is in Pakistan the next few months. I would like you to run our organization from there. Your duties will include taking phone calls, keeping track of our finances and membership lists and organizing the paperwork. You will also accompany me to our bi-weekly meetings and keep the minutes. To compensate you, I will pay you a weekly allowance of fifty dollars.'

My facial expression was set in stone.

'You must wear better clothes than you've been wearing,' he said. 'Dress formal. I want you looking professional. This is a professional organization.'

My mother was in the kitchen with us. She slid the hot, moist dishes out of the dishwasher and put them on the table for our dinner. She glanced at me sympathetically.

'Professional?' I said. 'Isn't it just you and a couple friends eating at a restaurant somewhere?'

'Yes, that is how it has been in the past. I will concede that,' he replied. I was startled, not to mention impressed, that my father both knew and used the word 'concede'. It meant he was treating me as an adult—that he was in a serious mood. 'We started off well,' he continued, 'but people get busy. We are gaining momentum now and I would like to restart our regular meetings.'

PAC-PAC, or the Pakistani-American Council for Political Action Committee, was a civic organization started and led by my father in the aftermath of 9/11. It was conceived at a time when fear of deportation, profiling and a rise in racism compelled members of the Pakistani community to organize. My father fell into the role of leader with ease, combining his recognition from the dealership and his popularity with the community to put the organization together. But I hadn't heard about the organization in months, years even. I thought it had met the fate of most well-intentioned civic organizations—something I saw happen all the time in D.C.—falling apart before ever getting off the ground. A still-born. Dead on arrival. In other words, something I safely assumed would never threaten my free time.

And now here it was, presented before me not as a side-venture, not something I could occasionally lend a hand to like I did at the dealership, but something I was expected to devote to full-time. A real job. With real responsibilities. When I broached this subject with Khalid, I didn't think anybody would *actually* have a suggestion for a job. Not yet! I thought we would all talk about it, mull it over for a while, keep an eye open, wait for something to come up, take it easy. I had just gotten used to this new, carefree lifestyle of mine and now that a real job was presented before me I realized I wasn't ready to give it up. The prospect of a new job felt like a threat—another life change, another upheaval when things were just starting to become peaceful for me once again.

This was sabotage.

No, it was worse. My mother had ceased unloading the dishwasher. My father was staring at me head on. And Khalid, now having entered the kitchen, was standing in front of me with his arms crossed, his lips curled slightly upward in joyous mockery.

This was an *intervention.*

5

It was Monday, 6:00 a.m. The previous eight, sleepless hours had been nothing but a continuous replay of old fights with Ethan and the images of him standing with Natasha in front of an office building. *My* office building. And then the line of orange cones. Then my car's tyres hitting the cones. Then two Capitol Hill guards running out of the booth as my car whizzed past them and then bright police lights and sharp-edged handcuffs slicing at my wrists and the piece of tomato skin stuck between the cop's two front teeth as he kept telling me, *You're in a lot of trouble young lady, you're in a lot of trouble young lady.*

Then two days later, the email from Ethan. The email that sealed the deal, capped a chaotic, other-worldly two-month period. Made me throw everything into that Founding Fathers storage unit and leave Washington once and for all.

'I'm marrying her. Just thought you should know.'

It was cold. A cruel, horrible way to tell me. I already knew they had started dating, soon after the day Ethan confronted me in my apartment. That was enough to deal with. But he had been with Natasha for two months. And he was already marrying her? Ethan and I were together eight years. We were practically kids when we met, sharing every experience as we grew into adults. Sharing families and meals and birthdays and vacations. Sharing fears and dreams and our darkest thoughts in the middle of the night while the world around us slept.

He couldn't have at least delivered this news in person? Was he that hell bent on punishing me?

No. There was something else going on. Something I didn't know. Something strange. It wasn't just the harsh, distant tone of the email. It had started earlier than that, at the precise moment when my car was screeching in the direction of Ethan and Natasha. It had only lasted a split second, less than a split second, but I could tell. Something was strange. Because in that moment Ethan saw my car coming towards him with my face peering from behind the steering wheel, he didn't have an expression of surprise or fear or shock or any other normal expression a person who was about to be ploughed down by his significant other would have, but he had an expression that communicated something else entirely.

Kill me.

I looked at the clock again.

7:00 a.m.

I let out a deep breath and pushed my hair away from my face. I had to stop this. All I did, every night, was rehash the incidents of the last few months, consciously and in my dreams, and I wanted out. I was sick of it, letting the memories dominate my life. My life had changed. There was no going back now. New things needed my attention. And I could either keep lying there on my bed, wretched and stunted, wallowing in the past while Ethan and Natasha and everyone else moved on, or I could get up. Get out of bed. Shower. After all, no matter what this new job of mine was going to be like, I now had a purpose again. I had somewhere to get up and drive to. I was needed.

A surge of energy flooded through me and I yanked the blankets off. I not only wanted to get up, hell, for this day, I wanted to look sharp. After a quick shower, I pulled my tan crêpe suit out of a clear plastic dry-cleaning bag hanging in my closet. I fixed my hair into work-mode—a low, sleek ponytail, dumped out some old papers and crumbs from my laptop bag and headed downstairs. My parents were sitting at the table having their usual breakfast of black tea and fried sourdough bread.

'Well, look at you!' my mother said. 'All done up and beautiful.'

My father gushed. 'My baby has always been beautiful. I am very proud of my baby today.'

The world had acquired a pleasant, perfect hue that morning. The family was happy, I was happy, and the rays of sunlight flooding the kitchen seemed to be rose-coloured instead of pale yellow. I walked to the table and grabbed a greasy slice of toast with a paper napkin. 'It feels good to be wearing these clothes again,' I admitted. 'Thanks for this opportunity, Dad. I'll do good work for you. I promise.'

'What time will you be home?' my mother asked. 'I'll make us a nice dinner to celebrate your first day. I have fresh bhindi from the garden that I can make with some baingan and paratha. And I can make your favourite dessert—kheer with coconut milk and pistachios.'

I told my mother that sounded great, but I wanted to get to the office early, to get a feel for the place, so I had better go. I reached over and gave her a kiss on the cheek, then my father. I grabbed some fruit from the fridge and headed out the door.

There was more traffic on the highway than I anticipated—I forgot how much the area had developed over the years. What was once farmland had been taken over by stripmalls, clumps of garden-style apartment buildings and office parks. The office park I was headed to was a good three miles off the highway in a somewhat isolated area. I pulled into the parking lot and saw decals hanging from the rear-view mirrors of all the cars. I didn't see why such a large and predominantly empty parking lot would require decals, but since I didn't have one I parked in a visitor's spot.

The park consisted of three identical, five-storey buildings. Punctuating their shiny black exteriors was a small white gazebo sitting on a patch of thick artificial turf. My building was the middle building, and the two on either side had banners hanging from the top that said, 'Office Space for Lease'.

I walked in, and immediately experienced culture shock. There was no security desk in the lobby, no lines to get through metal detectors, no watchful eyes on guests and their belongings—everything I had become accustomed to working in D.C. for five years. Here the lobby was empty, silent but for the clapping of my heels on marble. I walked freely to the elevators and double-checked the scrap piece of paper that had directions to the building. 'Suite 500'.

I stepped out of the elevators on the fifth floor. There were two heavy glass doors with a gold plaque that said 'Libby, Libby and McCrane.' I punched the code to let myself in. I walked down the hallway which looped in a big circle around the floor, peeking into every office, and found myself back by the glass doors again.

'What are you looking for, hun?' came a Southern female voice from a lone cubicle. I peeked in to see a plump and friendly-looking woman in a floral dress.

'I'm looking for Mr Kureshi's office.'

'You're fine, hun. Go about halfway down the hall to the left and you'll see it, right across from the kitchen.' I thanked her and walked around the circle again.

It was 9:00 a.m. and the floor was bustling. This was a very traditional law firm—all offices occupied by suited men of various ages and all cubicles, obviously meant for support staff, were housed by women who dressed much more informally. I eventually found the kitchen and Mr Kureshi's office, a white plaque with gold letters announcing his name on the door. The office was devoid of anything other than furniture. My office furniture was rather elegant—a large mahogany desk with a glass top, a black flat-screen computer monitor, an ergonomic chair, another black chair in front of the desk and some bookshelves. Not bad. At least this was better than the yellow cubicle I had in Congressman Bailey's office.

But my satisfaction with my new digs was brief. There were crumbs and other debris inside the keyboard and greasy fingerprints all over the glass top. I went to the kitchen and found a bottle of glass-cleaner and a couple of rolls of paper towels. I spent the next hour cleaning off the desk, computer and phone, getting into every crevice and wiping every surface I would have contact with, even the ones I wouldn't but were within breathing distance of me. I dumped the infected paper towels in the trash, washed my hands and returned to my office. I had used so much glass-cleaner that fumes lingered in my office and my hands were dry and cracking.

I glanced at my watch. It was almost ten o'clock. My father hadn't given me any tasks for the day, and now that the excitement of getting dressed and getting out of the house wore off I realized I wasn't sure what I was even supposed to be doing there. Just be present? Perhaps. Perhaps that's all my father wanted. Just be present in case any phone calls came in for PAC-PAC. I looked over at the black phone at the corner of the desk. It was the most frightening piece of Klingon weaponry I had ever seen, so I left it alone for the time being. I checked the desk drawers. All were locked except for the top middle drawer, which just had some erasers and paper clips gliding around in there. The lockdown made sense. An attorney wouldn't leave sensitive information lying around his office while on hiatus. I turned on the computer. Again, there were no files on there—just a few programs. Internet Explorer. Excel. Power Point. Word.

To kill some time, I played around with my ergonomic chair, experimenting with different heights and seat adjustments. That killed about another ten minutes. I locked my wallet and cell phone in that top middle drawer and went to explore the building.

I checked out every dull and identical floor and got a little too excited when I found some vending machines in the basement. When I returned twenty minutes later with a bag of Cracker Jack, I still had no idea what to do. I tried calling my father but couldn't reach him.

I walked about the office looking for something to read. On the shelves I found books on immigration tortes and a stack of rubber-banded pamplets that said in English and in Spanish, 'Immigration Reform and You.' I left them right where they were and walked around the hallways some more. At noon I munched on the fruit I brought with me and the bag of Cracker Jack.

It felt lonely eating at my desk, hearing nothing but the sound of my teeth gnashing popcorn and lumps dropping down my throat, and I realized what was happening. For the first time since moving home, I was starting to miss D.C.—the crowds, the tourists, the news crews, the excitement, the endless supply of young co-workers to lunch with. On Capitol Hill, I was surrounded by people in their twenties and thirties who never cooked and always had to eat out. Going out for lunch was the highlight of my day. You could step outside your building and be surrounded by dozens of great lunch spots and lunch buddies to fit every mood—the Spanish tapas bar when you want to socialize with a big group, the organic café when you want some intimate gossiping. Here there were no lunch spots nearby or even a common seating area for people to gather. The nearest place to grab a bite was a Subway in a broken down strip mall half a mile down the road.

I washed my hands when I was done eating. I read through the pamphlets on the shelf and some of the immigration books and it was now almost 2:00 p.m. I called Khalid.

'I'm bored out of my goddamn mind,' I said. 'What am I supposed to do here all day anyway?'

'I don't know,' Khalid said. 'Why don't you ask Dad for some work?'

'I can't reach him,' I replied. 'I'm going home then. He can't get mad at me for leaving so early, right?'

There was silence on the other end. 'Khalid? Are you there? I said it's not like Dad can get mad if I leave, right?'

More silence.

'Khalid? Hello?'

'Son of a bitch!' Khalid screamed, followed by the blasting of automatic gunfire. 'Take that! Take that, you little pussy!'

'Khalid . . .'

'Aww . . . fuckin' A. Fuckin'A, dude you massacred! Sweet!'

'Khalid . . .'

I stopped. I waited patiently for the sound of gunfire to die down before trying to speak again. When it finally did, I realized it was only because Khalid had hung up on me.

I got online and puttered around and wasted another hour on a website called 'Hitler Cats' where all the cats had little squares of black fur under their noses just like the Führer and then around three o'clock, I shut down my computer, slung my black bag over my shoulder and went home.

6

'Your father should be home soon, so set the table.' My mother turned the knob on a cooker and pulled a frying pan from the cupboard. 'Oh, how was your first day at work?'

I slid my bag off my shoulder, prepared and eager to tell someone my story. 'I sat on my butt for eight hours. I have no idea what I'm supposed to be doing there.' I threw my jacket on a bar stool and picked up a stack of mail. 'I think Dad just wanted me out of the house.'

My mother kept her eyes glued to the heat under the pan and shrugged her shoulders. 'Well,' she said in easy defeat, 'what can you do.' She put a handful of cumin seeds on the dry pan and the seeds started popping about. 'Well, at least I made a good dinner for you,' she said. 'Fresh bhindi masala and a pitcher of sweet tea. Go eat. You still need to put some weight on. And, oh . . . I almost forgot to tell you.' She picked off some of the hot seeds that had jumped onto the counter. 'Your cousins from Kasur are coming this weekend. You know, your Dad's sister Amila and Uncle Mumtaz? Their kids.'

'Cousins?' I asked. 'Are they staying at our house?'

'Yes, they're staying at our house. Where else would they go, huh? The Hilton?'

My mother chuckled at the mere thought of it as she slid the seeds into a plastic container. She always enjoyed the fact that while she grew up in the sprawling, modern city of Lahore, my father's relatives hailed from Kasur, a relatively quiet, third-world version of Mayberry, where everyone is still donkey-driven and plumbing is neither common nor necessary. I remember the one time we went to Pakistan as a family, when I was seventeen, and the five of us took the three-hour drive from Lahore to Kasur. Uncle Mumtaz had installed a shower just for our visit, but there was no toilet, so we had to do our business in a bucket in the backyard. While Khalid and especially Meena were taken aback at the prospect, I looked at the positive—at least we each had our own bucket. Uncle Mumtaz had taken us to the town bazaar as soon as we arrived and let us pick out our buckets, which came in a variety of colours. I chose a hot pink one and brought it home as a souvenir, much to everybody's revulsion.

I changed into a T-shirt and a pair of sweats, set the table as my mother asked and took my plate of food to the basement. My mouth salivated as soon as I breathed in the dense steam coming off the plate. The okra was sautéed with tomatoes, hot green peppers, onions and mint. Olive oil, stained orange from the peppers and spices, laced around the steaming hot veggies. I tore off a piece of dry paratha and used it to scoop up the veggies and oil into my mouth, making the crucial error of scraping up the thin slices of red pepper. The severity of the first bite activated my muscles, and my tongue and throat were on fire. I scooped more and more until I scraped the last piece of wilted mint off my plate.

'Thanks Mom,' I hollered from the basement. 'That was delicious.'

'Baby, you're here?' my father asked. I hadn't seen him when I was in the kitchen. He must have just returned from work. 'Come upstairs. We must leave now.'

'Leave for where?' I asked.

He repeated his order that I come to him. Once I reached the top of the stairs, he eyed me over. 'Yes, that is unacceptable, what you are wearing. You must change quickly or we will be late.'

'For what?'

Apparently, my first PAC-PAC meeting. My father was taking me to the restaurant where the three other members were already waiting. I asked him if he was sure I was needed at this particular meeting. Perhaps the men needed some time to get reacquainted—after all, this was their first PAC-PAC meeting in a long time. Perhaps they needed to do some catching up first, and my presence would just be an interference, a distraction. My father replied that he was paying me now and this was one of my duties and I should stop arguing with him because I was going. I went upstairs and changed into work clothes, taking much longer than my father liked because I was mentally resisting having to go and every movement of my arms and legs felt like I was dying.

In the car on the way to the restaurant, my father tried to reassure me. 'You will enjoy being part of this. This is a very important time for us. You will see. We are going to take PAC-PAC to a whole new level.'

My father explained that he wanted to take this local group national, to have it not only aiding Pakistanis in settling and staying in the US, but to have PAC-PAC recognized as the supreme voice of the Pakistani-American. There was a spark in his eyes as he spoke of his plans, and I always knew this organization was much more personal to him than just furthering the goals of Pakistanis. Through this organization, he could feel involved in American society, feel important and noticed. It would provide the only validation to his accomplishments in Pakistan that were lost the minute he stepped onto American soil—his rise from poverty in the aftermath of the India–Pakistan partition to a full-scholarship debater in college to the top law student at Lahore University. The skies were the limit for a young man like him. He could have gone into politics over there, become a diplomat, lived the high-life with drivers and servants in a gated home.

But to my father, none of that compared to living in America. Living here—where the water flowed clean and opportunities awaited his children—this was the ultimate prize, even if it meant having to start over. For years, after my parents emigrated from Pakistan, my father worked random jobs—hotel clerk, Radio Shack repairman. He fell into selling cars after the year he spent trying to sell vacation packages over the phone. Cold-calling people during their dinnertime is hard enough, but it's worse when you have an accent no one understands, or trusts. People always hung up on him. I was eight years old the night he finally hung up on someone himself, quitting the business altogether. I was with him at the kitchen table when he made his final call, my colouring books and crayons scattered around his business papers.

'Hello. My name is Tariq Tanweer, and I'm a representative of Starling Travel Agency,' he had said, using his standard introduction. 'If you have just a minute, I would like to talk to you about our wonderful family and couple vacation plans.'

'What did you say your name was?'

Maybe if my father hadn't given his name, the man on the other end of the phone might have done the polite thing like everyone else and simply hung up on him. Instead, I heard the word 'sandnigger' for the first time.

'Call here again and I'll hunt you down and your family of goddamn sandniggers,' the stranger yelled. 'You got that? You got that?'

My father didn't say anything back to the man. He just put the phone down. I tried to show him the unicorn I had just drawn in my book, but he didn't look at it. He pulled me onto his lap and kissed my cheek. Maybe he thought I was too young to notice, to understand. But I understood. I understood perfectly what had just happened, and I felt his hands tremble as he gently tucked my hair behind my ears, betraying the mask of calm on his face. He spoke so low I almost didn't hear him, but he promised me he would fix this, insha' Allah. That our family, that everything, would be okay.

The House of Tandoor was packed. It was hard to hear anything over the noise of chairs screeching and silverware clanking. Dinner, buffet-style, was being served to a private party in the back. Near the front, three men stood at their table when they saw us enter.

'Salaam!' said my father as he heartily hugged each of the men. 'Kya hal hai? How are you?'

'Who is the young lady joining us?' one of them asked.

My father grinned and puffed out his chest. 'Everybody, this is my daughter, Samira.'

'Ma sha' allah,' one of them replied, smiling and swinging his head left and right.

'She is the new office manager for PAC-PAC,' my father continued, 'and will be working out of Fahim Kureshi's office. Tonight, and for all our future meetings, she will be keeping the minutes for us.'

I was introduced to each of the men—Uncle Fareed, Uncle Mahmood and Uncle Abbas. Uncle Abbas had a moustache and a hard, rotund stomach like he was five months pregnant. He looked confused. 'She doesn't have a watch,' he said. 'How is she going to keep the minutes?'

'Keeping the minutes means she's going to record the meeting, yaar,' Uncle Fareed snapped. Uncle Fareed was clearly the youngest of the men, clean-shaven and stylish, with a glossy brown suit and a gold and ruby ring on his pinky finger.

'Uncles,' I said as we all sat down, 'my only request as I keep the minutes is that everyone speaks in English. I don't understand Urdu that well.' I made a big, youthful smile.

Uncle Fareed turned to my father and asked him, in Urdu, why his daughter didn't speak our language, a question my parents were used to getting from other Pakistanis. My father simply shrugged, always with the same answer. 'What good will Urdu do my children here?' he said in English. 'It is more important for them to master English. To be able to compete with the goras. To excel past them. And look,' he said, patting my shoulder. 'Now my daughter is the most successful civil servant in Washington D.C., working for powerful leaders and influencing this country.'

I noticed my father didn't refer to these things in the past tense, but I thought it best not to correct him. He broke off a piece of a crisp, peppery papad and spooned some mint chutney on it. 'My daughter has always been an important citizen of this country ever since she was a little girl,' he said, popping the dripping piece into his mouth. 'In fact,' he wiped his hand on his napkin and put it back on my shoulder. 'When my baby was eleven years old . . .'

Oh no. I *knew* this was going to happen.

'. . . she wrote a letter to the President of the United States . . .'

I cringed in my chair. I didn't know why my father insisted on telling everyone this story, about how when I was eight years old I wrote a letter to President Reagan and asked him why the world was so mean and what he could do about it. But what impressed my father so much was that one day, Reagan wrote me back! When I received the letter from him, little old me, in our mailbox with the White House insignia on it, my father told everyone—our relatives here and in Pakistan, the principal of my school and my third grade teacher, even our next door neighbours, showing them the letter if he could, about how the President himself responded to his little daughter's letter. It was extremely embarrassing. Even at the age of eight, I could tell Reagan's signature was made by a machine.

'Very impressive young lady,' said Uncle Mahmood, the eldest of the men. He dipped his napkin into his water glass and carefully wiped off some chutney from his plaid sweater vest. 'Very impressive, indeed.'

'My daughter, Neelam, she also worked in D.C.,' piped in Uncle Abbas. 'She worked for the Department of State.'

'I didn't know that,' I said. 'What did she do there?'

'Oh, you know, she did all sorts of things . . . you know, like . . . I don't know.' He stirred the straw in his frothy lassi. 'She's having a baby soon. I'm going to be a grandfather for the first time.'

'Congratulations,' I said warmly, the only person in the group that seemed to care.

Uncle Mahmood, cleared his throat. 'At any rate, we will do what the young lady asks and hold the meeting in English. But first,' he began as the the waiter brought out the dishes they ordered, 'let's eat.'

I had already eaten so I sipped on a glass of mango juice and watched the men dig heartily into their rice and curries, barely speaking to each other, barely looking up from their plates. About twenty minutes later, when the food was gone and the dishes were cleared, Uncle Mahmood belched without trying to be discreet, thus officially kicking off the meeting.

'We need to change our name,' said Uncle Fareed. 'I don't like PAC-PAC.'

'You don't like PAC-PAC?' asked Uncle Abbas. 'Why not? What is wrong with it? It is a fine name. The P-a-k-i-s-t-a-n-i A-m-e-r-i-c-a-n . . .'

Uncle Abbas began to restate the name of the organization, the strength of his argument laying in the slow emphasis of each word . . .

'. . . C-o-u-n-c-i-l f-o-r P-o-l-i-t-i-c-a-l A-c-t-i-o-n C-o-m-m-i-t-t-e-e. PAC-PAC,' he said.

Uncle Fareed dug a toothpick into his teeth with one hand and waved dismissively with the other. 'Don't like it.'

'Why don't you like it?' my father asked.

'Because, yaar, why does there have to be so many PACs in the name? PAC-PAC. PAC-PAC. PAC-PAC. Sounds like chickens on a farm,' he said. 'The Jewish American Council—they just go as JAC. Why can't we go as PAC?'

'Because everybody knows what is JAC,' my father replied. 'They've been around forever. We need to further identify ourselves.' He looked to the others. 'Don't you all agree?'

There was chatter among the group, prompting my father to say, 'Okay, let's take a vote. Who wants to keep PAC-PAC?'

Out of a sudden and unforeseen consensus, or perhaps just out of sheer indifference, no one in the group raised his hand. My father sighed. 'Then I guess it's PAC. Pakistani-American Council.'

I wrote all this down.

'Next issue,' my father said. 'We need to work on fundraising. I recommend we send out a mailing to all the desis in the community, laying out our mission and asking for donations.'

'But we need to raise funds to send the mailing out,' said Uncle Fareed. 'That needs to come first. Then we can tell every flauna and shauna about our mission.'

'What is our mission anyway?' Uncle Mahmood asked. 'So far all we do is sit around and eat samosas and talk like fools.'

My father took off his glasses and dropped his Mont Blanc on the table. 'How many times have we been over this?' he said. 'Our mission is to increase the visibility of the Pakistani community in this state and in America. To work with the government. To gain their respect. That way we get more laws that protect us and our interests.'

Everyone was quiet.

'I tell you what . . .' My father put his glasses back on. 'I will write a mission statement and bring it to the next meeting. Sounds good?'

The Uncles looked at each other and concurred. 'Sounds good to me,' said Uncle Abbas.

'Now, back to fundraising,' my father continued. 'We can initially use our own money to send out the mailing. In our letter, we can ask people for donations.'

'What good will these little donations from people do us?' Uncle Fareed asked crossly. 'Five dollars here. Ten dollars there. What good will this do us when we have to raise millions?'

'Millions?' my father asked.

'Yes, millions.'

'Why do we need millions?' asked Uncle Abbas.

'Because . . . do you know? Last year the budget of JAC—do you know what it was? Forty million. Forty million dollars! And do you know why? Because Israel throws money at them! And now look at JAC. They control this country. They are running this government. We should do the same thing and ask for money from the government of Pakistan.'

My father muttered an expletive in Urdu. 'The government of Pakistan can't find its own shit in the toilet,' he angrily replied. 'How do you think we're going to get any money from them?'

Uncle Fareed was unswayed. 'Pakistan should be funding us. It is the only way if PAC is ever going to compete with JAC.'

'Oh, yaar, what is your obsession with JAC?' my father asked. 'They have their agenda and we have ours.'

'If JAC sees a Muslim organization rising in this country, what do you think they will do? They will enlist every Jew here and in Israel to stop us. That is why it is imperative we raise millions of dollars.'

'Stop us from what?' my father asked, his palms flat out, begging. 'What do we have to do with any Jews? We aren't threatening them or anybody else. This is bakwas!'

'You obviously don't know JAC!' Uncle Fareed declared. 'The interests of PAC run counter to the interests of JAC.'

'What are our interests anyway?' asked Uncle Mahmood. 'We don't even have a mission statement.'

My father removed his glasses again and rubbed his eyes. I wondered if he was going to get up and leave. 'If you care so much, instead of running your mouth like a damn fool,' he told Uncle Fareed, 'why don't you look to them to see how they do it? That is your assignment. See how JAC raises money and bring that information to the next meeting.'

'Agh!' Uncle Fareed dismissively waved his hand again. I wrote down that his assignment was to find out about JAC's fundraising, but something told me he wasn't too keen on actually doing it.

The group moved on to the next agenda item—where was PAC going to hold its next meeting? After almost twenty minutes of bickering about locations, driving directions and who still serves daal makhani in the area, I picked up my pen and wrote down the words 'The House of Tandoor.'

On the drive home, my father told me again how proud he was of me. 'I am so proud of my baby today,' he said. 'For coming with me, being a part of this. I know you're tired and this was your first day of work. I appreciate you coming.'

'No problem, Dad,' I said. 'I was happy to help. I'll type the minutes and email them to you first thing tomorrow.'

He rubbed my cheek with the back of his hand. 'I have the best daughter in the whole world.'

I snuggled into the heated seat of his Honda Accord and looked out the window. I felt like a good daughter. Yes. After everything I did that evening, I *was* a good daughter.

'While you're at it,' my father added, 'since you're such a good daughter, can you write a mission statement for us too?'

7

All was quiet the next day at the office. The entire law firm of Libby, Libby and McCrane seemed to be out of the building, perhaps at a retreat. Only a few support staff stayed behind—answering phones, cleaning out file drawers—and even they came in wearing jeans and T-shirts and took extra long lingering around the coffee machines. I spent most of the morning wandering down the hall, peeking into darkened offices, swiping a handful of cinnamon candies off one attorney's desk, and checking out framed family photos, award plaques and other personal items of all these people I never spoke to.

Around noon I returned to my office and tried to do some work. I typed up the minutes from yesterday's PAC meeting and emailed them to each of the PAC members. That took two minutes. Then I typed in, 'How to write a mission statement' and started pulling a document together for my father. But for some reason now, I was having trouble concentrating. I just kept staring at the blank page, staring at it and staring at it until finally I pushed my keyboard aside and leaned forward, crossing my arms and resting my head upon them. I just felt so . . . tired. All the time, it seemed. Any small amount of exertion, mental or physical, seemed to wipe me out. I kept thinking that if I could just shut my eyes for twenty minutes, just lie down on something soft and rest my aching body, I'd be good to go. But it was occurring to me now that no matter what I did, I was never good to go. Meena had experienced something similar to this when she was a freshman in college. She wasn't sure what was behind her apathy or need to sleep until 2 p.m. each day and her crying fits when nothing in her life seemed to be wrong, but she went to the university clinic and they told her she had depression. She started taking a daily allotment of Zoloft and after about a month, she told me, she was waking up earlier. Paying better attention during class. Feeling energetic enough to check out local bands at night.

Maybe this was my problem. I didn't cry anymore. My crying days had subsided over the fall, and all that remained was the occasional aftershock—usually in the morning when I awakened after a night of dreams and the full force of the changes in my life would hit me—but even that was usually just a whimper and a trickle of tears. What I had now didn't seem like depression. This was more subtle—like a lingering malaise. But maybe I was wrong. Maybe this was indeed depression, just not as dramatic as I would expect. Maybe some medication would perk me up, get rid of some of this constant fatigue. Maybe that was all I needed. I could try some of that Zoloft for myself. Meena had told me it doesn't necessarily make you happy, just numb enough to make it through your daily activities.

I would take numb. A blissfully numb existence. Happiness was too lofty a goal for me anyway. Numb seemed the logical midpoint between miserable and happy. Numb seemed like the way to go. But getting a prescription drug wasn't an option for me. I was getting a small allowance for my PAC job, but I was still officially unemployed. No health insurance. What was I to do to perk up then? Try to find something to pique my interest? Start drinking coffee? Mentally coach myself into feeling excited about the world?

I closed my eyes and yawned. Sure, I could get to that. I'll give it a shot. But not today. Just not today.

I opened my eyes and sat back in my chair. This was uncomfortable. My desk was too high, and the sharp edges of the glasstop were scraping against my arms. I wasn't going to get any sleep at that desk if I tried. But maybe this was for the best. I moved my mouse, and the overwhelmingly blank document entitled 'Mission Statement' popped back onto the computer screen. I sat there for another minute or so, contemplating it, my eyes going dry, before grabbing my purse and getting out my car keys and locking the office door behind me.

Up the road about two miles was an aging stripmall. The mall consisted of a Big Lots store, some Korean groceries and a deli whose entrance was obscured by a large white truck that seemed to have found its permanent home as it was missing all its wheels. I parked and went into the Big Lots.

Once inside, I was greeted by a friendly obese African-American boy in a white T-shirt and shiny black shorts standing at the cash registers. There were only a few other customers in the store—a mother and her toddler, a retired couple, an apparent drunk with a flask shaking in his hand—nobody making a sound as they drifted through the aisles to an elevator version of Celine Dion's 'My Heart Will Go On'.

I headed to the discounted section. 'SUMMER DOLLAR EXTRAVAGANZA!' the sign above two large bins boasted. Beach towels. Swimming goggles. Barbeque tongs. Inflatable pool rafts. I picked up two of the inflatable pool rafts with fifty-cent price tags on the packages. A blue raft or a yellow one. Blue, yellow. Blue, yellow. I chose the yellow.

'Are you all set, ma'am?' asked the African-American boy in a voice as smooth as chocolate mousse, as he scanned the item and put it in a white plastic bag.

'I am,' I replied. 'I'm all set.'

Back at the office, I took out the yellow life raft from its package and unfolded it. I spent the next few minutes on the floor, blowing into the nozzle, until it was fully inflated. It was bigger than I expected—seven feet long—almost reaching both walls when laid flat—and after blowing all that air I found myself dizzy, almost high, by the time I was finished. I carried the raft to the far end of the room, having to move a guest chair to make room for it, and lay it down. I was getting used to the idea of not having anyone else in the office—no co-workers, no managers. There were obvious benefits to this. I took off my sweater to use as a blanket, switched out the lights and snuggled into my new bed.

It was three in the afternoon when I went home—another apparent benefit of my new job—and it was a beautiful drive. The afternoon sunlight pierced through low-lying puffs of clouds. Red, orange and yellow leaves drifted like confetti over freshly cut lawns. The streets in my neighbourhood were empty, peaceful, the only sounds being the soft, scattered chirping of birds and someone screaming from my house. I could hear the screaming all the way from the end of my street as I pulled in. I parked in the driveway and went through the open garage door into the kitchen, where Khalid was standing in front of my mother with his arms crossed. My mother was wearing yellow rubber gloves and holding a copper scouring pad.

'Clean up downstairs or get out!' she screamed, so loud and shrill it almost punctured my eardrums. 'I'm sick of you not contributing anything to this household! You kids just come and go and treat this house like a hotel!'

I picked up the day's mail and flipped through it.

'Mom,' Khalid began calmly, 'I said I was going to clean the basement after I was done with my work. How many times do I have to tell you? You need to calm down and try to listen instead of screaming.'

'You churail! If you would do what I say and not talk back to me, I wouldn't have to scream. This is my house and you do what I say or you get the hell out!'

'No. This is not rational. The basement will be cleaned but I can't do it right now. If you would *please* just stop screaming. God, I can't handle the screaming!'

'You are so rude to me, Khalid,' my mother replied with every ounce of regret in her voice she could muster. 'What did I do to raise such rude children? Oh, how my life would have turned out differently if I had just aborted you back in Pakistan like I had planned! Your father talked me out of it, of course, but my father, your Abbaji, did not approve of your father because he was a villager. No matter that your father is a Rajput, a member of royalty. His parents were poor, lived in mud huts, his whole village attacked during partition. Those Hindus came through one day and whoosh!' She made a sword sound again. 'Did you ever see the scar on your father's back? No, no. Your Abbaji was against this. He wanted me to marry a rich physician at King Edward Medical School where I was a nursing student. He had already moved to America and threatened he wouldn't let me come here if your father and I ever got married. And, well, by that point, your father and I had already married in secret and my belly had started to grow. So I panicked.' She started waving a yellow gloved finger at Khalid. 'Your father talked me out of it, and your Abbaji grew to love our first-born son, but if I'd have known what kind of man you'd turn out to be, Khalid, *if I'd have known*, I would not have gone through with it!'

Khalid tapped on his watch. 'Are we done with the Paki soap opera now? I believe *General Hospital* is on in a few minutes.' Tactically, this was not a correct move on Khalid's part. An insult, paired with a calm, condescending demeanour was the worst possible method of addressing my mother when her temper flared. But I continued to stay out of the discussion, trying to concentrate on the mail, when things took a turn for the worse. In one swift movement, like a tiger attacking her prey, my mother flung herself at Khalid, snatching his ears with her rubber-gloved hands and pulling his head in towards her. 'You go clean your mess right now or you get out and never come back here again.'

'Ow! Oww!' Khalid writhed in agony as she yanked on his ears, though not daring to use his strength to free himself of her grip.

It was coming on. I felt it.

I slapped the mail on the counter and ran out to the hallway where I let it release, all of it. I was laughing so hard I literally couldn't breathe. I bent over a potted palm, grabbing onto the leaves, just to steady myself. But it was scary laughing like that, risky. I had to stop before they overheard me or I'd be susceptible to their wrath. I calmed myself down, gently, easily, until I felt the last giggle escape. Then I peeked around the corner to see what was happening.

Khalid was holding both his ears with his hands. 'That's it!' he yelled. 'I refuse to stand here and take this! I'm going to finish my work and I will clean the basement on my own time!'

He stomped down the stairs. Seizing the opportunity to taunt him some more for my entertainment, I went after him. But all I could do when I reached the basement and tried to open my mouth was to keep laughing.

'Yeah, glad you got to see that, rat,' Khalid said, acting wounded but then laughing with me. 'Can you believe she said that to me? That she should have aborted me? That's fucked up!'

I was still laughing too hard to say anything, but noticed Khalid had immediately begun picking up the mess in the room. My chest ached as I wiped a tear smudge from my cheek. 'That was the hardest I've laughed in a long time,' I told him. 'Thank you very much.'

'Shut up, rat,' he replied. 'Preoccupy yourself with something else. I gotta clean up before Mom comes after me again. The Paki geek squad is on their way. Dad just called from the airport.'

My laughter ceased immediately. I had completely forgotten about my cousins coming to town. 'They're on their way now?' I asked. 'But they'll be too tired to do anything, right? They'll probably just want to shower and go to straight to bed, right?'

'I have no idea,' Khalid said. 'But I can tell you this—I ain't gonna be here to find out.'

'You're going to leave me alone with them? That's not fair.'

'Fair? While you're happily away at work I'm gonna be stuck here all week with them, showing them around and helping out Mom and Dad. I'll have to do my part too, you know.'

A noise from upstairs made us both stop abruptly and stare at each other in silence—the clunking and dragging of suitcases. Khalid and I didn't move an inch as we waited for the inevitable.

'Samira!' my father yelled out. 'Khalid! We are here!'

I let out a sigh and started up the stairs. 'Come on,' I told Khalid. 'Maybe they'll be too tired to talk to us. I mean, isn't it a twenty-hour flight from Pakistan?'

I turned around and there was no one behind me.

I continued upstairs anyway and as soon as I reached the top, my father winced at the sight of me. I was wearing conservative work clothes but my arms, tan and slim, hung naked outside my lavender tank top. It was probably the most skin either of my cousins had ever seen on a woman. My father cleared his throat. 'Samira, you remember your cousins, Hamid and Nasir. They are my sister's sons. Your *real* cousins. You met when you were younger, when we all went to Pakistan.'

I wasn't exactly sure of their ages now, but I knew Hamid was older than Nasir by two years and they were both in their mid-twenties. I had only the briefest memory of the two of them in Kasur—both dressed in the traditional white salwar kameez and dusty, tan sandals—taking my family through the narrow alleyways of the mid-day bazaars. Now Hamid and Nasir were both wearing identical khaki pants and stiff white shirts that, in spite of their twenty-hour journey from Pakistan, still smelled like they were fresh from the package. With their glossy, jet-black hair parted dramatically to one side and their thin moustaches, they looked like members of Ricky Ricardo's orchestra.

'Salaam alaykum,' I said to both of them, briefly pondering if I should hug them and then deciding not to.

'It's good to meet you again, Samira,' said Hamid, in perfectly enunciated English.

Nasir nudged his way forward. 'Samira, do you remember me?'

'Of course I remember you, Nasir,' I replied. 'How have you been? Your hair is longer than it was back then.'

'Oh. You remember me but only my hair,' he said, despondently. Nasir's English was a little rougher than his brother's.

'That's not true,' I said, trying to reassure him. 'I remember everything about you. Like, back in Kasur, you . . . uh . . . you . . . uh . . .'

'Where is Khalid?' my father asked, unintentionally coming to my rescue. 'He needs to greet his cousins.'

I heard the faint sound of a door closing in the basement, followed quickly by the sound of an ignition.

'Khalid had to run some errands,' I announced. 'But he'll be back soon. He said tomorrow he's going to take everyone around town.' My father sneered, not buying a word of what I was saying. 'That boy is a good-for-nothing. An absolutely good-for-nothing.'

My mother entered the foyer, and the four of us turned our attention to her, clueless as to what to do next, ready for her to step in and take over. I felt bad for my mother because as much as I always complained about having guests over, it was her responsibility to play supreme hostess—cook the guests' meals, be with them at all times, tend to their every need. It was a ton of work, a highly unenviable position, like being a servant in her own home.

'We're eating out,' she declared. 'I made a reservation at Nirvana for six o'clock. Everybody, chalo.' She snapped her fingers at us. 'Let's go.'

This was news to me and from the look on my father's face, obviously news to him. Like me, he probably assumed she had cooked dinner. It wasn't customary to take guests out to eat the first night of their arrival. My mother knew this. I guessed that's why she chose my father's favourite masala dosa restaurant to take us to—to avoid an argument with him about it later.

———

When I pulled out a chair at Nirvana, Nasir took the seat directly in front of me. As soon as we sat down, he asked me, 'Do you like living in America?'

I shrugged. 'Sure. I like living here. It's nice.'

I turned to watch another family being seated at a table to the right of us. I looked at the flecks of rice on the floor. I looked at the Mughal paintings on the walls, the forks on a waiter's tray, the pink paper added to my menu with the day's specials. But it didn't work. When I looked up, Nasir was still focused on me.

'Why do you like living here?' he asked.

I knew why Nasir was bringing this up, what the nature of the conversation was going to be. So to avoid having this discussion, I brought up travelling. 'Actually, I would love to travel overseas for a while. Southeast Asia. Maybe Europe. Khalid is going to Denmark and I may go there too,' I said, making this up, but realizing it wasn't such a bad idea. 'I've always been fascinated by Denmark. With their Viking history and their mountain ranges. I hear they have incredible mountain ranges.' I wondered if Denmark had any mountains at all.

'Why go to Denmark?' Nasir asked. 'Why not come to Kasur to live with your family?'

'Of course. Maybe one day.'

As expected, Nasir was wholly unsatisfied with that response and wouldn't look away until I said something else.

'I actually don't know, Nasir, about moving to Pakistan,' I said. 'It may be hard for me. There are restrictions on women. I remember what it was like. I couldn't shake hands with men, show my ankles . . .'

'Women have every freedom in Pakistan,' he declared. 'They vote and drive and go for educations. It's not Saudi Arabia. My sisters are happy. You judge the place when you go for a few weeks many years ago.'

'You're right,' I quickly agreed, because he had a point, but also because I wanted the conversation to end. 'It has been a long time since I've been there. I guess I really don't know if I could live there. I will take your word for it.'

Nasir gave a quick nod of triumph and I assumed our conversation was over, just in time for the waiter to slap a large white plate in front of me. Splayed across the plate was a thin, crispy dosa roll filled with piping hot curried potatoes, spinach and onions and three little tin cups, each filled with a different chutney—coconut, spicy tomato and a watery lentil soup. I tore off a piece of the dosa, dipped it in the coconut chutney and stuffed it in my mouth.

Within seconds I forgot all about Nasir and began devouring the food. The conversation at the table turned completely into Urdu, letting me off the hook. I quietly ate about half the dosa and sat back in my chair, letting my stomach expand while I sipped on a lukewarm glass of water. I tuned out everyone at the table to watch the rest of the patrons in the restaurant. I turned around again when my father started raising his voice at Hamid, in English.

'What good will that do you in this world, huh? You waste your time on such ridiculous studies.'

'But paijan, this is a very good field of study,' Hamid replied. 'It is a very classical field of study. It is history, art . . .'

'What art is there in Islamic Studies?' my father demanded. 'Are you studying the geometric tiles of mosques? There is no art. You should be studying economics, accounting, law. Or medicine. What kind of job can you get with your degree? Who would ever hire you?'

'Paijan, it is a very useful degree. I am going to teach with it. I can teach in Pakistan or I can teach here.'

'Ki bakwas!' my father shouted. 'What nonsense! You think you know these things? You don't know anything! America will keep you out if they hear you have a degree in Islamic studies. And you think Pakistan needs more religious scholars? No! You stop these studies right now. Such stupid boy.' The check arrived and my father slapped down some cash and hastily got up to leave. 'My money is being wasted on your education,' he told Hamid. 'I might as well send it directly to a madrasa in Peshawar!'

Just then my cell phone started ringing. It was Khalid.

'Hey,' he whispered, so low I almost couldn't hear him with the loud laughing and music behind him. 'Don't let them know it's me. Anyone upset I didn't come out?'

'Why are you whispering? They can't hear you,' I said. 'But, no. No more than usual.' I slowed down behind the group in the parking lot so I could talk to him freely. 'Anyway, I think you're in the clear. Dad's focus is elsewhere. He's yelling at Hamid.'

'That's excellent,' Khalid said, still whispering.

'Smile, baijee!'

A light flashed across my eyes, temporarily blinding me. I thought I had been struck by lightning.

'Smile! Smile!'

It took me a few seconds to make out Nasir's silhouette in front of me. I half-smiled as I patiently waited for him to snap another picture.

'Okay, now in front of this,' he said, pointing to a 'No Parking' sign.

8

Early the next morning, well before my cousins had a chance to wake up, I switched on the lights at my office and put my wax-paper-wrapped-everything bagel with cream cheese on my desk. I ate it slowly, scraping cream cheese off the paper with my plastic knife, then when I was finished, sprayed the glasstop with cleaner and wiped off every errant poppy and sesame seed I could find.

This would be the highlight of my day, the only productive activity I would engage in for the next eight hours. Just another day at the office, another day wasted sitting here waiting for something to happen before I would give up and hit the lights and retire on the life raft. By this point, I had just accepted that this was how life was going to be for a while, that I had no other job prospects and hadn't exactly been on the job-hunt anyway, and so there was no reason to complain or try to fight what was an inevitable phase of my life: inactivity. After so much activity, too much activity, perhaps this was a necessary part of my recovery. A total shut-down before reboot.

Speaking of shut-down . . . I grabbed the oversize sweater hanging from the coat rack . . . *there was nothing preventing me from taking a bit of a rest now, was there?* Sure it was early, but who would know or care? I pulled the raft from the far end of the wall, pushed the guest chair away and lay the raft down in the middle of the floor.

And that's when it happened—a ring so sudden and so loud it jolted me upright. My heart started racing. The green light on the phone was flashing. Someone was calling. No one ever called this phone. Who could be calling? I was unexpectedly excited, the drowsiness gone, all my senses piqued. I checked the caller ID. It was a long, strange number. I grabbed a legal pad and pen and picked up the phone.

'Pakistani-American Council,' I said in my most formal business voice. 'This is Samira. How can I help you?'

There was nothing. All I could hear was static, and the echo of my own voice. 'Hello?' I asked. 'Hello?'

More silence and static.

'Hello?'

'Hello ji!' a voice boomed on the other end. The voice was male. It was hurried, almost shouting. 'Mera naam Man Singh hai. Main ne phoon is wasle keeta hai-ji. Ke main Fahim Kureshi nal gal kerna chah na han America wich mera . . .'

Oh, shit.

The caller had launched into Urdu, obviously about something urgent. I was tempted to say, 'Whoah, whoah! Slow down there sport!'—possibly the most un-Urdu and unhelpful thing I could think of, so I grasped for something else.

'Uncle! Uncle!' I tried to say over his voice. 'Mera . . . oh, crap . . . I . . . um . . . nay Urdu . . . no Urdu . . . I don't . . .'

'. . . bhara mar gia hai. Oh-the koi mard nahi hai jo os the aakhri rasoomat puri . . .'

'. . . speak Urdu, so if you could please . . .'

'. . . kar ske! To hadi kirpa ho we gi je tusin ma nu visa dalwa dew! Bhai di kuri . . .'

'. . . speak in English . . .'

'. . . bil kul akeli hai . . . oh, ich minute . . .'

There was another pause, more static. I could hear some Urdu in the background. I started panicking, feeling utterly helpless, wishing more than ever that I knew Urdu. And suddenly angry with my parents for never having taught it to me. And from out of nowhere, a sudden revelation that maybe the reason my parents never taught us Urdu wasn't because they wanted us to master English, as they kept telling everyone over the years, but for the simple reason that maybe they were just too plain lazy to ever get to it.

'Hello?' I repeated. 'Salaam? Salaam?'

The line had gone dead.

9

My father flicked the newspaper he was reading to straighten it out. 'Samira,' he said, 'help your mother get ready for dinner.' As if on cue, my mother placed a plastic bag of onions in my hand and gave me a knife.

'You know how to cut onions, I presume?' she asked.

I had just gotten home from work, literally having just walked through the door. Any eagerness I had to deliver the news that someone, probably from Pakistan, tried calling the PAC office dissipated as anger filled my veins. 'Do I have to do this right now?'

'Yes, miss. I need them now.'

'Do I get a second to change out of my work clothes?'

'No. I need them now.'

'That's ridiculous!'

My father looked at me sternly. 'Samira . . .'

'Fine!' I yelled, slamming the bag of onions on the counter.

I quickly realized, as my mother went back to her pots and my father resumed his reading, that my act of protest of slamming the onions went unnoticed by both of them, so I hunched over the counter and did what my mother asked. I peeled the paper off the outer layers of three onions, trying not to get my clothes dirty, chopped each one in half, then paused as I stood above the six remaining chunks.

I bit my lower lip. I half-turned to the side to see if anyone was watching me, caught a glimpse of my mother's stare and immediately turned back.

'Well?' she asked, her hand on her hip, studying the hesitation and now fear spreading across my face. 'I need to fry them, bey. You going to cut them up or what?'

'Yes,' I snapped. 'I said I would. It's just . . . how exactly do you want them cut? In little square chunks or in, like, half-moon pieces?' I watched as my mother's face transformed from annoyance to resignation. She snatched the knife from my hand and nudged me out of the way. 'Go. I'll cut them myself.'

The potential for a fight that evening was evident the minute I walked into that kitchen. I could feel it—everybody was on edge. It was just one of those moments in any household where for no particular reason the chemistry between everybody is off and one wrong look or minor comment is all it would take to set a fight in motion. I was preparing to leave, grabbing my suit jacket and work bag before things got worse, but my mother was having none of that.

'Samira, don't you walk away,' she sourly remarked. 'I need to say something here.' She quickly chopped all three onions, and a fourth, with the precision of a sushi chef. 'You've seen me cook curry a million times. You should know how to cut onions by now. Men don't like women who can't cook. They may say it doesn't matter and they want modern women and all that, but they're lying. You're never going to find someone who will marry you. Men don't stay with women who can't do these things. They'll find any excuse to leave.'

Was she making some kind of veiled reference to Ethan?

'Is this some kind of veiled reference to Ethan?'

'Now she's getting paranoid,' she said to my father, who was half-paying attention over his newspaper. 'All I'm saying is that women who can cook and take care of a man, you know, the ones that are good at more traditional things, they are the ones men like to marry. Listen to what I'm saying. I'm trying to teach you these things.'

'Teach me what? How to be useless in today's world? I did just fine feeding myself when I was on my own. Not that you ever lived on your own to know what that's like.'

'Bandh kar!' My father slammed his newspaper down. 'Stop this shouting! We have guests in the house. Have you no respect?'

'Do you and Mom think you can say anything to me and it doesn't matter?'

'I said keep it down,' he yelled. 'Keep it down or get out of this house!'

I was frustrated beyond belief. I wanted to kick something or keep insulting my mother about her life or throw an onion at my father. This was the first fight with my parents since moving back home and it was an absolute buzz kill. All the doubts I had had about moving back home rushed to the surface. Any shred of optimism I may have acquired the last few months that things could get better living at home and that giving myself this rest period was a smart step towards my recovery was instantly replaced by the thought that my life wouldn't get any better and would, in fact, always be quite miserable as long as I lived under my parent's roof and their constant scrutiny. But I couldn't move out either. I wasn't ready. Moving out meant moving into town—too big a step for me to take. I didn't know how long I was going to stay in Cary or where I was going to go next. I was stuck in this fourth desi dimension—no longer dependent on my parents, yet in their eyes, still completely dependent because I was living in their home. Still expected to act as the quiet, obedient child.

I huffed out of there. Khalid, of all people, would understand my predicament. I went to the basement to find him, but upon reaching the bottom of the stairs, I could do nothing to hide the disappointment on my face. Only Nasir was there, sitting on the couch.

'Oh. Hey Nasir.'

'Hello. How was your day?' he asked.

I slouched down on the couch next to him. 'It was fine.'

'How is Khalid? I have not seen him lately.'

'Oh, I'm sure he's fine.'

'Okay. And how is Meena?'

'She's fine too.'

'She is at the school?'

'Yes. She is at school. At college. About two hours away.'

'What is she studying?'

'Engineering.' I pre-empted the next question. 'And she's doing fine at it.'

'And what are you studying?'

'I'm not in school anymore, Nasir. I'm actually twenty-seven years old so I've been out for a while. I work.'

'You work? So you are not in the school?'

It always puzzled me how Pakistanis think everyone is in school their entire lives. No matter a person's age, or the fact that there are jobs in Pakistan too, the only option it seems for anyone under the age of fifty is to be sitting in a classroom somewhere.

'And Khalid. What is he studying?'

The air in the basement was now laced with the sharp scent of onions, tomatoes and cayenne pepper. I could also hear a vegetable being grated upstairs, probably the zucchini I saw in a bowl of soapy water in the sink. It was at that moment that my stomach came alive and I could hear how hungry I was. But I wasn't going to dare eat any of my mother's cooking that night, not after what had happened. It would be too shameful, too pathetic for me to wander into that kitchen and help myself to a plate of food that I was incapable of preparing. I would not give my mother the satisfaction.

'Does Khalid attend the same school as Meena?'

My only option was to eat out, or else . . . maybe I could just swipe some food off Nasir's plate . . .

'Khalid must study very hard,' Nasir said to me, with a confident nod. 'He is always away from the home. Always very busy. His studies must be very demanding. But he is a smart boy. I can tell. A smart boy who studies hard. He will go far. He should get a Ph.D., I think. Yes. In his field. I will tell him this. As his cousin, I will encourage him to get a Ph.D. Maybe even two. He can be a Ph.D. double!'

I was about to explain to Nasir that Khalid wasn't in school anymore and that if he kept up this conversation for just two more seconds I didn't think I would survive it, when Nasir yawned. 'I am tired, baijee,' he uttered. 'Aunty and Uncle took us to see Shahrukh Khan movie today and I just sleep through it. I am tired still.'

We both slumped on the couch for a few minutes, silently watching a Lifetime movie where some woman was pointing a gun at what looked to be her husband. Then Nasir spoke up, turning to me with a smirk. 'Your mother say you do not cut onions.'

I felt my cheeks go red with embarrassment. Fights with my parents were not something I would want anyone to overhear, unwelcome cousin or otherwise. 'I'm sorry you had to hear that,' I told him. 'I shouldn't have yelled while you were staying with us.'

'Don't worry, baijee. It is okay. It is normal,' he replied. 'We are family. It is what we do.' He shrugged. 'We fight.'

I smiled back at Nasir. For the first time since his arrival, Nasir didn't seem so irritating. His comment was friendly, easy-going. Not what I expected. And suddenly I didn't mind sitting with him, there on the basement couch. I could ignore this strange instinct to flee in his presence, and I even found myself tempted to strike up a pleasant conversation with him—ask him what his interests, hobbies, favourite movies were, be the good cousin, get to know him a little better, perhaps loud enough for my parents to overhear my efforts and get back in their good graces. I was seriously thinking of doing this, and probably would have, if Nasir hadn't spoken again. 'Why you do not cook Punjabi food?' he asked. 'Why have you never learned? You do not like our food?'

That was the final straw, and I'd had it. What did this little dweeb or anyone else care if I cooked Punjabi food or not? Why was this suddenly such a profound shortcoming that everyone felt compelled to point out to me?

'I don't cook Punjabi food, Nasir,' I said. 'But I really don't cook anything at all.'

'How will you eat?' he asked. 'Who will cook in your house when you are married?'

'My husband will.'

Nasir's eyes lit up. He put the remote down and turned his full attention towards me.

'But on the nights that he can't, I can always cook soup.'

'Soup?' he asked.

'Yeah, soup. From a can. Canned soup.'

'I see,' he said, nodding his head despondently. 'I see. You will make the soup.'

'I can't sew either,' I said. 'My husband will have to do that for me and the children while I'm busy at work.'

Nasir didn't reply, but nodded that he understood, and my tactic effectively terminated the conversation. For the next half-hour, we sat there, quietly watching the rest of the movie together. The fact that he had no idea what the movie was about seemed to gradually lull him to sleep, and just as his eyelids slid all the way down, my phone vibrated. It was Khalid.

'Anyone notice I'm not home?' he asked.

I got up and walked away from Nasir. 'Don't think so. No one's said anything.'

'Sweet. See you later.'

'Wait . . . can I join you?'

'Really?' Khalid sounded surprised. 'Hell yeah. Come on out, rat. We're at the Tap Room.'

'I'll meet you guys there.'

I heard Khalid yell into the crowd, 'Hey, guess what? Samira's coming out!' followed by the collective chanting of his friends, 'Sammers . . . Sammers . . .'

I wasn't sure where the sudden desire to go out came from, but this little bit of spontaneity had me feeling good about myself again. While Nasir stayed planted in front of the television, I snuck upstairs to change into a pair of jeans and a hooded sweatshirt. Just when I got to the side door by the garage, I ran into Hamid.

'Hey, baijee. Where are you going?'

I was immediately faced with a moral dilemma. I could either tell Hamid I was going out to a bar and therefore reveal that I drink and spend time at such sinful places, but would be guaranteed he wouldn't ask to come with me, or lie about going somewhere else but risk looking rude that I didn't ask him to join me.

No. There was a third option. 'A pregnant girlfriend of mine is having early contractions and she may be going into labour soon,' I told him. 'I'm going to go look after her. Want to come with me?'

Hamid shook his head. 'Nahi, baijee,' he replied. 'I do not wish to go to that. I'm really very tired and I think Nasir is already asleep. But thank you anyway.'

'Then I'll see you tomorrow,' I said. Hamid still stood near me, almost blocking the door.

'I knew Paijan was not going to like my studies,' he said abruptly. 'But I've come too far to change my field now. No matter what, I will still study Islam. It's what I want to do, and I love it. I want to do good things with this degree, baijee. Nobody knows the real Islam anymore. It is being dominated by criminals, by thugs. But Islam is a deeply intellectual religion. A very modern religion. The world needs to know this. This is why I want to teach. I want to be a scholar, not a cleric. If Uncle doesn't like it he can stop funding me. I'll find another way to finance my education.'

I felt for Hamid. I didn't know he had been worrying so much when there was really no need for him to worry. My father may have disapproved of what he was studying, and probably always would, but there was no way he would ever pull Hamid's funding. Because the money wasn't just supporting his education, but feeding and housing him as well, something Hamid's parents in Kasur were scarcely able to do.

Still, hearing the defiance in Hamid's voice, his conviction to study what he wanted in spite of his social and economic circumstances, the way he was willing to stand up to my father, almost made me ashamed. Here we were, Meena, Khalid and I, growing up within the strata of American society where going to college wasn't a luxury but as much a given as going to the prom and having unlimited cell phone plans, and all three of us had gone right for the most boring and acceptable degrees around.

'My father won't ever stop sending you money,' I told Hamid. 'Promise. Just let him yell and scream for now if it makes him feel better. Eventually, he'll stop.'

'Are you sure, baijee?'

'Yes. And for what it's worth, I support what you are doing. Don't worry. I have your back,' I said, playfully hitting his shoulder with my fist, immediately unsure of the appropriateness of it.

To my relief, Hamid chuckled, not seeming to mind my overtly Western act of reassurance. 'Okay, baijee. If you say so. I will try not to worry then.' He yawned. 'I think I will go to sleep now. Uncle has big plans to take us through the mountains in the morning. I will see you tomorrow.' We said good night and he started back up the stairs. I headed for the door when Hamid turned back around and smiled wryly. 'Oh, please tell Khalid I said salaam.'

Khalid's party of six was the only noise coming out of the Tap Room, a relatively empty sports bar at the back of an American family-style restaurant about six miles from home. I could hear them all screaming 'Yeah! Yeah!' like their team had just scored a touchdown. But there was no football game on the flat-screen televisions above the bar, just a dog-diving contest, and I realized the screaming was because I had just walked in.

Under the dim glow of a million faux-Tiffany lamps, I could make out the guys—Cody, Cody's brother Eddie, Ross, Brian and Ken, all of whom were happy to have an outsider, especially a girl, join their party. I gave each of them a hug.

'Goodness. I forgot what a cute little thing you were,' said Brian in a motherly tone while he softly cupped his hand over my right butt cheek. 'Glad you're back in town. You should come out with us every night.'

I reached around and picked off his hand. 'Thanks, Brian. Glad to be back.'

'We hear you're working for your Dad,' Ken asked. 'How's that going?'

'Good,' I replied.

My answer was too quick and affirmative. These guys knew better.

'I'm not sure what I'm supposed to be doing all day,' I said. 'There's a lot of down time. But it's still a job and I appreciate having it. No drama like I had at the dealership that day. Sorry about that, Cody.'

The bartender placed a tray of amber-coloured shots in front of me.

'No problem, Sammer. We're just glad you're here safe,' Cody replied. 'Hey, let's have a toast.' He raised a fist and pretended to be behind a car steering wheel. 'Cuz little Sammer's here and she's got a new job. Beep beep!'

I had only just gotten there and already the night seemed too much to handle. I politely declined, preferring to wait a little bit, to ease into drinking with maybe a few swigs of beer first, when the collective yelling started all over again—Come on! Take it! Suck it up! Wimp!—a bunch of former frat boys who couldn't let go of the glory days of their keg parties. Not that any of them had the discipline or commitment to get into a fraternity in the first place. But it should have occurred to me that I was meeting a bunch of bored guys in their early thirties whose friendship would never have originated or been sustained without the help of alcohol. It was foolish to think I could join them and not drink.

I picked up a shot glass and smelled the liquid—coconut—which was promising, but I had no idea what it was. By now I was the only one still holding a full glass, and before I was ready to drink, another round had been ordered. The boys gathered around me, waiting for me to do my part. 'I just can't,' I said dramatically, like a stage actress asked to wear something she didn't want to. 'I'll go down fast. And then I'll start crying. Trust me on this.'

Brian wrapped an arm around my waist. 'What are you going to cry about?'

'Easy now. Easy,' Khalid warned him.

'Is it Ethan?' Ken asked.

'No, it's just that . . .'

I paused. They were all waiting for me, so I shut up and went for it. 'Aaahh,' I said in anguish as the liquor poured down my throat like battery acid.

'You're better off without him. Men like that can't be trusted,' Ross said, clearly and articulately, as he took another shot, probably his tenth or eleventh. Technically, you could call Ross an alcoholic, but it wasn't a very fitting term. He was more of an expert drinker. He could drink vast amounts of the worst alcohol and walk any straight line or talk to the cops with expertise on any subject. The only indication that he ever indulged was the shiny, red tip of his nose. 'We all liked Ethan, but he obviously turned out to be a dickhead. You should be glad you never married him.'

'Yeah, Samira. Seriously,' Eddie continued. 'So you fucked around a little. Had a one-night stand. Everyone does that.'

I looked at Khalid in disbelief.

'Sorry, rat,' he blurted. 'They were all asking about it. Couldn't keep it from 'em.'

'But getting off with your best friend?' Eddie went on, shaking his head. 'You don't want to be with a guy like that. That's pretty messed up.'

I was quite sure Eddie's sense of right and wrong was pretty messed up, and I would have to scold Khalid later for giving these guys all the personal, sordid details of my breakup. The less people knew about me and Ethan, the better. There was too much information to have to relay, too much blame to go around. It was impossible to pinpoint whose fault the breakup was, and that's what everyone wants—a victim and a perpetrator. But in our case, Ethan was both. And so was I. And even if I knew these guys were just trying to make me feel better, my instincts to protect Ethan still kicked in. No one could call him a dickhead except me.

'I miss him,' I told the crowd. 'I never thought we'd be here, talking about him this way.' My voice quivered a little. 'That he'd be gone.'

'All right, everybody back off,' Cody said. 'Let's not bring the Sammer down.'

Meanwhile, Khalid was holding his shotglass from Round Three. He was swaggering from side to side a little and his forehead glistened with sweat. But his face held an expression I hadn't seen on him in a long time, possibly years. It was concern. He looked like he was either about to give me a hug or pass out. 'Rat,' he began softly, 'are you okay?'

Whenever someone asks if I'm okay, of course I'm going to start crying. It's a combination of feeling grateful that someone cares enough to ask that question and the permission I feel it grants me to release my emotions.

I used my sleeve to wipe the water from eyes. Then my other sleeve as I cried some more. I just stood there, crying in front of them, switching between sleeves. Ken, who hadn't yet remarked on the breakup, seemed intensely in thought as he bowed his head low. Then his head shot back up, as if it came to him, some epiphany or perhaps he found the exact words he neeed to articulate a complex and thoughtful opinion on the matter. He put his hand on my back and said, 'Well,' with a pat so hard I was pushed forward a step, 'buck up, kid.'

Ross signalled for another round.

I didn't like this. I may have spent all my waking hours thinking about the breakup, but I didn't like talking about it so much, burdening others with it. It wasn't an efficient use of time. It was better to digest what happened in my own thoughts, without obstruction from people who didn't know and would never know the full story, so I blew my nose into a cocktail napkin, took another half a shot and changed the subject.

'You guys need to help me,' I told them. 'I need something to do in my spare time, to get away from my parents. Right now I just come home from work and sit on my ass.'

Brian's head fell back. 'And what a fine little ass . . .'

'Shut your trap,' Khalid interrupted.

'So, tell me,' I continued. 'What can I do around here that's interesting and I can meet new people?'

The crowd fell silent as they contemplated this with great seriousness. I had just given them a project.

'Do you work out?' asked Eddie. 'You could join a gym. Meet a bunch of meat heads. They'd love you.'

A gym? It wasn't exactly the after-school activity I had in mind. I was thinking more along the lines of a photography class or canoe club, even though deep down I resented these activities because they were precisely the kind recommended by magazines and websites telling you how to get out and meet people.

'A gym, huh?' I pondered this for a second. 'I haven't worked out forever. Where do you go, Eddie?'

'24/7 Fitness,' he replied. 'Up on Chapter Road near the Northpoint shopping centre. You should check it out. Maybe I'll get a discount for referring you.'

'Yeah, Eddie,' Cody snarled. 'Because twenty a month isn't cheap enough for your sorry ass.'

'Wow, twenty dollars a month?' I asked. 'That's pretty cheap. I'll check it out this weekend. And I'll tell them you referred me.' Eddie smiled, but by now all the others had lost interest in the conversation and were watching ESPN on the television above the bar, hypnotized by a post-game replay of the World Arm Wrestling competition.

'Hey ladies!' I yelled out, feeling the momentary exuberance of one and a half shots of liquor. 'Let's get one more round.'

Khalid got out his wallet. 'Nah. I'm heading out.'

Ken also took out his wallet. 'Guess I'll take off too.'

I looked back at the empty liquor tray and crinkled my brow. 'Just a minute ago you were all bursting with energy,' I said. 'What happened?'

'You wore us out, rat,' Khalid said, his hip hitting a bar stool as he tried to walk past it. 'You can't make us think like this. We get tired.'

One by one, the others followed Khalid as he passed the salad bar on the way to the front door. Ultimately though, it didn't matter if they wanted to leave. I got what I needed— not just a reason to get out of the house, but another purpose, another step towards building a new life with a new future, with all the new people I was going to meet along the way.

I was going to join 24/7 Fitness.

10

Saturday arrived and my cousins finally left to visit relatives in New Jersey. Even though it was a relief to both Khalid and me to have privacy in the house again, no one appreciated this more than my mother. Her good mood was on full display that morning as she surprised us with homemade apple cinnamon waffles, then put on her wide straw hat and went out to the garden, cleaning up and getting the plants ready for winter.

And me—I was doing what had solely occupied my mind for the last two days. The gym was an easy drive from my house, ten minutes tops. When I arrived, I rang the bell at the front desk and a muscular sales clerk came out from a back room.

'Hey there. How can I help you?'

'I'm interested in a membership,' I said.

He looked me up and down. 'Most certainly,' he replied. 'Have you been here before?'

'This is my first time.'

His eyes shifted over me again—at the mound of fresh, virginal gym meat before him. He jutted his thick hand forward for me to shake. 'I'm Ian. How about a tour of the facility?'

We did the walk-through, and I noticed the gym's decor hadn't been updated since the 1980s. There were big stars painted on pastel-coloured walls and two thin lines of pink and blue fluorescent lighting tracked along the ceiling. But the gym seemed to come with everything—an indoor track, an Olympic-sized pool, sauna and steam rooms, and every type of stair climber, stationary bike and treadmill available. The cardiovascular machines rested on a platform that overlooked the main floor, which was cluttered with aerobic equipment and free weights. Music blared from brightly lit mirrored rooms where aerobic classes were fully under way. Aside from the aerobic classes, however, the gym was virtually dead.

'It gets busiest during the workweek after five,' Ian said. 'That's when the real crowds come.'

'I don't like it being so crowded,' I responded. 'I hate waiting on machines. I prefer it this way.'

Ian nodded. 'A girl with true work-out goals. I like that.'

I smiled, pleased that I impressed this guy Ian with my serious approach to fitness. But the truth was that I was never going to come on a weekend again. Exercising around three or four hunched-over retirees wasn't exactly motivating.

I finished the tour, completed the paperwork, then hopped on a stationary bike for an easy fifteen-minute ride. Then I did some chest presses and pull-ups on the machines. I drank some water and started on some calf raises. Everything was going fine until I caught myself in the mirror—I was wearing my usual workout clothes—a pair of grey Georgetown University shorts and a loose navy blue T-shirt with the sleeves rolled up, and all I could think about was the fact that Ethan was not with me. He wasn't by the free weights, where he usually was in our D.C. gym, walking over to me when he found someone to make fun of—like the guy he called 'Ass Man', with the tight, green biker shorts that always gave him a wedgy. And 'Torpedo Tits', the woman with fake breasts so large and tight they pointed out like two . . .

I got off the machine. Tears filled my eyes, and I suddenly missed Ethan more than I ever had. I wasn't sure where the feeling had come from or why it had come on so strongly, but I wanted to be anywhere but in that gym. I wiped my eyes with my shirt, pretending to be wiping off sweat, and went to search through the box at the front desk for my keys. I untangled them from another set and headed for the door. A petite and overly tanned clerk gave me a look of both disappointment and superiority as I said goodbye.

'Leaving already?' she asked.

As soon as I got home, I threw away my Georgetown shorts and T-shirt. I returned triumphantly the following Monday with new blue lycra leggings that revealed every part of my behind and a sleek, brand-new gym bag. This time the gym was packed and every room was occupied. I peeked into one of the racquetball rooms and saw four equally hot guys sweating in all their glory.

I was thrilled. They were all over the gym. Hot guys. Everywhere. It was too much eye candy to take in at once, so the first thing I did was hop on a stationary bike that had a great view of the main floor. I noticed a lot of good-looking women around too but I was ready to compete—especially with my new black spandex tank top that gave me instant athletic arms.

'Hello. I've seen you here before,' said a thin, white-haired man with sneakers and black socks that came up his shins. He climbed onto the bike next to me.

'Yes. I was here on Saturday,' I replied.

'I was surprised to see you,' he said. 'Not many people come in on those days except us old-timers.' He unfolded a crossword puzzle in front of him. 'What's your name?'

'I'm Sam.'

'Well . . . oh my goodness,' he said, excitedly. '*I'm* Sam! We both have the same name! How about that! I'm short for Samuel. You short for Samantha?'

'No, I'm short for Samira.'

'Samira? What a beautiful name. Are you from India?'

'No, I'm from Pakistan.'

'Pakistan!'

Silence. Sam was in momentary shock. With trained patience, I waited for him to pass through the three stages typically experienced by someone coming face-to-face with a Pakistani: first, disbelief that someone from the world's most notorious brown country located way on the other side of the planet somehow ended up in the same room as you; next, fear and a little excitement that this Pakistani could have illicit ties to recent national and international news events; and lastly, the formulation and subsequent airing of a bone-headed comment.

'You gave Bin Laden a house before our boys took his left eye out!'

'Well, I didn't give him a house,' I replied. 'Personally.'

'Wow,' said Sam, eyeing with newfound scepticism my New Balance sneakers that were strapped to the bike pedals. 'What an *interesting* time to be from Pakistan. What with all the terrorists being from there and all.'

I smiled to put him at ease. 'It is an interesting time. But don't worry. I'm not a terrorist.'

'Well, I certainly wouldn't think you were,' Sam chuckled. 'My goodness. I sure hope I'm old enough to recognize a terrorist when I see one!'

My ass was killing me. I had entered a steep grade on my course and I leaned forward on the pedals with all my weight. Sam continued.

'Do you call yourself Sam to sound more American?'

'It's an easy, quicker way,' I said, short of breath. 'Samira's fine too.'

'I went to India once,' Sam said. 'My wife and I went a long time ago after we had our first son. We wanted the family to go on a spiritual journey together. Now that may sound strange to you but it was the 60s, and back then . . .'

I decided I had had enough of a workout as I could no longer feel my calves, and I was just about to dismount from the bike when something on the floor caught my eye.

Someone was watching me. I caught him and he immediately looked away, putting his weights down and walking over to a machine where some of his buddies were. There were too many other machines in front of him so I couldn't quite make out what he looked like, other than he had dark brown hair and seemed pretty fit. I stayed on the bike a little longer to try to see him again.

'. . . not a rite of passage I would recommend for anyone,' Sam said. 'Yes, sir. Won't be doing that again. If you ever go back there to India, I urge you, stay away from that brahmin. Stay far, far away.'

'Can't imagine that will be a problem,' I told him, smiling at his mistake, 'since I'm from Pakistan.'

Sam tapped on his temple. 'Oh, right. Pakistan. We're talking about Pakistan. Guess that's not the same as India, right?'

I looked around for that guy. As my heart-rate accelerated from the bike, I found myself aching for breath. The cool air from the vents was no match for the warm, sticky, evaporated sweat fogging the mirrors. I felt smothered. The gym was crowded on weekdays, indeed. Too crowded. And I had lost him.

'Lotta history in your country,' said Sam. 'I was reading the other day about that woman. The Prime Minister. You know, Buddah. How she was assassinated and whatnot. They brought in Scotland Yard to investigate her death. Thought maybe it was an inside job and didn't trust their own people to look into it. What do you think of that?'

'Bhutto,' I clarified.

'Yeah, yeah, Bhutto,' Sam said.

I rode a little longer until I spotted the pack of friends I saw that guy with earlier. He wasn't with them now and seemingly, as confirmed with a few more glances around, anywhere else, so I got up. The bike protested my early departure with a succession of angry beeps as I wiped off the handle bars.

II

Ethan was putting on his helmet—the one that matched his new silver Schwin that made him look like an oversized ten-year-old, when he said, 'I'm going. Be back in forty minutes.'

I looked out at the darkened sky. 'You're going now? It's ten o'clock. Isn't it kind of late?'

'Can you not question me all the time? If I want to go riding I'm going to go riding.'

'Then go!' I snapped, wiping water off the dishes before putting them in the cupboard. I thought about asking Ethan to help me, but I didn't want him crowding me in the crawl-space-size kitchen. He had no lights or reflective strips on his bike or helmet, something I kept telling him to get. After a certain point, I stopped caring. I wasn't going to baby him. I wasn't his mother. He slammed the door as he left.

About an hour later, I received a call on my cell phone. I had kept my phone by me on the pillow even though I needed sleep since I was leaving first thing in the morning. But I somehow knew not to fall asleep. I knew it was going to ring.

I drove to a narrow spot on a residential road where he was waiting for me. He was sitting on a patch of grass by his bike, a car pulled over near him, its emergency lights flashing. Other than the lights, it was pitch black outside.

I thanked the driver for letting Ethan use his phone to call me. Ethan had a bloody knee and limped as he and the driver put the bike on my roof rack. Luckily, no damage was done to the car or the bike.

We drove home without speaking to each other. Ethan dressed his wound and got into bed.

'Can you at least say thank you?' I asked.

'Thank you,' Ethan said, before continuing. 'You know, a little bit of sacrifice on your part, and you jump down my throat.'

'But it's always me sacrificing, isn't it? It's just expected of me to sacrifice, even though I'm the one working and in grad school full time. And the one who does all the chores.'

Ethan sat up to look directly at me. 'Chores? I transferred to this town to be with you. I took on thousands of dollars of debt to be with you. You *should* do more of the chores.'

'How dare you,' I said, crossly. 'You transferred here because there are more opportunities for you. And I told you when we get married or I get a higher paying job, I'll help pay it off.'

'That's low,' he said. 'You're trying to make me feel bad for my law school debts? That's really low.'

'No, that's not . . .'

'I don't need you supporting me,' he snapped.

'I'm sorry if it hurts your manhood,' I said. 'But that's our reality.'

'Our reality,' he repeated. He looked over at the suitcase on the floor, zipped and ready to go. He turned around so he wasn't facing me anymore. 'Have a good time in Atlanta.'

At the gym that evening, I spotted my unintentional friend Sam on the same bike he was on the day before. He seemed ensconced in his crossword puzzle, so I passed him, hoping he wouldn't notice, and hopped on a Stairmaster instead.

After twenty minutes of climbing towards heaven but never getting there, sweat dripping from my forehead onto the rotating steps, I dismounted and almost crumbled when I tried to balance myself on my legs. I wobbled over to the water fountain. Once there, I took my time, letting my heart rate slow as I slurped the lukewarm water. I was exhausted. It was the most intense workout I had yet and my knees hurt. I would surely strain or tear something if I didn't ease back into exercise, so I figured I would let my leg muscles relax for the rest of the night. Somehow that also excused me from doing any upper body exercises, so I decided to go home. I finished drinking and wiped the water off my chin.

When I turned around, I was met with a pair of dark eyes rimmed with long, chocolate-brown lashes.

'Is it my turn?'

He was holding an empty plastic water bottle in one hand, the cap in another, and he was looking right at me. I felt a jolt of lightning go through me when I realized who it was.

'Sorry,' I said, quickly moving aside from the fountain.

'No problem,' he said.

Seeing that the conversation was over, I should have walked away. Instead, I lingered, watching his tan body curve over the water fountain. I had never seen such a perfect body on a male in my life. His arms, his shoulders, his chest—everything was muscular—but in such a way that he was still slender, balanced. He could have been on the cover of a fitness magazine, gazing to the side while his slicked abdominal muscles bulged on the page.

I turned and took a step to my right, but there was nothing to my right except the day care centre, so I turned around again and stood at the water fountain.

'Do you know where the locker rooms are?' I asked, hoping that would explain my confusion.

'Yeah,' he said. 'Right here.' He pointed to two doors literally in front of me at the water fountain with a big sign above them that said 'Locker Rooms'.

'Oh, thanks,' I said, embarrassed but trying to look sweet to make up for it. I walked straight into the women's locker room and, still in a glorious, love-struck state of confusion, immediately walked back out, unsure of where I was going or what I was doing. He was still at the water fountain filling his bottle when he saw me grab my keys from the front desk and leave right away.

For the next two weeks, every day I went to the gym, I avoided him. He smiled and said hi to me a few times and I always responded with a hello before getting back to my routine. But the more I tried not to focus on him, the more I focused on him. I kept track of who he talked to (mostly males, to my relief, except for one French-manicured bleached blonde but she talked to everyone) and what his exercise routines were (treadmill and arms one day, treadmill and chest the next day, treadmill and legs the next day and so on . . .). I noticed he wore the same red muscle shirt twice in a row, and wondered how often he did laundry. On several days he wore a chunky silver watch. This pleased me, because it indicated he had just come from work. I didn't want to think he spent his life at the gym. He seemed to spend more time than the average person, but if he had a good job that required him to wear such a stylish and sophisticated watch, I could get past it. I was dying to know where he lived. One day when we left around the same time, I tried to see what direction he drove his Ford Bronco out of the parking lot.

'Stalker,' said Meena over the phone as I lay on the couch in the basement. 'I'm not stalking him,' I protested. 'It's not like he even knows I'm interested. I've been ignoring him ever since I met him.' 'Oh, that'll get him, for sure.'

From the other side of the basement door, I could hear someone jostling a key in the lock. I was about to get up and unlock it when Khalid burst through, carrying several large plastic bags from Best Buy. I caught a whiff of cold air and beer as he sat on the floor in front of me and started unpacking the bags.

'What are you doing?' I asked him.

'Got a projector,' he said. 'For my Halo. Now I can play on a big screen.' He pointed to the wall to the right of the television, where several velvet scrolls of Islamic art and drawings of Mecca were hanging. 'There,' he said. 'That's where it's going.' With some difficulty, he staggered up and went over to the velvet scrolls. He unhooked them from the wall and stuffed them behind the television. Then he sat back on the floor in front of his equipment, busying himself with plugs and cables.

'What's Khal doing?' Meena asked.

'Nothing,' I said. 'Anyway, if the gym guy wants to talk to me he's welcome to. But he hasn't, so what can I do about it?'

Meena sighed. 'You could try talking to him yourself.'

'That's a bad idea,' I said.

'Shit!' Khalid screamed.

'I'm going to take it easy,' I told Meena. 'I don't want to get too worked up over this guy because I have no idea how it may turn out.'

'Damnit!' Khalid screamed again. He was trying to connect a purple wire with a black wire, and they weren't connecting.

'I'm trying to be level-headed about this,' I said.

'You're stalking the guy in the gym parking lot,' Meena quipped.

'True,' I told her. 'Yes, that is true. But that was a one time thing. From now on, I'm going to be breezy and if he talks to me, great. If not, then so what.'

'You're being a wimp,' Meena said. 'But whatever happens, keep me posted.'

I spread out on the couch. All this thinking about my crush had drained my energy. I had also been working out at a frantic pace and my muscles needed the night off. There was no way I was making it to the gym that night. And besides, I didn't want that guy seeing me every day.

I opened a *Better Homes and Gardens* and splayed it across my face.

Better to create distance, I thought. Mystery.

I settled into the couch, and thoughts of kissing and lightly biting his thick neck cradled me like a warm blanket.

I was always the type to fall asleep on car rides. It wouldn't take much, just a half-hour or more until I would start to nod off. It was the gentle hum of the engine, the soft whiz of the wheels on the pavement—that reliable, monotonous noise that kept me locked in a deep slumber. What would wake me up, oddly enough, was silence—the sudden silence from stopping at a red light or reaching the destination, or as was the case in the basement, the sudden cessation of Khalid's commotion around me.

'Shit! Don't anybody move!'

I slid the magazine off my face and found Khalid frozen in the middle of the room, his face twisted in shock.

'The receipt! I can't find the receipt!' Khalid screamed. 'I thought I put it down here somewhere! Do you see it? It could be anywhere here. Do you see it?' Khalid dove head first into a pile of clutter on the floor and started picking up and throwing things around—plastic bags, empty boxes, cables—everything was flying.

I covered my face with the magazine and shut my eyes. 'No, I don't see it.'

'Help me,' he shrieked. 'If I don't find the receipt I'm out twelve-hundred dollars!'

I pulled the magazine off again. 'Twelve-hundred dollars? Good lord, your pastimes are expensive.'

'Can you shut your trap and help me look for the receipt?'

'Well, what's the problem?' I asked, sitting up on the couch and promptly tucking my legs under me. 'Nobody keeps receipts anymore. Just show them a copy of your credit card bill.'

'That's the thing,' Khalid replied. 'Ashley has access to my credit card statements. So I paid for it in cash. She has access to my bank account too, but this way I could withdraw the cash, tool around with the projector for a few days, then return it and put the cash back before Ashley noticed it was ever gone.'

I looked at Khalid in utter disbelief, and he looked back at me in panic.

'Well, it seemed like a good idea at the time!' he yelled. He slapped his forehead—a quick, crisp move that left a red mark. 'God, why am I such a dumbass? Why?'

I could only shrug in response. I didn't know what had inspired this whole projector scheme of Khalid's but one thing was certain—I had never seen him in such a state of despair. He frantically paced the room, searching his pockets, under the couch, and all the junk that was on the floor several times over.

'Look, don't worry,' I told him. 'We'll figure something . . .'

He slammed the basement door behind him. I watched as he retraced his steps to the car, then come back inside and search through everything once more.

Finally, after about twenty minutes of this, Khalid dropped to the floor, kneeling submissively before the Best Buy bags. 'No,' he said, the life draining out of his voice. 'It's gone. The receipt is gone.'

12

The following Saturday, out of a sense of solidarity and offer of emotional support, I accompanied Khalid to Best Buy. He was determined to return the projector, though I wasn't sure how he was going to do it without the receipt and with several parts already missing, but he had neatly repackaged everything to look new and seemed to have some sort of plan. When we walked through the sliding glass doors of the store, he stopped and turned to me.

'Listen,' he said. 'I'm about to make a huge stink to these Best Buy dorks and I can't have you snickering around the corner or I'll lose my nerve. So . . . you gotta get out of here.'

'What do you mean?' I said.

'A half-hour is all I need. Go on. Get lost.'

'I'm not going anywhere.'

'Just do this for me.'

'No! If you didn't want me around, why did you bring me here in the first place?'

Khalid grabbed a chunk of his hair in duress and released it. 'Please. Don't give me a hard time about this. You have no idea what I'm going through right now.'

I eagerly looked around. 'Where am I supposed to go?'

'There's a Target behind here. Hang out there and I'll pick you up when I'm done.'

I threw my arms up in defeat. 'Fine!'

'That's right,' he nodded. 'You're a good sister. I'll call you when I'm on my way.'

'Whatever,' I murmured as I pulled my hood over my head. I went back outside, back into the freezing cold, and began my trek along the highway to Target. Water droplets were starting to fall from the charcoal clouds. I wasn't pleased Khalid was sending me to Target. No good ever came from going to that store. I simply wasn't capable of leaving without accumulating at least thirty dollars worth of crap I didn't need, like hair barrettes and wooden candle-holders. And this time was worse—I was being forced to wander the store with no purpose. The situation was ripe for useless spending.

The heavenly, brightly lit warmth of the store beckoned forth across the acres of parking lot I still needed to get through. I slid between rain-slicked minivan after rain-slicked minivan until I finally reached the entrance, competing to get inside with clusters of young, suburbanite families for whom Target was a standard weekend destination. I removed my coat and passed the long lines at the cash registers to the women's clothing department. I found a pair of flannel pyjamas with frogs on them, tried them on and put them back. I looked at some bed linen, some Christmas decorations, then perused the frozen food aisle. Not long after that, while seriously considering a set of discounted suitcases, I remembered there was something I really did need to buy, something I could get at a good price there, something to occupy at least ten minutes of time. I rushed to the shoe department.

While the aisles of the rest of the store managed to remain somewhat tidy in the wake of the crowds, the shoe department was a chaotic mess. The floor was cluttered with boxes and single shoes torn from their plastic hooks. Kids ran rampant. All the shoes on the racks were misplaced, making it difficult to find what I needed. High heels, boots, work shoes, athletic sneakers . . . where were the casual sneakers? There didn't seem to be any in stock. I circled around the aisles several times and was almost ready to give up when I spotted two boxes of the type of black sneaker I was looking for on the top shelf of the sales rack.

Blocking the rack was a lone shopping cart. It was filled to capacity, practically overflowing, with canned food, diapers, toilet paper, towels sets, laundry detergent, and all other manner of household goods. I pushed the cart out of the way so I could reach the shoes. I stepped on the bottom shelf, pulling the two boxes forward. Size five and size nine. No size six. I was out of luck. *Damn. They were on sale too.* Feeling defeated and now back to having no purpose in the store, I stepped off the shelf.

When I turned around, there was a woman standing behind me. Almost waiting for me. And she stood close. So close, in fact, that I could see tiny red veins branching across her eyes. Her hair was dishevelled. Her eyes were fixated on me. Her cracking thin lips, pressed tightly together, were prepping to move.

I stood there waiting for her to talk. The way she was looking at me almost gave me the creeps, it was so intense. What the hell did she want already? She was holding a bag of diapers and a bottle of shampoo. They looked like items from the cart I had just pushed aside.

Then I understood.

Oh . . . I get it. It was her cart and when I pushed it aside, some of her stuff fell off and I didn't put them back on and now she's mad.

As offending behaviour goes, I thought this was pretty minor, and her anger toward me seemed a little misplaced. But this woman looked like she was having a bad day so I was going to give a simple apology, just a sweet and simple, 'I'm very sorry, ma'am,' to placate her and get her out of my hair.

But before I could say anything she threw the items back in her cart, rather sloppily because it caused some of the other items in there to bounce back off, and she finally unpursed her tight lips.

'Fucking Arabs,' she said.

She shook her head and started pushing her cart out of the aisle. Then she turned around to look at me once more.

'Welcome to America.'

She continued pushing her cart until her scraggly red bun was completely out of the shoe aisle.

I stood there for a second, confused.

What?

What did she just say? Welcome to America?

Welcome to America.

Welcome to America?

Just a few seconds earlier I had been thinking about shopping carts and shoes and detergent and diapers and now out of nowhere, all of a sudden all I could think about was the Statue of Liberty and people on little boats near Ellis Island and the red, white and blue of the American flag and Neil Diamond's chest hair.

Far!
We've been traveling far
Without a home
But not without a star
On the boats and on the planes
They're coming to America!
Never looking back again
They're coming to America!

Since I was too busy suddenly trying to recall the lyrics to this Neil Diamond song, the impact of the situation didn't start to crawl into my consciousness until I saw the woman nearing the cosmetics aisle.

Wait a minute . . .

Wait a minute!

Anger flooded me, almost drowning out my senses.

I didn't get to say a comeback!

She was getting away from me fast. And if I didn't think of something to say back to her and say it soon and say it now I would regret it for the rest of my life.

'Hey, lady!' I finally shouted across the shoe aisle. 'You can't say that to me . . . you . . . you're a dumbass . . . you know . . .'

But it was too late. She was already gone, out of my line of sight before I could even finish.

Not that I needed to finish. As comebacks go, mine was embarrassingly bad, hardly even qualifying as a comeback. On the other hand, if that woman didn't hear what I said, there was a chance for a do-over. I could find her in the store and say something good to her, short and witty. Something I could relay at parties among hearty rounds of guffaws and heaping praise for how clever I am.

I was mentally preparing for this, my clever comeback, when a petite blonde approached me. She was wearing the Target uniform of a red polo shirt and khaki pants.

'Oh my god,' she said, 'Oh my god. Like, I can't believe it. Are you okay?'

I looked around for the red-haired woman. 'Am I okay? Sure.'

'I'm so, so sorry. I'm so sorry that woman said that to you. Oh my god.'

'It's okay,' I reassured her. 'There's no need for you to apologize. It's no big deal. Did you by any chance happen to see where . . .'

'Yes, it is,' she insisted. 'It is a big deal. She had no right to say that to you.'

'No really, it . . .'

Two other shoppers had gathered around me. Before I knew it, I was in the middle of a small crowd.

'I feel ashamed,' one woman told me, her voice unsteady. She was holding the hand of small boy who was wearing one shoe. 'I don't want my son seeing things like that. This is not the country I want him to grow up in, where people treat others that way. I didn't think something like this would happen here. Not in this town. I pray every day that people in this world learn to love each other instead of hate.'

A man who was there with two kids gazed downward, his hands in his jean pockets.

I started getting nervous, unsure of what to do. I was upset about what that red-haired woman said to me, but to be honest, I wasn't *that* upset. Her comment didn't really penetrate. I saw it more as a frazzled female shopper making a bitchy comment to another female shopper. I wanted to tell the crowd her comment was stupid, because I wasn't even Arab, but I knew that wasn't the point. I wanted to tell them there were worse things she could have called me, like towelhead or carpet driver or terror monger, but that wouldn't have helped either. I don't know, maybe what she said upset me more than I was letting myself feel. But I couldn't let myself feel anything other than the overwhelming emotion at hand, which was just . . . embarrassment. I was in the middle of a group of people, the centre of attention, and whether I liked it or not, I was ultimately the reason everyone was so upset. And now they were waiting for a reaction, for me to say something, to address the situation, when all I wanted to do was get out of there, curse Khalid for making me leave Best Buy and become an anonymous shopper again.

'That woman was probably just having a bad day,' I tried to explain. 'She looked stressed. And then I moved her cart and some things spilled off and it made her mad. She was probably just taking it all out on me, that's all. I guess I was an easy target. Oh . . . "target". Get it?' I laughed slightly at the pun, hoping others would join in and it would lighten up the situation. No one laughed.

From across the aisle, the blonde employee was hurriedly walking over a man who looked to be in his fifties. He was holding a scanner and wore a name tag that said 'Butch Sutton. Assistant Manager'. 'On behalf of Target,' he announced, 'I want to apologize for what happened today. People like that are not welcome here.'

Embarrassment was now slightly giving way to gratitude. I was touched. How could I not be? Although I still wanted nothing more than to get the hell out of there.

'I hope you feel comfortable at our stores and will continue to be our valued customer,' he said.

'Of course I will, sir,' I assured him. 'What happened doesn't change my view of Target. I love this store.' I thought about adding, 'I love America too!' to make everyone feel better, but that would have just sounded odd.

'We're at your service,' the store manager added. 'Please let us know if you need anything.'

'I will. Thank you, sir. Thank you everyone,' I said, my hand waving to the crowd like a magician at the end of a performance, hoping that would disburse them.

But they wouldn't leave. They all stood there in front of me, in need of more comforting. So I turned to the person who was the most upset—the woman with the little boy, and I spoke to her gently, motherly. I told her it's over now, that that woman was gone and she wouldn't be bothering us again, and ma'am, are you going to be okay?

She nodded yes. I smiled and even rubbed her shoulder a bit, to try to assure her that everything was going to be okay.

Ten minutes later, Khalid picked me up.

'So, a woman in the shoe aisle made a racist comment to me,' I announced in the car.

'Oh, yeah?' Khalid asked with interest. 'What happened?'

I gave him a quick recap of the incident.

'Welcome to America?' Khalid asked. 'Why did she say that? What does it even mean?'

'Who knows.'

'And what did you say back?'

This was it. The moment I had been waiting for—to finally say the witty comeback I thought of back in the store. I straightened my posture and took a deep breath.

'So I said to her, 'Hey bitch, didn't you hear? It's called Americastan now!'

'Good one!' Khalid yelled, holding up a flat hand. 'Nice comeback, rat. High-five!'

'Yeah!' I cheered on, slapping his hand back and proudly settling back into my seat.

'What a bitch,' Khalid said. 'How did she react?'

'Oh, she didn't like that,' I said, continuing with the lie. 'She was outta there so fast.'

'Nice.'

'But listen, don't tell Mom and Dad. They'll get upset if they hear about it.'

'I won't.'

'So what about you?' I asked. 'What happened at Best Buy? Did you return the projector? Did you get your money back?'

'Nope.'

'Oh.'

I turned to look at Khalid. This was not good news. I didn't know what he was going to do now and I wanted him to see the look on my face, the sympathy, the acknowledgement that his predicament was understood. But he gripped the steering wheel tight, not averting his attention from the road.

We stayed silent the rest of the drive home.

13

Back at the office the next morning, I felt oddly energized—my ego having been slightly elevated on the heels of thinking of that great comeback. I was really getting off on the idea that even though I didn't manage to say the comeback to that woman in time, the fact is, I *could* have. I had just been seconds away from thinking of it in her presence. And I imagined scenarios of her bursting into tears, people overhearing my comeback and laughing with me at her expense—bitter, angry feelings of retribution that gave me a hit of energy. For the first time in a while, there was no urge to nap. No need to slide the life raft from the side wall and switch off the lights. I left the door open. The buzzing sounds of lawyers filing affidavits and shouting through conference calls drifted into my office and it felt good. There were things to do. Things I had been procrastinating on and now was the perfect time to get started. Starting with this: from my work bag, I pulled out a letter I had received in the mail a few days earlier. The light blue envelope had three stamps of Muhammad Ali Jinnah, the founder of Pakistan. The letter was written in blue ink on plain cream paper.

Dear cousin.

Salaam.

Hope you are fine. We are safe here in Kasur and fine by grace of Allah. How are Khalid and Meena? How are their studies? How is Aunty and Uncle? Please pay my regards to all and I pray for them. Salaams from my family. Regards to Khalid's fiancée. I am still on my job for fixing computer parts in a company in Karachi. I must travel long distances but it is good. Hamid is coming back to Pakistan after a long trip to Amman for his studies.

I keep photo of you eating masala dosa. It is a good picture and reminds me of my trip to USA. What about you???? Do you plan to come to Pakistan?? OK take care and if possible please do send me email address so we may speak every day.

Thanks. Awaiting your kind reply.

Nasir

I picked up my peanut-butter- and jelly sandwich and took a bite, mulling this over. *Hmm.* I swallowed. *Interesting.* This was not a letter I would have expected. I was actually quite surprised, not just because I didn't know Nasir had taken a picture of me eating that masala dosa, but because his letter was sweet. Genuinely sweet. After his last visit, I thought Nasir wanted nothing to do with me. I would have to show the letter to my parents, I decided, as yet more evidence that I was capable of having friendly relations with my own kind.

I found some stationery in my desk. I wrote back that I was fine, the family was fine, the fiancée was fine, and that I would love to come to Pakistan when I had some vacation days but couldn't for a while because I started my new job helping people, and so on. I deliberately neglected to mention my email address, and signed my name at the bottom.

My second order of business—checking my email. I had been avoiding it for months, scared shitless of whatever awaited me in there. Certainly enough time had passed that it was safe to check, that whatever was in there couldn't hurt me anymore. I logged on. Three hundred and fourteen new messages piled my inbox, mostly junk or mass emails from friends.

There was one I opened and read with interest, entitled, 'I'm waiting for you'. It was a service for hooking up with 'dirty, horny housewives' in my area. It even gave the address where my horny housewife was waiting for me. I went down the list of emails, checking all to be deleted except this one so I could later check if the address was legitimate and if so, who lived there. It would be a fun little nugget of time to waste if I ever got bored at work.

I found my last email from Congressman Bailey's office. It was from Bailey himself, describing what a great staffer I had been, and how much he and the rest of the office were going to miss me. Following that was a message from a friend in another Congressional office. He had forwarded me a small *Associated Press* article about a traffic incident at the intersection of Independence Avenue and South Capitol Street, the right side of the Rayburn building. 'Samira, is this you?' he asked. 'Heard you got arrested??!!'

Delete. Both emails gone. Now my eye was roving for one email in particular. Ethan hadn't made any contact with me since I moved back home, so I scrolled up and down, looking, and felt a shock pierce through me when I saw an email from him. Then, not a second later, felt my stomach sink when I realized the message was five months old. I opened and read it.

Hey babe—this is that speech Byron Baker gave at the National Press Club. Read the part where he says "Security cannot be realized without a holistic approach to a country's economic needs." That's an exact sentence from my Foreign Affairs article! This guy plagiarized me! Oh hey, since you're on the rag can this be hummer week?

Ethan DeWinter

White House

Assistant to the Special Assistant on Legislative Affairs

'Senior White House Official,' the cops called him.

My ass.

I checked his email for deletion, the last normal email Ethan had sent me before we broke up and deleted en masse, including the horny housewife email, all three hundred and fourteen messages. I had been doubtful Ethan was going to email me and so didn't really check to see if he would. But now that it was confirmed he didn't, I still felt let down.

I went to the trash folder. I found Ethan's message, unchecked it, and moved it to the Saved folder. When I returned to my inbox, a new message had popped up: 'Samira, this is your Dad. Please remember to write the mission statement. You are the best daughter. Daddy.'

I brought up the Mission Statement document I had already started, and just as my fingers hit the keyboard, I saw it—a red light flashing above the message button.

It must have been flashing there all morning. For some reason, I didn't notice, and for some reason, I was sure it was the same person trying to call from Pakistan a few days earlier. I pressed the message button and thankfully it took me right into the message centre. There was one message, and I listened as the same harried voice I had heard the first time went on again, in Urdu.

I didn't know what to do. At first, I replayed the message, constantly rewinding it, trying to write down everything I heard phonetically. Maybe my father could parse out what the caller was trying to say that way. But it was no good. Even trying to phonetically translate Urdu proved too difficult a task. I gave up. There had to be some way of saving the message and replaying it for my father to hear himself. I thought about it for a couple of minutes—I could bring my father to the office, or . . . get a tape recorder. I did work at a law firm. Someone around here must have a tape recorder.

Someone did. The very same administrative assistant who spoke to me my first day at the office. She always called me 'hun' so I went to her and smiled and she pulled an old recorder out of a filing cabinet and told me to keep it as long as I needed. I thanked her and returned to my desk. Turning on the speaker phone and upping the volume, I replayed the message from Pakistan, catching every word on my tape recorder, and took the recorder with me to the next PAC meeting.

'This time I have secured a conference room at the Sheraton,' my father said in the car. 'The hotel manager is a good friend of mine. I gave him and his family good deals on their Hondas, so he owed me a favour.'

I would soon realize that the manager must have loved his Hondas, because the room he gave my father at the hotel was huge and quite formal—crystal chandeliers, lowered to a soft, amber glow, hanging above tables centred with foggy pitchers of ice water. A stage and podium had been set up in front, along with several white boards with pens. Though the room was big enough for a conference of several hundred people, there were twelve of us there.

Nevertheless, my father stood in front of the podium and spoke through the microphone.

'Ah . . . Yes. Hello. Welcome everyone, to our bi-weekly meeting of the Pakistani-American Council. Today, we are to discuss the following agenda items . . .'

I reached into my bag and pulled out my thick cotton cardigan. As elegant as the room was, it was freezing in there. These ballrooms were all the same. Freezing. In fact, as I looked around—the carpet, the chandeliers—the ballroom was almost an exact replica of the one at the hotel in Atlanta, at that conference on government reform. I had kept my sweater on over my suit during the entire conference because I couldn't bear the chill. I couldn't have cared less if it looked inappropriate. I was hardly there anyway, hardly paying attention to any of the speakers or socializing with the other participants.

During the third session of the first day, I had taken a seat in the ballroom and leafed through the programme brochure to see who would be speaking next. It was someone from Citizens for Fiscal Responsibility. They were an important group. I would be asked what they had to say, and this was a session I absolutely needed to pay attention to. I put the brochure in my bag and reached for my notepad and pen.

When I caught a glimpse of my phone, the knot in my stomach tightened. Ethan still hadn't called me. He hadn't called to see how my flight was or if I had even arrived at the hotel. I thought he wouldn't have cared if we were fighting or if I had said nasty things to him before I left. This was supposed to be the one thing that trumped all else for him—my safety. The thought both angered and terrified me. If Ethan no longer cared about that, I wondered if he and I had anything left.

'Is this seat taken?'

I looked up at what was about to irrevocably change the course of my life. He was standing above me, holding the conference brochure. Dark blue eyes. Brown hair. Black suit. His name-tag mentioned some law firm in Chicago. My workbag was on the chair he wanted.

I put my bag on the floor. 'Not at all.'

He sat next to me and also put his bag on the floor. As he took out a pen from his suit jacket, he smiled. 'I like your sweater,' he said.

The drinks were strong at the reception that night. And free. Mojitos, gin and tonics, bourbon and gingers. Who knew what you were drinking and after a while who cared. The evening became a blur—a crowd of business people getting louder and louder and jackets being thrown on chairs and coiffed hair swinging free from rubber bands. We had stood together all night by the same tray of drinks. Talking, laughing, flirting. Finding common interests. 'You like Space Ghost too? Nobody watches Space Ghost! I have it on my laptop upstairs!' and using what we both knew was a convenient excuse to go back to his room.

The next morning, I lay under his blankets and watched him move about the room, gathering his belongings. His movements were swift, bird-like. I was on my stomach, my head on the pillow, laying to the side. I tried to sit up, and it felt like someone had placed a crate of bottles on my head. I'm not sure why of all things I thought of a crate of bottles but I just did. I put my head back down and shut my eyes.

'Check-out is in a half-hour,' he reminded me. 'You should probably get a move on.'

There was no pretence of this being more than it was. We exchanged no information, made no plans to see each other again, had barely probed each other's personal lives to begin with. We were both at the right place at the right time and that was how it was to remain. I left his room and once in my room, packed my suitcase, including my toiletries. And then I unpacked my toiletries and took a shower. I heard the maid knocking on my door, so I quickly ended my shower and put on my clothes and left the hotel.

On the plane, the flight attendant wouldn't let me change my seat. I had an aisle seat, and I needed a window seat. If she knew what was good for her she would look at my face and understand what was going on and give me a damn window seat but the plane was full and she wouldn't relent. So I sat at the aisle, looking at everyone looking at me—the girl with wet hair not discreetly crying into the side of her sweater. I had minutes before take-off, so I called Natasha. I told her I think I just cheated on Ethan.

'You *think* you cheated on him?' she asked.

I had to clarify myself with everyone in aisle four and aisle six looking at me and listening. 'No,' I said. 'I just cheated on him.'

Natasha said some things to me after that, things that are now forgotten. Probably just words to calm me down. But maybe something more than that. I was in too much of a daze to really know, and I was still in a daze when I reached my apartment and unlocked my door and found Ethan sitting on the couch, remote in hand, the television on mute.

'You're back,' he said. 'I'm glad.'

I rolled my suitcase into the bedroom and came back out.

'How was your conference?' he asked.

'It was . . . uneventful.'

Ethan looked up at me. He waited for me to say something else. His eyes wide, his shorts a size too large, he looked like a little boy. Overwhelmed, scared. Someone who had managed to leave his small town and go to law school and accumulate credit card debt and receive job offers from big places and have a big serious relationship, but somewhere along the way, forgot to age first.

'I called the hotel,' he told me. 'I called the day you arrived, to make sure you got there safely. You know I'm always worried about your safety. I was just . . . too angry to call you directly.'

I watched a tear glide down my nose and fall off the tip. I was hardly aware that I had been crying. 'You should have called me, Ethan.'

He must not have understood how seriously I meant that. He got up, gave me a hug and told me he had prepared dinner. Spaghetti but with a side salad, he laughed. So it's fancy this time. Was I hungry?

'I am,' I said.

'You look tired,' he said.

'I didn't sleep much.'

As soon as those words were out, even though he had quietly gone on to take the plates out of the cupboards and get the vinaigrette from the fridge, I knew I had just carelessly, perhaps knowingly, planted the seed of doubt in Ethan's mind forever.

I looked up from the notepad. My father was going over the agenda, and I wondered if he noticed what I noticed—that three of the men in the room were admiring the watch of one of them, another man was concentrating on his sub sandwich, one was leaning back in his chair already asleep, and another chatted on his cell phone. The rest, including one female sitting alone, seemed to be paying attention. The girl looked about my age, so I walked over to her table.

'Salaam alaykum,' I whispered. 'Mera naam Samira.'

'Hey,' she responded. 'I'm Neelam. No need for Urdu here.'

'Good,' I said. 'That's the only Urdu I know.'

Neelam held her stomach as she laughed, and I noticed under her green and gold salwar kameez that she was pregnant. 'Twins,' she said, upon seeing me notice her stomach. 'Ready to pop in two months.'

'Congratulations,' I said. 'Are you Uncle Abbas' daughter? The one that worked at the State Department?'

'Right girl. Wrong job. I worked for the Maryland State Troopers Association.'

'Sorry. I thought he said State Department.'

'He probably did,' said Neelam. 'But that's desi information for you. There's a thirty per cent accuracy rate.'

We both started laughing but looked toward the front of the room when we heard the PAC men raising their voices. My father was now standing in front of a white board where he had crudely drawn a table. They were still on Agenda Item Number One, which was how to raise money.

Uncle Fareed spoke up. 'The problem with this society,' he began, 'is that Muslims are still afraid to give to Islamic charities. Nobody will give money if it means the police, Homeland Security, the FBI and every other gora agency in this country starts watching you. These goras say things have changed for us but nothing has changed. I was just reading how mosques are suffering, having to cancel activities because they lack funds. Everybody is scared.'

My father pointed his dry-erase pen at him. 'Good,' he declared. 'That's good news. That means more money for us.'

'Did you not hear me?' Uncle Fareed asked. 'I just said people aren't giving money to Islamic charities.'

Uncle Mahmood piped in. 'Yes, that definitely poses a challenge for us.'

'Look at this,' Uncle Fareed said, tapping the piece of paper in front of him. 'This mission statement you gave us. It mentions upholding rights for Pakistani-Americans, but it says nothing about building mosques, recruiting Islamic leaders, supporting our Palestinian brothers . . .'

In a move that I think startled every person in the room, my father threw his dry-erase pen across the chequered ballroom carpet and pulled off his glasses. 'How many times do I have to tell you people?' he yelled. 'We are *not* an Islamic charity! We are here to promote the Pakistani-American, not the religion!'

'And Islam is not part of their lives? Is it not a part of your life?'

'Ki bakwas! Are you questioning my devotion to Islam? You don't know. I've been twelve times to Mecca over my life. Have you ever been once?'

'Yes, I've done Haj,' Uncle Fareed defensively replied. 'Many, many times. Even my children have done Haj!'

That last remark caught my attention. Khalid, Meena and I had never done Haj, and come to think of it, I never knew my father to have done it either. But I stayed quiet.

'Why doesn't everybody relax,' said one of the men. 'We are all in this together. No need for all this fighting.'

I wasn't sure if I should have spoken up or not, come to my father's defence, or if he just wanted me to keep quiet and take notes. I had already pleased him with how I had drafted the mission statement—with lots of references to preserving rights and promoting livelihoods, all with my father's vision in mind. It actually wasn't as hard to write as I thought it would be. I modelled most of the mission statement after one I found for a west coast conservation society, cribbing whole passages, sometimes the task as simple as replacing the words 'sea-turtle' with 'Pakistani-American.'

I walked over and picked up the dry-erase pen and handed it back to my father. 'Thank you, mera laal,' he said before turning back to the group. 'Okay. No more arguing. We'll get nothing accomplished this way.' He slid his glasses back on and turned to the white board. 'All right—back to our Agenda.'

My father looked down at the printed page I gave him. He noticed, probably for the first time, that I had written down an agenda item of my own, entitled, 'Call from Pakistan'.

'Baby, what is this?' he asked.

I cleared my throat and spoke up. 'I received a phone call at Uncle Kureshi's office the other day. I think it is from Pakistan, and the caller sounds like he's in trouble. He left a message in Urdu and I recorded it onto this tape recorder.'

I showed the tape recorder to everyone, and the PAC men all huddled in as I played back the message.

When it was over, my father took off his glasses, wiped his brow and said, 'I see.' I felt a great relief, immediately unburdened now that he had heard the message and understood the content.

'Baby,' he explained. 'This man is calling from Karachi. His name is Man Singh. He is calling Fahim Kureshi because he needs his help coming to America. He doesn't know Kureshi is in Pakistan. We don't even know where Kureshi is right now.'

'Why does he need to come here?' I asked.

My father explained that a cab driver from Pakistan, living here in Tennessee, was driving his vehicle on the interstate when a truck slammed into him. He unfortunately passed away from his injuries, leaving behind a daughter, the only family he had here. These were Sikhs, my father explained, not Muslims, and according to their customs, only a male can perform the funeral, the final rituals. The caller was his brother, trying desperately to get a visa to come to the US so he could take over the final rituals. He spoke in Punjabi, my father told me, not Urdu, which was probably why none of Mr Singh's words sounded familiar to me.

'Can we help him?' I asked.

Uncle Fareed jumped in. 'We're not immigration attorneys. There is nothing we can do. Kureshi should have handled his business matters before he left.'

'Now, now, let's not be hasty,' Uncle Mahmood responded. 'I'm sure there is something we can do to help this chap.'

I looked at my father for his response. 'Dad,' I asked, 'what do you think?'

He shrugged. 'I'm sure there is something we can do. I have some people I can call. Kureshi is really the only immigration attorney in this group, but maybe someone will know another who can help.'

Uncle Fareed shook his head. 'Oh, yaar, why do we even want to help this guy? He's a Sikh! We don't want to ship more of them here. What is he even doing in Pakistan? Bakwas! He should go back to India. Let him perform his rituals there.'

A mild argument broke out, with my father and Uncle Mahmood defending the need to help the Sikh and Uncle Fareed disagreeing. No one else in the room was getting involved. They were just sitting as they were, watching the fight unfold. Uncle Abbas wasn't even pretending to pay attention—he was in the back of the room with Neelam, listening to her stomach.

'It will be a disgrace to this organization if our first act is to help a Sikh. Bah!' said Uncle Fareed. 'Do not include me in any of this.'

It struck me as odd that the two men defending helping the Sikh had the most history of strife with them—having been young boys during the India–Pakistan partition, actually having lived through the mass migration and the violence, pain and racism that broke one country in two. Uncle Fareed couldn't have been older than forty-five, born during progressive and peaceful years in Pakistan, and the only one in the room still cocking his rifles and wanting to continue the feud.

'If you want to do nothing, then you do nothing,' my father scolded him. 'But that is not the spirit of this organization.'

On the drive home, I spoke with my father about Mr Singh. My father said if Mr Singh was calling Uncle Kureshi it meant, for some reason, he was having difficulty getting a visa. But there must be some way to get him here, I stated. He wasn't asking for a green card, just a temporary visa. How hard could it be?

'Baby,' my father began. 'It is very, *very* hard to come to this country. We only managed to come here because your mother's father was a diplomat. Most people try for years and their green cards, even temporary visas, are rejected. It breaks your heart. It takes much courage to try to start over in another country, especially when you have no money and barely know the language, but people everywhere still want to come here. The government knows this, and that is why they can be picky. They only want doctors or business owners or engineers. If you're an average person, a nobody, forget it. You're staying right where you are. And right now, insha' Allah, it will change, but people from Pakistan, even from the top tier of society, have virtually no hope at all. Not with all the paranoia and suspicion towards us. You children are very lucky. You were born here. You will never have to face this kind of rejection in your lives.'

My father exhaled, like he was unburdening himself finally of years of difficulties in getting to America. He had set out to help others this way, in fulfilling their dream of making that flight or sea voyage to the land of opportunity, but insha' Allah, this was no longer *his* problem.

He turned to me and smiled, cheerful now. 'You know, I almost didn't make it here to America. Even with your Abbaji's status, they almost didn't let me in. You see, I have no birth certificate. I lacked the proper documentation to apply for citizenship. You kids won't understand this, being born and raised here, but in Pakistan, back in the day, there were no files kept on these things. Sure, maybe I once had a small document announcing my arrival into this world, but if I did I'm sure it was burned or lost during Partition when they moved us from Hyderabad in India to some town in Pakistan whose name I can't even remember now. That's what they did, you see. During Partition, all Muslims living in the east came to a newly formed

Pakistan and all Hindus and Sikhs living in the west went to what is now India. Anyway, when I tried to come here to America, I wrote on the form that my birthday was 15 January 1941. The American authorities looked at it and said, 'How can you declare a birthdate when you have no birth certificate?' And I told them that one day, when I was five years old, my mother, your Ammaji, took me to the village teacher to enroll me in school. She gave my name, her name and my father's name.

'"What is the date of birth?" the school teacher then asked.

'Since there was no birth certificate, my mother, my Ami, had to go by her memory. And she had a terrible memory. Ami would go to the bazaar and come home with daal when she was cooking mungra that night, she was so forgetful. So she thought about it for a while and said, "Well, he was born some time after that epidemic in India, and it was rainy and cold the night he was born."

'The village teacher then gave this some thought. "Epidemic?" he said. "Hmm. Sounds like famine. Maybe it was the famine in 1939. Yes, that must be it. We'll add two years and say his birth year was 1941."

'Then my mother said, "I also remember there being lots of ber on the ground. All over, as I was giving birth to my little Tariq, there was ber."

'The teacher said, "Okay, it was cold and rainy and there was lots of ber around. Sounds like January. We'll just say the middle of the month then. January, 15, 1941."'

My father laughed. 'And that is how we calculated my birthday.'

'Dad,' I said, impatient and eager to get back to the situation at hand, 'is there anyone you can call to help Mr Singh?'

My father ignored my question, still enthralled by his own story. 'I don't know how the authorities ever accepted that explanation. They wouldn't today, that's for sure. But they said okay and let me in. Such a crazy world, isn't it?' He continued chuckling, and I realized I was about to take matters into my own hands.

14

At work the next morning, I dropped six books onto my desk. I spent the next hour flipping through pages upon pages of information, rubbing my eyes several times, trying to absorb everything pertaining to immigration law. There was a lot of information in this new world of mine: the Naturalization Act of 1970, the Immigrant Act of 1990, the Illegal Immigration Reform and Immigrant Responsibility Act of 1996, state versus federal jurisdiction, current legislation, the debate on healthcare for illegal immigrants . . .

After about three hours of this I pushed the books aside. This was a waste of time. There was no way I would get up to speed on the intricacies of immigration law in time to help Mr Singh. He had a funeral to attend. Time was of the essence here. There was an easier way to get things done. The D.C. way. And I knew this way quite well.

I picked up the phone. I surprised myself when I dialled my friend's number straight from memory, without hesitation. This was the first time I was calling a Washington number in months. A part of me wanted to be scared, to feel that anxiety that I was re-entering a world I had totally extricated myself from and never planned to return to, but there was simply no time for that.

A familiar voice answered immediately. 'Congressman Haisley's office.'

'Tony?' my voice was a little shaky, wary. 'Hey, it's me. Samira.'

Tony was a legislative aid for a prominent Congressman from Tennessee. I never worked with him personally, but prominence fraternizes with prominence. Our bosses were buddies, and Tony and I always took time to chat with each other in the hallways and at receptions and hearings. At first Tony said nothing, and some of that anxiety started drifting to the surface. Then he spoke, 'Sam? No way! How have you been?'

My shoulders relaxed a bit at his friendly tone. 'Good,' I said. 'I know it's been a while.'

'Hell yeah, it's been a while,' he replied. 'Heard you left D.C. Moved back in with the folks. How's that going?'

'Oh, it's good and bad,' I said vaguely, wanting to get past the chit chat and onto the purpose of the call. 'How are you?'

'Pretty much the same as you last saw me,' he said. 'But I heard some rumours about you that I've been wanting to ask you about.'

Here it comes . . .

'A couple of people said you were arrested outside of Rayburn, that you ran your car into a couple of guards and passersby.' He laughed, a sign that he was both unsure if it was true, and a sign of disbelief that someone as bland and well-behaved as me could have ever pulled that off.

'Little old Sam in handcuffs!' he laughed. 'I could hardly believe my ears!'

I was tensing up. I could feel my stomach and back ache suddenly but I tried to respond with as much levity as my voice could muster. 'I know people said that,' I replied, 'but it was just a car accident. I slipped on some ice and lost control a little bit. They totally let me go and all.'

'Didn't it happen in August?'

I needed to put an end to this conversation quickly, for my benefit and the Sikh's. I told Tony I didn't have much time, but the reason I was calling was to ask a favour.

'Anything,' he replied. 'Shoot.'

I told him the situation—that Mr Singh's visa application was most likely sitting with the State Department, and I gave his name, address and whatever other information I could provide about his identity to Tony. Tony said he would look into it, and if need be, ask his boss to do something about it. Maybe make a call to the State Department or something.

'Thank you so much,' I told him. 'I really appreciate this.' Then, unable to help myself, I had been out of the loop for so long, I asked him, 'Anything new over there?'

I heard a beep on Tony's phone indicating he was getting another call. 'Congressman Finkle's scheduler was caught with his hands down an intern's pants last Thursday,' he told me. 'It didn't make any big news but it's all we're all talking about over here. From what I hear Stafford's furious. Oh, hey, I gotta take this call.'

He told me he'd be in touch about the visa application and we hung up. Afterwards, I sat back in my chair, grinning. I had accomplished much by making that phone call. Not only did I just help out a total stranger, I had just broken the barrier I had put up between me and D.C. Once stripped of all the regal monuments and advanced degrees, D.C. was really a small, gossipy town. I remembered that now. And I was all too happy to remember that one scandal in this town supersedes another, and that there are so many scandals that maybe my little adventure with the cops was no longer at the forefront of anyone's mind.

As a reward to myself for my highly productive day, I took a long nap when I got home that evening—shutting the blinds, getting under the quilt, eventually being roused by the concentrated aroma of garlic and onion drifting from downstairs. I got up. I was starving and hoped my mother was cooking something normal and not a weird Bengali dish like stuffed bitter gourd. But when I stepped in the kitchen, it looked less like dinner and more like a bombing. Pots and pans and dishes were scattered everywhere and scraps of peeled vegetables were piled in different colours by the sink. At the counter was my mother, wiping emptied drawers and cabinets with a damp cloth that smelled of disinfectant. On the floor was my father, banging heads of peeled garlic into a heavy, stone bowl with a wooden club.

'Your mother is crazy,' my father said upon seeing me, scowling as hard as he could. 'I can't come home from work and get any peace in this house. She has to put me to work, always.'

'Well, if I had any good daughters they'd be doing this instead of you,' she said to him. 'One is busy chasing boys, the other sleeps all day.'

For once, I wasn't sure which was Meena and which was me. 'Mom, why are you cleaning out the cabinets now?' I asked her. 'Isn't it a little late at night to be doing this?'

'I would have done it earlier but your father made me go to work with him.'

'Okay,' I said reluctantly, still sceptical of finding any logic behind this. 'I understand the need to clean the cabinets, but couldn't it wait until tomorrow? Is there a reason they all had to be cleaned out before the stroke of midnight?'

'Samira, I didn't ask for your help. Why is this any of your business?'

I looked over at what was cooking on the stove. Nothing. My mother was frying a heap of onions and garlic in olive oil so she could freeze it and use it later.

'There's no dinner made,' she said upon seeing me gaze into the pot. 'I was too busy tonight.'

'What are we going to eat then?' I asked helplessly. Then, realizing this was an opportunity to assert my age and demonstrate my problem-solving abilities to my parents, I said, 'How about I order us a pizza?'

My father scowled as he pounded the garlic. 'I don't want no pizza.'

'I fried some shimla mirch for your father so he can eat those,' my mother said. 'You know we don't eat junk like pizza.'

'I've seen you eat pizza before, Mom, and why does he have to do that?' I asked, nodding in my father's direction. 'Don't we have a garlic press?'

'You know what a garlic press is? Ha. I'm amazed.'

I turned to the cro-magnon with the wood and stone tools. 'Dad, give me that stuff. I'll do it.'

'Oh, let him do it,' my mother offered. 'He likes doing it. He just won't admit it.'

'Such a crazy woman,' he said.

I took another look around, grateful I had somewhere else to go.

'Hello, stranger. Haven't talked to you in a while,' Sam said as he mounted the stationary bike next to me. Since these bikes were the newest and most comfortable of the collection, I figured if I ever wanted to use them, I would have to get used to him.

'Doing well . . . *Sam*?' he chuckled.

'Doing great,' I replied. 'And you?'

'Doing great!' he bellowed. 'Doing great! My son and his kid are in town this week. I'm taking them to the river Friday. His little girl has never been canoeing. I figured I'd take them on Cape Fear on Friday and then take them to the new dinosaur exhibit in Raleigh. Boy, I'd better pack some warm clothes for the canoe trip.'

'Sounds like a wonderful plan.'

'Do they have canoeing in Pakistan? I can't imagine . . . it being the desert. Is Pakistan a desert?'

'Parts of it are dry but I'm sure you can go canoeing up north.'

'Yeah, up north. There's always mountain climbing. K-2. Some people claim it's higher than Everest. Do you think it's higher than Everest?'

'I'm not sure,' I said, already panting heavily from having to chat and ride at the same time. I got off and stretched my legs. I quickly surveyed the gym. No sign of my crush.

'Well, that's one place the terrorists can't go,' Sam continued. 'Good old K-2. Need a lot of energy to climb that big boy. Don't think that bin Laden fella ever made it up there . . .'

I stretched my arms over my head. I was disappointed my crush wasn't there, but also relieved. He wouldn't see the wimpy four-pound weights I was about to use for my bicep curls.

Nevertheless, my heart stopped when I felt a tap on my shoulder.

'Well hey, look who's here.'

The voice sounded Indian. Thick Indian.

I turned around and looked at the five foot three, ninety-eight pound Bangladeshi before me. It was Pranab, one of the few South Asians that went to my mostly white high school. When he was my physics lab partner in eleventh grade, people started rumours that we were dating. The rumour was founded on the belief that since we were both brown and from the same part of the world, it was reasonable to expect that we were in love. The rumour embarrassed me, not because it gave a false impression to the school body that I only dated my own kind, but because Pranab looked like he would never achieve puberty.

'How are you, Pranab?' I asked.

'I am doing good, you know?' he said. 'Just living and working like a slave like everyone else. I am a technician now for IntelSat. Where are you?'

'I work for my father's organization. PAC. We try to improve the lives for Pakistanis here in America.'

Pranab's eyes widened. 'Oh, that is very, very good. I am very proud of you. To be working to improve humanity, you know, that is to be admired. Most people, they don't care about others,' he said, the last word sounding like 'udders'. 'But I knew even in school that one day you would serve the greater purpose.'

'Thank you,' I replied, busy concentrating on a red shirt with a muscular arm sticking out of it. Over the bulging forearms and past the shiny, round biceps, I followed the arm back to its owner, and it was my crush. He was by the arm machines, chatting with a friend as he did lat pull-downs.

He looked up, right at me. There was no mistaking his eye contact—it was direct, intense, meant only for me. I felt like my heart was going to explode in my rib cage. Was he going to come over and talk to me?

'You know, Samira,' Pranab said, 'people suffer greatly in this world. It is much better in America than in India and Pakistan, but you know, I have seen many, many people go through hardships here. For example, there is a Pashtun woman in my office, who is *this* big,' he said as he spread his arms out wide. 'So fat she cannot move anywhere, and . . .'

I had to get rid of Pranab.

'Oh, Pranab,' I said, feigning stress. 'I just realized what time it was. I have to be home soon to help out with my, um, dog. So I need to hurry and finish my workout.'

'You better go then,' he replied, sounding more stressed about it than me.

I told him we'd catch up later, when my dog was better, or whatever, and Pranab blessedly went back to his own workout. I took a moment to stretch my arms while discreetly glancing around. I was becoming good at this—spying in the gym. Without turning my head, I would dart my eyes back and forth, using the mirrors on the walls to see what was happening in every corner. But once again, I had lost him. It was getting late—my crush and I were part of the five o'clock crowd, and most of us were gone by seven. He must have left. And if he was gone, I figured there was no point in my being there either. I grabbed my keys from the front desk and hit the water fountain one last time.

I drank heartily even though the water was disgusting—warm with a heavy metallic taste.

'It's nasty, isn't it?' came a voice from behind me.

I swung around. A basketball tucked under one arm and an empty water bottle in his hand, he stood right before me.

I puckered my face like a little girl. 'Yeah. Pretty nasty.'I was still standing in front of the water fountain, my exhausted heart quickening its beat again, when he walked in close and started filling his bottle.

It was a definite violation of my personal space. It was pure bliss.

'How are you?' he asked.

'Good,' I said. 'So . . .'

He looked up from his bottle.

'Let's get a drink sometime.'

'Oh.' He lowered his head and paused.

Blood rushed to my head. My ears were on fire.

Who was this guy? I didn't know his name. I had never spoken a word to him in my life. Did I just ask him out? I couldn't help it. The words spewed from my mouth like bullets.

'Uh . . .'

I felt all that blood drain from my head and pool in my gut.

'Well . . .'

And now this stranger was thinking of how best to reject me—*I have a girlfriend, I'm busy these days, I think you're a gym whore.*

He raised his head and looked straight in my eyes. 'Sure,' he said. 'I would absolutely love to.'

I could hear the screaming in my head. *What an accomplishment! What a proud moment! Congratulations!*

I smiled, and for a second I think I might have softly laughed. All at once, I felt valid and confident and beautiful again. Impressed, I did something that I never would have done before, and more specifically, didn't think I knew how. I had no experiences with men other than Ethan. This was a sign to me. Personal growth. I was growing, changing. I wasn't the same person that I was in D.C. I could leave that whole life behind. Tonight, with just this one, simple little act, I just proved that to myself.

He held out his hand. 'I'm Brad.'

I took his hand in mine, thrilled to be touching a part of his body. 'I'm Sam. Well . . . Samira.'

'Samira,' he repeated. 'Gorgeous name.' He spoke in the upbeat, athletic tone of popular high school boys everywhere. 'Hold on,' he said. 'I don't have anything to write with. I'll go to the front desk. Be right back.' When he returned from the front desk with a piece of paper, he added, 'I'm just . . . I'm just so glad you asked me. Wow.' I was beaming. I had developed an embarrassing perma-grin. I was so pumped with adrenaline I could have hopped on one of the treadmills and run twenty miles. He said yes, and he seemed pleased with me that I asked him out. An ultra confident, go-getter type of woman who works out on top of that. What an impression I must have been giving off! I was on a roll. First the call to D.C. and now this. As I stood there, my hair in a messy ponytail and sweat stains on my tank top, my self-esteem was miles high.

'I have to run,' I told him, planting the impression that I was a busy woman on the go. 'I'll be in touch. It was nice meeting you, Brad.'

'Nice meeting you too, Samira. I look forward to talking to you again.'

I ruled out wiggling my ass as I left the gym, not sure I could pull it off, afraid I would just look like an electro-shock victim trying to walk again, so I walked as normally as possible to my car. Once home, I lay on my bed, holding up the piece of paper Brad had given me. His email address was long: bradley.g.turner@inx.commoditytrading.com Commodity trading. This gave me an exciting new task. At work the next day, I would have to read all about commodity trading and research the education requirements and average salary statistics for the job.

I put down the piece of paper. I imagined for a moment what his bed looked like and what I would wear the first night I slept with him. A nightie? A pair of underwear and a tank top? There was so much yet to discover. I picked up the piece of paper again, this time analysing his handwriting. It was small and square, typically male. Nothing to decipher there.

But I did find it odd that on that wide piece of paper, Brad started writing his email address two-thirds of the way to the right-hand edge. He ran out of space, and instead of starting on a new line, he wrote the rest of his email address down the right-hand edge of the paper, one letter at a time.

15

At work the next morning, the office phone rang. I put my Google search of Brad Turner, Bradley Turner, Bradley G. Turner, INX Trading, etc . . . on hold. I wasn't getting anywhere with my search of all things Brad Turner anyway. I found the website for INX Trading, but only clients could get past the main page. And my search for his name produced a million other Brad Turners here and in Europe, with nothing on my specific research subject.

'Pakistani-American Council,' I said, noticing the number was a D.C. area code. 'This is Samira.'

'Sam, Tony here,' said Tony. 'Got some good and bad news about

Mr Singh. The good news is that we located his visa application over at State. I got Haisley on the phone with them and he got his application approved.'

I smiled broadly. 'Just like that?' I asked.

'Just like that,' he responded. 'So he's good to go. The problem is that Mr Singh has failed to pay the 131-dollar application fee in order for them to process it. Is there any way you can reach Mr Singh and let him know?'

I told Tony I would look into it and thanked him for all his help. I thought about what to do next—I could call my father and ask him to get back in touch with Mr Singh, call him in Pakistan and tell him about the application fee, but I didn't want to. The man had faced tragedy, and trying to reach him again and arrange for him to make this payment would be time-consuming. It had now been several days since his brother died, and plus the time it would take to travel . . . something had to be done sooner. My father was wrong about something. I knew what it was like when the American government didn't want you. I had experienced some of that rejection. But I was in a place now where I could prevent that from happening to someone else. I grabbed the piece of paper where I scribbled the name and number of the State Department contact Tony gave me. I dialled the number.

'I'm Samira Tanweer with Congressman . . . with the Pakistani-American Council,' I said. 'I'm calling on behalf of Mr Man Singh's visa application.'

'Oh, I think I have his application right here,' the girl replied. 'Oh, wait a minute . . . maybe it's here.' I heard a stack of papers being moved around. 'I know I have it somewhere . . .' The voice on the other line sounded just like me.

I pictured this girl in a cramped cubicle, inundated under a pile of stapled application forms, some typed, most of them probably handwritten in different coloured ink, some of them in pencil, some barely legible, and trying her hardest to keep it all together. Probably with no direction from her supervisors, feeling like this was nothing like the life she envisioned when she graduated summa cum laude and moved to the nation's capital to make a difference.

'Got it,' she eventually said. 'Yes, Ms. Tanweer. How can I help you?'

'I would like to pay Mr Singh's visa application fee,' I said. 'If it is okay, I have my credit card ready.'

Later that morning, I called my father and delivered the good news. Mr Singh's visa application was approved, there were no more hurdles, and he was free to come to the United States immediately. 'I am so impressed with my baby today,' my father told me. 'I will call Mr Singh in Pakistan and deliver this wonderful news. How impressed everyone will be when I tell them! How successful my child is, how quickly she was able to pull strings in Washington. How she has the ear of prominent leaders, the movers and shakers of this world . . .'

Someone beeped on my other line. It was Meena.

'Hey, Dad,' I interrupted. 'This is an important call. Can I call you back later?'

I got off the phone with him and clicked over to Meena, immediately snapping at her. 'I called you four times last night. What took you so long to call back?'

'I was busy,' she said.

'Doing what?'

I didn't expect Meena to provide an honest answer, and to be honest myself, I didn't have the time or any real interest in getting one, so I was glad when she replied, 'None of your business. What's going on?'

'Well, guess what?' I said. 'I asked him out.'

'Asked who out?'

'That gym guy.'

'You asked him out?'

'Yes! And he said "Absolutely!" and said he was glad I asked him out and that by asking him out, I wowed him.'

'He said you wowed him?'

The conversation was already becoming tedious. I lacked that girlish tendency to dwell on details or further examine the minutia of voice inflection or body language of boys which I feared Meena was going to want to do. I delivered my news and now there were more pressing matters at hand. I got off the phone with Meena and wrote a draft of the email I was sending to Brad to set up our date. I wrote that it was nice meeting him, cracked a joke about the lead in the gym water fountains and how they were intentionally poisoning us so we would have to restore our health at the gym and that was how they got people to renew their memberships, immediately erased every line of the joke about the water fountains, and recommended we grab drinks at Stoney's at the Town Centre around eight on Friday.

I sent the email, then checked my sent box to ensure it went. Then I pulled my squashed, ziplocked peanut-butter and jelly sandwich out of my workbag and tossed it in the trash. I was riding high on a sense of accomplishment, first the visa application and now this, and I deserved some hot take-out. Schezuan. Maybe some spicy pasta. I was almost out the door when the bell rang on my computer, indicating I received a new message. My heart started pounding. Less than a minute had passed since I sent the email. Had Brad responded already?

I checked my inbox. The new email was the exact email I had sent to Brad, with the subject heading, 'Undeliverable'.

I re-sent it. Ten seconds later it was returned again. I tried sending it once more, against my better judgement, and it came back again. I tried calling Meena, couldn't reach her, and sent it again, once more against my better judgement.

Idiot! If the emails eventually went through to Brad, I'd have four desperate messages awaiting his inbox. I should have stopped at one and waited. Why didn't I just stop? This had me rethinking myself. My previous act of asking him out, what I considered a bold, assertive gesture, now seemed less like personal growth and more like a growing impetuousness. Bummed by this revelation, I retrieved my squashed sandwhich from the trash and tamely picked at it. I tried calling Meena again to no avail. But then finally, around five o'clock, Brad responded.

'Hello, Samira. Sorry about the email situation. Technical difficulties here. I would love to hang out tomorrow night if that's okay.'

'Holi holi! Slow down,' my mother said as I rushed past her in the kitchen. Plucking, waxing, manicure, pedicure, wardrobe selection—there was much work to be done in preparation for my date. I wouldn't have time for any of this after work the next day so it had to be done tonight. Wardrobe selection was causing me the most anxiety as I scoured my closet. Nothing seemed right. All my clothes reminded me of Ethan, and there was no time to go shopping.

Then it hit me. I had purchased a brown, cleavage-enhancing tank top on a recent shopping trip with Meena. Still brand-new, it should have been hanging in my closet with its price tag on.

But it was nowhere to be found. Wearing a towel and leaving a trail of water droplets from my hair, I fervently searched every inch of my closet, dressing table and trash bags that still had some unpacked clothes. 'Where is that damn shirt?' I said to myself, yelling out the word 'shirt' as I threw a bag back into my closet.

'Meena, I need you to call me immediately,' I said to her voicemail.

Another fifteen minutes passed and I left another voicemail. The next morning, I left yet another voicemail and finally heard from her at lunchtime.

'Meena! Thank God.'

'What is it? I lost my phone last night and just got your messages. You sound terrible. What's wrong?'

'Do you have the brown titty shirt?'

'Oh my god,' she said. 'I thought there was an emergency.'

'There is. I have a date with muscle head tonight and I can't find that goddamn shirt,' I explained. 'Do you have it?'

There was a pause on the phone.

'Meena? Did you take it or not?'

'I did. I took it.'

'Damnit!'

'Don't be mad at me, sis,' she said. 'I should have asked you first. I'm sorry. But I ran out of outfits and needed to wear it over for . . . my friend . . . because it was a special night for us and, well, never mind that, but I tell you what—Mom and Dad wanted me to come home this weekend, so I'll leave now and bring the shirt with me. I'll do your make-up too.'

I started to calm down a bit. I was not adept at make-up and hair applications, not entirely hopeless, but not as skilled as Meena, so I agreed. Meena told me she'd get home around five and asked that I not touch my face until she got there, that she would need a clean palette, but that I could go ahead and bleach my moustache.

'There,' Meena said as she finished smearing my black eyeliner. 'Perfect.'

I looked in the mirror. I felt a tingling sensation in my arms. Wow. I had forgotten how good I could look when I try. Damn! I twisted my body, very much pleased with what I was seeing. Meena had applied a lot of make-up on me, more than I usually wore, but I liked it now. Dark, exotic eyes and shiny lips. Dewy, bulbous cleavage. My hair, longer by three inches since moving back from D.C., glistened and draped down my back. For months I had avoided anything that could make me look this sexy. The cheating and lies between Ethan and me killed my sex-drive, and I had since neutered myself, preferring the dress of ten-year-old boys. Anything to bring back my innocence. Anything to make me feel like I was still a decent person. Now, all that decency seemed to be going out the window as Meena shoved a pack of condoms in my hand.

'I don't want you using these tonight,' she said. 'Remember your track record. But I want you to have protection just in case.'

'What track record? I've only been with two guys.'

'Exactly,' Meena said. 'And look at how you got with them. You're a good girl bottled up, and when the cork goes so does your moral compass.'

I laughed, a bit condescendingly. 'Moral compass. Don't be preaching to me about any moral compass. I'm not the one giving BJs to drug dealers. Your moral compass points in every direction simultaneously.'

Meena's voice raised. 'I gave that BJ for you, okay? And that's not even the point. The point is that yeah, I've had my fair share of shacking up, but my bad girl tendencies are measured. You keep it in and keep it in and then *poof*, one day you explode.'

I squirted some peach-scented lotion into my hands and rubbed. I didn't like being confronted with my character flaws this way, especially not minutes before a date, and especially when deep down, I knew part of what Meena was saying was true. 'Thanks for the psychoanalysis,' I responded. 'But I can handle myself.'

'No, you can't,' Khalid said upon entering my room. 'What are you two cackling on about? What's going on in here?'

I shoved the condoms in my purse before he could see them. 'I have a date tonight. Don't I look gorgeous? Meena did my hair and make-up.'

'You look like a cheap hooker.'

Meena could dismiss Khalid's comment with an adolescent roll of her eyes, but I was in a very delicate state. The wrong comment, just about anything going wrong, could easily push me over the edge. 'This is an important night for me,' I told Khalid. 'I don't need your negative energy so get out.'

'Okay, sorry,' said Khalid. 'Sorry, I take it back. But listen, real fast, if Ashley calls, tell her I'm not here.'

'Ashley never calls here,' said Meena. 'Why are you avoiding her?'

'I can't deal with her right now. There's some stuff I gotta work out.'

'You're not marrying her, are you?' she asked.

'Of course I'm still marrying her.'

'Then why are you avoiding her?'

This was beyond frustrating. I was meeting Brad in less than an hour and I needed Meena's full attention back on me. I directed Khalid to the door. 'Yes, fine. If Ashley calls, you're not here. Got it.'

I shut the door behind him and locked it. To my relief, Meena immediately returned to fixing my hair. After one last fine misting of hair spray, she put the can down. 'Beautiful! My work here is done. Too bad Ethan can't see you right now. He'd regret marrying that skanky troll.'

'Thanks,' I said, giving myself a once-over before putting on a black velvet jacket. 'And thanks for the condoms. You certainly have a generous supply. Why so many?'

Meena took a pair of tweezers and began working on her eyebrows. 'Don't have much use for them.' She turned to look at me. 'You better go. Traffic's getting bad. But remember now—moral compass.'

16

Nine years prior to my date with Brad, almost to the day, was the night I met Ethan at a motel in South Carolina. It was the last debate tournament of the semester, and the rooms were packed with drunken coeds brought together from all over the country. I was in a room with four of my teammates and a couple of UPenn students. Sprawled out on the bed, I was running through the second negative construction I would have to use if I was paired against Brown while everyone else sat in a circle on the floor, passing a bong around.

'Dude, can someone turn this shit off?' asked Tucker from the UPenn team. 'We've been listening to the same CD all night, waiting for this Alice and Chains mother fucker to get out of his fucking box.'

Quentin, one of my teammates, tossed Tucker a Soundgarden CD. 'Here, bitch,' he said, then glanced up at me on the bed. 'Hey, Sam, we think you and that new guy on the WVU team should hook up.'

'Which guy?' I half-heartedly asked. I was concentrating too hard on arguments, my head too foggy with pot, to really care.

'The hot one,' said Michelle, another one of my teammates. 'He's the freakin' hottest one on the team. Probably in the whole debate circuit. No offence to any of you.'

'No offence taken,' Quentin said, wrapping his shoulder-length brown hair in a rubber band. 'Dude, I will totally concede that point.'

'I heard he's deep,' said a girl from UPenn. 'He's all into Pink Floyd and shit.'

'Let's call him over here. Anyone know his room number?'

'No,' I protested. I sat up and rubbed my eyes, dried out from the smoke in the room. I put my plaid shirt over my cropped black T-shirt and tied the laces of my Doc Martins. 'If I don't get some sleep I'll fuck up the first round. I'll see you guys in the morning.'

I stepped out into the clean, misty air on the balcony and headed for my room. I was halfway down the stairs when I saw him walking up, wearing a navy blue jacket over a polo shirt, khakis, and a Pink Floyd baseball cap. He was holding a small plastic trash can.

'Hi,' he said.

'Hi,' I said back. I stopped in my tracks. When he reached my step, he also stopped. We both just stayed there on that step.

'Hey, do you know where I can get some ice?' he asked.

'I think there's an ice machine on the ground floor.'

'Thanks.'

He didn't move.

'Are you from the WVU team?' I asked.

'Yeah. And you're on the GU team, right?'

'Yeah,' I answered. He had green eyes and light brown hair with a tiny bit of wave. And he was smiling at me.

'I'm Ethan,' he said, putting his hand out for me to shake.

'I'm Samira,' I replied.

Three hours later, at roughly 2:30 a.m. at the Motel 6 off highway I-85, I lost my virginity.

I took a wrong turn on the way to Stoney's. I was having a hard time concentrating on the roads—too busy wondering where Ethan was that night, how he was doing, if he was with Natasha at that very moment and what he would think if he knew I was on my way to a date. I could hardly believe it myself. Me. On a date. I was only twenty-seven and had never been married, but I felt no different than any fifty-year-old divorcee starting over—a woman who married her high-school sweetheart, never spending a minute without him, now awkwardly trying to learn for the first time how to pump gas in her car on the way back to her lonely apartment after the first day of her new temp job.

I ended up getting there almost twenty minutes late. Brad was waiting at the bar with an Amstel Light in his hand, chatting with the bartender. His muscular physique was slightly visible under his clothes. He turned when he saw me and smiled.

'Hey Samira!' He hugged me, and he smelled like green marbled soap.

My hands lingered a bit over his hard shoulder blades before I detached. 'I'm sorry I'm late.'

'No problem. I'm just happy you're here. What do you want to drink?'

I told him a Seabreeze, and he gave our request to the bartender. We sat in a corner table of the bar and my posture was stiff. I still couldn't get over it. I was on a date? Who goes on dates anymore? I felt like I was on a cheap sitcom that was out of touch with how romance really plays out these days. I was even sure everyone was watching us, that people knew we were on a first-date. Ethan and I would do that at restaurants. We would sit side-by-side at our table, trying to spot the first-daters and laugh at them. You do these things when you're with someone so long you've run out of things to talk about.

Brad and I looked at each other while waiting for our drinks, both of us smiling without saying a word to each other.

'So . . .' Brad fiddled with his watch. 'Um . . .' He paused again after that. 'How are you?'

That served as some sort of icebreaker and I started laughing, prompting Brad to laugh with me.

'Good,' I replied. 'And how are you?'

'Good,' he said, still laughing. 'Well, someone had to say something here, or this was going to be a very long night. Okay, let me ask you a different question. Where are you from?'

'Well, originally Jersey.'

'No, I mean, like, what country?'

'Oh, sorry. Sometimes when people ask where I'm from I'm not really sure if they mean what state or what country . . . anyway, I'm from Pakistan,' I said, pronouncing it 'Pack-i-stan,' the pronounciation used for white audiences, rather than the correct pronounciation used amongst desis, 'Pock-ee-stan'.

'Pakistan?' Brad repeated. He seemed surprised, but pleased.

'You're from Pakistan? Oh, yeah.' He started nodding slowly. 'Pakistani women are beautiful.'

'You know other Pakistanis?'

'Um . . . no.' Brad fiddled with his watch again. 'Guess . . . I guess not.' He looked up for our bartender, who was nowhere around, and I thought that had concluded our conversation about Pakistan when he said, 'So your parents don't mind you dating a white guy? Isn't this really taboo? Don't they do arranged marriages and stuff like that in your culture?'

I nodded. 'Some families do. Sure. You've probably heard the child bride horror stories, but usually it's just two sets of parents arranging for their kids to meet, putting them in a room together and stirring. But my parents never even tried that. I think they learned early on they had no control over us, especially our romantic lives.'

Brad's eyes widened. 'Wow. You and your siblings must be super rebellious.'

'Rebellious?' I said. 'Oh, it's nothing that glamorous. We're just suburbanites.' I laughed, but Brad didn't laugh with me, and I took this to mean the conversation was increasingly going over his head. I wasn't surprised when he changed the subject back to something safe.

'So . . . the gym,' he said. 'You're pretty new there, right? Believe me, I would have noticed you a long time ago.'

I flirtatiously hit his knee with my knee under the table. 'I joined a few weeks ago,' I said. 'It's a nice gym. I want to take advantage of the classes and squash courts, but I just end up doing the same routine every time.'

'I know what you mean,' he said. 'I started playing basketball with some of my buddies, but that seems to be falling apart. Whenever the weather gets cold, people start losing motivation to work out.'

'I know what you mean,' I said, immediately and painfully aware that I had just parroted him. 'So . . . how long have you been at the gym?'

He said about a year, that he was in New York before that but moved to North Carolina to start his own business. I asked him what kind of business, with mock curiosity, of course. After all my on-line research, I probably knew more about Brad's business than he did.

'Commodity trading,' he said. 'I was a trader on Wall Street. But I hated it. It wasn't my thing. I'm not the kind of person that can have a boss screaming orders at me. And everyone else I worked with was too consumed by it. They lived for the highs. But if the market turned, these guys plummeted to the lowest of lows. I mean depression, drugs. God-awful stuff. That's not what I want. I want to sit back and enjoy life. Having my own business is much more satisfying.'

I liked him. I liked everything I was hearing. As the night progressed, our bodies moved in closer together as we covered everything from our travels to movies to gym gossip—he told me stories of mid-workout trysts and steroid parties in the spinning room. Three hours passed easily with him. By now I was on my third Seabreeze, or fourth. I didn't know and I didn't care. I was having a great time. I was also still wearing my jacket, not maximizing the benefits of the shirt, so I took it off. I brushed my hand through my hair, trying to look appealing, while Brad reached into his pocket and pulled out a large white pill.

'What's that?' I asked, immediately realizing the inappropriateness of my question. 'Wait. Sorry. I shouldn't have asked that.'

Brad grinned. He popped the pill in his mouth and started chewing it enthusiastically. 'It's my crazy pill,' he said, his eyes widening, his lips smacking.

'Gotta take it before I get . . .'

He raised his arms menancingly, transforming into Frankenstein.

'Like this . . .'

He came at me suddenly, grabbing both my sides and tickling. I fake screamed and laughed along, even though his fingers were too thick and strong. It hurt. He let go when our waiter asked if we wanted another round. 'Samira, what do you think?'

I was drunk and knew I should have refused but I couldn't. I didn't want the night to end. The bar started closing as the waiter brought our next and final round. Brad paid the bill after refusing to take my credit card, as I hoped he would, and he leaned in towards me.

'Samira, what's your story?' he asked.

'My story? What do you mean?'

'You have a story. You never really explained why you moved back from D.C. You said it was to be closer to your parents, but there's more to it, isn't there?' he said, slyly. 'Come on. Spill it.'

'No. No story at all.' My speech slurred a little.

'Uh huh.' He gave me a suspicious but playful smile. 'I'll get it out of you one of these days.'

I wasn't too drunk to dissect that last sentence. He wanted to see me again.

'What should we do now?' I asked. 'I don't feel like going home yet.'

Brad shrugged. 'Want to go to my place?'

I paused for a second, then laughed.

'What?' he asked. 'What did I say? Why are you laughing?'

'You know why I'm laughing,' I replied. 'I don't think I should drive right now anyway.'

'All we're going to do at my place is drink some coffee,' he coyly remarked. 'Nothing sinful or anything. And you can meet Mr Chips, my golden retriever.'

It turned out Brad lived in the very townhome development that Ethan and I were eyeing to move to one day. These were expensive townhomes encased in cul-de-sacs with dozens of other exact replicants—the kind of safe, bland luxury suited for post-city yuppies eager to settle down and reproduce. Brad, however, didn't seem too eager to begin that kind of life as the inside of his home was decorated solely with electronic equipment. There was literally nothing else in there—no rugs, no furniture, no knick-knacks in the hallways and kitchen and nothing in the living room but a denim futon and the most massive television, stereo and DVD system I had ever seen. Boxes and boxes of black equipment with not a speck of dust on them were sprawled across the floor, wires cobwebbing through and around them. A lone BOSE speaker hung above the empty and undecorated fireplace.

I read the word on the speaker. BOSE. The next thing I knew someone tossed a bear-skin rug onto my back, the enormous fluffy weight of it pushing me forward, hurtling me towards the fireplace. A dull pop sounded as my forehead hit the mantel.

'Hey, get off her!' Brad yelled, grabbing his dog's harness and yanking him off me. 'Oh shit. Sorry about that, Samira. You okay?'

My forehead was throbbing, but I resisted the urge to rub it. 'Fine,' I smiled. 'Hey, don't worry about it.'

'Mr Chips gets a little excited when someone new comes over. Chips! Down! I'm really sorry about that. I'm still training him not to jump on guests.' Brad steadied the dog, then dragged him to another room and shut the door.

'Oh, don't do that,' I pleaded. 'Leave him out here with us. I don't mind at all.'

'You're a trooper. I'll bring him back out then. Just give him a second to calm down.' Brad gave me a peck on the cheek as he walked by me on the way to the kitchen. I was sure I had just passed some sort of test. 'Want some coffee?' he asked. 'I've got every type you can imagine. Starbucks, Devalia, even Folgers.'

I looked up the stairs. I wondered what, if anything, was up there. 'I wouldn't mind something with hazelnut.'

'Hazelnut,' he said. 'Got it. Hey, you hungry? I can whip us up something too.'

Wow. Brad could whip something up? On top of all his other outstanding qualities, he knew how to cook? Ethan couldn't cook. The only culinary skill Ethan had was adding peanut-butter and Taco Bell sauce to ramen noodles, and he was very proud of that.

I walked back into the kitchen and found Brad carefully reading a box of microwave popcorn.

'I can make us some of this,' he said, pointing the box towards me.

I thought it was so cute that the food Brad was offering to whip up was microwave popcorn, and that he had to read the box to learn how to make it. This was, of course, a complete reversal of what I had been thinking about him a mere second earlier, but I was love-struck. Brad could do no wrong.

For the next hour, we sat on the futon and ate popcorn and skipped coffee. Brad had painstakingly searched his cabinets in front of me, baffled he didn't have any of the coffee brands he mentioned, even more baffled that he actually had no coffee at all, and he apologized for his mistake and gave me bottled water. The water and our conversation flowed easily. At one point we found ourselves talking about past relationships and admitting to each other that neither of us had had sex in a long time. Silence followed.

Finally, Brad spoke up. 'I can't believe I told you about my break-up with Nicole. Isn't that a big faux-pas on a first date? You're not supposed to talk about your exes?'

I shooed this with my hand in the air. 'That's ridiculous,' I said. 'It's an outdated social norm. The way I see it, everyone is in and out of relationships these days. It's such a big part of our lives. Not talking about it is disingenuous. Almost like hiding something.' My mouth went dry as soon as I said that.

'Well, good, because I spilled a lot about my relationship with her.'

'Not a problem,' I said, giving Brad a reassuring pat on the knee. From the sound of it, though, there wasn't much to spill. In comparison to my drama with Ethan, Brad's story about how he and his ex broke up because she wanted to live in Florida and he didn't was so mind-numbingly dull it could have been bottled and used as an anaesthetic.

'You on the other hand,' Brad said with a sly smile, 'you didn't say very much about your ex. Only that his bike riding got on your nerves.'

'Well, there isn't much to tell, I guess. That's about it.'

'How long were you guys together?'

I knew better than to answer that question. 'Not long. Really, not that long.'

'Why did you guys break up?'

'I tried to kill him and got arrested for terrorism.'

Brad was silent, then I burst out in drunken laughter. He shook his head. He drew in closer with a serious look on his face, took my hands and said, 'It's okay. I like a little mystery.'

He leaned in and kissed me. All at once my senses registered soap and cologne and wet lips and freshly shaven cheeks. We kissed and kissed until the bowl of popcorn I was holding on my lap fell on the floor. Brad moved until he was on top of me, his weight pushing me further into the couch.

As soon as his lips made contact with my neck, I lost all control. My hands dug underneath his sweater and T-shirt, and I rubbed the smooth and tight skin on his back. It wasn't much longer until I grabbed his sweater and shirt and pulled them over his head. Laying there with his gorgeous half-naked body on top of me, he reached up and pulled my straps over my shoulders, pulling down my top and levelling the playing field between us.

He grabbed me and pulled me over him until I was on top. In no time, I was in nothing more than my black underwear. 'You're a knock out!' he said, playfully slapping my bottom. 'Where in the world did you come from?'

Brad was single-handedly curing me of everything bad that had ever happened to me. I didn't utter a word as I lay paralysed on his chest, my eyelashes swiping against his skin, afraid of saying or doing anything that would ruin the moment. He gently touched my hair, gliding his hands through it. 'And God, your hair is gorgeous.' That did it. I wiggled away and reached for my purse.

I held the condom in my hand and studied his face, waiting for a response.

'Later,' he said. 'I was thinking of doing some laundry.'

I smiled and ripped the package open.

Two hours later, I awoke from a nap in his arms. I checked my cell phone for the time. 'I need to go home,' I said.

Brad put his hand over his mouth to yawn. 'Want me to drive you back home or to your car?'

I was nervous. I imagined my father in his bathrobe, sitting on a lawn chair at the end of the driveway waiting for me. It was close to three in the morning. I had never stayed out this late while living in my parents' house before.

'You can stay here if you want,' Brad said. 'Me and Mr Chips wouldn't mind.'

'Thanks for offering,' I replied. 'But I really should get going. My parents might freak out if I'm not there. I told you I lived with my parents, right?' I asked, horrified at my admission.

'Um, no. You didn't. But everyone does these days.' Brad lazily sat up, lifting his arms, twisting his neck left and right. 'I'll take your sweet ass to your car then. Mr Chips! Come on, road trip.'

The three of us got into his truck and headed to my car. When we were parked beside my Honda, he started kissing me again. 'Now I can check you out at the gym without feeling guilty,' he said. 'You look hot when you're on the calf machine, all bent over in your itty bitty shorts.' I giggled and he kissed me some more. 'I want to see you again,' he said. 'I had a great time tonight. Maybe next time we can get dinner or catch a concert. How does that sound.'

'That sounds great,' I said. I opened his door and started to step out. 'Give me a call or let's chat at the gym.'

'Absolutely, babe. You drive carefully, okay?'

I told him I would and waved to the furry mass in the back of the truck. To my relief, when I got home, no one was awake. I crept through the house and carefully locked the door to my room, my head immediately hitting the pillow. But I knew I wouldn't be getting any sleep. I was too wired, running through every detail of the night, repeating every line of conversation, wondering why after such a wonderful and perfect evening there was a small knot in my stomach.

And then I felt my head on Ethan's pillow, his blue sheets slipping under my skin, my feet trapped between books by Hegel and Wittgenstein, his Berber carpet scattered with dirty tissues and stacks of stapled academic papers. Ethan was standing naked before me—his damp body glistening. His hazel eyes had transformed to dark green. He picked up a small towel from the floor. He was about to head for the bathroom when he turned around and leaned against the wall, facing me. He crossed his feet, then hung the cloth over his still full erection. 'Excuse me,' he said to a pretend passerby. 'Have you seen my towel?'

I buried my head in the pillow and burst out laughing. 'Oh, hey, I just got this classical music tribute to Pink Floyd,' he said, dropping the towel and approaching the bed again. He leaned over and popped a CD into the player on the windowsill above me. 'It's a string quartet. Listen. It's *Echoes*.'

For a few minutes, we listened. Ethan contemplated the sound, studied it. 'I don't know,' he said. 'Can't tell if I like it or not. It's too smooth, not raw like the original. Let's listen to the original. Fuck it.' He leaned over me again and put in another CD, the original *Echoes*—the house of horrors sounds immediately filling his cluttered room. 'You know, Roger Waters was one sorry son-of-a-bitch,' he said. 'I love the dude, but you can feel the misery in his voice. His father left him for the War, and his wife left him for another man. This guy made millions and had groupies all over him, but he never got over it, the abandonment. I mean, listen to this shit.' Ethan changed the CD again, this time to 'Don't Leave Me Now' off *The Wall*.

'See what I mean?' He crouched in front of the bed, still naked, and buried his face in his hands. 'I have to tell you this. Okay, this is going to sound lame, so don't laugh, but the only reason I can listen to this dude is because I know I'll always have you. I know I'll never be a fucking Roger Waters.'

I grabbed Ethan's hand. He was drunk. We had just finished celebrating his acceptance to law school over two bottles of drugstore Merlot. But with a genuine seriousness, I looked back at him and said, 'You will never be a Roger Waters.'

He clutched my hand tight and put his other hand over his heart. 'Mother, will she tear your little boy APART!'

'Shut up,' I said, pulling his large body under the covers with me. He snuggled up to my side, nestling his head within my cleavage. After a few minutes and a few deep breaths, he started drifting off to sleep. A soft whistle escaped his lips. I wrapped my arms around him tight so he wouldn't slide off, and lowered my chin over his head until he was as encased within me as he could be.

'Babe.'

Brad called me 'babe'.

17

My stomach growled as I descended the stairs. I could smell breakfast cooking—a mix of Indian spices and sweet vanilla. I walked into the kitchen and found my mother tossing spiced potatoes in a skillet. A pan of cinnamon rolls was baking in the oven.

'You came home late last night,' she said.

I grabbed a mitt to take the rolls out of the oven and saw my reflection in the oven door. I hadn't fully washed off my black eye make-up and it had smeared all around my eyes.

'I went to a friend's party,' I said. 'It went late.'

'I mean, you came home *really* late,' she repeated. 'But don't worry, your father was asleep so he didn't notice. But I certainly noticed.'

My mother sprinkled some cumin seeds onto the potatoes. 'I'm glad you're finally going out and enjoying yourself,' she said. 'Young people should go out, live life. If I wasn't married to your father, I would be out and about all the time instead of always going to these boring people's homes. I'm sick of sitting in these homes, watching these women shove kebabs in their fat faces.'

My father walked in and said nothing to my mother as he helped himself to the potatoes. I smeared frosting on a cinnamon roll, using my finger to lick off whatever dripped onto the plate. I was counting the minutes until Meena woke up, desperately needing to talk to someone about the night before.

My father loudly dropped his plate of food onto the table. 'My children don't care about me,' he grumbled. 'Everything I do for them . . . for what? What good does any of it do me?' He turned to me. 'Why did your sister leave? She doesn't like it here? She doesn't like being with her family anymore?'

'Meena left?'

'This morning. She got up and said she had to go back to study. For what? She can't study here? This house is not good enough for her? She'd rather be at that party school on the beach than go to the perfectly good schools around here? For what, I ask you? To be as far away from her parents as possible? God knows what that girl is up to. She's so mysterious these days. Coming then going. Coming then going. Never does it seem to be about spending time with any of us.' I was disappointed. I couldn't believe Meena had left. I was so sure she would wake up dying to hear all about my date. I would call Meena later and demand to know why that wasn't the case, but for the moment at least, I had a sibling obligation to defend her. 'I'm sure she had an important exam to study for, Dad. She probably thought she would be distracted at home. Don't you care more about her doing well in school?'

My father just shook his head in response.

'Your father is angry at everyone today,' my mother said as she sat down with us. 'Ignore him.'

'Should I go get Khalid?' I asked.

My father scowled. 'No. Leave him alone. He's another good-for-nothing.' He ate his food quietly, then looked up and started talking to my mother like I wasn't there. 'All my children are big disappointments. All of them. They dilly dally around. No direction, no ambition. None of them married to anyone worth knowing.'

From almost out of nowhere, but I suspect maybe around the corner where he had been eavesdropping, Khalid marched into the kitchen and yanked out a chair at the table, sitting straight ahead of my father.

'We can either talk about this like adults or you can continue to form your own opinions and argue with me about it.'

My father threw his hands in the air. 'Who is the adults? There are no adults. I am the adults! I am your father! I tell you what to do and you shut up about it and do as father says.'

'Who do you think you're talking to, Dad? "Do as father says"' Khalid replied, mocking my father which was never a good idea. 'Are we going to have a discussion about this or not?'

'No!'

'You're being totally unreasonable,' Khalid asserted. 'Fine. If that's how you want it, Ashley and I will just count the two of you out of our wedding completely.'

My mother immediately straightened her posture. 'Don't you drag me into this, Khalid. I have nothing to do with this. This is your father's doing.'

My father appeared wounded. 'My doing? This is all *my* doing? If it wasn't for my involvement with the people in this community, you would have no food to eat, no friends, no gossip, no parties. You've never appreciated how much I do to provide for this family.'

Khalid spoke up. 'Dad, I understand the importance of the Pakistani community. I do. Okay? I just don't want this dictating how I have my wedding.'

My father raised a flattened hand. 'Khalid, I am no longer speaking to you.'

As I debated whether or not to get involved, Khalid turned to me, dragging me into the conflict anyway. 'You know what Dad wants us to do? He wants a maulvi to perform our ceremony. Ashley and I don't mind wearing the traditional clothes and having hundreds of people at the wedding that we don't even know or care about,' he said directly to my father, 'but neither of us want anything religious in it. I mean if we did, we would at least have a Catholic ceremony, because that's how Ashley was raised. But she and I don't want any religion that day because that's not who we are. This is our wedding. We don't want to spend it pretending to be something we're not.'

'You would have a *Catholic* ceremony?' my father asked, homing in on that one detail, shocked at what he was hearing. 'A Catholic ceremony? In a *church*? And Bless the Lord!' he said, mockingly stretching his arms towards heaven and jiggling his fingers. 'Bless the Lord! Save me! Save me, Jesus! *This* is what you would do? And ugly old fat women sitting at the organ? You would put your mother and I through that?'

'How many times do I have to tell you,' my mother snapped. 'Don't drag me into this. I told you. As long as I can dress my children in their outfits and have a stylish wedding, show these other desi women how a real Pakistani wedding is done, I'll be happy. I don't care about the maulvi. I don't care who marries them. You see all this fighting? Such unenlightened and unsophisticated people. Catholics, Muslims, Hindus, Jews. To hell with all of them.'

'What nonsense you speak,' my father snarled. 'You are a Muslim. You were raised your whole life as a Muslim. Don't act like you're not one now.'

'I live here. Things are different,' she said, and then quite unexpectedly, pounded her fist upon the table. 'I am no longer a Muslim. I am an antagonist!'

I opened my mouth, which was full of potatoes. 'You mean an agnostic.'

Khalid hurriedly got up from the table, almost knocking down his chair. 'We will do everything you want for the wedding except the maulvi. Now I think that is being very reasonable and fair. You can think about it for a while and get back to me.'

My father shook his head. 'I don't have to be reasonable and fair. This is my son's wedding. My only son!' he yelled, as if Meena and I were second-tier. 'And I will not embarrass myself in front of the community by having an improper wedding. What will I say when they ask questions about it? You know how nosy these people are. They will gossip and tell everyone my children are not Muslims.'

Khalid walked back to the table and sat down again. 'Then why do you call them your friends, Dad? Why do you care what these people think?'

'I have business relations with these people. The food that feeds your big, fat mouth comes from these people.'

'That isn't true, Tariq,' my mother interjected. 'Plenty of white people come to your lot all the time. Don't bend the truth because you suddenly want to impress these people.'

'You are no longer a part of this wedding,' he announced to her.

My mother waved her hand in the air as she sipped from her teacup. 'Okay then. I'm no part. Jo merzi ker lo.'

I had been quiet this whole time, but could no longer resist the urge to get involved. 'Dad, it's hard for us to understand. None of the kids of these other parents act like Muslims. They all drink and party. We've seen it. So why do we have to pretend anything?'

My father's voice calmed down a bit when he spoke to me. 'I know what these kids do. Okay? But they still have an Islamic ceremony to please their parents. It saves their reputation in the community. It's all because of a few, nosy people in the community that we have all these pretences. They will go and tell everyone in Pakistan that we are Satan worshippers if we don't do this.'

'Can't we pretend we had the Islamic ceremony at an earlier date, then just have the reception?' I asked.

My father shook his head. 'No. Others have tried that. They don't believe it anymore.'

'This is ridiculous, Dad!' Khalid shouted. 'Don't you see that?' I knew it was a bad idea to say what I was about to say, but I had to say it anyway. 'Khalid . . . I can kind of see Dad's point.'

Khalid squinted at me. I was his general who had just stabbed him on the battlefield. 'You little kiss-ass.'

'I'm not being a kiss-ass.'

'Do not use this language!' my father snapped.

I clasped my hands together, very adult, very negotiator-like, and rested them on top of the table. 'Dad, you want the maulvi. Khalid has agreed to do everything but the maulvi. There must be some middle ground that can be reached here.'

'No middle ground,' he flatly stated. 'Either they have the maulvi or they don't have the wedding. Not with my blessing anyway.'

'Okay, Dad,' Khalid said as he got up and walked away for good this time. 'Then I guess we won't have your blessing.'

18

Later that day, Brad called me.

'Hi honey!' he said. 'How are you? I wanted to call and check up on my girl.'

I was shocked to hear from him. I had expected the requisite two-to-three-day waiting period that I thought most guys adhered to. I was also a little surprised at the 'my girl' reference, but maybe this was normal when you date later in life. Maybe this was a good sign. Brad was mature. He didn't hide his feelings or play games.

'Did you get any sleep?' he asked me.

'I did. And you?'

'Not much,' he replied. 'But who needs sleep when you can have a beautiful girl in your bed every night?'

I awkwardly giggled.

'So,' he said, 'what does my girl want to do tonight?'

'Tonight?'

'I want to take you to this great Italian restaurant overlooking Lake Jordan. You have to try their pasta. They have a killer Penne Arabbiata. I remember you said you liked that dish. And they have a great wine selection. We can gorge on pasta and wash it all down with bottles of wine, throw it up and eat all over again. Just like the Romans. How does that sound?'

'That, uh . . .'

'Pick you up around seven?'

'Seven?'

'Seven,' he confirmed. 'It's a date.'

'But wait . . .'

I paused. Brad wanted to see me again already? I wasn't counting on this. Not that I didn't want to see him. I did. But the night before was so difficult to pull off, technically. All that effort Meena put into my appearance, my clothes, my hair—I would have to do it all again already, by myself?

'Seven not okay?' he asked.

I reluctantly answered. 'No, seven sounds good.'

'Great! I'll pick you up then.'

'No, don't pick me up,' I told him. 'My parents are old-fashioned. And Pakistani old-fashioned is worse than normal old-fashioned. I'll drive to your house.'

'No problem, sweetheart. I'll wait for you here.'

For a second, I thought I couldn't breathe. I sat on my bed and dug my face in my pillow just to calm down. What the hell was wrong with me? Last night had gone smoothly enough and it wouldn't be a big deal to see him again. Brad was a great guy. There was nothing to panic over. What was I panicking over?

I had little time to dwell. I had to get up and scrounge together another outfit and do my make-up all on my own. I ended up doing a much less vixen-like job than Meena and wore jeans with a simple cream pull-over sweater. When I met Brad at seven, to my relief, he was just as happy to see me as he had been the night before. He drove us to a large, brightly lit Italian restaurant that was overridden with pink and white balloons for a five-year-old's birthday party. It wasn't exactly a romantic setting, but Brad was in good spirits. He ordered an expensive bottle of wine and told me about his plans to go treasure hunting for some lost gold coins in the Nevada desert with his buddy Keith, but that his buddy Keith was having a hard time taking off work because he was a lawyer at that big shot law firm in town where they drive its young attorneys to the ground—Libby, Libby and McCrane.

'That's where I work,' I informed Brad. 'Where I'm temporarily using an office.'

Brad put down the wine bottle, astonished at what he was hearing. 'You're at Libby too? No way!' he replied. 'That's so . . . *ironic.*'

I waited for Brad to explain the irony of that, to give a reason why he used this word to describe what was really a coincidence and nothing remotely approaching irony and allay this inexplicable nugget of loathing growing in my chest, but he enthusiastically went on to list the camping and metal detector equipment they were going to have to purchase for the trip. Then around eleven Brad and I got back to his house and started doing things we both knew would lead to sex—drinking more wine, sitting close on the couch, touching each other innocently as a precursor to more intimate touching. I felt nervous and was talking more than usual. 'Oh hey, I was meaning to ask you,' I said. 'Did you hear about that guy in Lancaster, Pennsylvania who won the Lotto? He got three hundred and sixty million dollars. I mean, how the hell do you suddenly adjust to having that much money? And he said he's going to keep his job at his accounting firm. Who believes that bullshit? The media, that's who. He's everywhere now. Getting paid even more money for giving interviews. They're treating him like he's some kind of hero.'

Brad slipped his hand up my shirt. One look at the bicep that was further north of his hand and it was no use. I shut up and gave in.

That was our routine for the next few dates—Brad and I would go out to dinner, go back to his place, drink, have sex, and I would drive home. One evening, as I was checking my email on Khalid's computer, I received an email from Brad. He had sent me three recipes and asked me to choose one. He was going to cook dinner for me at his house the coming weekend, and was going to call me that night to find out which recipe I chose.

This was happening awfully fast. It hadn't even been two weeks since my first date with Brad and already I felt like I was seeing him too much. The adrenaline rush, that elusive, priceless, wonderful dreamy state of falling in love with someone was being replaced with tedium. I didn't want to see him this much. I wasn't looking for someone to hang out with every day, cook dinner with, talk about my daily routine. I had already had that with Ethan for eight years. I wanted everything that comes with a new romance—excitement, instability, obsessive and irrational fear.

I could hear Khalid raising his voice, practically yelling on the phone in his bedroom. His door was closed, so I put my ear up against it.

'Ashley, will you calm down!' he screamed. 'I can't speak to you when you're like this. I told you already . . . I needed the money to buy a new laptop. Yeah, I know. I know! Yeah. I don't know why it says that on the account either. I'll call the bank and straighten it out with those bastards! I'll call you back and let you know what they say . . . . .Yes, *of course* you can still reach me. My phone was broke for a while but I told you, I got it fixed.'

Khalid hung up the phone. I quickly scuttled away before he opened the door. 'Shit!' he yelled. 'Ashley saw my bank account. Is she watching it every freaking day?'

'Maybe if you used your money for your wedding instead of your toys she wouldn't get so angry,' I said.

'Mind your own business, rat. And who are you to judge? From what I hear you've been putting out for guys all over town.'

I started to laugh. 'Hear from whom? Meena? Like that little tramp should talk. And by the way, this guy I'm seeing, his name is Brad. He's actually a really decent guy. He's attentive and wants to see me all the time. I mean, maybe he wants to see me a little too much. But why is that a bad thing? He likes me and he's not afraid to show it. I mean, if you really like someone . . . what's the problem? You should show it. That's how romance between mature adults should be.'

Khalid had already lost interest in what I was saying. 'You know what this means, don't you? I have to set up a new bank account at Carolina First. It's *my* money, after all. I should get to spend it how I please. Ashley and I aren't married yet, so let me enjoy this last bit of independence until then.' He paused, and then added, 'Not that we're having a wedding anyway. I'm not getting married by some friggin' maulvi.'

'Why don't you just do it and get it over with,' I asked him. 'Cross your fingers during the ceremony and it won't count.'

'I don't think Ashley would be happy doing that. I don't know . . . maybe I'll ask her if she really has an objection. It would be worse if she was a real Catholic, but since she's not, maybe she won't care.'

'Well, I think a good way of buttering her up is to stop going to Best Buy. That's a good start.'

'Ashley's not the type of woman that butters up. So I might as well do what makes me happy. I mean, when I'm happy, she's happy. She just doesn't need to know what's making me happy, you know, specifically.'

I sat on the couch and leaned against the arm rest. This was stressing me out. I could feel Khalid's struggle for independence from his pending wife, and I felt sorry for him. I would never want someone watching over me as much as she watched over him. But Khalid was, by his own previous admission, an utter dumbass, so I felt sorry for Ashley too.

Mostly, though, I was feeling sorry for myself, because in a few minutes I was going with my father to another PAC meeting.

'Today's PAC meeting is being held at your Aunty Gazala and Uncle Abbas's house,' my father said in the car. 'Their daughter Neelam has had her babies. We must go as a respectful gesture. Your mother should have come with us. Everyone else's wives go and support their husbands. I don't know why your mother insists on staying home and embarrassing me. Always people ask, "Where is baijee? Where is baijee?" And what can I say? Baijee would rather stay home and scrub the toilets than come meet with you and your children?'

I nodded every now and then to let my father know I was paying attention, but I was fixated on my cell phone. Brad hadn't called yet to see which recipe I had chosen. But it was still early, only eight o'clock, so I put my phone on vibrate and stuck it in my pocket.

We could hear babies screaming the minute we walked in. Neelam and her husband were in a corner of the living room with the crib, looking frazzled as they tried to chat with doting community members and feed and care for their babies at the same time. Neelam's hair was a frizzy mess that she obviously tried to tie into a neat bun. Her husband, who had a boyish face with a generally bewildered expression, did most of the work tending to the babies. Neelam was smiling and thanking everyone for coming when her husband accidentally dropped a pacifier onto the floor.

'No!' she yelled, as her husband wiped the pacifier on his shirt and was trying to stick it back in the baby's mouth.

I thought I would wait to say hello to them a little later, when the crowd dissipated and things cooled down a bit. My father made the rounds as I perused the dinner table—kofta curry, samosas, fried spinach pakoras, onion and tomato salad, julebi and pink rice for dessert. I grabbed a crispy samosa with a paper napkin and drizzled some sweet and sour imli chutney over it. Uncle Abbas came by and told us the meeting could start whenever we were ready. My father and I promptly sat on the living room couch and waited for Uncles Fareed and Mahmood. The two eventually joined us and encouraged everyone else to have a seat as well. Once everyone was settled, my father stood up and walked to the front of the room.

'I would like to make an announcement,' he said. 'The most wonderful news. Samira,' he gestured towards me, 'will you please come up here?'

Everyone's heads turned in my direction, and I had half a samosa in my mouth.

'Come up here,' he ordered.

I had no choice but to obey. I had to finish chewing my bite in front of everybody as my father paused to ensure he had the room's undivided attention, then rested his hand upon my shoulder. 'I would like everyone to know that my daughter, Samira, has accomplished the first official act of the Pakistani-American Council. Through her wisdom, intelligence and powerful Washington D.C. connections, she was able to convince the United States government to approve the visa application of a Mr Man Singh of Karachi.' My father paused a second to look directly at Uncle Fareed, whose nose was turned up in disgust like someone had just farted. 'Yes, Mr Singh is a Sikh. But he is also first and foremost a Pakistani who, under the most tragic of circumstances, needed desperately to come to the United States. Because of Samira, Mr Singh will now be able to attend the funeral of his late brother and care for his brother's family. We at PAC are very proud of this accomplishment, and I would like everyone to offer a hand to congratulate my wonderful daughter.'

The group applauded, some also nodding their heads in approval. One Aunty with a pink dupatta and giant tortoise-shell sunglasses resting atop her swaying head said, 'Ma sha' allah! Ma sha' allah!'

'Maybe you should make *her* president, Tariq,' someone joked from the crowd.

My father laughed along, then patted my head. 'My daughter as President? Insha'allah, that would be a dream come true.'

I fielded a few questions from the crowd about who I knew in Washington and how I managed to 'convince' the United States government to approve the visa application. I wished my father hadn't exaggerated my efforts. In the end, all I did was make a few phone calls and pay a relatively minor fee. But I understood this was an act done on behalf of my father's organization, and it was good publicity, and if membership increased so would the opportunity to help more Man Singhs in the future, so I went along with it dutifully and answered everyone's questions the best I could. I thanked everyone again before heading to the back of the room where Neelam was standing with an all-knowing smirk.

'That was quite a display,' she remarked.

'You better not mess with me,' I told her. 'I'm powerful.'

I asked her how she was doing, how the babies were doing, and she said aside from lack of sleep and nipples that felt like they were on fire, the babies were in good health so she was happy. We spent some time huddled in the back with them, a boy and a girl. I picked up the boy for a while and cradled the gloopy mess in my arms and cooed at him a little bit, when Neelam spoke up. 'Did you know your Dad asked me to hook you up with someone? Said he wants me to find you a decent boy.'

I looked back at her puzzled. I thought my parents still believed I would repair things with Ethan. Why would he ask her to find me someone else? 'My father doesn't know I just started seeing someone,' I told her, putting the baby back in the crib. 'This guy I met at the gym.' I removed my phone from my jacket. 'In fact, he's supposed to be calling me about some dinner plans. Maybe I'm not getting enough reception in here. I'm going to step outside for a second and check. Can you fill me in if anything happens here?'

'Go for it,' she said. 'Take your time.'

It didn't take me long. As soon as I stepped out of the house, all bar signals appeared on my phone. I had no missed calls or voicemails.

For the rest of the meeting, I kept my phone accessible in my suit pocket. By the time I got home around ten o'clock, Brad still hadn't called. I thought about calling him but couldn't make up my mind. It was late and it was a work night. If I call and he's asleep, I thought, I could annoy him. If I call in spite of him saying he'd call me, I could look desperate or insecure. I decided it was best to just wait and let him do the calling. After all, the dinner was planned for the weekend. It was only Tuesday.

I plugged my phone into the charger on my nightstand. I got into bed, tucked myself in, took my blankets back off and picked up the phone.

'Hey,' he answered.

'Hey,' I said, somewhat apprehensively. 'Hope I'm not calling too late.'

'Not at all,' he said. 'I was just about to call you, so you read my mind. Did you pick a recipe? I was starting to think you didn't like any of them and that's why you weren't calling.'

Oh. He thought *I* was supposed to call *him*. I dropped my defences and spoke daintily. 'No, I loved the recipes,' I said. 'Especially the stuffed green pepper dish . . . with the orzo. That sounds really good.'

'Ah, you make my life so easy!' he said. 'I already have all the ingredients for it. Can you be here Saturday around seven?'

'I'll be there,' I replied. 'Should I bring anything?'

'Just your sweet ass,' he said. 'And maybe a bottle of wine.'

Saturday afternoon, I showered, blow-dried my hair and applied my make-up.

Around six o'clock, he rang.

'Hey!' I answered.

'Hey,' he replied. 'But . . . Samira, let me call you right back.'

I was confused there for a second. Did I call him just now? No, he called me. Why would he call me if he was in the middle of something and couldn't talk?

'I'll call you right back,' he said. 'Two minutes.'

'Sure. I have my phone with me,' I told him. I finished getting dressed and sat on my bed. For the next half hour, I stared at my cell phone.

I would continue staring at it for the next week.

19

Not only did Brad never call me back that day, he didn't show up at the gym all week either. I tried emailing him but the message bounced back. To make sure I wouldn't miss his call, I carried my phone with me everywhere I went—to the bathroom, to the kitchen table, to the shed out back when I thought Merlin got stuck in there.

When I finally struck up the nerve to call his cell phone, it was turned off.

'Stop acting desperate,' Meena said on the phone when I complained to her about it. 'Guys can sniff that a mile away. He has to think you're busy and don't care. You can't be waiting by the phone.'

'No girl has ever not waited by the phone,' I declared. But I knew Meena was right. I called Brad one last time and left a simple message. 'Just wanted to say hi. Give me a call.' The pit in my stomach felt tight as I flung the cause of my despair, my phone, under the couch and out of reach.

I hadn't even bothered to change out of my work clothes that evening. In my black pants and two-hundred-dollar cardigan, I lay on the Persian rug in the sunroom and hugged a giant silk pillow. My father was also in the room, seated on a low plastic stool. He had his shirt off, and his head was sticking through a hole in the middle of a newspaper page. My mother stood above him, holding a paintbrush and a cup of Just For Men hair dye. She dipped the paintbrush into the cup and carefully brushed strokes of black dye all over my father's head.

'Sit still,' she commanded him, grabbing both sides of his head. 'Stop moving so much.'

'I'm not moving, woman.'

'Yes, you are. You're trying to read the articles.'

'Hi, Mom. Hi, Dad,' I said wearily from my pillow.

My father turned his head around. 'Oh, Samira. I have the best news to tell you.' He got up from the stool and approached me. 'I have managed to get Senator John Marshall to come to our next PAC meeting. He's going to speak to the entire community. This will be an especially important event for us.'

'Will you come back and sit down?' my mother yelled.

My father was unperturbed as he continued walking towards me. 'He is the most prominent Senator in all of Washington. Been Senator in North Carolina for twenty years. So incredibly powerful. You see?' he asked me. 'You see how powerful our organization is becoming?'

'That's great, Dad,' I said. 'Senator Marshall is a very respected man on the Hill.'

'Did you ever meet him?'

'No.'

'Well, now you will be able to.' He pulled out a piece of paper from his pocket with scribbles on it. 'I've already started writing my speech. I will be introducing him. Oh, hey . . . how do you say that word, you know, when you say 'without further . . .'

'Adieu?' I asked.

'Yes, that word. How do you pronounce it?'

'Adieu,' I repeated slowly.

'Adoo,' he said.

'No, Dad. It's "ad-ee-you".'

'Add-ee-you.'

'Okay, but say it faster.'

'Add-ee-oo.'

'No, "you". You say, "you" at the end.'

'Add-ee-YOU!'

'Will you two stop this already?' my mother yelled.

My father stuck the speech back in his pocket and turned to my mother. 'Do you see once and for all, woman? Do you see the value of this organization?'

My mother waved her paintbrush. 'Sure. See the value. Now sit down so I can finish you.'

My father obediently resumed his seat on the stool as my mother painted over his eyebrows. His body was turned to the side as she did this, and the scar on his back was in full view—a deep V-shaped gash by his right shoulder. The edges of it had melted into the rest of his skin, but it was still visible—a slightly purple centre, underneath thin wisps of grey and black hair. 'Everyone in the community will be coming to this meeting,' my father informed us. 'This will be our biggest of all. All because of *me*.'

'What will be the biggest of all?' Khalid had nonchalantly entered the kitchen.

'Nothing.' My father's face turned sour. 'I'm not speaking to you.'

'Fine. Hey, Mom, what's for dinner?'

My mother shook her head. 'You two need to stop this fighting and start behaving like real men. I need to know if we're having this wedding or not because I need to order the girl's outfits from Lahore.'

Khalid searched the fridge. 'No wedding, Mom.'

In a quick flash, so quick I almost wasn't sure it happened, my mother and father exchanged a glance. My mother put the paintbrush down and went over to the dishwasher. As she emptied it, my father took a seat at the kitchen table.

'Khalid,' he said. 'Come sit down.'

Khalid twisted the cap off a Diet Mountain Dew and sat at the table. He sighed, a sign that he knew this conversation was coming. 'What is it, Dad?'

'All my life, *all my life*,' my father began, 'the only thing I ever wanted was for my children to have everything they needed. Proper schools, the best education, the best clothes. I left behind my entire family in Pakistan to come here, just so my children would not have to live the life I did. Just so my children could grow up with the things they wanted and needed. Your mother and I have worked so hard. This wedding is so important to us. To see our child getting married, it fills our hearts. It validates what your mother and I have struggled for all these years. We have sacrificed so much . . . our families, our own enjoyment, so that we could give everything to you. And all we ask in return, bismillah, all we ask is one thing. Just one little thing to make us happy. Your mother and I . . . we're getting old. We don't have much to live for anymore . . . just our children . . .'

My father stopped, covering his face with his hands. Still wearing the newspaper and with dye all over his head, tears spilled out of his eyes, and he quickly wiped them away with the back of his hands.

'I love you, my son. Please do not be angry with me. You know . . . you are my heart and soul . . .'

'Dad . . .' Khalid walked over to my father and put his arms around him. Some of the dye got on Khalid's T-shirt, but he didn't seem to notice. ‘It’s okay, Dad,’ Khalid said. ‘I don’t want to keep fighting like this. We will do the wedding. Of course we will.’

‘Thank you, my boy,’ my father whispered.

I looked on in amazement as the two of them embraced, not believing what was before my eyes. For all the years I had spent growing up with Khalid, all the ways that I thought I knew my brother backwards and forwards, I couldn’t believe he had just been duped by the worst acting job in desi history.

20

The next morning, there was a soft knock on my bedroom door.

‘Samira, may I come in?’

It was my father. I quickly covered myself with my blankets as he walked in. He was already dressed for the day, looking dapper in a navy-blue suit and striped tie under a heavy black coat. Bulova watch and freshly applied cologne. He sat on the edge of my bed.

‘Sorry to wake you, baby,’ he said. ‘I know it’s early. But today is a very important day. It’s ’Eid-ul-Adah. Do you know what that is?’

I rubbed my eyes. ‘Uh . . . yeah. I know what it is.’

He smiled. ‘I don’t think you know what it is. I’m your father. You think I don’t know my own children?’ He patted my head, as if to assure me he wasn’t mad about it. ‘There are two Eids,’ he began. ‘’Eid Fitr and ’Eid-ul-Adah. ’Eid Fitr marks the end of the month of Ramadan, or the month of fasting. Fasting is the one of the five pillars of Islam. You know what the five pillars are right?’ Before I could respond to say yes, that I vaguely remembered something about pillars from my sophomore year Religious Studies class, my father counted with his fingers. ‘Faith in Islam, praying five times a day in the direction of Mecca, giving to charity, fasting during the month of Ramadan, and making the Haj to Mecca. ’Eid-ul-Adah happens about two months after ’Eid Fitr. It marks the end of the Haj and is considered the biggest Muslim holy day.’

'Okay,' I said.

'So this is a very important day for us. Your mother and I are going to the mosque for prayer, and I want you and your brother to join us. You can drive separately, but you must come soon, because prayer starts around eight. I want the community to see my children there. It is especially important for your brother if he is to have this wedding.'

'Okay, Dad.'

He smoothed down my hair and gave me a kiss on the forehead. 'You were always the most responsible of my children. Your mother and I are leaving now. We'll see you there.'

He left the room and joined my mother downstairs. A few clacks of their dress shoes later, I heard their car pull out of the driveway.

I slid back under the blankets and shut my eyes. I pretended for a minute that my father entering my room and talking to me about Eid was all just a crazy dream. Then I opened my eyes.

Dammit.

I looked at the darkness outside and cringed.

Godammit.

I reluctantly stuck my feet out of the warmth of my bed and rested them on the cold, hardwood floor.

About twenty minutes later, I was at Khalid's door, pounding. 'Khalid, wake up!' I said. 'Khalid!' It was getting late. I had already taken too long finding an outfit to wear and if we got there late my father would blame me. No reply was coming from Khalid's room, so I opened the door and walked in.

All at once a blast of arctic chilled wind smacked across my face. The windows were wide open and the sheer white curtains that covered them billowed about wildly. Khalid, in what could only make sense to him, had wrapped his blanket into a tight ball to lay his head on, and was shivering under the cover of a pile of pillows.

'What!' he yelled as I approached his bed. His face was flushed red and his hair was matted to one side. 'Get out, rat!'

'Listen, it's Eid and Dad wants us to go to this mosque thing.'

'I'm not going anywhere.'

'Get up! If I have to go, you have to go. I mean it, Khalid.'

'Oh, god!' he yelled dramatically as he buried his face in his blanket.

I continued to stand over him and waited for a sign that he was going to get up. 'Come on,' I said. 'We have twenty minutes to get there. Get up.'

'Why is Dad making us go to the mosque all of a sudden?'

'He wants everyone to see us participating with the community. He said he especially wants you to go so everyone will think you're a good Muslim boy . . . you know . . . as a prelude to your wedding.'

'He's such a hypocrite! He never goes to the mosque and today, all of a sudden, the world depends on us going? I can't stand this!'

'He asked me nicely and said this would be a favour to him.'

'Wasn't it Eid just like two weeks ago?' Khalid asked. 'It seems like it's always freakin' Eid!'

'That's because before it was 'Eid-ul-Fitr. Today it's 'Eid-ul-Adah.'

'How do you know that shit?' he asked.

Because Khalid was continuing to lie on his bed with no sign of moving, I started shoving him. 'We need to leave so we can get there for the eight o'clock prayer.'

Khalid curled his body up in a ball. 'Fine. You go and I'll meet you there later.'

'I'm not leaving until you get up.'

Finally, resigned to his fate, Khalid angrily threw the pillows to one side and got up. As a way of punishing me for this terrible intrusion, he belched loudly into the air and blew it towards me. I swung my arms up to protect my face but it was too late. I breathed it in.

'How do you like that, rat? Beer mixed with two chalupas and refried beans, all fermenting together overnight.'

I hastily retreated from the room. Finally, twenty minutes to eight, we were in the car. I was wearing a plain red salwar kameez, the most conservative I could find, and a simple black dupatta. I couldn't even look at Khalid. Just the sight of him was enough to make me gag. Under his reflective sunglasses he was obnoxiously smacking mint gum and guzzling Mountain Dew at the same time. His hair was still all matted up and he had hastily thrown on the same wrinkled, smoke-infested slacks and collared shirt he had worn the night before.

Squeezing the plastic bottle of Mountain Dew, Khalid cocked his head back and swallowed a large gulp of liquid. 'Buuurrpp!' he said, belching and saying the word at the same time. 'See, that's talent.' He took another swig and immediately let out another loud belch, this time accidentally causing his gum to drop out the side of his mouth. He bent down to the dirty car mat under him, retrieving the little green ball and popping it back in his mouth.

'Dad owes me big time for this,' he said, resuming his chomping. 'Making me go to a mosque like this. I'm damned to hell in this religion. I'll probably burst into flames the minute I walk in.' He laughed and nudged my side with his elbow. 'I can't even remember the last time we went. When was the last time we went?'

'I don't know,' I snapped, cracking my window open to get some fresh air.

But, of course, I remembered clearly the last time we went to a mosque. A corner of my dupatta was still caked with dried mud from that day. It was my grandmother's funeral— a cold day in December, just like today. After prayers at the mosque, everyone went to the cemetery, and I looked down at the mud square that was reserved for her—the only colour on the frozen grey landscape that day. They brought over her frail body in a plain wood coffin. The coffin was not anything more than four planks of raw wood nailed together, and her body, cleaned with soap but forbidden by Islam to be preserved, was wrapped in a plain white sheet.

All the women, including my mother and her two sisters, stood on the periphery of the grave with their heads covered, gently sniffling into the cheap white tissues provided by the funeral home. The men stood in a single-file line, each ready to shovel a small amount of dirt onto the grave. No one remarked on Ethan's presence in the line. Everyone was used to seeing him with our family at weddings and parties. He was my brother's best friend, my parents had told everyone. Ethan and I always kept a good physical distance to keep up the appearance.

When the Imam finished reading from the Koran, the sheet was pulled away from my grandmother's face, and the women were allowed to view her one last time before the shoveling began. As I slowly walked towards her, in the corner of my eye, I could see Ethan taking wide steps towards me from the other side of the grave. His shiny black dress shoes and the bottom of his black wool coat were caked with mud. Just as I reached my grandmother for the viewing, Ethan grabbed me and put his arms around me, turning me away from what lay beneath. But it was too late. I had already seen my grandmother's face, mangled and disfigured after three days of decomposing.

I gripped my hands around Ethan's red tie and sobbed into it, leaving no doubt in anyone's mind that he was more than just my brother's best friend.

The mosque where we were headed was brand-new, considered the largest in the state. Over the tops of the trees I could see the freshly painted minarets poking the sky like gold spears. A huge, shimmering gold dome capped the middle walls of the complex. Every desi in the world seemed to be there, and most of the nearby streets had been closed off, so Khalid and I parked several blocks away. By the time we walked up to the crowds socializing around the entrances of the mosque, I realized I had made a huge mistake.

All of the women, from the frailest matriarchs in wheelchairs to the littlest girls in pigtails, were dressed to the nines. Silk and chiffon in bright orange, ruby, royal blue, emerald green—every colour of the rainbow—laden with sequins and beading and heavy embroidery, all worn with layers upon layers of diamond and gold jewellery. My mother, clad in a silver chiffon salwar kameez with gold and black beading, immediately spotted me in the crowd.

'*This* is what you're wearing?' She stepped towards me, her head shaking in utter disbelief. 'I have a million beautiful salwar kameezes in my closet, and *this* is what you chose?'

I glanced around furtively, paranoid that people were noticing me. 'I thought you were supposed to look all humble for Eid. Isn't Islam about looking humble?'

She sighed again. 'Chalo. Never mind now. You're here.' She took another look and shook her head. 'You look like an old woman. But what can you do? Come now. I want you to meet your Aunty Tahmina's kids.'

'Nice going,' Khalid whispered to me, still smacking that same piece of gum, as we entered the mosque.

Inside the crowded hallway, Khalid and I were introduced to Syma and Bashir, both of whom looked to be in their mid-twenties and seemed far more comfortable at this venue than we did.

'After all the festivities today,' Syma said to us, 'you guys should come over to our place.'

'We're having a bunch of people over, desis and non-desis,' Bashir added. 'It'll be a good respite from all this.' And, as Bashir would tell me, leaning into my ear, 'with plenty of booze.' I took a respectable step back from him, wanting to avoid any further cultural mishaps, and started wrapping my dupatta around my head. The call to prayer began over the loud speakers in the mosque and out on the streets.

'Shit, the Azan's already started?' Syma cried out. 'I won't have time for a cigarette.' Syma grabbed my hand, leading me into the prayer room. Everyone else on the property joined in the procession, including my father, who had been chatting with his own friends down the hall.

At the entrance to the prayer room, we took off our shoes and placed them side by side on large, wall-mounted racks, and I peeked inside. I wasn't sure why, maybe because I had heard the financiers behind the construction of the mosque were Saudis, but I was expecting an opulent, Arabian-nights décor. Instead, the prayer room was just a plain square room with white walls, mats on the floor and basketball hoops on both ends. There was a small stage up front and to my curiosity, a white picket fence towards the back.

Once inside, I quickly learned what the fence was for. Syma, my mother and I were directed behind the fence as Khalid, Bashir and my father walked in front of it with all the other men. My father was scowling and I knew why. He didn't approve of women and men being separated like this. And I knew he especially didn't like having to see his own wife and daughter relegated to the back of the room. As he passed by us, I nodded to him knowingly, ready to hear his sarcastic remark about the segregation.

'Somebody's feet in here stink!' he said before looping around to the front.

Syma laughed. I noticed her trying to conceal a box of Marlboro Lights in her hand when she asked me to save her a seat, that she'd be right back, and she squeezed out of the room as more and more people streamed in, everyone immediately forming into neat lines facing the front. Some people had their hands cupped to their faces, already praying. I was surprised to see such a buffet of races in there—South Asians, Southeast Asians, whites, Middle Easterners, Hispanics. Two African-American boys in matching basketball jerseys and backward baseball caps were standing together when one answered his cell phone.

'Wassup y'all?' he said, before the other grabbed his phone and clasped it shut. They started lightly shoving each other when the doors banged shut. It occurred to me I had no idea what to do next.

'Just follow me,' my mother said, somehow reading my mind. She reached into her purse and pulled out a tube of expensive, old-lady-looking lipstick. 'But first . . . please. Put this on your lips.'

I furrowed my brows, irritated at the request. But I opened the tube anyway. The lipstick was burgundy with flecks of gold in it. 'No way I'm wearing this.'

'What's wrong with it?'

'It's purple,' I said. 'Nobody has purple lips. Purple lips don't exist in nature. Not with gold sparkles.'

'But you look so plain Jane right now. Please. I don't want to be here, sitting like a leper behind this ridiculous fence. I'm just doing this for your father. But if I have to be here with my daughter for all these desi women to see, I want my daughter looking pretty. Whatever happened to you, Samira? Your sister is into nice things like jewellery and make-up . . .'

'Mom, please . . .' I was about to protest further when suddenly everyone kneeled down. A young bearded man, no older than twenty, stood in the front of the room and began the prayer, reciting the Koran in Arabic. I got on my knees and kept a close eye on my mother, following her every move. I leaned forward, touching my forehead to the ground. Then I got on my knees, then I stood up and cupped my hands together in front of me. I was the only person in the room with my eyes open, and I felt like I was cheating on an exam. I was relieved when it was finally over.

But my relief was short-lived. A minute later, a different maulvi, a much older one, walked on stage and everyone sat down again. This maulvi had an almost cuddly look to him—high, rosy cheekbones, thin wire-rim glasses, a white beard—Islam's version of Santa Claus.

He spoke professorially in English. I listened for a while as he talked about Eid and Islam and what this day meant. My mind started wandering immediately, hunting for something more interesting. I found my father and Khalid in the crowd, both sitting with their knees pulled up, listening. I looked over at my mother who was mindlessly watching the floor in front of her. Two women in the very back were huddled together, chatting. All this went on for about half an hour when a little boy who had been sitting quietly with his mother clearly had had enough. He sprang up from the floor. His arms shot up, raised high, and he started weaving through the women, bumping into them and buzzing like a bee. When he ran in front of me, he noticed I was smiling at him and he stopped. I whispered hello, then he picked up my purse and took off with it.

I got up and quietly tiptoed after him, but his mother, clad in a sky blue burqa with blue lacing around the face, caught him before I did. 'I'm so sorry,' she whispered, handing the purse back to me. I nodded that it was no problem and returned to the spot near my mother. A few minutes later, while the maulvi was still speaking, the boy came back.

He stood in front of me this time and grinned. I kind of liked having him there, pleased he picked me to focus on. He was a fun distraction from the service and the other women seemed relieved he was finally standing still. I waved to him and said hi again, and he held out his hand.

He was clutching a small object. He kept his hand in front of me, clasped shut. My curiosity was growing as to what he was so secretive about, so I very gently leaned forward to get a look, careful not to disturb the others listening to the maulvi. 'What is that?' I whispered. The boy slowly raised his arm back, revealing a tiny purple package in the soft brown puffs of his hand. In one sudden movement, he threw it towards me. I jerked my head around in time to see one of the condoms Meena had given me flying over my shoulder.

'Jesus Christ!'

I twisted backwards, awkwardly, probably very unnaturally, and caught the condom before it landed on the ground. Everyone in the room—Muslims and maulvis, Koreans and Persians, burqas and sport jerseys—turned around to see who bellowed out the name of the Good Lord in the middle of the service. The little boy, oblivious to the commotion he had just caused, buzzed around in circles again. I quickly stuffed the condom back in my purse and looked around too, acting just as curious as everyone else to see who caused this terrible disruption. The boy's mother grabbed him when he came near her and made him sit down again, and the maulvi resumed his sermon.

'What was that all about?' my mother whispered, the anger in her voice as palpable as if she were shouting. 'Can't you sit still and be quiet?'

I was half-relieved she didn't seem to notice the condom, but half really, really annoyed. Didn't she just see what that little brat did? Is everything in her eyes my fault? I refused to even pretend to listen to the service anymore. I took out my phone and reviewed the pictures I had on it that I had already seen a million times.

Finally, the service ended for good, and everyone got up. There was a mass exodus for the doors, and my mother and I scooted to a corner to wait for my father and Khalid.

'Hey, Samira,' Bashir yelled out from across the room. 'See you tonight?'

I nodded yes. As my father and Khalid approached, my mother nudged me out of the room. 'Shoo, shoo!' she said to me. Out in the hallway, everyone descended on the shoe racks at once, creating a small chaos. Children were picking up other people's shoes and throwing them around at each other, making their parents scramble after them. I inched my way through the crowd and found my shoes buried under what looked like Paul Bunyan's leather sandals.

When we reached the parking lot, Khalid asked my parents, 'So are we done?'

'No,' my father replied. 'Now we join everyone at your Uncle Naveed's house for lunch. You two follow us in your car.'

Khalid let out an exaggerated sigh and looked up towards heaven. 'Almighty Allah!' he cried out. 'Will this day never end?'

21

A feast was spread on two tables put together with every meat and vegetable curry imaginable, along with naan, rice, tomato and onion salad, and platters of pink and orange blocks of sugary ledhu. I filled my plate and sat in a corner of Uncle Naveed's living room, watching as my parents made the rounds, introducing Khalid to everyone and announcing his upcoming nuptials. After finishing three blocks of ledhu, still licking the sticky sweetness off my fingers, I got up to wash my hands.

I bypassed the crowd in the living room to get to the kitchen where a large, yellow bottle of soap sat by the sink. As I approached it, to the right on the kitchen table, something else caught my eye—white plastic grocery bags filled with large, foil-wrapped objects. I had seen these bags already. When I first walked into the house, I noticed people congregating around them, and from what I could gather from my passive skills at understanding Urdu, they were deciding what to do with them. Now that I was alone in the kitchen, I could finally see what all the fuss was about. My hands still sticky, I reached into the first bag and pulled out an especially heavy piece. I unpeeled the foil, carefully unpeeling layer after layer until I found myself gazing down at a pair of ears, a nose, a tongue and a pair of wide, unblinking eyes.

It was the skinned head of a lamb, the rest of its body sectioned into foil-wrapped pieces in the other bags.

I found my father in the living room and tugged on his shirt. 'I'm going home,' I said.

'Home?' he said. 'It's too early.'

'I want to go home.'

'Why? It'll look rude if you leave.'

'I don't care,' I said. 'I just realized I want no part of this.'

'No part of what? What nonsense are you speaking?'

I pointed to the bags in the kitchen. 'That. Over there.'

My father looked perplexed. 'Why all this hulla-goola you are making? For what? I still don't understand.'

As I looked at my father, I felt a little bit of Khalid in me—a rising resentment that I had participated in something I would never otherwise participate in, just to please him. I had always known what happens on Eid. Actually, with all the festivities we had to attend and panic over what to wear and how to pray, what happens on Eid, besides the praying and the lunching and the socializing, was somehow lost. But now that I was reminded, as it was presented before me in the kitchen, staring back at me, I realized my duties to my parents were officially over.

'I don't want to pretend to celebrate over a sacrificed lamb. I went to the mosque and did my part so let me go.'

'But you didn't kill the damn thing.'

'Dad . . .'

My father contemplated me for a second and then, much more quickly than I would have anticipated, nodded his head that it was okay to go. I wanted to believe it was because he had such enormous respect for me, for my beliefs, for my wishes, that he gave in so quickly, but something told me he was more afraid I was going to cause a scene and he wanted me gone.

'Take your brother's keys,' he said.

I looked at my mother for her approval. 'Yeah, go,' she said.

As I clicked the front door shut, I could hear Khalid pleading his case on the other side. 'No fair. I'm not down on the lamb thing either.'

'Too bad,' my father told him.

Bashir and Syma's house, a good forty-minute drive away, was a little, white rambler, completely unkempt, with cigarette butts littered under the hedges in front. I could hear loud voices inside, so I let myself in. I found the interior of the house to be equally disgusting, with permanent brown stains on the linoleum kitchen floor and stuffing coming out of the drab, sectional couch.

'Samira, you made it.'

Bashir greeted me as soon as I walked in. He grabbed me a beer from the fridge.

'Hey everyone,' he announced to the group, 'this is Samira.'

'Eid Mubarak!' the crowd shouted, raising their beer bottles.

'Don't mind the house. It's a shithole,' Bashir acknowledged. 'But Syma's getting married and I'm moving to my own townhouse, so why bother with it?'

'Congratulations, Syma,' I yelled over to her in the living room. 'I didn't know you were engaged.'

'Yeah . . . engaged,' she sneered as the other four people sitting around her started laughing. I didn't know what was so funny, and rather than clueing me in, she took a long drag from her cigarette.

Bashir introduced me to the other six partiers—Mustafa, Irfan, Jill, Susan and Vince. 'And that's Andy,' he said, pointing to a tall, lanky white guy with dark brown hair. 'Andy's Jewish, but that's okay. He's self-hating.'

'I suck,' Andy said.

I laughed. The weight from earlier eased a bit. This felt nice, being around a bunch of young people, drinking and cutting loose. Andy and I chatted for a few minutes in the kitchen as the conversation between Syma and the friends on the couch resumed. Eventually, we joined in. As the night went on, as the conversations frequently referenced events and people only they knew, I realized this was a very tight group of friends. I was definitely the outsider. Bashir made several attempts to explain backstories to me and include me in the conversations, but he would get sucked in and forget about me as the stories progressed. I drank and smiled and laughed with their stories and pretended I cared as much as they did about the time Jimmy Wehmann got wasted after a Duke/UNC basketball game and slipped off a gargoyle at the top of the Four Mile Junction Tavern and missed the awning by three inches and landed in his puke that had unfortunately reached the ground before he did. But I felt lonely sitting there, unable to fully engage with the group, reminiscing about my own friends in D.C. who were now estranged. Ethan and I used to be the parental figures of our group, the centre of it. Everyone always came to us for advice and crashed on our couches. I wondered what the others thought of Ethan and Natasha together, if they were liked as a couple, if they hung out with the gang or if the gang was even intact anymore.

My thoughts came back to Bashir and his friends when I realized there was a lull in their conversation.

'Heard you left Uncle Naveed's house early, that you were upset,' Bashir said to me, breaking the silence in the room.

'How did you know I was there? Or that I left early?' I asked.

'News carries fast in this community. Don't you know? We all keep track of everyone,' Bashir said. 'There are no secrets with us. Gossip reigns supreme.'

'Word got through the community that I left? That's kind of embarrassing.'

'Actually, no. My mom was there. She said you left early.'

I playfully hit him. 'You jerk.'

'My mom said something about how you saw the lamb,' Bashir continued. 'She said you were complaining about it.'

'Why were you upset about the lamb?' Mustafa asked.

Everyone turned to me. It was clear that it was my turn to speak, the stranger in the room, the part of the night when the friends are tapped out of their own stories and want to learn about the new person. But I didn't want to talk about the lamb or Eid. They were heavy, and I didn't want heavy. I wanted light, and that's the kind of response I gave.

'I just got a little upset,' I explained. 'I don't see why they have to kill lambs on this day, just for a ritual.'

'It's Eid,' Irfan replied. 'It's just what we do on this day as Muslims.' He took a swig of beer.

'And it isn't *just* a ritual, as you say,' Susan briskly asserted. 'The sacrifice holds important symbolic meaning for you guys.' I stopped, and looked at this white girl like I hadn't before. She was wearing a pair of black boots, a heavy wool skirt and a black sweater set. Adorning her eyes were a pair of red triangle glasses that tried too hard to say 'I'm funky'.

'Susan's in the doctoral programme at Duke,' Bashir said. 'Cultural anthropology. Writing a thesis on religion and stuff. She knows her shit. She knows Islam better than we do.'

'So, like I was saying,' she continued, 'sacrificing the lamb is an essential part of Eid. It commemorates Abraham's willingness to sacrifice his own son, Isaac, for God, and how God replaced Isaac with a . . .'

'Lamb,' I interrupted. 'I know this story. No need to explain it to me.' I was smiling as I said this, a broad, friendly, easy-going smile, but it was the kind of smile Delta Delta Delta girls greet Chi Omega girls with at Saturday tailgate parties. Fake.

'Don't you agree?' she asked me. 'It's part of the religion. A part of Muslim culture.'

'Female genital mutilation is a part of Muslim culture in some places,' I said, still trying to smile. 'But you don't approve of that, do you?'

'Zing!' said Andy.

Susan appeared slightly miffed. 'I don't approve of genital mutilation. But they're not the same thing, obviously.'

'Why?' I asked her. 'Why is it so obvious that one's bad and one's good? Both seem like useless cruelty to me.'

'Well, that's because you think like an American, who . . .'

'I what?'

I stopped. I was about to say something to this Susan girl that I knew would deeply disturb her, and possibly everything she represented, which was a worldview predicated on neatly carved-out categories. 'I don't think like an American,' I told her. 'I don't think like a Pakistani. And I don't think like a Pakistani-American.'

'But . . .' she said, sounding increasingly exasperated, 'it's not about labels. It's about embracing your heritage. It's a great and wondrous thing to come from such a rich background. It's like you're trying to escape it or are ashamed of it. Ashamed of being Pakistani.'

I responded with a vague, simplistic shrug. If she wanted an argument to exercise her degree, she wasn't going to get it from me.

But she continued anyway, determined to show off her knowledge of foreigners to her drunken, captive audience. 'Immigrants and their children are often part of what is called the "diaspora"—people who feel in between cultures, not knowing where they fit in, not belonging to any one group or the other. They feel pulled in different directions. Can they adapt to their new countries without sacrificing their original cultures and value systems? These inner struggles are at the core of their identity crises. It seems evident that perhaps you, too,' she said, directly to me, 'suffer from these feelings to some degree.'

I knew things were about to take a decided turn for the worse, and I knew exactly what I needed to do, what would have been the right thing to do—to stay, to let this girl continue her diatribe on my shame and suffering and the inner struggles she believed I should have. To refrain from challenging her over-romanticized view of immigrants. To blow it off, smile, grab another beer and accept that beggars can't be choosers and I had to do whatever it took to make these people like me and accept me and want to hang out with me. To penetrate the group. To make new friends. To please my mother.

Or I could try the other option.

'The only thing I suffer from,' I said as I arose from the couch, 'are tedious conversations with overzealous doctoral students. A better way to spend your time?' I nodded to the others in the room. 'Ask the Eid-loving Muslims here why they booze it up and treat their religion like a joke.'

A hush fell over the crowd. It was definitely time for the outsider to leave.

'Nice meeting you all,' I said, grabbing my keys.

That night, I fell into a deep sleep, the kind of blank, dreamless sleep that comes from utter defeat. I had reached the relatively painless conclusion that I was never going to make friends again so I could just stop trying, and that I was never going to hear from Brad Turner again. So I was fully relaxed under my thick covers, unconflicted and unagonized, my body not on edge from expecting to be roused in the middle of the night by a phone call from him or anyone else.

Then around one in the morning, my cell phone rang. Ignatius was snuggled by my side, gently snoring. In my hazy state, I decided I wasn't going to answer it. No one would be calling me except Brad, and I didn't care to talk to him, hear him give some lame excuse for not calling.

I reached over Ignatius and picked up the phone anyway, for the satisfaction of watching his name on my phone and ignoring it.

But it wasn't Brad.

It was a 202 area code. Someone from D.C. A strange number. I hesitated before answering it. Could it be Ethan? No, he wouldn't call me this late. And not from his home. I was sure if he ever did call, he would do it from work so as not to upset the wife. Could it be my former landlord? Did he find out I didn't really have Rocky Mountain spotted fever which is why I had to break the lease and move back to North Carolina to be under the care of my parents?

I flipped the phone open. 'Hello?'

'Samira.'

It was a female voice. I could hear my heart beat in my chest. I wasn't prepared for this at all.

'How are you?' she asked.

It took me a second, then I said, 'I'm fine, Natasha.'

There was more silence on the phone.

'Can I help you?' I asked.

'I don't know if I should be calling you,' she said. 'But I just decided to go ahead and do it. I've just been wondering—how are you?'

'Fine,' I repeated.

'I'm glad,' she said. 'It's good to hear your voice.'

If I was in front of her, I would have slapped her hard for saying that to me.

'Eid Mubarak,' she said. 'Just wanted to call and wish you and your family well today.'

I raised my eyes from the phone to watch Ignatius's stomach rise and fall with every breath.

'It's late, Natasha.'

'I know,' she said. 'But I wanted to call and see if there's any way we could, you know, talk about things.'

'Does Ethan know you're calling me?'

'No. He's asleep in the other room.'

Of course he is.

'I need you to hear me out,' she said. 'Understand me better. We were such good friends, Sam. Like sisters. I can't believe how things went down.'

'How "things went down"?' I replied, mocking her attempt to sound hip. 'If I recall, things went down because of you.'

'I know you're still angry. And I understand that. I really do. But I don't want you thinking I'm a bad person because I'm not.'

I cleared my throat. 'Of course you're not a bad person. You betrayed your so-called sister by revealing her secrets to her boyfriend, then slept with him. Good people do that all the time.'

'But you two were already having trouble. It's not like everything was fine.'

'How we were doing was none of your business,' I said. 'We were going through a rough patch. All couples do. Don't make excuses for your trashy behaviour.'

'Sam . . .'

'Listen' I said, trying my hardest to remain calm, 'don't bother me in the middle of the night. If you need to clear your conscience, do it on your own time.'

'You're being cruel.'

'Excuse me?' I was genuinely surprised she said that. For a second, I wondered if it was true. 'Go away, Natasha.'

Her voice rose, and her words quickened in pace. 'He deserved the truth, Sam. You couldn't give that to him. I gave that to him. Is it any wonder he chose to be with me?'

'What?'

'Sam . . . it's not like I forced him into my bed.'

I wanted to scream. I almost hung up, right then and there, but I didn't, because doing that, simply hanging up, pressing a button or closing the phone—it wouldn't have been enough. None of it would have been a harsh enough response for the wound from which she had just ripped the scab off.

'I was only helping him. If you truly love Ethan, maybe one day you'll see that. And maybe you can find it in your heart to forgive me. But I guess for now, I'm still being punished.'

I took a deep, unsteady breath. 'You don't need me for that, Natasha. I think you're being punished enough already.'

She was silent for a second. 'I don't know what you mean.'

All the tension I had been feeling for months, everything I had been keeping inside of me ever since Ethan's email—I wasn't going to pretend I didn't know anymore. I knew. I knew damn well. And now, not needing anger in my voice, not needing to resort to name-calling or accusations or yelling, all I had to do was state the truth, the simple truth, to get back at Natasha utterly and profoundly for everything she had done to me.

'You got pregnant by a man who doesn't want you.'

It was a few seconds later, when I saw the time flashing on my phone, that I realized she had hung up. I turned around on my bed and crawled over to Ignatius who was now lying at the foot, trying to get away from all the loud talking. I stroked his head until he awakened with a slight purr. Warm tuna breezed past me as he yawned, and I lay down next to him, burying my face in the fluffy orange and cream fur of his stomach.

'I'm sorry, Natasha,' I said. 'I can't forgive you.'

22

On the drive to work the next morning, I came up with a list of everybody I hated: Ethan, Natasha, Muslims, babies, doctoral students—and now especially, most of all, Brad Turner. Still no call from him—not even to apologize for blowing me off that Saturday. He was clearly playing games and I wasn't going to take it. I mean, really—some steroid muscle-head with his stupid little online business and his cliché golden retriever—why was I going to let myself get so upset over such a loser? Plus, he had a small dick. I decided that. It was much smaller than Ethan's and probably most of the male population.

As I rounded the hallway at work and approached my office, I could hear my phone ringing in my purse. It was early, and I was sure it was my father calling about something PAC-related. But when I pulled it out and saw the name on the screen, my heart went wild.

Brad T.

I scrunched my eyes shut and then opened them again, wide, to make sure I wasn't hallucinating. I wasn't. Brad was finally calling me. But why now? Did he feel bad for ignoring me? Was it weighing on his conscience to apologize? Did he want to tell me, officially, that he was through with me? I had planned on ignoring him for the rest of eternity, but curiosity trumps bitterness.

I locked the door to my office, leaned back and flipped open my phone. 'Hello?'

'Samira,' Brad said. 'Hey, it's me. Brad. How are you?'

'I know it's you,' I replied in a somewhat business tone. 'I'm fine. How are you?'

'I'm fine,' he said.

For a few seconds, there was a palpable silence.

'So what's up?' I asked, trying my hardest not to sound angry or cold, although I knew I sounded both.

'We haven't spoken in a while,' Brad said, 'so I was just calling to see how you are.'

'I tried calling you. But your phone was turned off. I left a message too.'

'You know what happened? I lost my charger, so my phone went dead,' he explained. 'I got a new one but I didn't get your message until now.'

Different thoughts raced through my head simultaneously. He lost his charger. His phone went dead. Couldn't he have called me from a different phone? Would he really let a week pass without his cell when he works from home? Wouldn't he have come to the gym to see me, to tell me all this was going on?

'I couldn't make it to the gym all week either,' he said. 'Work has just been killing me. One of my big clients went under and I was scrambling all week to minimize the damage. It's just been nuts over here. But it's over now.'

'I'm sorry to hear that,' I said, my voice softening a bit.

'I thought you were coming over for dinner last Saturday,' he said. 'What happened? I waited all night for you and when you didn't show up, I thought you were blowing me off.'

My heartbeat started to slow to a normal pace, but I was still lost in confusion. 'You called and said you were going to call me back,' I said, 'so I waited for you to call . . .'

'No, I didn't,' he interrupted. 'You were supposed to call *me* back. And when you didn't . . .' He started to laugh. 'I guess we just had a miscommunication.'

I wasn't so ready to agree with him. I could have sworn he said he was going to call me back. But . . . I don't know . . . maybe I could have heard things wrong. Maybe it was possible. And even if I was right, that he was the one who was supposed to call, he could have just been confused. An honest mistake. But I started to take comfort that regardless of who was supposed to call who, the most important point was that he still wanted to be with me, that he wasn't rejecting me.

'Guess it was just a miscommunication,' I said. 'But . . . let's forget about it now.'

'I'm going to call you later,' he said. 'I have to run, but let's try this dinner thing again. I miss my sweetie.'

The planets were slowly realigning to their proper spots in the galaxy. My heartbeat slowed back to normal. 'That sounds great,' I said.

'Can't wait to see you. I miss your warm body.'

I hesitated for a second before responding. 'Can't wait to see you, too.'

For years, up until my breakup with Ethan, I had always considered myself a smart and independent woman. After all, I had managed to get a full scholarship to Georgetown, got through all my accounting classes without the help of Adderall and landed a full-time job with a Congressman without connections or starting as an intern. I felt self-made, self-motivated. Like my father. Accomplished.

Now my only accomplishment seemed to be my infinite capacity to sit on my ass and wait. Again, Brad had promised to call, and again, almost an entire week had passed without hearing from him. I lay on my bed, staring endlessly at my cell phone which was right on my pillow, hating myself for it.

I could wait no longer. I grabbed the phone and dialled. A surge of nerves coursed through me as Brad picked up on the first ring.

'Samira.'

'Hey,' I said. 'How are you?'

'Good,' he said. 'Good. Just working hard.' He gave no acknowledgement to the fact that we hadn't spoken. 'So what's up? How are you?'

'I thought we were going to hang out this week,' I said. 'Try to have dinner again. But if you're really busy right now . . . I know you had that client and all . . . so if you can't, that's fine. I'd just like to know so I can plan my weekend.'

'Are you crazy? Of course I want to see you,' he replied. 'And . . . no, the thing with my client is over. Did we say we were going to hang out this week?'

'Yes, we did.'

Brad was quiet. 'Oh.' I heard the shuffling of papers. I heard him breathe heavily through his mouth several times into the phone. 'See, that's why I gotta regulate,' he said. 'With my pills. I have this problem. Sometimes the thoughts in my head . . . sometimes things race around and jumble up, tangle, like a big tangle, and I get *confused*. I get all . . . I get all . . . but yeah. Of course I want to see you.'

'How about tonight?' I suggested, tested. 'We could stay in and get take-out.'

'No . . . I can't tonight.'

I waited for a reason, and he didn't give me one.

'Tomorrow night's better,' he said. 'We could check out this new French café. I heard they have live music there. I have to run but I'll call you later tonight to set things up. Sounds good?' he asked, enthusiastically. 'You on board?'

My stomach was queasy. There were too many unanswered questions, too much that was going wrong, and I knew I needed to leave this situation now while I still had some remnants of self-esteem. It just wasn't healthy for me to stay, not when I was still raw from past events, still being crushed under a heavy load of emotional baggage. After all, in the end, what was worse, I asked myself? Being alone or having to deal every day with this soul-killing mess?

'Sure,' I said. 'Call me tonight.'

Later that night, I felt anxious, wondering what time Brad would call, if he was going to call at all. I stayed on my bed with some magazines, trying to read, but only stewing over him, running through what happened the last two weeks and picking apart everything he said and all our apparent miscommunications. I was starting to realize something was off about the guy's mental faculties but I didn't know what. Or perhaps the only thing off here was that I was refusing to face what was right in front of me—an obvious and inevitable rejection. I put my magazine down and checked my watch. Seven o'clock. My bedroom door pushed open, suddenly revealing Merlin's shiny black coat. He jumped on the bed, purring, his head turned sideways as he waited for me to acknowledge his presence. I reached out to pet him, scratching under his neck and around his ears and all along his back. Merlin bared his teeth and yelped a thank you. I picked him up, kissed his head, and started to scratch him some more but he slipped through my hands to walk to the middle of the bed, where he jostled his hind legs apart, arched his back, and in quick, successive motions began humping a throw pillow.

I had to get out of the house. If I didn't get out and do something and occupy my mind I was going to go crazy. I had no friends to call up, so I invited my family to dinner at Dungrats, my treat. My parents accepted. Khalid politely declined.

'You'll like this food,' I told my parents once we were seated at the restaurant. 'It's like Chinese meets Indian.'

'We'll see,' my mother said, looking around at the relatively empty restaurant.

My father put on his glasses and studied the menu. 'Samira, what is this,' he said, knocking the menu with his knuckle. 'Pad thigh?'

'Pad Thai,' I said, correcting him. 'It's a noodle dish with vegetables. You'll like it.'

I jumped in my seat.

My cell phone was ringing. My purse was hanging on the chair and I grabbed for it. I stuck my hand in and wildly searched. My phone wasn't in there. I checked the floor. Maybe it fell out. No, it wasn't there either. I felt my pockets . . . then my coat pockets . . . where the hell was my goddamn phone?

'Hello?' my father answered. 'Hello?' He clasped his phone shut. 'Nobody's there. Wasted my minutes.'

I rested my forehead in my hands when I realized I had left my phone at home.

'What's wrong with you?' my mother asked.

'Samira, what is this?' my father said. 'Plah gong . . . goong . . . gang?'

'Dad, there's a description by each menu item,' I impatiently explained. 'Just read it and it'll tell you.' I turned to my mother, who sat upright but blankly in her chair like a robot switched off. 'Mom, are you going to look at the menu?'

'You know this stuff. You order for us,' she said.

My father cleared his throat and pointed to the menu. 'What is this—'pad pik pow?'

'Okay, just let me order.' I regretted the entire excursion. Now all I wanted to do was get the hell out of the restaurant and get back home to my cell phone. When the waiter came by, I quickly ordered our food—a salad for me, three springrolls, a noodle dish and two curry dishes—when a well dressed, suited couple walked into the restaurant. I recognized the man as an attorney from my floor at Libby, Libby and McCrane. He was with a blonde and overly tanned companion who looked thirty years his junior. They were seated at the table next to us.

'Samira,' he said, waving. 'Hello.'

'Hi, George,' I replied. 'Nice to see you.' I introduced him to my parents. George and his companion walked over to our table.

'Nice to meet everybody,' George said. 'This is Angie.'

'Hello,' we all said to her. Angie wore a tight black pencil dress with a plunging V-neck, putting her burnt, industrial-sized cleavage on full display for my parents. My father furrowed his eyebrows and my mother raised hers. Even though I didn't even know this woman, I knew my parents were judging me for being associated with her, no matter how minuscule the connection.

'Eat Thai food often?' George said.

My mother shook her head. 'No. But Samira says it's good. We'll see.'

'I can't understand the menu,' my father said. 'I don't recognize any of these things.'

'I believe they include a description by each menu item,' George said, trying to be helpful. 'They do, right Angie?'

Angie nodded.

'You must be careful. These people eat strange meats,' my father said, to my outright horror, as the waiter walked by. 'At least at Indian restaurants, you know beef is beef and chicken is chicken.'

'Are you from India?' Angie asked. Her breasts collided like two boulders as she bent over me.

'We're from Pakistan,' I said. 'But Pakistani food, Indian food—same thing.'

A torrent of blood rushed to my father's face, changing his skin colour from muddy brown to clay red. 'No, it is *not* the same,' he declared. 'Pakistani food is based on Islam. Islam is the only religion that forbids the eating of certain meats.'

George and Angie nodded politely.

'No it's not, Dad,' I said. 'Jews and Hindus forbid certain meats too.'

'You didn't let me finish,' he said, angry at me for correcting him in front of strangers. 'It is the only religion that forbids the eating of animals that eat other animals. Like in Islam, you cannot eat animals like squirrels and opossums.'

'What? That doesn't make any sense,' I said.

'Are you questioning my knowledge of Islam?'

'Dad, squirrels don't eat other animals. They eat nuts.'

'I would never eat a squirrel,' my mother said, waving her hand about. 'Not for me, thanks.'

'Well, anyway,' said George, 'I'm sure you all would like to get back to your dinner and enjoy your evening.'

I was eager for them to leave our table. 'Yes. Nice seeing you both.'

'Good to meet you all,' Angie said, politely.

My mother half-smiled and my father grunted a goodbye. Thankfully, after George and Angie walked back to their table, the waiter finally arrived with our appetizers and set them in front of us. I was dismayed to see that my salad came with big chunks of prawn.

'What is that?' my father asked.

'I didn't know it came with prawns,' I said. I felt the tension rise in me as I tried to pre-empt what I knew was going to happen next. 'This is what I ordered,' I told my parents, 'so it's not their fault.'

'Excuse me!' my father yelled out to the waiter. 'Excuse me! This is not what we ordered.'

'No, Dad, I just said it's not their fault. Please.'

My mother sniffed my plate. 'It looks disgusting. What is that?'

'It's just a salad and I didn't know it came with prawns. It's not a big deal. Please, can both of you let it go?'

'How can I help you?' the waiter said.

'My daughter didn't order this thing,' my father said. 'Looks like aliens on a salad.'

The waiter checked his notepad, and I interrupted. 'Please, sir. This was my fault. I ordered it by mistake.'

'Is there anything else I can get for you?' he asked.

'Not really,' my father sneered.

We finished our food with minimal conversation, my parents occasionally speaking in Urdu together while I chewed in silence. George and Angie kept their conversation to a delicate hush, sprinkled with a few smiles and chuckles as they leaned in lovingly toward each other. We were still the only ones in the restaurant.

My mother started touching her face. 'I have a *huge* pimple on my chin.'

'Mom, please,' I whispered. 'People don't want to hear that while they're eating.'

'Well, if they don't want to hear it they can still see it.' She spoke at full volume. 'What's wrong with you, Samira? Why are you so uptight? You're making me nervous.' George and Angie turned around.

'I'm not uptight. Just . . . please . . . do you have to speak so loudly?'

'Boy, I'm never coming out with you again,' she said, while my father pulled a half-chewed leaf out of his mouth and examined it. He presented it to me.

'Samira, what is this?' he said.

My mother peered out of her backseat window. 'Where are we going? This isn't the way home.'

'I want to check something out,' I said.

'Samira, where are you taking us?' my father asked.

'I just want to see something, okay? It'll only take a second.' We were seven miles in the opposite direction from home. I made a right turn into a townhouse development.

'This place looks familiar. Didn't you and Ethan want to buy a townhouse here?' my mother asked.

'Yes. That's why I want to come here. I want see how the development is going.'

My father turned around in his seat to face my mother. 'You see how intelligent our children are? They keep up with real estate development so they can make smart investments. Do you know any other Pakistani children who do that?'

I backed off the gas pedal to slow down. We had just entered Brad's street. We started approaching his townhouse . . . and anger filled my veins like acid—parked in his driveway was a glossy, red Chevrolet Grand Prix. The kind of car that only girls drive. I knew it! That bastard. That two-timing, muscle-headed, pencil-dicked . . .

Oh, wait. Wrong townhouse. This one had gnomes in front.

'That townhouse over there is up for sale,' my mother said, pointing to one across the street. 'See? See the "For Sale" sign in the front? You see it?'

'Yes, I see it,' I shouted back. I needed to concentrate. We were now directly in front of Brad's townhouse. His upstairs lights were on, but his truck wasn't in the driveway. Maybe it was in the garage.

'Samira, you could still invest in one of these properties,' my father said. 'It would be a good idea for you. You're not getting any younger. And since it doesn't look like you'll have a husband anytime soon, I could help you with the down-payment. You should really think about this. This is the time you should be thinking about your future.'

I turned the car around and drove past Brad's house again, this time to get a better look at the upstairs windows.

'Why do you keep looking at *this* house?' my mother asked, referring to Brad's. 'This is not the one for sale.' From the backseat, she leaned forward and stuck her pointed finger in front of my face. 'That one over there is.'

'I see it, Mom!' I shrieked, shooing her hand away. I slowed us down, almost coming to a full stop, in front of Brad's house. My eyes were fixated on the upstairs windows. The lights up there were dim, like he had candles glowing. Why would he light candles if he was alone? What guy does that?

A second later, my eyes dropped to the ground floor. A light in the kitchen had just turned on. I watched, with a steadily growing terror, as a dark silhouette approached the window, and then looked down.

'Shit!' I screamed, pressing the gas pedal and turning the steering wheel hard to the right. The tyres screeched as I rounded the corner and sped through a stop sign and out of the neighbourhood. My mother, not wearing her seat belt, swung from one side of the car to the other.

'Are you trying to kill us?' my father shouted. 'What is wrong with you?'

'I'm sorry. I thought I saw a dog on the road.'

'You could have killed us!' he screamed.

'I'm sorry. I said I'm sorry.'

'And I don't like you using such foul language in front of me.'

'I know, Dad. I'm sorry. Mom, are you all right?'

My mother pulled her seat belt across her lap and buckled it. 'Samira,' she said calmly, smoothing her hair down, 'let me say something here . . .'

'Mom, please. Don't say it. Whatever you're going to say to me, just don't say it. Please? Just this one time.'

'Okay,' she said. 'Okay. I won't say anything. Just get us home alive.'

I practically burst into my room the minute we got home. It was now ten o'clock. Brad should have called by now. My phone was resting on my nightstand, plugged into the charger. I picked it up and saw that I had three missed calls. I breathed a sigh of relief when I saw that. In fact, I felt so relieved I almost wanted to laugh. No one else ever called me, so the probability that one of the three calls was Brad was too high to not be him. Maybe even two out of the three, or even three out of the three were him. He probably got upset when he couldn't reach me, I thought. Ha! That's a nice turn of events! I flipped open my phone and read the missed calls.

Meena

Meena

Meena.

'Damn you, Meena!' I screamed, throwing my phone onto the bed.

23

I decided to go back to the gym for the first time in almost a month, and all I wanted was some exercise. I didn't want to chit chat. I didn't want to run into anyone. I especially wasn't counting on running into

Brad. It had now been three weeks since I had last spoken to him, since he last blew me off, and I was relieved when I walked in around six o'clock and he wasn't there. Sam wasn't there either, so I was able to ride my stationary bike for almost forty minutes without interruptions.

I was breaking a good sweat, banging my feet against the petals to some angry German metal, when my ipod started skipping. I unclipped it from my waist and checked the battery. It was full. Nothing seemed to be wrong with it. I unplugged and replugged the cord several times to see if that would fix it. I was facing forward, concentrating on my headphones, when I heard Sam's voice. I turned to look. Sam was approaching the stationary bikes, his pace brisk and deliberate, a crossword puzzle rolled tightly in his fist, his eyes locked onto mine. There were mounds of intention on his face, and I felt a pang of distress when I realized it meant one thing.

He had something to say, and dammit, he was going to say it.

He climbed onto a neighbouring bike and whipped his head towards me. 'What in the heck are your peeps doing over there in Pakistan?' he demanded. 'I was just watching the news and there was another truck bombing in that northwest province area. Took off an entire side of a hotel.' He made a chopping motion with his hand. 'Bam! Gone! Eighty people dead!'

'I didn't hear about that,' I replied. 'That's awful.'

'Awful? It's more than awful. It's barbaric!' he cried. 'What's with all the killing over there anyway? You tell your peeps to quit all this fighting and killing and find peaceful solutions to their problems!'

'I'll try,' I responded.

For a second, Sam turned to his bike consol and punched in the settings for his ride, and I thought he was done. But then as he started slowly pedalling, he turned back to me. 'I tell ya', first it was Bin laden fighting the US, then it was the US fighting the Taliban, now it's the Taliban fighting the Pakistanis. When is this all gonna end? Who's even in charge over there? Now I hear the people in those villages are getting in on all the action. Picking up their guns and firing out of their own homes. What the heck are they doing that for?'

I slowed the pace on my bike. I would have given anything to ignore Sam, to just get off the bike and walk away, but I didn't. I knew he would just follow me to another machine. So I tried to do the best I could with the knowledge I had to provide him a satisfactory answer and get him off my back. 'The villagers are fighting over the incursions the Taliban are making onto their lands. At first the Taliban came with promises of money and education, which the villagers welcomed. But soon they realized it was just a ploy for cover and the only thing the Taliban brought with them was gunfire from the Pakistani military, and now their villages are war zones. So they're taking their own guns and fighting back against the Taliban.'

Sam slapped his crossword puzzle over the bike console. 'If I wanted that kind of answer I would have gone to CNN.' He unfolded the newspaper and began smoothing out the creases. 'I want to know the *inside* scoop. How do the people of Pakistan feel about what's happening? What's the government going to do about this new uprising? Tell me what's really happening over there.'

What's really happening over *there*? I could sure tell him what was happening over *here*. Which was that some old fart on a stationary bike was looking at me like I was a spokesperson for Pakistan or that somehow a suburban North Carolinian such as myself had privileged access to information about Pakistan's internal and foreign affairs that the media did not, and that every Pakistani on earth knew each other and we tweeted each other daily. What was really happening was that I didn't have a clue about what was happening over there any more than anyone else and I was growing tired of the expectation that I should.

'Kinda hard for me to get the inside scoop,' I told him, 'since I'm stuck in this gym talking to you.'

I put my headphones back on, and miraculously, my ipod was working again, so I resumed my German metal. Sam was uttering something at me in response, his mouth sure was moving fast, but all I could hear now was the lead singer of Rammstein screaming, '*Ich hab euch etwas mitgebracht! Ein heller schein am fermanent! Mein herz brennt!!*' I didn't like being rude to Sam this way, but honestly, he started it. He had always been an ally, so nice and sweet to me every other day. But today, he was unfriendly, even aggressive. The old bastard. Senile mother fucker. What was happening?

I took a look around the room, and suddenly started feeling weird. Displaced, even a little unwelcome. The people, the equipment, the yoga balls, even the towels—everything felt different, like there was a negative charge in the air.

The gym was turning on me.

And then, right away, my mind picked up something to the left. Over by the front desk. A red tank-top with a muscular arm sticking out of it. Brad was checking in, his gym bag over his shoulder, smiling to the clerk as if nothing was wrong. And standing next to him—a girl with long platinum hair.

She checked in immediately after him. My eyes followed them as they walked together to the locker rooms, chatting until they separated. A few minutes later, they both emerged from the locker rooms about the same time and hopped on treadmills next to each other. My heart pounded deep in my chest as I continued to observe them, every glance between them, every brief word exchanged, every laugh. Brad eventually finished his run and got off first, heading straight to the floor. Then she got off and joined him on the floor. Everywhere he went, she went. They stood closely. She touched him. They both went to the free weights and started doing bicep curls. Then Brad glanced up and saw me.

We locked eyes for a few seconds.

Then I got up.

Drenched in sweat, my hair a sticky mess, I walked until I was directly in between the two of them, forcing her to take a step back. As I watched his face go blank when I did this, just as Ethan's had that day on Capitol Hill, I briefly relished the fear he had of what I was about to do.

'Hi, Brad,' I said, calmly.

'Hey,' he replied. I noticed he didn't say my name. 'How are you?'

'Great. I've been doing just great,' I said. The platinum-haired girl pretended to be preoccupied with her arm curls, not listening to us. I felt like pushing her long body into the dumbbells. 'It's good to see you.'

'Yeah, sorry I haven't called in a while,' he replied. 'Been really busy. I haven't had much time to hang out.'

I waited. I stood there and intentionally prolonged the awkwardness for as long as possible. Then, I smiled. 'Have a nice workout, Brad.'

I turned to walk away, to leave it at that, but I turned back. That woman at Target may have gotten away easy, but Brad wasn't about to. No way. His injury to my ego was prolonged and insidious. He of all people deserved one. And my mind was clear, sharp, already prepared. I hardly even needed to think about it.

A comeback.

'You know what Brad,' I said. 'You should lay off the weights. You don't need bigger biceps, sweetie. What you need are bigger balls.'

A random meathead who had been within hearing range, clearly amused, said, 'Suh-nap!' I turned around for good this time without seeing the expression on Brad's face or that girl's face, and walked away.

I showered when I got home and dozed off on the couch downstairs. But it was a fitful, dream-clustered sleep. As I started waking up from it, bit by bit, the cloud of pride I had at telling off Brad started to dissipate. Did I make a mistake? Did I jump to conclusions? What if Brad wasn't seeing that girl? What if she was his cousin? Will I ever talk to him again? Will I ever be able to go back to that gym again?

Oh, god.

The mere thought of that gym made my stomach churn.

'Hey, get up,' Khalid said, nudging me off the couch. 'You're infringing on my territory.'

'Where's your game chair?' I asked.

'I had to return it. I need the couch back.'

'No,' I said, pushing him away. 'Leave me alone. I just told off that guy.'

'What guy? There was a guy?'

'You know there was a guy!'

Khalid ignored me and placed his headset over his ears, sitting Indian style on the floor.

I sat up. Then I immediately lay down. Then I sat up again. I needed a distraction, something to take my mind off Brad and what had just happened. My workbag was on the floor next to me, and I pulled out a letter I had received from Nasir three weeks ago but had never bothered opening. It was weighing on me to respond, and now was as good a time as ever to get that out of the way. I tore the envelope open and read it.

Dear Cousin,

Salaam. How are you? I am fine, alhamdulillah. All is fine in Kasur and here. How is Khalid, how is Meena? How are their studies? How is Uncle and Aunty? Please pay my regards to all.

I have been anxiously awaiting your reply. I await every day for your mail. I want to know what you are doing in USA. How is the weather in USA? How is job??

Now a days, I am very reserve. That is because I have discover new feelings, the feelings of love. I stay up all night at my window, looking at the moon and stars to think of this. I cannot think of anything else. I cannot work. I cannot eat. Never have I felt this way. And, dearest cousin, it is because of you.

My dearest Samira, by the grace of Allah, peace be upon Him, it would do me great honour if you are to become my wife. I have picture of you eating masala dosa and keep it with me at my pillow each night. But it is not enough. I want to see you every day. I have much to offer woman and I feel you will be happy with me. It is ok if you cook only soup. As husband I will oblige this.

I eagerly await your answer.

Love always, Nasir.

'Suck my hairy balls!' Khalid yelled into his headset. 'I'm gonna crouch down and teabag you, you little punk-ass bitch!'

'This is your father's fault,' my mother said later at the dinner table. 'He gave Nasir the impression you were looking for a husband. I know that's why those boys came. They wanted to see you and Meena because they were scoping out wives.'

'I never gave anybody the impression of anything,' my father insisted. 'Don't listen to your mother.'

She turned to him. 'You told your sister Amila when our daughters were born that they were available for her sons. You were very backward those days, Tariq. You may have forgotten but I haven't.'

I looked at my father to see if it was true.

'Okay, maybe I said that in the beginning,' he admitted. 'But it was a long time ago. I didn't think they were still holding onto the idea. Just ignore Nasir and he won't bother you again.'

Before the unpleasant realization could kick in that Meena and I could have been married off, living in a rural village in Pakistan and having sex with our cousins, I was actually more shocked that my father was telling me to ignore the son of his sister. Even I thought that was rude. I couldn't ignore Nasir. Whatever my feelings were about the whole business of being promised off to family members when my umbilical cord was still attached to my mother, and no matter how grating I found Nasir's inquisitiveness during his visit, his marriage request was still genuine. He deserved a prompt and proper response. I told my parents that I had already written to Nasir and put the letter in the mail.

'What did you say in the letter?' my mother asked.

'Well, first I told him thank you for the marriage proposal and that it meant a lot to me. Then I told him that while I appreciate his offer, I love him like Khalid, like a brother, and I could never see him as anything else. And then I said it wasn't a good idea for first cousins to marry anyway because it increases the odds of having children with genetic deformities. You know . . . to make it about *science* and not about him.'

'But it is about him,' my father said, scraping the remaining daal in his bowl with a piece of dry roti. 'What do you think he is?'

'What he is?'

'His mother and father are first cousins.'

'See how backward your father's family is?' my mother said. 'You see?'

'Bandh kar!' he snapped at her. 'This woman has a mile-long tongue!'

'I didn't think about that,' I said, getting back to Nasir. 'The possibility that he was . . . it never occurred to me.'

My mother waved her head back and forth. 'And now you've insulted him worse than if you had just ignored him. Good luck with that one.'

'But everybody knows diversity strengthens the genetic pool!' I let out a moan and cupped my hands over my face. 'I feel terrible. What do I do?'

'Is the letter gone?' my father asked.

'I posted it today.'

'Well,' my father said, letting out a slight hiccup. 'You should have ignored him.'

24

The life raft was comfortable again. It had begun to lose air from all its use over the last few months, plus a bit of weight gain on my part, but all it needed now was a few more puffs and it was good to go. I inflated it to its maximum volume, having decided a few weeks prior that I prefer a stiffer mattress to a softer one, and laid it flat on the floor. I literally had nothing else to do at the office that day. Nothing. And I was sick of surfing the net. I just wanted an escape, a time-out from everything—from my family, my cousins, PAC and everything else that came with being back home. I switched off the lights, pulled a sweater on top of me, and within minutes started having an unusually pleasant dream about Ethan.

It was about that time we had gone to the coast with our friends. We were all poor so we stayed at some shitty motel about a mile from the beach, but since all we did was get drunk, play cards and play in the surf, our accommodation didn't matter much. Then one night the toilet in our room stopped working. We had called room service over and over again, but no one ever showed up. And that's when Ethan grabbed an ice bucket.

He filled it with water. Holding it high over the toilet, he slowly began to pour the water in the bowl, trying to flush afterwards. Then he looked at me, overcome with excitement. Giggling outrageously, he quickly stuck the bucket under the fawcet, filled it again, and poured it into the toilet. I didn't understand what was so funny until he was on the third bucket and I heard an elderly guest next door comment that someone in our room 'has a bladder the size of Texas.' Ethan signalled at me to shush when I burst out laughing, his own face bright red with amusement, his cheeks puffed from trying to stay quiet. We huddled together by the sink as he did this several more times, going into hysterics about something that could only be funny after one too many cheap beers. The toilet still didn't work, but Ethan and I went back to the bedroom and collapsed on the bed together—holding hands, amazed at how funny all of that was—at the prime of our love. Just laying there in each other's arms giggling.

A finger poked my shoulder. I let out a few more giggles and turned to the side, snuggling one side of my face into the warmth of my sweater. Then the finger poked me again.

My eyes flung open. The lights in the office were on, and a man was crouched beside me.

'Excuse me,' he said.

Three white file boxes were stacked on the desk. A metal briefcase was leaning against the wall, and a strange cologne permeated the air.

'I believe this is my office.'

In a startled fit, I shot up, missing Fahim Kureshi's head by a few inches. He was a sophisticated man with black and silver hair cropped short and shiny black shoes.

'I see you have enjoyed full use of my office,' he said.

I got up fast, grabbing my purse and the three bags of Cracker Jack I kept in the top drawer of his desk.

'I presume you are Tariq's daughter?' he asked.

I replied that I was. 'Nice to meet you,' I said.

Then we both looked at the floor.

It was still laying there, never looking so massive and radioactive yellow than it did at that very moment. 'Um . . . I need to, uh . . .' I told him, pointing to the raft. I kneeled on the floor and popped open the plastic valve. A hiss of air started escaping.

Just a hiss. It was so goddamn slow. Barely anything was coming out—I had just added a pint of new air that morning and was now cursing myself for it. I tried squeezing the raft with my hands, trying to wring the air out that way, but it was still taking forever to deflate.

So I sat on it.

'Please,' Mr Kureshi begged me. 'If you don't mind, I have important business to attend to.'

I slid to another corner of the raft and put my full weight on it there, bouncing up and down a little bit, trying that out. The corners seemed to deflate first and that was helping, but overall the raft was still as inflated as ever so I slid to the middle to try that out and then just decided to try sitting everywhere and . . . did he have to just stand there like that and stare at me while I did this?

He cupped his hands together and begged me once more, 'Please,' he kept saying. 'Please.'

It was no use. I stood up. With one end of it sagging, I picked up the life raft and carried it with me out of Mr Kureshi's office and into the hallway of Libby, Libby and McCrane.

For the first time since moving back home in August, I found myself alone in the house. Khalid was out with the boys, and I didn't go with my father to his next PAC meeting. I told him I wasn't feeling well, clutching my stomach for emphasis. Luckily he bought it and asked my mother to go in my place. She grumbled for a good five minutes but finally relented and got in the car. After they left, I went up to my bedroom and locked the door.

I sat at the desk my parents had bought me when I was in fifth grade—cheap, hollow wood painted white, its brass hardware tarnished green with age. I opened the top drawer and pulled aside some old letters, postcards and some scented flower-shaped erasers, and took out the joint Meena had given me months earlier. I sat backwards on the chair and lit it. One deep breath. Slow release. Then another deep breath. Slow release. The chair was wobbly and uncomfortable. It was too small for me now, like a piece of dollhouse furniture. But I remembered so clearly the day I got it. There was so much I was going to do sitting at that desk—curing cancer, solving the world's ancient mysteries.

I took a few more sucks off the joint and stared at the little-girl wallpaper. Blue and purple flower bouquets against cream and pink stripes.

I got up from the chair and walked over to my bed, the joint hanging from my lips. I pulled from underneath a heavy cardboard box and opened it. Right on top of everything was the green silk pillow Ethan had thrown at me in my apartment. When I picked it up, the beads hung loosely by their threads and scatterered like raindrops on the hardwood floor. I put it down. Next in the box was a picture of me and Ethan from my twenty-third birthday. He had taken me to one of those mansions where someone gets killed and the guests have to figure out who did it. 'Murder on the Menu' I had scribbled on the back. I put the picture on the floor and reached into the box again, this time pulling out a small plastic object with a big head.

'Hello,' I said, flicking my thumb under the chin, opening and closing it, opening and closing it, opening and closing it. I took another hit off the joint.

I reached into the box again, this time to get what I really came for—a half-filled bottle of Grey Goose vodka. I wasn't sure why I kept it—probably too cheap at the time to have thrown away good vodka. I took the bottle back to my chair and twisted off the cap. Looking straight at the wallpaper, I took a heavy swig. It was disgusting, like warm auto lubricant. I closed my eyes and took another swig. Then another. My eyes stayed shut. Then another.

In the darkness, a horizontal line appeared behind my eyelids. A circle around the line, and then my hands on the circle. A steering wheel. A big white building ahead of me. Marble steps, orange cones. And people. There were so many people around, but it was only them I could see, standing together, him in a dark suit and laptop bag over his shoulder, her in a pair of tight jeans and a cropped shirt. What was she doing there? On a regular workday? She didn't belong there. They were talking intensely, leaning into one another. And then I saw it. He embraced her, pulled her in close, mere seconds before my wheels were knocking into the cones. I wasn't trying to run them over. I wasn't trying to hit anyone. In that moment, without thinking of consequences, without embarrassment or fear, I just wanted them apart. To tear his arms away from hers.

I opened my eyes.

My cell phone was ringing.

I reached for it immediately, eagerly. It was in my purse on the floor. For six whole days, not a single call came to my phone. Finally, someone was calling me!

But when I grabbed it, the screen was dark. Blank.

Fuck. I took a few heavy breaths.

This shit is messing with me.

I crumbled the joint into bits, my hands shaking.

But it wouldn't stop. The images. Flooding back to me. The memories. That piece of tomato skin stuck between the cop's two front teeth . . .

'Now tell me, young lady,' he said, setting a file folder down and adjusting his hefty thighs on the seat next to me. We were at the

Capitol Hill police station and it was lunchtime. An empty bag of Quiznos rested atop the desk I was handcuffed to. The cop's finger, jabbing in my direction, hinted of pickles and tobacco. 'Just what did you think you were doing this morning?'

'It was an accident,' I said. 'That's all it was.'

'Oh? An accident? It looked pretty deliberate to Officer Reynolds, who saw the whole thing.'

'Well . . . he saw wrong.'

'He saw wrong? Are you questioning the memory of one of D.C.'s finest officers? A decorated officer, protecting the United States Capitol and its residents for over twenty years? You're in a lot of trouble, young lady.'

I tried to explain what had happened—that I was driving to work when I saw a couple of friends of mine near my building. That I tried to steer closer to them to say hi, and I hit some of the cones. That it was just an accident.

'Multiple witnesses, including the officer who arrested you, said you deliberately accelerated your car upon seeing these friends of yours,' the cop replied. 'You drove through the cones, right past the guard post at the Rayburn building and into a crowd of civilians. Witnesses say one of your targets was a senior White House official.'

That's when that other man stepped in. The one in the grey suit. No badge. 'I'm Special Agent Robert Stafford. Homeland Security.'

He opened the file folder and started asking me questions. Bizarre questions.

'Are you a Muslim, Ms Tanweer?'

'Excuse me?'

'Are you a Muslim?'

'I don't know. Why?'

'You don't know?'

'No, I don't. Why?'

'When were you last in Pakistan? Do you have any allegiance to Pakistan? We need to take you somewhere else. Do you want to be proclaimed America's newest terrorist threat? You're young, pretty, no accent. Mideast terrorists are old news. Bin Laden is dead. Kept alive longer than the bastard deserved because your country harboured him. It's Pakistan now. The media will have a field day with you. Recognize him?'

From the folder, Stafford pulled out a photo of a young bearded man in a tan salwar kameez and a puffy black jacket sitting at a table. In the background was a plaid couch, some bottles of Coke on the carpet, an old poster on the wall of Arnold Schwarzenegger displaying his Mr Olympia biceps, and a few DVDs stacked by a small television on a metal cart. I had no idea who the man in the photo was.

Stafford spoke again. 'You have a unique name, Ms Tanweer. So unique, in fact, that the Capitol police immediately identified it on the FBI Terror Watch List.'

'My name is on that list? Why is my name on that list?'

'Chief Long here alerted our Department, right after you tried to drive your car onto restricted federal property with probable intent to harm administration officials and innocent civilians.'

'But what does this have to do with me? Why is my name on the list?'

They would never tell me.

You're in a lot of trouble, young lady. You hold it in and hold it in and then one day, poof!

I coughed up a speck of the weed, the bitter taste strong on my tongue, and picked it off. I wiped the back of my hand across my forehead. My heart pounded so hard my chest felt like it was caving in. I took a few more breaths, hoping the oxygen would dilute the pot, but all it did was wear me out.

I needed to lie down, but I didn't want to lie down, because if I did, I might fall asleep.

I had already ruined my reputation, gotten fired, risked everything for a stupid stunt. And yet, in spite of all that, I got off easy. I got the handcuffs removed. I got to go home. No way would I take something like that for granted again. Things would be different. I would start over. Build myself up again. Think before I act. Stop making dumb mistakes.

And now, I didn't want to fall asleep. I was downright terrified of the idea. Because in the morning, when I woke up, I would have nothing to do. I would have nowhere to go, no job, no friends. And no one to blame but myself. No Ethan, Natasha, cops, cheating or lies that I could hide under. I was the one who lost a guy that at one point seemed to like me back. I was the one who insulted a bunch of partiers I barely knew. I was the one who called the only man who had ever proposed to me a genetic mutant.

I picked up the bottle of vodka and rested the glass tip on my bottom lip. I breathed in its warm vapour and felt sickened. Repulsed. Everything was repulsive, the room, the wallpaper, the box of crap, myself . . . *this fucking bottle.* I threw the bottle as hard as I could at the wall above my bed, shattering the glass all over the floor, soaking my blanket and pillows in warm alcohol.

And in one easy heave, threw up under my little white desk.

Part 3

25

I was crouched in the jungle. Four men in blue and red armour and heavy boots pounded the ground, lifting the dense green fauna as they ran past me. Someone was going to see me. There was no way I could stay hidden for long—not with my jeans and pink My Little Pony T-shirt.

'Reload!'

Several bullets whizzed by overhead and one grazed the top of my shoulder. I screamed, but when I looked at it, I wasn't bleeding. And it didn't hurt. I crouched lower within the plants, almost tasting the moist soil. A man ahead yelled to another one. 'Get out!'

I got up and ran. I ran so fast, in every direction, not knowing where I was or where I was going. Deafening explosions sprayed the jungle through the air. Gunshots fired all around. My legs felt like they were filled with cement. I strained to run. I was out of breath and almost ready to collapse when the jungle finally cleared.

I had reached the edge of a cliff, where I saw a small, dark man standing alone.

'Samira . . .'

His white salwar kameez was stained red.

'Help me!'

'Nasir?'

'Samira . . . I thought you loved me.'

'Get him!'

Six armoured men ran towards us and fired . . . ratatatat!!!! Nasir clutched his chest and tipped over the side of the cliff, blood spilling out of his body as he drifted towards the infinite blackness underneath. Cloaked monks marched in a circle around me, chanting as all guns were raised again.

'Don't shoot me!'

Ratatatat!

I screamed, but it came out as a whimper as I bolted upright.

Ratatatat!

'Jesus Christ.'

Khalid was on the floor with his headset on, the wireless control in his hand. 'You're awake?' he asked.

Ratatatat!!

Each round of gunfire drilled a nail in my head.

'Why did you sleep here last night, rat?'

When I tried to sit up, sour fluid filled the back of my throat. I yanked down my My Little Pony shirt, which reeked of vodka. 'I . . . had a little accident last night.'

'Gross! I don't want to hear about your feminine issues.'

I lay back down and turned my head to the side—boxes were piled up in one corner of the basement. Everything of Khalid's was packed, except his X-box equipment and projector.

'You gotta get ready,' he said. 'We're all going to the PAC meeting today.'

'You're going to a PAC meeting?' I asked.

'Yeah. Dad got Senator Marshall to come.' A bright explosion illuminated the television screen, and it when it was over, Khalid's avatar's head was in a million crimson pieces on the ground. 'Fuck you, kid!' he shrieked into his headphones. 'Did you know I fucked your mother last night? But, anyway,' he said, turning back to me, 'it's a big deal for Dad that we all go.'

I carefully propped myself on my elbows. 'Well, look at you,' I said. 'You two are certainly chummy these days.'

'Someone woke up on the bitter side of the bed this morning.'

Several more rounds of bullets shot out. 'Aww fuck! That was close.

Anyway, Dad's happy with me because I agreed to do the wedding, maulvi and everything.'

'You sure caved easy,' I said. 'You were so principled before. What happened?'

'I realized it wasn't worth fighting with Dad over this. I'm a pretty reasonable guy, you know.'

'And Ashley agreed to this too?'

'She agreed.'

'She said yes to it all? The wedding, the maulvi . . . everything?'

'Yep,' he said. 'Maulvi *et. al.*'

'Wow.'

Khalid turned around. He winked at me.

'What was that for?' I asked.

'We gotta get going, rat. You should take a shower. You look like hell.' He leaned in close and sniffed. 'Smell like hell too.'

Khalid was right. I was a mess. I went back to my room, tossed my clothes in the hamper and took a long, hot shower, scrubbing every inch of myself with the loofah, shampooing my hair twice. I stayed for seven whole minutes under the massage setting—a powerful single stream shooting right between my shoulder blades—and felt the tension melting away.

After I got out, I quickly dressed and took out some stationery, writing down everything I thought of in the shower.

Dear Nasir,

I hope you are well. I have received your letter. Thank you for asking me to marry you! I am very flattered. I love you very much too. But I am not ready for marriage, so I must turn down your proposal. But I know you will make a great husband one day, and I am sure you will find a great woman who will make you very happy. I will always be here for you, and I hope you will continue to write me.

I signed it, 'Love always, Samira,' then folded the stationery and stuffed it in the envelope. Nasir would probably receive this letter after the first one I sent. There was nothing I could do to erase what I said in that first letter, so my best hope at this point was to just confuse him.

'Samira!' my father screamed from the kitchen. 'Let's go! We are running late!'

'Hold on!' I screamed back.

'We must go now! I can't be late!'

'I'll meet you there,' I hollered, securing my damp hair in a bun before licking the envelope.

The ballroom at the Sheraton was packed with desis, faces I knew and names I once learned but as always, forgot. While my father and the other PAC members took photos with Marshall out in the hall, Khalid, my mother and I took our seats to the far left inside the room. I spotted Bashir sitting alone and smiled at him. He motioned me to come over and I did. We chatted for a bit. He told me he was impressed my father was able to get Marshall to come to the meeting and look how many people showed up—we weren't even serving these desis food—and I laughed and apologized for yelling at his friends. Bashir said not to worry. He said he thought what I did at the party was pretty funny and that his friend Andy got turned on by it and no one really liked that girl Susan with the glasses anyway.

'Hey, looks like it's about to start,' Bashir said.

I looked around. My father, the PAC men and Marshall were now in the room and the doors started closing. Everyone took their seats. I quickly scooted in between my mother and Khalid, and my father stepped up to the podium.

'Salaam alaykum,' he said. 'Welcome, everyone. Thank you for joining us for this most important meeting of the Pakistani-American Council. Tonight, we have a very special guest, and first, I would like to say a few words about him.'

My father cleared his throat and began. 'Senator John Marshall began his political career in 1946, when he was elected President of his high school class . . .'

I could tell my father was nervous. He was slowly and carefully enunciating every word like he had just learned English that morning. Overall, he was doing fine, but when he neared the end of his introduction, my heart nearly stopped.

'So . . .'

I looked nervously at Khalid.

'Without further . . . uh . . .'

My teeth clenched. 'Adieu, Dad,' I said to myself. 'Adieu.'

'Without further . . .'

He paused again, each second of silence stretching for an eternity.

'Doo . . . no . . . ad . . .'

He receded from the podium a bit, deliberating in his own mind, keeping the audience waiting. Finally, he came forward and he waved his hand about. 'You know . . . say anything else . . .'

Khalid and I burst out laughing, crouching so our heads were in our laps. My mother gave Khalid a sharp whack in the shoulder. 'Don't make fun of your father,' she said. 'Bandh kar. Shut up.'

Khalid and I still were sniffling as my father concluded his speech. 'Now, I would like to introduce our guest of honour. Everybody . . .' He gestured towards the stately, snow-haired gentleman in the front. 'Senator John Marshall.'

I was relieved when the applause broke out and Marshall took over the podium. Marshall's speech consisted of the usual appreciation for being invited to speak and the chance to meet with Pakistani-Americans during this crucial stage in the relationship between our two countries. He spoke about the role our community can play in fostering greater understanding between Pakistanis, Muslims and the rest of America. I tuned him out almost immediately.

About forty minutes later, my body seemed to remember it was desperately hung over. I shifted uncomfortably in my seat. My forehead broke out in a sweat. My stomach felt like it was rotating whatever food was in there like a concrete mixer.

'You look beat up,' Khalid whispered to me.

I wiped my forehead. 'I don't feel well.'

As Marshall finished his speech, the question-and-answer session began. Members of the audience asked about racial profiling, visas, deportation, relations with Israel and foreign aid, and Marshall responded to everything politely and blandly. The only time I really listened in was when someone brought up arrests of US citizens under the Patriot Act, making sure no one mentioned my name or looked my way. But even then, something more interesting was catching my attention.

Khalid was typing furiously on his Blackberry.

'Hey sweetheart,' he wrote. 'We're all set for the big day BEFORE the big day. Our appointment is at 11:00 a.m. with the Cary County clerk. Remember to bring your birth certificate. Can't wait to see you. I love you sweetheart. I love you so much. I know I can be an asshole. Sometimes I don't know why you put up with me. Sometimes when I'm alone I look up at the stars and wonder how a guy like me got so lucky. You always seem to make it right, and I want to be a better man for you. I WILL be a better man for you, my darling. I will give you the life you want. I will be the husband that you want. I promise I won't let you down. You will see. I miss you. All I want to do is to wrap my arms around you, revel in the silkiness of your skin, the smell of your . . .'

'Move away, rat!' Khalid demanded, pushing me to the side and shielding his Blackberry from my view.

'Don't push me,' I angrily replied. 'I said I don't feel well.'

One man from the audience stood up and cleared his throat. 'Senator Marshall, as a businessman and a US citizen, I feel the United States has done very little to protect Muslim–Americans. If the government wants better relations with the Muslim world, with countries like Pakistan, they need to change their policies. Change how they treat Pakistanis living here. Right now we are blamed for everything other Pakistanis do on the world stage. We are victims of racial profiling, we get pulled aside on roads, at airports. Americans, sometimes our very own neighbours, fear us. And the media and government do nothing but promote that fear. I ask you now, what can you and our other representatives do about this?'

Before Marshall could speak, my father reached for the

microphone. 'Senator Marshall, if you don't mind, may I address the audience on this one?'

'Of course, Tariq,' Marshall graciously replied.

My father looked around. 'Why do we need the government to step in and do something about this? If our image is tarnished, isn't that our responsibility? Right now, Pakistanis are only known for being anti-Israel, anti-India, anti-America, anti-this, anti-that. But not for what we can *offer* this world.'

Some people in the room applauded.

'It is *our* duty to change this image we have,' my father continued. 'To show that we as Pakistanis and Muslims are proud to be living here, and can contribute to American society al-Hamdu-lillahi. Our literature. Our textiles. Our engineering. We have much to offer America, the world. This is not the responsibility of any government. This is *our* duty as citizens. And this is the mission of this organization. To make ourselves visible, to make our voices heard. To take this first step. And I hope you will join us here at PAC-PAC, I mean PAC, to make this happen.'

The room broke out in applause again, some people even knocking on tables.

'Here, here!' Uncle Mahmood proclaimed.

My mother leaned into me and Khalid. 'Look at this,' she said. 'How respected your father is, how much the community looks up to him. Hai hai hai. This is why I married him. He is a natural born leader.'

She admiringly gazed up at my father, who was now beaming at the front of the room before all the applause. She caught his attention and smiled, and my father smiled back, a warm, loving return of affection.

Suddenly, a sour, acidic fluid rushed up my throat and I thought I was going to throw up. I held my hand tightly over my mouth and stood up.

'You okay?' Khalid asked.

I quickly stumbled away, passing row after row after row of heavily perfumed Aunties and Uncles, accidentally stepping on shoes and purses and extra-long dupattas until I was out the door and into the hall and through the door of the women's bathroom. I slammed open a stall door and bent over the toilet. I gagged but nothing came out. I gagged twice more but still nothing came out. I stayed on the floor for a good six or seven minutes, getting dirt and bits of toilet paper and god knows what else all over my black suit. Eventually, when my stomach calmed a little, stopped contracting, I went to the sink and rinsed my mouth with cold water.

There was a dimly lit lounge in there with a large mirror and velvet couch pushed up against the wall. I sat down, leaning my head against the cool wall. My stomach relaxed completely, and the nausea started to disappear. My breathing slowed down. It was quiet in there—dark, cool . . . calm.

I must have passed out, because suddenly all manner of Aunties were bursting through the doors, going to the toilets and checking themselves in the mirrors. The session must have ended. I smoothed my hair down and went outside. Everybody was in the hallway now, taking photos with the Senator and noshing on the crudités and crackers on the banquet table. I put a cracker in my mouth and very carefully chewed. Then I grabbed a handful more and stuffed them in my mouth all at once. Uncles Abbas and Mahmood joined me.

'The evening was a great success!' Uncle Abbas proclaimed. 'Many people liked what your father had to say and now want to join our organization. But some people, you know, they did not like what he said so much . . .'

'Ah! Forget those goondas,' Uncle Mahmood said. 'We don't want those types anyway. Is this all there is to drink?' He pointed to the bowl of bright orange punch.

'You know,' Uncle Abbas continued, 'Now that our organization is expanding we could use someone like Samira to do our PR. We should make her our spokesman.'

'Not spokesman—spokeswoman, yaar!' Uncle Mahmood proclaimed. 'You're going to scare her away.'

I swallowed a lump of chewed up crackers. I was starting to feel better, the starch soaking up my stomach acids. 'Nobody's scaring me away, Uncles.'

'Looks like your father needs you,' piped in Uncle Abbas.

I turned to look down the hall, and my father was waving, trying to get my attention. He was standing with what appeared to be the only white woman in the vicinity. I said goodbye to the Uncles and walked over.

'Samira, I would like to introduce you to Deborah Banks,' he said. 'She is Senator Marshall's Chief of Staff.'

I shook her hand. 'Good to meet you.'

'Likewise,' she said. 'I've been looking forward to meeting you for some time. I have to ask—how are you?'

I felt sick to my stomach again, the crackers clogging in my throat.

'Do you two know each other?' my father asked.

'We've never met,' Deborah said. 'But I know what happened to your daughter on the Hill. And I think it's a shame what they did to her, arresting her like that, treating her like a common criminal, especially after years of public service. I think it's a prime example of our overzealous attitude towards Muslims, and this is why the Senator is here today. He thinks this is a very important issue and wants to take the helm in addressing it.'

My father's eyes bulged as she handed me her card.

'I would love to talk to you about your experience. If the police or Homeland Security mistreated you in any way, there may be some recourse you can take.'

The sweat of my unsteady palm soaked through her card. 'Thank you,' I said.

I glanced at my father. He was thoroughly and uncomfortably shutting down. *Police, arrest, Homeland Security, common criminal. Your daughter.* System overload. He looked back and forth between me and Deborah Banks, his lips quivering, trying to utter a word, not being able to find one. I knew I had a few more seconds of this before he would start to come to, so I needed to bolt.

'It was a pleasure meeting you Deborah,' I quipped, taking off down the hallway, walking steadily but briskly until I was past the front desk and out of the hotel doors, not daring to look back once. I knew this moment would come eventually, one way or another. Actually, not this way. I was sure if my parents ever found out about the arrest, it would have been because someone in the community found out and the information leaked to my parents. This was worse. This was coming from a white woman directly. A United States government person. This was *official.*

There was no escape for me now. I had to come clean. About everything.

26

At breakfast the next morning, my father staggered as he clutched his chest over a plate of fried toast and sliced melon. 'Oh my god!'

The night before, after I got home from the PAC meeting, I parked my car up the street and slept under Meena's bed, successfully avoiding my father the rest of the night. Then in the morning, first thing, I called Deborah Banks. In spite of the fact that I was lying on my back under Meena's bed and whispering, Banks seemed delighted to hear from me. The conversation went well. I told her about myself, my work with Congressman Bailey and gave her a rundown of everything that happened during my arrest. She listened with great interest. When I told her about my name being on the FBI terror list, she said she couldn't promise anything, but they would look into it. She liked me.

Or pitied me. I couldn't tell. Actually, I could. She pitied me. But whatever the reason, it helped give me the courage to do what I was about to do next.

I asked if she would hire me.

It was a long shot. This was a powerful woman working for a powerful Senator. People with even more experience and advanced degrees than I had scrambled for unpaid internships just to get a foot in their door. I was pretty sure if the Hill incident had not happened and she and the Senator didn't have a profoundly noble sense of morality, she wouldn't have expressed her pleasure that I wanted to return to D.C. and told me to fax my résumé over later in the day, that they could always make room for bright, young, fiscal policy analysts in their Hall of Justice.

Whatever the reason. All I knew was that now, armed with this nugget of information, I could confront my father.

'Dad, are you having a heart attack?' I asked him.

'Yes!'

'No, you're not. Will you please calm down?'

'I will NOT calm down!'

'When I drove through the guard post,' I explained, 'it was just an accident. I wasn't really trying to kill anyone. I just wanted to . . . you know . . . scare Ethan a little. It was a one-time thing. The cops let me go. No big deal.'

'No big deal? This is a very serious offence!' he yelled. 'You are a Pakistani! Do you know what they do to Pakistanis they suspect of terrorism?'

I told him I did, but he answered anyway.

'They put masks over their heads and beat them with sticks and dogs!'

'Nobody will do that to me, Dad. They know I'm innocent. They were probably confusing me with another Samira Tanweer, someone connected to that guy in the photo. And besides, I'm a US citizen. I have rights.'

'Your citizenship means nothing, bey! This government is very powerful. They will strip you of your citizenship whenever they want. Even if they don't beat you or deport you, after what you've done, now you have a file. On *you*, not some other Samira! You're going to be under suspicion for the rest of your life! They're going to follow you around and bug your phones. This whole family is going to be watched. Our phones are probably already bugged.' My father whizzed around in his plaid bathrobe and picked up the phone. He listened in for a second, and then said, 'Hello? . . . Hello?'

'Nobody's listening in, Tariq,' my mother said. 'And even if they were, why would they talk back to you, idiot.'

My father hung up the phone and pointed his finger at my mother. 'It is because of you my daughter is in this mess. You filled her head with liberal ideas when she was growing up and let her run around with boys and cigarettes, and now look what happened.'

'You're blaming me for all this?' my mother said, indignant. 'You raised your daughter the same as me. I don't appreciate all your yelling and accusations.' She took a sip from her teacup and shook her head. 'Boy, you really are a terrorist.'

'You stupid woman! Don't say such things out loud!'

'Both of you stop,' I said. 'I'm sorry I caused all of this. This is nobody's fault but mine. I'm really, really sorry.'

My father shook his head and lowered his voice. 'Listen to me, Samira. You are young and stupid. You've never had to struggle in this world. I've been here much longer than you. And I've seen things you cannot imagine. *Seen with my very own eyes*. Even in this country, bad things can happen to you. I have heard stories. Stories of desis appearing on that FBI list and suddenly vanishing when they didn't get their emissions inspections done, sent them to god knows where now that they shut down that place in Cuba. The police in this country are very corrupt. They will do anything to come after you, use *any* excuse. They can ruin your entire future over this if they want to!'

'My future won't be ruined, Dad, because . . . guess what?' I grinned broadly at both of them, ready to announce the news. 'I talked to Marshall's office this morning. Banks, his Chief of Staff. Remember her? I just spoke to her about a job.'

My father looked at me cautiously, like he wanted to believe what he was hearing. 'You did?'

'Yes.'

'It is confirmed? You have a job?'

'Yes. It's another legislative aide position. Fiscal policy. But maybe this time I can branch out into something new. I've learned a lot about immigration policy.'

'So you're leaving?' my mother asked, making no attempt to mask her one and only interest in my story. 'You're abandoning us again?'

'Christ, Mom. Can't you ever be happy for me? It's not like I have many career options with my background.'

'Why can't you work with PAC?' she said. 'I thought you liked attending those meetings, helping your father.'

My father seemed to be calming down now, muscle by muscle, as he poured himself a second cup of tea. 'She can't work for PAC, honey. That's not a real job.'

'But this job with Marshall is,' I explained. 'See, Dad? Isn't this what you wanted? For me to get a job there? Everybody wins. Marshall looks good for having a Pakistani on his staff, my reputation is saved because I can't be a terrorist *and* work for a Republican, and you win because the desi community will see that your connections got me a job with a powerful leader.'

My father took a moment to reflect on what I said. 'It would be good for you to work for Marshall. He can protect you if the police come after you again.' He sighed, and relaxed his shoulders. 'Okay. Your mother and I support this.'

'I don't support any of this!' my mother protested. 'Did anybody ask me if I support this? Do I have a say? No. Go to your job then. Jo marzi kar lo. These kids come and then they go.'

'Come on, Mom,' I said impatiently. 'You knew when I moved back here it was only temporary.'

'Do whatever you want,' she snapped. 'I have no control over you kids anymore. Dufa ho! Are you at least going to honour us with your presence at the wedding?'

'What kind of question is that?' I asked, pouring myself a bowl of cereal. 'Of course I'll be there.'

'Well, at least one of my girls will. If your sister is not there she is no longer a part of this family.'

'Of course Meena will be there. Why are you acting this way?'

'Your mother's just trying to pick a fight with someone,' my father interjected. 'She's angry because she doesn't like the way Ashley looks in her wedding outfit.'

'How does Ashley look?'

My mother scrunched her nose. 'Too . . . I don't know . . . *American*. She's obviously uncomfortable in the lehnga and doesn't want to wear it. I spent six hundred dollars getting this lehnga hand-sewn and shipped from Lahore. And she won't even let me put her hair up. She insists on wearing it down, like she's going to the office or something. Blah.'

'Go easy on her, Mom,' I said. 'She's doing the nikkah and wearing all the clothes and jewellery so what more do you want?'

'A Pakistani wife for my son. Or at least an American girl that was a warmer person.'

'Well, it's too late,' my father said. 'All you can do now is support them. They're getting married in a week so don't bring up any issues or cause for argument.'

'Oh . . .' my mother waved with her hand, 'I'm not going to cause any trouble. I'll just put on a smile and drink my wine.'

'No wine or alcohol at the wedding. I'm cancelling the bartender.' My mother stopped chewing her toast. 'What?'

'No alcohol.'

'Says who?'

'Says me. This maulvi is coming from Pakistan just for my son. He is a very important man. I will not have my family disrespect him by drinking alcohol and acting like awaras.'

'Listen, Tariq. If you don't have alcohol at this wedding I will bring some myself in a flask. How would that make you look then, huh? In front of your maulvi and all your community?' She turned to me. 'Samira, tell your father. You of all people are going to need a drink that night.'

I snickered. 'Why, Mom? Because it'll be a reminder that I'm not getting married?'

'No, because Ethan will be there.'

I swallowed a whole ball of Cocoa Puffs. 'What did you say?'

'Ask your brother. He's insisting on it.'

'Be quiet, woman!' my father yelled. 'See? I told you she's trying to stir up trouble.'

'What do you mean he's insisting on it? Khalid!' I swivelled my chair in the direction of the basement. 'Khalid! . . . Khalid!'

He didn't reply, so I got up from the table and went downstairs. Khalid was sitting on the floor, headset on, reading the post-game carnage report on the projector screen.

'Dude, it was total and utter annihilation,' he said into his headset. 'Nipple Flick didn't stand a chance against our artillery. Right . . . I totally agree. Next time we're going to have to . . .'

I came up behind Khalid and yanked the headset off him.

'What the hell?' he said.

'Why did you invite him to your wedding? What gives you the right?'

Khalid made a giant paw-swipe for the headset. 'Can we talk about this later? I'm about to start another game.'

'No!' I said, stepping away so he couldn't reach me.

'Give me back the headset,' he said.

'No.'

'Give it!'

'No!'

Khalid stood up and came towards me. I held the headset close to my chest and bent over.

'You're not getting this back until you tell me why you invited Ethan.'

'Give it to me first and I'll tell you.'

I bent over further, my arms crossed tightly over the headset.

'Give it back to me, rat!' he said. 'I'm about to start a new game. My partner in Amsterdam's waiting for me.'

'Your partner can kiss my ass!'

'All right. That's it . . .'

Khalid came at me with both hands, trying to pry my arms apart, prompting me to hold onto the headset tighter. But he was strong. It was getting more and more difficult. His hands were over my wrists, my legs were kicking aimlessly about, and soon we were fully entangled.

'Give it back to me!'

'No!'

'Give it back!'

Khalid wrapped my ponytail around his hand, gripping tight. He pulled my head until my face was parallel with the ceiling.

We were locked in position, screaming at each other to let go. Merlin, who up until that point had been curled in a corner of the couch, had enough of the commotion and darted up the stairs, just as my mother came running down, her dupatta flying behind her as she clutched a bright blue bottle of Windex. She raised her arms, aiming the bottle at the mass of limbs that were me and Khalid and sprayed. A clear blue stream went on my hair, in my mouth, in my eyes. Khalid and I immediately let go of each other, using our arms to shield ourselves from the spray.

'Stop it! Stop it you two! All this hulla goolla!' she yelled as she pumped the bottle. 'You two stop this right now!'

My eyes stung as I dropped the headset. Khalid immediately picked it up, using his shirt to wipe off the Windex.

'What is this nonsense?' my mother asked. 'Are you children or adults?'

Khalid shot a nasty glance towards my mother. 'I told you I would tell her about Ethan myself.'

'Forget Mom and answer me!' I shot back, my eyes squinting, leaking fluid from the intense pain.

Khalid sighed and tossed the headset on the couch. 'Look, rat. I know everything that happened between you and Ethan. Okay? I do. But he was like a brother to me.'

'So what? He was like a boyfriend to me,' I said, doing air quotes around the word 'like'.

'I was in a weird position,' he explained. 'I felt I should invite him out of, you know, courtesy. I thought he'd say no.'

'So he said yes?'

'Yeah. And he said he's looking forward to seeing everyone again.'

My next question, to my utter surprise, was pre-empted by my mother.

'Is that bitch he married coming?'

I swung my head in her direction, in total disbelief. 'Mom, you know? You know about Natasha?'

'Of course I know,' she snapped.

'Meena told them,' Khalid said. 'A long time ago.'

'Them? Dad knows too?'

'Meena was being a good daughter,' my mother said. 'You've been here for months now with no talk of Ethan. No talk of going back to D.C. You think your father and I were born without brains? We knew you were hiding things from us. Someone had to tell us what was going on.' She turned to Khalid. 'So, now, what are you going to do about Natasha? Because if she comes to this wedding, she won't be allowed in.'

'I told Ethan he couldn't bring her,' Khalid said. 'But he said he still wants to come.'

I couldn't believe I was hearing this, any of this. My head was spinning.

'Listen, rat,' Khalid said. 'If you don't want him to come, I'll respect that and tell him.'

'You can't do that now!' I shot back. 'It'll look like I'm not over him and can't handle being around him.'

'This is true,' my mother added. 'Better to let him come and see you've moved on. Made new friends. Wearing make-up again.'

My mother had a good point. Ethan's last impression of me was terrible. I had been so distraught over our breakup and lost so much weight that during the last few weeks before the Hill incident I was nothing more than a crying stick figure with tangled hair. If he came to the wedding, he could see me looking beautiful and happy again. Colour in my cheeks.

I turned to my mother. 'Would Dad care if he came?' 'You know your father. He'll do whatever you want.'

With my mother and Khalid standing before me, I weighed my options. Now that I was moving back to D.C., I was probably going to bump into Ethan one day anyway. Wouldn't it be better to see him on my turf? And besides, actually most importantly, Ethan would be driving five hours to spend the evening alone with me and my family. Surely that would upset Natasha.

'Fine,' I told Khalid. 'Let the bastard come.'

27

Three hours before the wedding, I was in Meena's room struggling with my heavy and complicated lehnga. I wasn't used to wearing clothes that I had to think about or take great care just to put on—the sequins and beading kept scraping against my skin, leaving thin white tracks along my arms and stomach. But I had to admit, my mother had great taste. The outfit she chose for me was stunning—a cropped purple top that exposed my bare midriff and a long, matching scarf that draped around my arms and shoulders. But the best part was the skirt—light blue with purple sequins scalloped along the edging. It dragged when I walked, for once making me feel like a Mughal princess. I placed about a dozen silver bangles on my arms and a tiny diamond bindi over my forehead. I looked positively exotic.

But Meena, as usual, looked better. She had a sexy red and black lehnga that hugged her curves better than mine, and I was jealous. I needed to look perfect that day. I was seeing Ethan again after almost a year and I had gained about ten pounds. There was a new deposit of fat on my stomach—a loose slack of blubber I hoped was merely awaiting distribution to the rest of my body. I would have to remember to suck in.

I practised my sucking in while I was seated on Meena's bed, my face raised up as she traced liner around my eyes.

'I brought a date,' she said.

'A date?'

'Yes.'

'You brought a date?'

'I can't say it any simpler than that for you, Sam.'

I pushed her hand away from my eyes. 'Meena, you can't bring a date to this wedding. This desi function of all desi functions. What will Dad think?'

'You're letting Ethan come. What's the difference?'

'These desis already know Ethan,' I reminded her. 'I broke him in slowly. And he knew foreign affairs and could talk to them about Kashmir. How are you going to parade around some strange boy in front of the community?'

Meena brought part of her hair forward and brushed through it with her fingers. 'That won't be a problem, given that my date is a she.' I felt my mouth grow dry. I immediately looked over to make sure my bedroom door was shut. 'What did you just say?'

'Remember the Halloween party we went to?' she asked. 'I was going to introduce you to Anna. I wanted you to be the first person I told. But we were having problems back then. She thought I wasn't serious about it. That I was just experimenting. So she blew me off and didn't come to the party. But she's here now and we're working things out.'

I tried swallowing, but there was no lubricant to swallow. 'And . . . are you just experimenting?'

Meena leaned in towards the mirror and started applying liner around her own eyes. 'I'm not sure. Maybe.' She turned around and shrugged. 'I might just be bi.'

A wave of relief. I didn't know what it was about weddings, why they encouraged family members, friends and former lovers to suddenly unearth themselves from all corners of the globe and air their long-held grudges, undying passions, deepest regrets in life and in this case, secret identities. If Meena was gay or bi it wouldn't make a bit of difference to me. Meena would always be Meena, no matter what her sexual label. But her timing was lousy. I was seeing Ethan for the first time since my arrest, since his marriage to someone else, and my drama cup was full. Brimming over. But if Meena was still confused, I figured the conversation didn't need to happen right away. It could be put off for another night, maybe when she's figured things out a bit more. A more appropriate night when the entire world wasn't waiting for us at the hotel.

I leaned into the mirror and wiped off some of the eyeliner with my finger. I had to admit, Meena showing up with her girlfriend presented an interesting prospect. A Pakistani wedding is a complicated social affair, with customs and formalities similar to a ball in a Jane Austen novel, where the room is segregated into women in their finest jewellery and men gravely discussing politics and all eyes are scrutinizing any exchanges between the non-married. But a girl and a girl? No one would suspect. Just friends, everyone would think. Cute and harmless. Nothing haraam about that. Unless, of course, Meena tried to pull something stupid.

I got up and looked at myself in front of the mirror. I was going to say something to Meena, probably remind her not to do anything stupid, but forgot about it the minute I saw my stomach again. I twisted and sucked my gut in hard, privately vowing to forgo food the rest of the day.

At the hotel, Meena, my mother and I and two random Aunties stayed in the honeymoon suite with Ashley to help her assemble her lehnga. My mother was wearing a white and silver sari. Her diamond jewellery clung to her ears, forehead and fingers like hexagonical ice crystals, and her hair was curled and pinned up on one side, 1940s style. She looked radiant, and it was a much simpler and classier look than I would have expected. This was her first family wedding in front of the community, and I had expected her to go full-on gaudy, spread her peacock feathers for all the desi matriarchs to marvel at. But I guess gaudy was being saved for the bride. Somewhere underneath folds and folds of sparkly gold and burgundy fabric and thousands of dollars worth of heavy gold jewellery studded with rubies, diamonds and emeralds was my brother's fiancée.

'No, I appreciate it very much,' Ashley said to everyone, 'but I think I'm going to leave my hair the way it is.'

'But it would look better up,' said one of the Aunties, scooping Ashley's shoulder-length dark auburn tresses in her hands. 'Let me put it in a bun. One simple bun.'

Ashley visibly recoiled from her. 'I do appreciate all the time and effort you have spent helping me, but I would feel better with it down. Thanks.'

My mother tried to knowingly glance at me and Meena about this, but I avoided looking back, not wanting to promote any drama. Ashley was cooperating as much as anyone could expect in this situation, and with all the Aunties focused on her, fussing and bustling around her, I would want the night to be over with as quickly as possible if I were her. But I hated to admit one thing my mother was right about—Ashley had one look. No matter if she was lounging at home or working out at the gym, every time I saw her, her hair was coiffed and business ready. In her sparkly gold gown she looked less like a bride and more like she was going to a costume ball at the office.

'You look beautiful,' Meena said to her.

'You do. You really do,' I added, touching her shoulder. I think it was the first time I had ever touched her.

'Is there anything we can get you?' I asked.

'Maybe a glass of wine. It would really help right now.'

'I'll go,' Meena volunteered. 'Can I get you anything else?'

'I think that's all I need,' Ashley replied. 'I really appreciate your Dad keeping the bar open. I don't know what Khally's friends would do with themselves if there weren't any booze here. Probably leave for another party.'

I forced a laugh. Ashley never did think too highly of Khalid's friends. None of us did, to be honest, but there was something different whenever Ashley spoke about them. It wasn't affectionate and teasing like it was with my family. With Ashley it was serious, dreadfully serious—like Khalid's choice of friends had some greater meaning and impact about the world. Plus, and I wasn't sure why, it was creepy to hear her call my brother 'Khally'.

'Meena and I will make sure all the guests are taken care of,' I tried to assure her.

My mother jumped in. 'Don't be worrying about the guests right now. We need to make sure Ashley is properly ready for the maulvi. He should be here any minute.' She held up a wallet-size mirror and swiped on a last layer of lipstick. 'You're going to be married in a few minutes!' she said. 'Aren't you excited?'

'Oh, very. I'm very excited, Mom,' Ashley said.

Meena and I shot quick glances at each other. I couldn't tell if Meena was looking at me because Ashley had just called my mother 'Mom', but I was looking at Meena because my mother, my father, the maulvi and almost all of the three hundred plus guests had no idea that Khalid and Ashley were already married. They had gone the day before to a non-denominational justice-of-the-peace and tied the knot. The nikkah, after all, would officially marry them under Islam but they would still need to get paperwork under the state. Khalid and Ashley just reversed the order. Now the Islamic ceremony was just an enhancement to their already official, non-religious marriage.

There was a soft knock on the door, and before anyone could answer it a herd of women and giggling young girls burst through. Ashley's mother was in the crowd, a slight and quiet older woman in a simple brocade dress, and she quietly scooted to the side of the excited crowd.

'The maulvi is here,' one of them said.

'Good,' my mother replied. 'But this is private. So I'm sorry, but we request that all of you go back outside. We will be out shortly for the reception. Not you, Mrs Harris,' she said to Ashley's mother, pulling her back in the room. 'You belong here.'

In spite of my mother's request, most of the women stayed. Seconds later, the maulvi walked in, a frail man in a black cloak and a black crochet prayer cap, clutching a copy of the Koran. He bowed his head and introduced himself to Ashley. My mother took Ashley's mother's hand, and both of them stood on either side of the bride.

The maulvi recited a few verses in Arabic, then looked at Ashley and asked if she would marry Khalid Tanweer.

'Yes, I will,' Ashley answered.

'Then I pronounce you married. Congratulations!' the maulvi said.

'I have already done the nikkah with your husband, and he is waiting outside to meet his new bride.'

All the women rushed to Ashley's side, hugging her and stepping all over her lehnga.

'Thank you, thank you,' Ashley said. She tried to hug everyone back, and by the time she reached her mother, she held her for a solid minute. I wondered if her mother was in on the fake marriage.

'Okay, everyone, out!' my mother yelled. 'Time for Ashley to make her entrance. Are you ready, mera laal?'

Ashley cleared her throat and pulled her dupatta over her head. 'Yes, Mom,' she said.

The lights went down. The drums beat. Ashley straightened her posture then lowered her head, a symbolic gesture of the bride being distraught over leaving her biological family. My mother and Ashley mother's each clutched one of Ashley's hands, and the three of them glided across the room—between rows of tables with royal blue and gold dinnerware and a bouquet of flowers so large you could hardly see the people on the other side—underneath sheets of sheer purple, pink and blue fabric, glittering with sequins, that swung across the ceiling from chandelier to chandelier. Meena and I, along with all the other females, held candles as we trailed behind. Ashley arrived at the stage where my brother was already seated. He stood up when he saw her. It was the first time I had seen him in his wedding outfit—a cream-coloured jacket that fell below his knees, cream leggings and sequinned slippers that curled at the toes. A part of me wanted to laugh at how ridiculous he looked, but I couldn't. Khalid was beaming, the happiest I think I had ever seen him. He kissed Ashley in front of everyone, let her go and kissed her again. When they finally sat down together and a hearty round of applause and whistles broke out, I felt my throat tighten. I wiped my eyes before any tears came out.

Then the flashbulbs went off, blinding like paparazzi. Everyone gathered for pictures of the newlyweds on their thrones. When that eventually died away, everyone approached the stage, family by family, for another round of photos with the couple. In the meantime, the wait staff had just begun placing food out on the buffet tables and my mother asked the DJ to play music. Prepubesent girls literally screamed and ran to the dance floor when the DJ started playing 'Dancing Queen'. Everyone turned their chairs around to watch.

'Sammer,' Cody bellowed from behind me. His hair was slicked back and he was clutching a Heineken. 'Beep Beep! Watcha doing?' He came at me, bear arms akimbo, and I quickly stepped back.

'Not here, Cody,' I said. 'Gotta keep a respectable distance.'

Cody stepped back himself, a little more than he needed to. 'Right. Sorry. Hey, gonna sit at our table tonight?'

I looked over at the three tables filled with Khalid's and Ashley's friends, way in the back, pink dots in a sea of brown.

'Where's your woman?' I asked.

'Things didn't work out with her. I'm flying solo. Lots of nice ladies here, though, to distract me.'

'Sorry to hear that. But yeah, save a seat for me. I've got some things I need to do first.'

Those things I needed to do consisted solely of finding Ethan. I scanned the ballroom—the PAC men were seated with their wives near the front, Neelam and her husband were at another table, each with a baby on the lap, Abdul and Bilal from the dealership had just walked in late, the buffet table was filling up in the back . . . but no signs of him. Nothing. I don't know why the idea hadn't occurred to me before but . . .

What if he doesn't show up?

My thoughts were interrupted by an angry voice behind me.

'Samira!'

I turned around. My father was looking at me intently, furious.

'Hi Dad,' I said sweetly. 'The reception is really nice, isn't it?'

'What is your sister doing?'

I looked over at the dance floor, and Meena's backside was up against her girlfriend, her knees bending and unbending as she bumped and grinded, totally out of sync with ABBA.

'That girl is embarrassing me in front of everyone!' he said. 'Go tell her to sit down.'

'Come on, Dad. Everybody's dancing. Just let her . . .'

'I said go!'

'Okay, okay.' I gathered my skirt and shuffled over to the dance floor. I caught Meena's eye and made a cutting gesture across my neck. She nodded her head in acknowledgement, and before I could feel relief that she was going to do as told and sit down, Anna gave her a long, sexy dip. Then they sat down.

'Samira,' Meena said happily upon my arrival at her table, ignoring the scowl on my face. 'This is Anna. Anna, Samira.'

Anna shook my hand vigorously. 'I've heard so much about you. The big sister!'

'Good to meet you, Anna,' I said, looking down at her plump hand. Anna was nothing I would have expected. Kind of a blonde and blue-eyed mall rat, wearing a simple blue sari that looked like one of Meena's, the ink of a fairy tattoo peeking above the folds of fabric on her waist. Anna seemed sweet and innocent, vastly different from Meena's taste in boys.

Meena asked Anna if she would get them a couple of sodas. She obliged, and as soon as she left I scolded Meena. 'Boy, you are pushing the limits of this, Meena. Dad saw you on the dance floor and he's pissed. Don't you know what he'll do to you if his friends start asking . . .'

'Hey, there's Ethan,' Meena said casually.

I whipped my head around.

'There,' she said. 'By the bar.'

In his back pinstripe suit, white shirt and silver tie—his fanciest outfit, Ethan stood with Khalid and my parents. My mother picked up Ethan's left hand. She shook her head. I watched them for minute or two. And then as if they knew I was watching, all four stopped and looked across the room at me.

'You better go over there and talk to him,' Meena said.

I looked on as my father patted Ethan on the head, and then both my parents walked away. Khalid leaned in and said something to Ethan and they laughed, and then they embraced. After a few masculine thumps on the shoulders, they let go of each other, and Ethan straightened his tie. He started walking towards me.

'I can't believe he's here,' I said to Meena. 'Why the hell did he even want to come tonight? Why?'

Ethan's sporty cologne arrived several seconds before he did. He looked at Meena and spoke to her first. 'Hey, Meena. How are you? You look really beautiful.'

Meena gave a chilly response. 'Thanks. So glad you could make it.' Ethan knew Meena enough to know that was about as good a response as he could hope for. He turned to me. 'Samira . . . um . . . long time no see.'

I shook my head. He started laughing.

'Long time no see?'

'I know,' he said. 'But it could have been worse, right? Like, hey, long time no see, you crazy bitch.'

'At least it would have been honest.'

We kept smiling at each other. I felt oddly at ease in his presence, completely at home, like no time had passed and nothing had happened.

'Nice cuff links,' I said.

'You remember them?' he asked. 'I got them with you at the mall, after that night we watched *The Godfather* trilogy. Remember?' I was pleased he shared a memory with me. 'I remember, Ethan. What do you think of the wedding?'

'I think Khalid looks like a douche in that get-up,' he said. 'But it's great. I'm surprised to see so much booze here.'

'Well, it's just for the whites, the goras,' I said, 'so take full advantage of it.'

'Actually,' Ethan said, 'I won't be staying here for long. I have to drive back to D.C. in a little bit.'

Immediately, I felt my ego deflated. I thought Ethan was going to stay with us, spend time with my family and be with us for the entire event, maybe even stay the night.

Then for the first time, I saw his wedding ring.

'Oh, should I take this off?' He started sliding it off his hand.

'Leave it on,' I said sharply. 'We know you're married. No use hiding it. Let me see it.' I grabbed his hand and pulled it up to my face. Just a plain, gold ring. How *boring*. I would have gotten him white gold or platinum.

'Want to go somewhere and talk?' he asked. 'Catch up? I'll get us some wine.'

'I'm not allowed to drink but get yourself some,' I said.

I fluffed my hair with my hands until Ethan returned with a glass of red wine. We stepped onto the patio outside the main reception hall. The sky was overcast and it was a bit chilly, but there was a moist, warm breeze that drifted through—a harbinger for a thunderstorm. I sat down on a small wooden bench with red geranium pots on either side. The large, potted plants out there gave us total privacy from everyone inside. Ethan sat next to me. Our hips touched.

'How have you been?' he asked.

'Fine,' I replied. 'It's nice being back home. I really connected with a lot of new people here.'

Ethan raised an eyebrow. 'Connected?'

'Yeah . . . connected.'

'Huh . . . connected.'

He looked pensive. I knew saying those words would get this exact reaction out of him.

'When you say connected,' he continued, 'do you mean, like . . . a guy?'

I purposely circumvented the question. 'I connected with lots of people.'

'Oh. Huh.' Ethan was quiet again, then he changed the subject. 'So, what are you up to now? Are you working?'

'Yes. Well . . . I was. Actually . . .' I looked up at him, prepared to study his reaction for what I was about to say next. 'I'm moving back to D.C. I got a job offer with Senator Marshall.'

Ethan straightened his posture. 'You're moving back?'

'You seem surprised.'

'I am surprised,' he said. 'I thought you wanted to get away.'

'I did get away. And now I'm going back.'

'You're not worried about the Hill thing? Returning to the scene of the crime?'

I shrugged. It had been some time now that I had conquered my phobia of D.C., so I was able to respond with conviction in my voice. 'I'm not worried at all,' I said.

Ethan reflected on this, then smiled. 'There's also such a high turnover rate on the Hill. I bet a lot of people who knew about it are gone anyway. Well . . . congratulations,' he said. 'On the job.'

'And congratulations to you too,' I said. 'On your marriage.'

Narrowing his eyes, Ethan said, 'Don't be fake with me, Samira. I know you too well. Don't say congratulations.'

I didn't respond.

'You know why I was with her. I was messed up. I wanted revenge. I know it was wrong but I was never . . . you know . . . interested in her . . .' Ethan stopped talking and gazed down at the small fish pond below us with no fish.

'Why are you here, Ethan?' I asked abruptly. 'I'm sorry if I sound impatient, but I haven't talked to you in months and suddenly you show up.'

Ethan looked at me cautiously, and I prepared myself to get emotional over whatever he was about to say. 'Samira, I'm here to tell you . . . I want to tell you . . . well . . . why I married her.'

'You knocked her up.'

Ethan looked shocked. 'You know about that?'

'Yes, Ethan,' I said, feeling exasperated with him. 'It was all very honourable of you, marrying her like that. Me? I would have pushed her down the stairs.' I shifted on the bench, the cold and the conversation making me tense up. 'Is this why you came?'

Ethan was still confused. 'But . . . how did you know?'

'I was with you for eight years,' I said flatly. 'I know you inside out. I know that's the only reason you would marry her. So this is why you came? Just to tell me this?'

'Of course not,' he replied. 'I also wanted to see you again. I haven't seen you in a long time, not since . . .' His voice trailed off. He stiffened his posture and raised his voice. 'That was the fucking worst day of my life. That day on the Hill. She showed up, right as I walking into your building. I don't know . . . maybe she was following me or she knew I was coming to see you . . . and she tells me she's pregnant. And then not a second later, I see you barrelling towards me in your car with that maniacal look on your face . . .'

'I didn't look maniacal,' I said. 'At that point, I was calm in my resolution to kill both of you.'

Ethan started to laugh, then immediately stopped. 'I'm sorry what they did to you,' he said. 'I contacted Homeland Security and the cops, pulled some of my White House weight to get you out of there. Thank god it worked. Boy, I . . .'

'Why were you coming to see me that morning?' I interrupted. 'We hadn't spoken in almost two months.'

'Because . . .' Ethan stopped and took a breath. 'I came to tell you I was over it. That I wasn't angry with you anymore, and that I did some dumb shit too.'

I sat there quietly, unsure of how to react.

'I was going to ask you if we could start over.'

He pulled in close and brushed some of my hair away from my forehead. I noticed a light smattering of freckles on his cheeks. They weren't there when I was with him. They were new.

Too much was new.

I scooted away. 'Guess you're going to be a father soon.'

'Samira . . .'

'When is he or she expected?'

'I'm already a father,' Ethan said. 'Aadil was born last month.'

I wasn't prepared to hear the kid's name.

'Do you want to see a picture?'

This time I paused for a while, a really long while, and Ethan let me. It was one thing to have thoughts of him and his new family, but now I was confronted with seeing real people, real faces. It probably wasn't good for me, but there was no way I could refuse. 'Let me see it.'

My heart started pounding as Ethan pulled out his wallet. It was a picture of Natasha and the baby at a small picnic. She was stretched out on the blanket, their son tucked under her left arm. I blurred her out and looked at the baby first. He looked just like Ethan. Same nose, same crooked upper lip. And there was something else. It surprised me that my first reaction wasn't one of sadness. Instead, I wanted to laugh.

'This baby is white,' I said. 'It doesn't look mixed at all.'

'He,' Ethan said. 'Aadil. Not it.'

'Oh, right. Sorry.'

Still holding the photo, I concentrated on her next. It had been almost a year since I'd seen her. Natasha looked pretty—less make-up than she usually wore and her hair was back to its original state—natural black, pulled into a simple curl of a ponytail. But there was something different about her face. Her birthmark. That small purple discoloration near her right temple. It had grown, maybe from pregnancy, maybe from stress. Now it went past her right eye and onto her forehead.

It pleased me to see it.

Ethan abruptly put the picture back in his wallet. The last few rays of the sun glistened over the water droplets on his eyelashes. Ethan wiped them away, thinking I didn't notice, then gripped my hand so hard his wedding ring dug into my skin.

He saw me wince and let go.

'You should know, Sam, that in spite of everything, I do care about her. I don't want to hurt her, to treat her bad.'

I looked back at him. Somehow the tone of his voice, the expectation that accompanied what he said, made me feel small. It was one thing for me, for a part of me, to still hate Natasaha, to not wish for her happiness. But underneath my anger, I didn't want Ethan to feel that way. It would have been wrong, beneath him. Not suitable for a man I could fall in love with.

'I don't want you to treat her bad either,' I said. 'She needs you. That little boy needs a good home. I know, and you know, you have a duty to give that to him.'

Ethan nodded along with what I was saying. He looked around and then took a sip of wine. And then he held my hand again, gently this time. For a few moments we sat that way, saying nothing to each other. I looked at the fleshiness of his soft, freshly shaven cheeks, the hazy green of his eyes. Memories of our past years flooded back. Summer nights of crickets and wet grass and wine coolers, quick, dry kisses under a weeping willow, Chinese take-out on his bed while a storm raged outside. And then I remembered something else.

'Ethan, I have something for you.' I reached into my blue beaded purse and pulled out a plastic object. He literally squealed when he saw it.

'The Emperor!' he yelled, grabbing from my hand the special edition Emperor Palpatine Pez dispenser—the one he bought when *Star Wars Episode IV* came out—that he said was a collector's item. 'I knew you had it this whole time!'

'I'm sorry,' I said. 'I wanted to keep it because it reminded me of you.'

Ethan got up and dusted off his pants. 'Bullshit,' he said. 'You kept it because it's a friggin goldmine!' He fitted his thumb under the head and made the Emperor talk to me. 'Always two there are, a master and an apprentice.'

'He didn't say that. Yoda did.'

Ethan laughed and put his arms around my waist, lifting me off the ground. My skirt twirled as he spun me round and round. I hadn't eaten all day, and I felt my stomach in my throat. I rested my head on his shoulder and shut my eyes until my feet touched the ground again.

Ethan reached into his pockets for his keys. 'Well, I want to stay. I do. But I've got a long drive back and she'll start to worry.' I nodded my head.

'So . . . shit . . . I don't know what to say here, Sam. I'm glad we talked. And . . . I guess I'll see you.'

I turned my head to sniff my shoulder.

And the world stopped.

Ethan's scent was on my clothes, it was on my skin, it was all over me, and it was going to stay there all night while he drove away, leaving me to go back to her and his new kid, and it all felt so wrong and I didn't know how I was able to make peace with it seconds earlier because now . . . . .

That's it for us? That's fucking it? Eight years ends with guess I'll see you?

I grabbed the pez dispenser from his hand, bent it over my knee, and in one swift movement, snapped off the head.

Ethan's face went pale.

'Here's your goddamn pez dispenser,' I said, throwing the pieces at him.

Ethan fell to the ground, scrambling for the pieces. 'What the hell did you do that for?'

'It's worth a dollar fifty, Ethan,' I said. 'A dollar fifty. In all the years you had it, you never bothered to look up its price?' Tears layered over my eyes, then dripped out.

'You know what? No one forced you to do it,' I said. 'She was my best friend. No one forced you to sleep with her.'

Ethan rested on the balls of his feet, then stood up and put his arms around me again. He wiped my eyes and tucked my hair behind my ears. 'You're right,' he said. 'No one forced me. It was malicious, and I'm sorry.'

His response startled me. I had grown so accustomed to combat with him, it was hard to hear him agree with me. I expected excuses, rationales, more pinpointing that it was because of me he did what he did. Which is what, deep down, I still believed.

'I made you Roger Waters.'

I said it, knowing how ridiculous it sounded, but it seemed to perfectly summarize *my* malicousness—his biggest fear, realized because of me.

'What?' Ethan said.

'Roger Waters,' I said, my voice sounding unnaturally deep from trying to control my crying. 'I left you first. You were only reacting to me. I'm sorry. This was all my fault.'

Ethan leaned his mouth against my forehead. 'That's not true, Sam. I had choices. I didn't do things right either.' Several tears dropped from my chin and streaked down his dress shirt. 'And I'm no Roger Waters. Shit. Wish I was, then I'd have so much cash I wouldn't have to worry about some fucking little . . .' He paused and shook his head. 'A dollar fifty. Are you sure?'

I nodded. 'Probably less than that since you ate the candy inside.' I gently pushed him away, not wanting to soak his shirt and not wanting any more of his scent on me. 'You should probably get on the road,' I said nodding, and adding solely for his benefit, 'so you don't make her worry.'

I could tell Ethan appreciated that. He flickered a smile, but then immediately looked down at his keys. 'I don't want this to be it. When you're back in D.C., think we could meet up? We could grab coffee. Even though you know I hate coffee.'

I tried to smile. 'Of course we will. That would be nice.'

'So no goodbyes,' he said. 'No goodbyes. Just a . . . see you later?' I nodded and smiled, a fraction more comfortable with his parting words this time. He turned, started to walk away, but then he stopped and turned back. Still clutching the pieces of the pez dispenser, he fitted the head against the stem and swung the parts in the air, examining them up against the sunlight.

'Maybe I can crazy-glue them together,' he said.

I walked back into the ballroom alone, relieved no one seemed to notice my prolonged absence. I picked up a silver knife to check my reflection and wiped off my make-up the best I could. Luckily, no one would notice my messed-up face because the lights were dimmed low, everyone now focused on Khalid and Ashley slow dancing to 'Unforgettable'. The videographer was right up in their faces and both of them were trying to gracefully shield their eyes from the floodlight of his camera. They were quietly laughing to each other about it, an intimate moment before hundreds of watchful eyes. I walked over to the buffet table where my father was standing next to Cody. My mother was busy gabbing with Aunty Ruby and some other random Aunties at a table near the front, and Meena was snapping pictures of Anna with her pink camera phone. I let my stomach hang out freely as I turned to the buffet of curries and rice, scooping some on my plate. I went and stood right behind my father and Cody, joining everyone in watching the couple of the night, all of us watching Khalid whisper something in Ashley's ear, making her crack up and whisper something back. Cody affectingly put his arm on my father's shoulder and my father returned the gesture and put his arm on Cody's shoulder, and as I was chewing off a large piece of naan, my father leaned into Cody and said one word.

'Divorce.'

28

It felt lonely downstairs. The room was just too clean, too barren, with only the couch and television and freshly vacuumed rug. All the boxes, papers, pens, dirty T-shirts, X-box equipment and beer bottle caps stuffed into the cushions were gone. Khalid and Ashley would just be unpacking their wedding gift ramekins in their apartment in Vødesværk, and Meena was back at her apartment at school, already having broken up with Anna and back to dating boys. I pulled the television forward. I reached behind it and pulled out two velvet Islamic scrolls and put them back on their hooks.

'Samira!' my mother yelled from upstairs. 'While you're out running errands, can you get me a large sack of potatoes and a few cans of tomato paste?'

'Sure, Mom,' I replied.

'And a box of dhania?'

'What's dhania?'

I could hear her mutter something in Urdu. 'Never mind,' she sighed. 'I'll get it myself.'

'Will you just tell me what it is?' I yelled back upstairs.

Coriander powder. Now I had to go to two stores—a regular one for trash bags, potatoes and tomato paste and an Indian store for the dhania—and one gym. Now that I was leaving, I had to cancel my membership. I could have done it over the phone, but I thought, since I was cancelling my membership early, it would be better to do it in person in case there were any problems. What I didn't have to do was intentionally show up the same time Brad usually did.

'We're going to miss you,' said the beefy 24/7 clerk in an unexpectedly high-pitched voice. 'We've enjoyed having you. So sad you're leaving us.' He reached under the desk and pulled out some guest passes. 'If you're ever back in town, stop by and see us again.'

I thanked him for the passes and he went off to print my cancellation forms. While I waited there, just as I expected—timed, actually—I had waited out in the parking lot until I saw him pull up, then gave it another ten minutes before going inside—Brad walked out of the locker rooms. He looked in my direction, started to fill his water bottle, and did a double-take.

'Samira?'

He started walking towards me. I straightened my posture and tried to look casual.

'Wow,' he said. 'I didn't expect to see you just now. How are you?'

'Your cancellation form,' the clerk said as he slid the paper in front of me. 'There's no fee since you're moving out of state. Just sign here.'

'You're moving?' Brad asked, looking surprised and, at least what I wanted to believe, upset.

I scribbled my signature on the form. 'Moving back to D.C. I got a new job. I'm leaving in two weeks.'

'I'm happy for you,' he said. 'But . . .'

He paused. I waited.

'I just wanted to say . . . things got weird there, huh?'

Yeah, things got weird. Part of me wanted to clarify to Brad, remind him perhaps, that things 'got weird' because he started acting like an asshole. And as we were standing there, a possible explanation behind the 'things got weird' part walked right between us, just like I had done to her earlier.

'Are you coming?' she asked Brad, her toned legs towering over me, and, quite curiously, almost towering over Brad. He seemed a good several inches shorter than I remembered him. Had he shrunk?

'I'll be there in minute,' he responded. There was a twinge of annoyance in his tone. She stood there for another second, eyeing me up and down, before walking away.

'Is that your girlfriend?' I asked, forcing a smile, not wanting to appear jealous.

He watched her walk away. 'Not a girlfriend per se . . .'

'It's okay,' I told him. 'I felt you pulling away, and now at least I know why.'

Brad appeared startled. 'I pulled away? No, Samira. *You* pulled away. I wanted to keep hanging out with you, see where this was going. But . . . come on,' he said. 'You were never really into this, were you?'

My response was immediate. 'Of course I was.'

'No you weren't. Sometimes it was like, I don't know, you didn't want to be there. We had a good vibe in the beginning, you know, we really connected. But then it was like you were forcing yourself to hang out with me.'

As I kept looking back at him, listening to what he was saying though far more perplexed as to why I never noticed he was barely an inch taller than me, it smacked me across the face.

Brad Turner was a rebound.

I crinkled my eyebrows, stuck for words. I wanted to deny what Brad was saying, fight it, offer him proof that it was his behaviour that messed things up between us, but now that the fog of rebound-land had lifted and I was seeing things for what they really were, I knew he was right. I wasn't over Ethan. Clearly I wasn't. The thing is, I knew that all along, but I thought I could date Brad anyway, that the two could exist simultaneously. Obviously they couldn't, because no matter what Brad did, whether he attached himself to my hip or flat out ignored me or found a peaceful middle ground, I would have been miserable with him. I would have found a way.

'I'm sorry about what happened,' I told him. 'I did like you. I still do. But yeah . . . things just got weird.' I shook my head and grinned. 'I never should have insulted your balls, huh?'

Brad laughed, his teeth glowing white against his newly tanned skin. 'No, you shouldn't have. But who knows. Maybe I'll forgive you one day and come to D.C. for a visit.'

'Anytime,' I said. 'I'll be back in town too.' I held out my guest passes. 'Can't escape my parents for too long, you know.'

Brad smiled. A drop of sweat glided down his right temple. He lifted his shirt to wipe it off, revealing his taut, rippled stomach.

At least I didn't imagine that.

'You better call me sometime,' he said.

I knew that realistically, I probably never would, that I wanted to put this chapter of my life well behind me, but I grabbed the pink copy of my form and said, 'I will.'

My room was all packed—clothes, toiletries, alarm clock. It didn't take long. I just put everything back in trash bags. I dragged them down the stairs and slapped them all into the trunk of my car, one by one, sometimes two at a time, noting how much stronger I was this time around, not needing Khalid's or Meena's help.

I went back up to my room to get the last remaining item of mine—the cardboard box under my bed. I slid it out. It was much lighter now that the bottle of Grey Goose was gone. I closed the flaps and picked it up, carrying it downstairs and outside, past my car and to the trash can behind it.

I opened the lid of the trash can and threw the box in there.

I closed the lid and walked away.

I walked back and opened the lid again.

With the moist scent of rotting banana peel drifting upwards, I unfolded the flaps of the box. I retrieved the picture of me and Ethan from the Murder on the Menu night. I thought of the picture he showed me at Khalid's wedding, of him and Natasha and their baby. He has new pictures with new people now. And Natasha's birthmark. I thought about her birthmark again.

I didn't feel better thinking about it. I didn't want Ethan to be unhappy. And for the first time since this had all started over a year ago, I really didn't want her to be unhappy either. If they were going to be stuck together, what was the point of wanting them to be unhappy? Their suffering wouldn't cancel out mine. It wouldn't make my life any better, make my problems go away or my friendships or relationships with men easier. My life was going to be my life regardless of whether he slept on the couch or not. Which I hoped he did.

No, I didn't really hope that.

Actually, I did. I really did.

I ripped the picture I was holding in half, keeping the side with Ethan. I knew I still had a lot of work to do before I was over him, but it felt easier to mourn the loss of him instead of the loss of us. Start with this first step. Approach my healing incrementally. I put the picture in my back pocket and closed the lid of the box and the lid of the trash can, this time for good.

'Baby! Mera laal!'

My father was standing in the driveway by my car, holding out his cell phone and yelling out to me. 'Stay right here. A very important phone call is coming.'

'From who?' I asked.

'You will see.'

I walked over to him and looked down at his tan sandals and black ankle socks. 'I'll be back soon, Dad. I won't let as much time pass between visits anymore.' I reached over and hugged him. I gave a full body hug. And I felt the indentation under his shirt. 'Hey Dad.' I looked up at him. 'Where did you get this scar?'

He looked down at me, and read my eyes. I could tell that he knew how to read them. They were wide, curious, but stern. He knew they implored, 'Just tell me the truth this time.'

My father nodded his head. 'I got it during Partition,' he admitted. 'I was a little boy when the Hindus raided our village. They cut me while I hid under my parent's bodies . . .'

I dug my face in his chest. The thought was too much to imagine, and I just wanted to be near him, his heartbeat. I asked through a muffled voice, 'Why did you tell us it was a moped accident?'

He laughed. 'Oh, you know how these things go. Over the years, these stories get confused. But it is true. And this right here,' he pointed to a thin, white line above his eyebrows. 'This is my other scar. How your mother and I met. I flew off my moped in college. But I only got six stitches on my face.' He put his hand under my chin and pulled my face up. 'You know, you have taken after me. You are truly your father's daughter. Meena, she has taken after your mother. The same rebellious spirit. And Khalid? God only knows who that boy took after . . .'

My father seemed to lose whatever train of thought he was going on, and then he lifted my chin again. 'The scar is not important, Samira.' He let go of me and patted the spot on his back. 'Sure it's here. I am always aware. It is a part of me, of my history, and it follows me wherever I go. But all I have to do is put on a shirt, you see. Cover it up, and I can start over. This is what is important. When I came to America, I was able to leave one life behind and start a brand-new one here. This is why everybody comes. To this land of opportunity. The opportunity to try something, and if it doesn't work, if you fail or quit or just change your mind, you start over. You know? It's not the money or the cars or the big houses. In this country, you can keep starting over.' My father flashed a smile. A fresh, healthy peelu smile. He raised his arms, one arm pointing to the O'Donnell's house on the right, the other pointing to the Wolynski's house on the left. 'Where else in the world can you do these things?'

I went over and hugged him again—the perpetual optimist, my unstinting supporter, and he wrapped his plaid arms around me too. 'It won't be the same without my baby here,' he told me. 'Even your mother has gotten used to it. She's sad now. You need to go give her some attention.'

'Mom doesn't care if I leave,' I said. 'She probably doesn't want me back until I can cook masala.'

'What nonsense you speak. Go to your mother.' He started pushing me towards the house. 'Go.'

I turned to walk away, and then he immediately called out to me again. The phone, still in his hand, started ringing. He handed it over to me, and I took it with a puzzled expression. The number on the screen was a US area code.

'Hello?' I asked.

'Hello ji!' The voice was exuberant, excited, and on top of that, crisp and clear. 'Tussy Samira, he?'

I looked at my father, more puzzled than before.

'Gee,' I replied to the caller. 'Yes.'

'I am Man Singh!' he said in barely decipherable English. 'You get me here! I know this! I ask people at visa office and they say you pay for me! I now stay here for longer with work visa and take care of my brother's daughter. They offer me my brother's job here with cab! Shukria, baijee!' he said, the most generous and heartfelt thank you I had ever heard anyone give my entire life. 'Shukria! Shukria!'

I looked back at my father, the proud expression on his face that meant I was the best daughter in the world again. I smiled, and welcomed Mr Singh to this country.

My mother was in the kitchen tossing peeled potato chunks into a pot of boiling water. She was quiet when I initially walked in. 'Are you staying for dinner?' she eventually asked.

'I have to get on the road, Mom. Before it gets dark.'

'Uh-huh.'

She took out a bag of peas from the freezer.

'I told Dad I'd be back soon. I'll come home more often than I did before.'

'Sure. Fine,' she said.

While she clutched the bag of peas and a pair of scissors, I walked behind her. I wrapped my arms around her, pressing my cheek against hers. Her skin felt slimy from the cheap aloe vera lotion she'd been using for years—the huge two-dollar bottle that always sat near the kitchen sink.

I didn't know what was going through her head. She didn't turn around or say anything to me. I didn't expect her to say anything, not on her own anyway. And I never asked. I never asked her what was on her mind or how she felt. It always felt weird doing that, almost inappropriate. Too adult. Like I was her peer, not her child.

But that could change. I was older now. Things change. Didn't I realize that after everything that happened? This was simple. All I had to do was open my mouth and ask her how she was doing and what was on her mind. Ask her if she was happy, if her life had turned out how she wanted, if there was anything she needed, and everything I was conditioned to think about her could change.

'Mom . . .'

'Shhh . . . it's okay,' she said, putting her arms over mine. 'Don't worry about me. You know, you're my little girl. I just want you to be happy. Wherever you are, whoever you're with. Just to see my little girl happy. That's all I ever want.'

She gripped me tighter and I rested on her shoulder. I stayed that way, silent, easily succumbing to my expected place in her world.

All my things were packed in the car. I had a bottle of water in the cup holder, my ipod connected to the radio, orange and black fur stuck to my shirt from kissing Ignatius and Merlin, and my new address scribbled on a piece of paper. I felt a mix of emotions thinking about it—living in a new apartment in a new neighbourhood, a new office, new projects, new co-workers—that mix of excitement and loneliness that comes with starting anything new.

I backed out of the driveway. As I started down the road, I glanced in the rearview mirror. My parents' house was getting smaller and smaller.

And I pulled a U-turn.

I wanted to see them one more time. My mother, my father. Kiss the cats a little more. I knew I'd be back for visits, but I wasn't ready to leave just yet. I wanted to stay for dinner. And I wanted to remind my parents, promise them again, that I'd be home soon.

I pulled back into the driveway and got out of the car. I ran to the front door and swung it open.

'How many times have I told you?' my mother screamed in the living room. 'It needs direct sunlight!'

'Ki bakwas! It's blocking the vent!' my father screamed back. 'You stupid woman! You don't care about these things because you don't pay the bills for this house! You have no respect for the money I earn for this house!'

'You keep your filthy hands off my hydrangea,' my mother warned him. 'By God, if anything happens to it, *by God*, its death will be on your hands.'

I quietly shut the door behind me, buckled myself in the car, and backed out of the driveway.

Acknowledgements

First, a huge thank you to my editor at Penguin, Diya Kar Hazra, for her perfect blend of enthusiasm and warmth. Thanks also to Paromita Mohanchandra, Rachna Kalra and the entire team at Penguin India for making the publishing process downright enjoyable. To my tenacious agent, Erin Cox of Rob Weisbach Creative Management, thanks for always believing in me and saying that day, 'We're going to publish this goddamn book!'

For the times I was convinced I would never see this through, thanks to my family and friends for taking my panicked, desperate phone calls from coffee shops, bars and that one time from the Virginia unemployment office: Kamran Akhtar, Bill Wojtach, Sahar Akhtar, Stella Guillen, Kate Choban, Sam Stafford, Adam Linzey, Matt Geller, Meg Figley, Dawn Pace, Mike Payne, Scott Goodnow, Zerka Moreno, Hodayah Finman, Marta Montoro, Layne Hanson, Brian Williams, and Wendy Namisnik. A special shout-out to Patrick McVicker, Halo extraordinaire, who ignored my calls but let me watch him slaughter people on screen sometimes.

Thank you to my first readers for thinking I was a good enough person to take harsh criticism: Aysha Akhtar, Shannon Ravenel, Molly Travis, and Greg Goodale. They may have improved this book tremendously, and it likely would never have been published without their input, but that didn't stop me from cursing them the whole time.

I'd like to thank Siglinda Scarpa and all the cats at the Goathouse Refuge for providing me a magical environment to think and write, all for the small price of scooping some litter boxes.

Finally, I owe this novel to my parents, who encouraged me to forsake stability to follow a recurring daydream. Mom, Dad . . . you are the most fearless duo I will ever know. For inspiring me with your sense of adventure, I thank you most of all.

Read More in Penguin

The Wish Maker

Ali Sethi

Zaki Shirazi returns to Lahore to celebrate the wedding of his cousin and childhood companion Samar Api (who has finally, it seems, found her Amitabh). Home is not what it used to be; Musharraf is in power, there has been a boom, and Lahore seems to have seen 'too much too soon'. Zaki's estrangement, amidst the flurry of wedding preparations in the house he grew up in, takes him back to his past: his childhood as a fatherless boy growing up in a household of outspoken women, and his and Samar's intertwined journeys from youth to adulthood.

As children, they often attended dangerous political protests with Zaki's journalist mother. Surrounded by the mysterious talk of adults, only Zaki seemed to share his older cousin's yearning for the perfect world. Inspired by American soaps and Bollywood films that they watched together, their world held the promise of all sorts of forbidden love. Then, when Zaki supports one of Samar's romantic schemes, the family suffers the disastrous consequences. But as his fate diverges from Samar's, he comes to understand the world around him better, and to cherish the bonds that survive the tugs of convention, time and history.

Fiction
Hamish Hamilton
Rs 499

Read More in Penguin

Beautiful From This Angle

Maha Khan Phillips

Amynah Farooqui writes 'Party Queen on the Scene', a weekly anonymous gossip column for a Karachi magazine. Amynah, who makes no apologies for her life of casual sex and recreational drugs, is the polar opposite of her best friends, Mumtaz and Henna, whom she wishes would lighten up—especially Mumtaz, who is too uptight to be the daughter of a drug baron.

When party regular Monty Mohsin starts raking in the moolah producing a reality TV show called *Who Wants to Be a Terrorist?* Mumtaz decides to cash in on the trend by making a documentary on violence against women in Pakistan. And the ever-resourceful Amynah finds the perfect subject in Nilofer, Henna's childhood friend from the village. As filming begins, it becomes obvious that each of them has their own agenda including Nilofer, who's not as helpless and innocent as she seems. The stress of the project, along with pressure from Henna's politician father, draws the friends apart. Then tragedy strikes and changes their lives forever.

Maha Khan Phillips's *Beautiful From This Angle* is a sensational debut that serves up a cocktail of Chanel and cocaine, fundoos and feudalism, while on the search for love and happiness among Pakistan's swish set.

Fiction
Penguin Books India
Rs 250

Read More in Penguin

The Good Muslim

Tahmima Anam

One hot afternoon in a remote Bangladeshi village, a telegram arrives for Maya Haque. Eight years before, a devastating war tore Maya's country—and her family—apart. Now she realizes it is time to return home at last. Maya arrives to find that everything has changed. Her old friends have been seduced by the lure of new money, her city's streets have been renamed and the freedom she had once yearned for is a long-forgotten dream. Worst of all, her beloved brother Sohail has become a stranger to her, abandoning his liberal beliefs to become a strict religious leader. As she attempts to come to terms with her brother's radicalism, Maya will be forced to rethink what it means to be a good daughter, sister, friend and citizen—and to be a good Muslim. She must decide where her loyalties ultimately lie.

Set in the dusty streets of Dhaka and the villages and river-islands of rural Bangladesh, at a time when the rise of religious fundamentalism was a whisper in the wind, *The Good Muslim* is an epic, unforgettable story of the challenges of peace in the long shadow of war. It is a novel that cleaves to the simple truths that shape all of our lives: that the bonds of family and love often strain to bear the weight of history.

Fiction
Hamish Hamilton
Rs 499